A Cabinet of Wonders

Renee Dodd

A CABINET of WONDERS

The Toby Press

First Edition 2006

The Toby Press LLC

POB 8531, New Milford, CT 06776-8531, USA
& POB 2455, London WIA 5WY, England
www.tobypress.com

Cover art work by Reginald Marsh, American, 1898-1954,
Wonderland Circus, Sideshow, Coney Island, 1930. Tempera
on canvas stretched on masonite, 48 ¾ x 48 inches, SN951.
Museum purchase, Collection of The John and Mable
Ringling Museum of Art, the State Art Museum of Florida

ISBN 1 59264 164 4, *hardcover*

A CIP catalogue record for this title is
available from the British Library

Typeset in Garamond

Printed and bound in the United States
by Thomson-Shore Inc., Michigan

To my parents

Welcome, Rubes

On April Fool's Day, 1927, you hurry to buy your ticket, shoulder to shoulder with a flock of flapping early birds. As the throng shoves along, jostling, elbowing, eager to catch the Starlight Carnival Royale's first Freak Show of the evening, your imagination creates a slideshow that begins with some scamp's firecracker and ends with your body and bones being crushed beneath the stampeding herd. A shiver of fear hits your gut, but then you catch sight of a man, tattooed head to foot with religious pictures, pitching the show from a wooden platform outside the tent. When the tattooed man turns to entice the bodies pressed against the opposite side of the stage, you push through the crowd, your eyes fixed on a tribute to the book of Revelations inked onto the man's back: above the clouds, an army of angels waving wings and weapons gathers around a sword-wielding Jesus dressed in blood-dipped robes, while below, in a fiery hail that consumes the land, the Beast rises up from a bloody sea, shaking the ten crowns on the ten horns that sprout from its seven heads. You can hardly believe that this, the most amazing picture you have ever seen, is tattooed on a man's skin. You move closer to listen.

I

"Step right up, ladies and gentlemen, and approach the blessed marvel of Dugan's Cabinet of Wonders," he says, with the power and persuasion of ten honey-tongued revival preachers. *"These canvas walls enclose much more than a mere Freak Show, much more than mere entertainment. They enclose the very evidence of the presence of God. Purchase a ticket for a dime—a bargain at twice the price—and you may enter and witness a collection of human oddities that truly displays the great variation and inspiration included in the Lord's plan. Within this tent are Dwarfs and Wolf Girls and Siamese twins—prodigies you must see to believe. For just one single dime, you may stand in the presence of these incomparable Freaks, these Wonders of God's creation, and feel His very presence sanctifying the air around you."*

Your heart pounds as you're swept toward the ticket booth on the current of the crowd. Unexpected, isn't it? How every nerve-ending prickles at the prospect of actual Freaks, those most marvelous marvels of God's creation, hidden, waiting, just shouting distance from the sawdust that cushions the soles of your shoes? Inside the tent are new and better reasons for that expectant fear still quivering in your gut.

When you purchase a ticket, you aren't entirely certain if you receive the correct change, but the man at the ticket booth is a vast Negro with dockworker muscles and indisputable iron eyes, so you scuttle along, the ticket clutched in the pocket of your clenched fist, where it grows moist and pliable. At the tent's threshold, you peer inside at a series of small, black-cloaked stage platforms, trying to moderate the overwrought chuffing of your breath.

A loud, disembodied voice calls out, "Welcome, one and all!" the timbre expanded and hollowed by a megaphone. A man's voice, his words emerging crisply, marching with a Yankee abruptness antithetical to the tattooed preacher's fluid, southern drawl.

"Welcome to Dugan's Cabinet of Wonders," the hidden man continues. "I am the great Dugan himself, your able guide into the strange and wondrous world of Lusus Naturae—Freaks of Nature—gathered here to thrill and amaze the common man."

The horde rushes forward, surging as one into the large tent. The white canvas is thick enough to provide shade and shelter, but thin enough for the gentle glow of sunset to filter through, softening the electric glare from bulbs strung overhead and smoothing the coarse faces of friends, neighbors, and out-of-town strangers. With the ticket holders now packed in rows, Dugan says, "Finch, if you will," and the immense Negro appears through a previously unseen gap in the wall of the tent.

The show is about to begin. Blockaded by flesh on all sides, the fear in your gut whispers, there's no turning back now.

"Our first exhibit," Dugan continues, his voice carrying through the black cloth curtain of the foremost platform, "is me, the World's Smallest Scholar! Although I am smaller in body than many grade school children, my genius can match or exceed that of any academic, from Harvard to Oxford."

The Negro called Finch strides forward and pulls the curtain aside, and you gasp, all of you gasp, for there on the stage, pedestalled on a wooden schoolhouse chair, stands a living, breathing, speech-making Dwarf—with squat legs and arms sprouting from a sturdy, barrel-like torso, a squarish head disproportionately large, and chiseled adult features. Just like a miniature Dapper Dan for a Silkum ad, he wears his brown hair slicked back with pomade and sports a tiny, elegant suit cut perfectly to his unusual proportions. Every inch of him is strong with masculine lines, making his smallness all the more incongruous, but the dapper clothes and hair do not seem incongruous at all because (for a moment the feathery thought tickles your mind) this Dugan is quite handsome. Uncomfortable with yourself suddenly, overly aware of your skin brushing against the coarse warp and weft of your inelegant clothes, you cross your arms over your chest and listen.

"Do not be fooled by my slight stature, for the dimensions of my skull belie the breadth of my intelligence. Do not be fooled by my misshapen body and graceless form, for my soul is lovely and sublime—made of music, art and poetry."

Though much deeper than you would expect, the Dwarf's voice is still small; the sound of a large man's voice confined and attenuated by a child-sized ribcage. One of your nervous hands plucks at your own ribcage as he continues to speak. "I would like to recite a few words from Ralph Waldo Emerson, a great American writer and a very practical man."

He rumbles his throat clear and says, "Dear to us are those who love us, but dearer are those who reject us as unworthy, for they add another life; they build a Heaven before us whereof we had not dreamed, and thereby supply to us new powers out of the recesses of the spirit, and urge us to new and unattempted performances."

The words are pretty, you suppose, but you can't quite grasp the scope of their meaning, and it discomforts you to hear rejection and Heaven and power connected by some sort of logic that doesn't make easy sense, so you expel what you remember of the words from your mind as the corners of the Dwarf's mouth twist into a smirk, and his eyes skim the surface of the crowd.

Hopping to the ground, his ungainly form alive with surprising grace, Dugan leads the way to the next black-curtained stage. Beside it, as beside all the platforms, is a set of rustic library steps, which he climbs in order to be seen and heard above the herd of spectators.

"Meet Molly and Faye, Siamese Twins with beguiling faces and angelic manners. As close as close can be, these two lovelies are joined at the hip. Like the late Chang and Eng, Molly and Faye once stood nearly back to back, but after years of stretching the band of flesh which yokes them together, they are now able to stand side by side as two sisters should."

He parts the curtain, and there, standing side by side as promised, is a pair of identical, pretty young girls. You blink, digesting the thought that they stand so close, wearing a dress with two bodices and one large skirt, because they are fused at the hip. The sight of their four slender calves and knobby ankles tucked snugly into pristine white stockings and shiny patent leather mary-janes is suddenly simply too bizarre to accept, and you look away until a man shouts, "It's a fake." The suggestion calms you. As your shallow breathing deepens, your eyes return to Molly and Faye.

The girls giggle, and one twin exposes and widens a slit in the top center fabric of their shared skirt while the other tugs their white ruffled underpants down low enough for you, and the man, and the crowd, to glimpse the joining place where it becomes impossible to define where one hip ends and the other begins. Apprehension cyclones through your skull like a gust of cold air, making you doubt your footing, doubt even the sawdusted ground beneath your shoes.

While the girls readjust and smooth their skirt, and then blindfold themselves with black scarves, Dugan says, "Molly and Faye have a clever trick for you. Will somebody pass up to the stage an object that you have with you, any object at all."

A well-dressed woman from the back yells, "I have something," and passes up a mother-of-pearl notepad fettered to a thin silver pen by a delicate chain. "Give it to Faye," the woman adds. "My mother's name was Faye."

Dugan hands the object to Faye, the twin on the right, who has lowered her blindfold. She smiles at the notepad and pen, lifting them closer to the lightbulbs strung overhead, running her fingertips over the nacreous cover, then flips the pad open and ruffles the creamy, unlined pages.

"It's a notepad," her twin Molly declares, still blindfolded. Then, as Faye holds the silver pen and writes on the air in big looping cursive script, she says, "and a pen, too!"

Impressed, the crowd murmurs breathlessly, but you're too amazed to make a sound. Then Molly adds, "And it must be really pretty, because it makes Faye happy."

Your hands begin to clap of their own accord; applause fills the tent like an ascending cloud of birds.

Once the notepad is returned to the woman, Dugan asks, "What else?"

"*I got something!*" *a man shouts. Grinning like a bald monkey, he fondles his crotch with one grimy, pink hand. "But they'd hear my pants unzip, and it'd give the whole game away, which is a real shame, 'cause I got enough for both!"*

Shocked and offended by the man's words, you turn to the Siamese twins, expecting horrified cries, brows furrowed with confusion, or perhaps the onset of weeping, but instead Molly yanks her blindfold down around her neck and both girls burst into laughter.

Together they study the man, from his oily hair down to his boots. Then Faye says, "I don't think hearing your zipper would give anything away," and Molly says, "We'd probably need as much help as we could get," and Faye concludes, "since you probably don't have enough for us to tell what it is, even without blindfolds and our hands right on your thing!"

Squawks and squeals shake the crowd, and even Dugan seems to stifle a chuckle as he hides the twins once more with the curtain, then moves briskly along to the next platform. But you're disturbed by Molly and Faye's words. True, the man deserved it, but where did these girls learn such vulgarity? Or were they simply born that way? Wrong on the inside, same as the outside?

Taking hold of the black cloth that conceals the next platform, Dugan closes his eyes for a moment as if offering a silent prayer, then opens them and says, "Our last marvel is Saffron, the amazing Wolf Girl of India."

He pulls the curtain aside. The tent walls ripple with a collective intake of breath.

The creature, garbed in a stylish yellow dress of the sort seen on stage or in moving pictures, is molded in the shape of a voluptuous young woman, but her entire body is furred in thick, reddish-brown hair. The fur on her ankles grows shorter, then very sparse at the top of the feet, which are decked out in yellow high heels. While her hands are nearly bald, her face is so covered with fur that it's difficult to discern if the features are animal or human. Her eyes seem human, but the irises shine a strange and feral gold that would make you fear for your safety if you encountered her while alone in the dark.

"When our Saffron was still curled in her Indian mother's womb, her family journeyed from Bombay to Calcutta to visit relatives. Halfway there, their party was attacked by a pack of vicious wolves, and her mother was mauled. The woman held on just long enough to give birth to Saffron—no one can say if she even saw her own child before she passed on—and the baby was taken in by the wolf pack and raised as one of their own. Until, that is, a group of explorers captured the girl, presuming her to be a completely undiscovered species of creature. They brought her to the United States and sold her to an animal menagerie—one right outside of this town, in fact—until one night, during a full moon, she escaped into the woods nearby, where she met up with others of her kind."

Exclamations of disbelief and fear simmer through the crowd. As for yourself, you don't think it's likely that a pack of half-wolf/half-human folk live anywhere near the place you were born and bred. But then again, if there's one creature like that right here in front of you, who's to say there can't be more?

"Luckily for us," Dugan went on, "she grew bored with her life in the forest and joined our traveling carnival. A true blend of beast and woman, she boasts a graceful and feminine form, as well as a thick coat that any wolf would envy. She never learned to speak, but she did marry—"

—The crowd voices your own feelings in spurts of surprise and wonder. *This creature has a husband? I can't believe it. How can that be?*

"It's true," Dugan says. "A perfectly normal man, as you shall see."

He nods to Saffron, who lifts a black cloth from an easel beside her and uncovers an unbelievable sight—a large photo of the Wolf Girl in a wedding dress, standing beside a handsome, well-formed man in a tuxedo. Inconceivable—and yet there it is before you.

"Like I said, she never did learn to speak, but when her husband died five years ago, she was so stricken with grief that she acquired the ability to mimic any song of love she hears."

The Wolf Girl steps forward into the collective disbelief and begins to sing, "There's a somebody I'm longing to see...I hope that he...turns out to be..." and the music is prettier than hearing the song on the radio, prettier than the choir on Sundays. Certain that the tune never sounded so wonderful, you feel your eyes fill, wet and salty; your cheeks radiate heat. The song and the singer fill you with a tart lemonade ache and the vague memory of something you can't picture or name, but that you regret nevertheless, with every drop of blood in your veins.

As the last note fades from the air, the Wolf Girl curtsies. You suppose that the audience remains still and silent because, like you, they are overcome, breathless, aching. Your palms itch to applaud, but the heavy sadness that saturates the air makes clapping seem somehow inappropriate, and then Dugan closes the curtain, and it's too late anyway.

Raising his hands in the air, he says, "The main show is over folks, but for those with a taste for the exotic, an extra treat awaits. For just a small fee extra, you can see the most amazing, the most shocking, the most unbelievable human being you will ever encounter. Alexander-Alexandra, the Marvelous Morphodite. This is like nothing you've ever heard of—an individual who must be seen to be believed. Keep in mind, this is an adults-only show. The kids can go on and play at the petting zoo, and the more delicate ladies can visit the gypsy fortune-teller for a private reading. But for those remaining mature adventurers, for just one nickel, the Hermaphroditic Marvel of Alexander-Alexandra awaits! Step right up and buy a ticket, and experience the Mystery behind the Indigo Tent!"

The Dwarf pulls aside a flap in the back wall of the canvas to expose a much smaller tent dyed the deep blue of midnight skies.

There are so many reasons not to buy a ticket. You had

8

wanted to fill your gurgling stomach with fried green tomatoes and blackberry cobbler after the show, and you had heard that you could ride on an elephant's back for a nickel, and you really hadn't planned on spending much money today. But it isn't every day that the carnival is in town, and your body scarcely feels like your own anymore, with sweat soaking your collar, trickling down your palpitating chest, and dampening your underwear; and the fact remains that there is a genuine half-man-half-woman waiting just a short walk away.

You wonder if this Alexander-Alexandra will be entirely naked.

It's possible. Even likely.

You thrust your fingers into your pocket, fish out a nickel coated with flecks of lint and the grime of hardworking hands, and rub the coin between the calloused pads of your fingertips. To walk away from this chance would be lunatic. A line is rapidly forming, rapidly growing. You step forward, the nickel cupped in your clammy palm like a baby in its cradle.

Part One: The Family

Chapter one

A Boil Up

April 3ʳᵈ, Hurford, Alabama

On a Sunday afternoon in early April, on the lichen-encrusted granite bank of a pool fed by streams burbling like babies and drunkards, Dugan sat close behind Saffron, inhaling apple cider vinegar, hot charcoal, and musk, and fought a swell of yearning as he pulled a fine-toothed metal comb through the vinegar-drenched fur of her back. As the tines slipped through her glossy pelt, he glimpsed the fertile outer curve of a breast, and gazed down at the beginning of the cleft between the tawny and hairless skin of her buttocks, and even this partial view of her nakedness—these small morsels, this tease—when combined with the rare chance to touch her body, was sufficient stimulation for him to be glad that he hadn't yet removed his pants for the boil up.

But beneath his yearning lurked a rising dread. If by some strange, bad luck a boil up and delousing failed, what would be a mundane discomfort—a mere aggravation—to most carnies, would cause Saffron a great deal of suffering. And Dugan feared anything that might weaken the bond between his beloved and his show. The urge to clutch her fur and pull her against his chest flooded his muscles, and his fingers stiffened around the comb. He breathed deeply and slowly until the craving passed.

It was the Starlight Carnival Royale's first day on the new lot, and the other carnies were boiling and bathing at a larger, less picturesque lake downstream, giving the members of Dugan's Cabinet of Wonders, the carnival's biggest moneymaker, the rare privilege of privacy—a show of respect, a luxury, for which Dugan felt grateful.

"I'm glad we aren't going too far north until summer," Saffron said as she studied the Starlight's route card—blurry, blue-black ink printed on the sort of flimsy cardboard used to manufacture candy boxes. "I like warm weather. West Virginia in July suits me fine, but it's still winter up there now."

Her nakedness affected only Dugan; his group had been together for three years now, and any astonishment the troupers had once held towards their fellow anomalies had been quashed by living so claustrophobically close that not even menstrual cycles or bowel movements were private experiences. And yet no matter how many towns he toured, no matter how many boil ups he endured, and no matter how commonplace nudity was in carnival life, Dugan could not become inured to the marvel of Saffron. Every day, his wonder—and his desire—stubbornly renewed itself.

Alex was the first to dive into the cerulean pool, letting out a whoop of joy upon surfacing. "The water is absolutely divine! Hurry up and get in here!"

"We'll be in soon, I hope," Faye called back. "You almost finished, Finch?"

"I'll be finished when I'm finished," Finch replied.

Molly and Faye were sitting on the bank near Dugan and Saffron, their light brown hair fanned in vinegared clumps across the sheet they had wrapped around their shoulders and tented over their bent knees. Two identical, pale faces pouted above the damp white cloth held closed by one petal-pink hand (maybe Molly's hand, maybe Faye's), so that to an outsider they would have appeared to be a single, two-headed girl—a beautiful, valuable, impossible Freak that Dugan might summon in his most acquisitive dreams.

Finch sat behind the twins, combing out their hair with another fine-toothed metal comb. Sunlight traced the contours of his brown body so that the curves of his shoulders and tightly muscled back gleamed like polished rosewood and the gray filaments woven in the tight ebony curls of his head shone like silver—the graying hair the only clue that he was nearly forty, almost ten years older than Dugan. Every so often the comb's teeth would snag a knot or snarl in one twin's hair, and both twins would mewl in protest. Whenever this happened, Finch would wince, nauseated by the blurry, shifting nature of the line that divided one girl's identity from the other's.

Dugan combed his way down Saffron's back at the pace of an eighteenth century British epistolary novel, but eventually he reached her hips. Longing to be given access to even more alluring territory, he placed his palm against the warm flat of her back and asked, "What about…?"

Saffron glanced at him over her shoulder and said, "Oh, the twins got my rear and the backs of my thighs—it was the least they could do—and I did the rest. If you've finished my back, then I guess we're done. No, wait. You should check my scalp. I combed it, but I couldn't really see if I got all the nits at the top of my head and behind my ears."

Overcome as he was by Saffron's lush flesh, his own flesh swollen with yearning, Dugan anticipated that even after the less exciting scalp inspection he would still need to wait before he could strip down and add his pants to the large iron pot at the bank's edge. But as he stood to reach the top of her head, an all-too familiar pain scorched the marrow of his bones and killed his erection. Most dwarves had convex spines—swaybacks—but not Dugan, whose back was gradually, painfully, caving in, while his knees and hips ached like a man's twice his age. The unknown nature of his debilitation made the pain so terrifying that he had become accustomed to a constant vibration at the crown of his head, an inquisitive buzz forever questioning, Will the pain ever cease? Am I destined to be crippled? Is the condition life-threatening? Having never met another dwarf with the same problem, and being unwilling to see a doctor (the eugenics movement, an obscene scientific quest to scour out the human gene pool with a wire brush, was quite popular, and Dugan did not wish to undergo a surprise sterilization), he had no way of knowing what would happen to his body until it happened, and no way to take charge of the problem and solve it. The helplessness terrified him most of all, so he defied it in the only way he could, by keeping the condition secret, and suffering alone.

He stood very still, resisting his body as it goaded him to lean on Saffron for support, and waited for the agony in his joints and spine to subside to an ache. Once it did, he lifted his almost steady hands, parted her damp locks in sections, and began to search for the telltale fuzzy whitish flakes cleaving to the roots.

"No," he said at last, his voice worn thin by pain and fear, "you didn't get them all. And too much of the vinegar has evaporated. Lean back."

Saffron tipped her head back and closed her eyes as Dugan lifted a bottle and poured the cool cider vinegar over her scalp, the sharp-scented fluid washing away the last hint of her skin's musk. "It serves me right," she said, "for comforting two little girls who don't know better than to play with dirty rube children."

"We're not little girls," Faye said, at the same time that Molly said, "They didn't look dirty."

Saffron laughed. "Well, all I know is the next time you two wake me up because you had a nightmare, I'm checking your heads before I let you sleep in my trailer."

Molly and Faye frowned and looked out over the water, which reflected the sunlight that fell between wind-stirred oak and maple leaves in shifting splotches as changeable as the twins themselves. The scent of charcoal intensified as the fire beneath the iron pot crackled higher and hotter, the water bubbling within.

"Alright, finished," Finch said, tapping the twins on the head as he stood.

"Finally!" Faye said, then paused and added, "Thanks, Finch."

"Well, someone had to help Dugan with your infestation."

"Yuck," Molly said. "Don't say infestation."

Ignoring Molly, Finch walked to the edge of the bank, shucked his pants and dropped them into the pot already churning with clothes and bedding. Then he ran and cannonballed into the pool with a far-reaching splash that dripped cold fingers over the carnies still onshore.

When he surfaced, Saffron shouted out to him, "Hey! You got the route card wet. And I'm not buying Dugan a new one."

Finch smirked and did a lazy sidestroke as he replied, "Well I looked over the books yesterday, and I think we could spare a penny for a new card."

"How about some cash for a new truck?" she asked. "I drove the blue one on this past jump, and it handles like it's held together with rubber bands and chewing gum."

"Up to Dugan. I don't know his *priorities*."

Finch was irritated because Dugan wouldn't consider the cost of a new camera part of the show's nut, or operating expenses. Dugan knew it should have been; in addition to keeping the books, Finch took all of the photographs for the souvenir postcards sold after every performance. But money was tight at the moment. The '27 season had barely begun and there were few funds left over from the season before, which had been hurt by the rapid proliferation of movie theaters, among other things. Coast to coast, moving pictures had bewitched the masses away from older forms of entertainment. Dugan hoped it was just a fad, but knew in his heart it was not; on the few occasions he'd gone to the cinema himself, he had been as enchanted as any other man, merging with the flickering images dancing before him, images no less alive for their lack of dimension or the absence of color and sound.

"Well," Dugan said, "our first priority is a new wardrobe for Molly and Faye—"

Happy hoots came from the twins as they bounded into the water with synchronized hops. Dugan looked away. Until Saffron pointed out a month ago that not only were the girls outgrowing their dresses, but that it was high time that they had brassieres, he hadn't noticed the twins' changing bodies; he had looked at them and seen the same sweet little doves who flew from their mother and alighted in his nest when they were only twelve years old. Dugan had acquired familial perfection three years ago, and would have given anything to keep each of his Wonders locked inside that perfect time forever—a time he could not admit was already lost.

"—after that," Dugan continued, "Finch and I will continue to set aside a percentage of the take each week, and by May we should have sufficient funds to buy a new truck. I think the old jalopy should hold out until then."

"Have you driven that thing lately?" Saffron asked. "Don't *think* it'll hold out. *Pray* that it will."

At the word *pray*, Finch's eyes slid towards a grove of willow trees on a hill about twenty yards from the pool. Patches of tattooed skin glimmered there from behind the languid droop of long green branches. He frowned and said, "Shadrach must be pretty desperate to take that spit bath up there. No sweet springwater, no heat from the pots, just him and a crick and a rag."

"God's work is never done," Dugan murmured, concealing a fresh wave of fear with sarcasm. Finch's enduring feelings for the show's tattooed talker distressed Dugan. Although he had met many of Finch's more casual paramours through the years, he knew little about the man's past loves. What if Finch were the sort who flees the scene of his heartache, putting as much distance as possible between himself and the object of his thwarted desire? Even if Finch *were* able to withstand the torment of unrequited love, the odds that Shadrach would remain unaware of Finch's feelings were slim. Some sort of stubborn subconscious denial kept Shadrach from seeing his friend as a complete and sexual being, and if the day ever came when that denial shattered, Shadrach was sure to abandon the Starlight Carnival. Dugan was loath to lose either man, and in the meantime, he grieved to see Finch suffer. Finch didn't have the temperament to savor one-way passion as Dugan did—as Dugan was doing that afternoon, moving ridiculously slowly to prolong his contact with Saffron.

Still, eventually, despite any man's effort, all things must end, and so he told her, "We're done here. You are officially louse-free."

"Thank God," Saffron said. "Do you know how many hours it's taken to put a fine-toothed comb to every root of every hair on my entire body?"

"Three," Molly said, neck-deep in the water, her lopsided smile of contrition doubled on the surface of the pool. Beside her, Faye tried to appear less penitent, but succeeded only marginally.

"Yes, three hours. And five bottles of cider vinegar," Saffron said.

Dugan watched her walk to the far end of the pool and raise her arms above her head. The silky, russet shoulder fur thinned over her torso as it did on her buttocks, the bare brass-brown skin of her breast and belly punctuated by the chocolate medallions of her nipples and the protruding nub of her navel, the fur growing thicker again where the swell of her hips met the fecund fullness of her thighs. An unbearably delicious sight. Dugan had loved women before—and was usually loved in return—but he had never loved this acutely, his body's craving so potent it was nearly spiritual ecstasy. If someone had asked him why he loved Saffron, he would have said he didn't entirely know, but in truth, as a connoisseur of curiosities, he had found in Saffron such divine singularity that loving her was as natural to him as loving the printed page, as natural as breathing. And yet there was also something more to his love, something deeper, indefinable, inescapable—something in the core of her that called out to the core of him.

He watched her execute a perfect, shallow dive, then swim the modest length of the pool, before she angled up and broke the water's surface, the sheen of her pelt ornamented with crystal drops of spring water, and then he looked away, too frightened of losing her to become aroused again, gazing instead at the scenery as if he'd simply paused to take in the view.

At the edge of the pool not far from Dugan's feet, Alexander/

Alexandra stretched out naked, back against the warming granite, shapely calves and wide feet underwater, and the lingering ache in Dugan's bones did little to dim his pride at the sight of his blow-off goldmine. Hardly a single rube—not the men anyway—managed to resist coughing up an extra coin for the chance to see Alex. That was what a blow-off was all about: holding the public by the scruff of the neck until you squeezed out that little bit more. This marvelous morphodite, this most profitable of blow-offs, was the closest friend that Dugan had in the Starlight Carnival Royale. And what a beautiful picture Alex made, with the double allure of two-sexed flesh. Her firm, slender limbs and small, pert breasts; his short, wet blond hair in tousled spikes; her blue eyes contrasting with the patches of emerald moss and milky lichen growing on the bed of granite; and between those two supple thighs, anything that anyone might desire and more. When Dugan started out on his own, his very first act was a single-O, a one-performer show featuring Alex. His Cabinet began and ended here, with this Wonder.

Alex shifted, feeling the gaze, and so Dugan looked away, knowing how important it was for Alex to use each Sunday to disgorge a week of staring strangers before returning to the blow-off tent to be filled once more. Alex loved working the Freak Show, and adored the hungry crowds fraught with curiosity and fear and lust, but without this Sunday respite, this day free of gluttonous eyes, the following week of shows would be too overwhelming. As Dugan thought on these things, his fear rose up again, his terrible, infuriating fear. Alex had not been herself lately, every show weighing upon her heavier than before. But the true source of his fright lay in the aching marrow of his bones. Last season, Dugan had been unshakably confident, even cocky, when it came to his Wonders; now his feelings were as variable as a weathervane. How could he pretend to be able to will immutability when his body daily defied him by deteriorating at this slow but constant pace?

Forbidding his emotions to keep him paralyzed, Dugan calmed down his fear to its usual mild simmer, then removed his pants and added them to the boil. Spring breezes infused with fire-and-iron heat skimmed the surface of the pool, stirring the flora with a rustle like taffeta and slipping softly over the bared skin of Dugan and his *phenomènes*. He waded into the water, then floated on his back, the large rugged features of his face warmed by the sun, his broad pale trunk and short thick limbs soothed by the cool liquid. As the buoyancy took pressure off his bones, easing the infirmity that had become progressively more difficult to hide, his physical relief permitted his fear to fade until he scarcely felt it at all.

"How about a blanket game this afternoon?" Saffron asked the group. "I left the last one holding, so I got some cash burning a hole in my pocket."

Dugan, enjoying his swim so much that not even Saffron's obsession with gambling could trouble him, volunteered: "I've got the cards."

"And the whiskey," Faye giggled.

"Can we play?" Molly asked.

Saffron said, "Of course you can. It's about time you learned how to play poker."

"Absolutely not," Dugan countered. He loved Saffron, but he would not allow her to corrupt the twins. "Molly and Faye are far too young to gamble."

"We're almost sixteen," the twins said together. "Practically adults," Faye added, with a toss of her pretty head. Frowning again, Molly and Faye dropped underwater.

Finch said, "I don't know if anyone should play poker. Believe it or not, there's another carnival in Hurford this week, so we'd better prepare for a skimpy take. They've got a pretty good line-up, I hear. The Freak Show calls itself Smythe's Traveling Museum of Curiosities."

"I think I've heard of them," Dugan said. The cogs and wheels of his mind began to spin as he floated, watching wispy clouds cross the sky like white glaze streaked over blue ceramic. If that week's stop proved to be a bust, then the show wouldn't make enough money for the twins' new clothes, which would mean putting off the purchase of a new truck for even longer. Rubber bands and chewing gum—

Saffron was right about that, and unfortunately the truck was one of three essential vehicles without which Dugan's Cabinet of Wonders would be unable to jump from town to town. The other carnies with the Starlight might assist for a time; they already pitched in to transport a number of the Freaks' sleeping trailers, but not without resentment, and their charity would likely falter after a few weeks of stuffing in extra passengers and towing extra weight. In the minds of their fellow carnies, the Freaks were rich; they wouldn't understand if Dugan tried to explain that his show struggled too. True, his Cabinet of Wonders squeezed more money from the rubes than any other show, but even in times as hard as these, Dugan still paid his performers far better than most bosses did, and his expenses had been unusually high of late. So the truck was a big concern, but if Dugan were honest with himself, he would have to admit that the delay of the twins' wardrobe troubled him most; it wouldn't be long before the demure frocks they now wore would become so small as to be indecent, and Molly and Faye already disliked the dresses. Last season he would never have worried that something as insignificant as clothing might drive a wedge between him and his girls, but while his family endured the stagnation of over three immobile months in winter quarters, the twins had terrified him by evolving into unpredictable adolescents, acting like children and women at once, changing inclinations and preferences like long grasses in a whirlwind. He would do whatever was necessary to keep them happy—to keep all of his Wonders happy. His love for them shook his weary bones like the shifting of tectonic plates, a vast natural force far greater than any pain.

As for Smythe's Traveling Museum of Curiosities—Dugan had heard of them, but wasn't too impressed. A man of genius like himself should have little trouble thinking of ways to keep competing shows from eating into their profits. Perhaps he could convince Shadrach to do his fire-eating bit during his ballyhoo to draw a few more suckers into the tip. Or maybe Saffron could extend one furry arm through the tent flap behind the bally platform, enflaming the rubes with a burning need to see the rest of her. Dugan was not about to let a peasant like Jimmy Smythe interfere with his family's well being. He recalled a speech concerning war reparations made by Sir Eric Geddes many years ago. It had been reprinted in an American paper, and Dugan had copied a portion of it down, thinking that it made an excellent aphorism for a showman contending with a challenging stop.

"'We will get everything out of her that you can squeeze out of a lemon and a bit more,'" Dugan proclaimed aloud, his bombastic speech-making voice skating across the blue water. "'I will squeeze it until you can hear the pips squeak. My only doubt is not whether we can squeeze hard enough, but whether there is enough juice.'"

Dugan's carny family always used to find his impromptu quotes and soliloquies amusing—Alex most of all—but this time, no one laughed.

Something was changing here, and Dugan could do nothing to stop it; Alpha and Omega, change is essential to the movement of the tides, the cycle of breath, the shackling specter of self-awareness.

Nothing lasts forever.

Chapter two

Introducing Baby Beatrice

April 9ᵗʰ, Hurford, Alabama

The trees huddled close to the sides of the road and reached across until they touched branch tip to branch tip in the middle, casting a broad shadow that made the dim of evening seem more like the dark of midnight to the frantic woman who ran below. Beatrice Smythe's heart flung itself against her ribs like an animal against the bars of its cage, and yet she ran on, her accreted rolls of flesh joggling under the powder pink ruffles of her costume, her strawberry blonde ringlets wilting, plastering themselves against the cherry flush of her baby-smooth forehead and cheeks, the jute croker sack holding her belongings wearing a groove into her left shoulder.

It isn't as late as it seems. The words sang in her mind, kept her running, but truth was, she'd be very lucky if she managed to catch up to the Starlight Carnival Royale before it made the jump from Hurford to whatever town was next on the route. If she missed them, she'd be left homeless, jobless, hopeless. Jimmy would track her to the empty lot, find her huffing and puffing on the ground with her fearful heart still pounding, and she'd be forced to swallow her pride, apologize for trying to run off, and make things up to him by pretending not to mind when she noticed the tang of another woman's cunt perfuming his cock.

As the tar road became gravel and clay, her footing became less steady over the shifting rocks, but she didn't dare slow down. When the trees thinned and the road opened onto a wide field, she filled with relief to see that although the canvas was down, the banners stripped and rolled, and nearly every ride and concession had been sloughed and loaded, the carnival's fleet of trucks remained standing by. Beatrice scanned the carnies through a saltwater glaze of shock and gratitude until she spotted a tattooed man and a dwarf next to a rusted out, rattletrap blue truck.

Panting and grinning, she staggered towards the men, extending her hand to the handsome, dark-haired dwarf who she was certain must be the man she sought. "Mr. Dugan, I'm Beatrice Smythe—Baby Beatrice. I just ran off from my husband, Jimmy Smythe of Smythe's Traveling Museum of Curiosities, and if you ain't got a problem with the fact that he'll cast about a thousand kittens when he figures out I left him, then I'll make you a hell of a lot of money."

Dugan stared in surprise, recovered his composure, then said, "Just call me Dugan." He vigorously shook Beatrice's sweaty hand in his small, powerful grip, and added, "Your presence here is more than welcome." He took a deep breath and smiled. "To tell you the truth, I think it's exactly what we need right now. As for your husband, don't worry yourself. If he tries anything, he'll have to deal with Finch." Dugan pointed toward the heavily muscled photographer single-handedly loading a ticket booth into the long trailer of the Freak Show's largest truck.

"My, ain't he a bruiser! A regular strong-armed bimbo." Beatrice smiled. Her Jimmy couldn't lift anything heavier than his bankroll. "So I guess I'm in then?"

"You certainly are." Dugan's teeth flashed in the moonlight like the candle behind a jack-o-lantern's grin, his expression warm and hungry, (here was fresh blood to strengthen his family), and it relieved Beatrice to see that their eagerness was mutual. There would be no need to crawl back to Jimmy. At least not yet.

"You got a pickup with an empty flat bed?" she asked. "There's no passenger seat made that'll work for me. Traveling with my husband, I used to ride in the pickup that toted hay for the acrobat horses." She shrugged and smiled awkwardly; only at times like this did her fat embarrass her. Beatrice's imposing and ostentatious bulk was her livelihood and her pride, but traversing a world designed for much frailer forms did have its difficulties.

"I assure you, dear, that you are under my care now, and whatever you need to stay happy and healthy, I will provide. First on my list shall be a comfortable ride for your journey."

To be welcomed with such enthusiasm, kindness and chivalry robbed Beatrice of speech, and again her eyes glazed over with briny gratitude, although she did not actually cry—few carnies allowed themselves tears for anything except manipulating the suckers.

When the caravan was ready to commence the night's jump, Dugan led Beatrice to the hay-cushioned flatbed of the show's third truck, a white pickup. She boarded the vehicle by climbing a heavy-duty stepladder, and after the ladder was taken away and a sleeping shack was hooked up behind, a furry head and shoulders peered over the wooden sides of the truck's flatbed and said, "If you don't mind, I'd like to ride with you. They call me Saffron—the Wolf Girl of India," she added with a wink.

Although disconcerting, it was also quite lovely the way that auburn fur fuzzed the woman's forehead and nose, becoming less sparse and more silky at her cheeks and chin to form a beard that reached just past her shoulders—the same length as the sleek, wavy hair of her head, the resulting mane more leonine than lupine. Beatrice whistled a tuneful slide of respect, and said, "Saffron, sugar, you are really somethin' else. I've been around, but I never saw anybody like you. Bearded ladies, sure, but nobody like you. Get on up here. Call me Bea."

As Saffron climbed into the pickup, Bea observed that she wore men's clothing—work boots, denim pants, a plaid flannel shirt—

and smiled. Bea wasn't fond of the frou-frou type of woman; when she wasn't performing in her frilly little girl clothes, she dressed much the same as Saffron was dressed now—or she used to. She had left most of her clothes, along with everything else, behind with Jimmy.

As the caravan of trucks revved their engines and began rolling down the road, Saffron settled herself on the hay. The only unobscured features of her face, two eyes glowing like polished citrine in the moonlight, crinkled at the corners with an answering smile.

Bea leaned against the cool metal and glass of the cab, careful not to put any pressure on the wooden sides of the truck bed. Watching the winding headlights of the caravan following behind, she asked, "What's the next stop on the route?"

"Columbus, Georgia," Saffron replied. "We played there last year. I planted some tomatoes and cucumbers on the lot, so if we're lucky, we can look forward to some fresh vegetables."

Bea nodded. "Sounds delicious."

"So, what's your story, Bea? Tonight's a big jump. It's nearly two hundred miles to the next lot, and we've got a lot of time to kill."

With her back against the deep cushion of scratchy hay, Bea inhaled its dusty, sun-baked smell and took in the star-strewn sky above. She felt good; she liked conversation and getting to know people, and it had been a very long time since she'd had a female friend.

"Well, I've been fat pretty much my whole life," she began. "No decent Fat Man or Woman ever had a thin time, and my whole family was just as pursy as me. At fourteen I hit four hundred and was still packing on the pounds. That's when I met my husband, Jimmy. I didn't know shit from shinola, so I was an easy mark once he laid on the charm. He swooped in and took me off with his show, working hard to fatten me up, pushing me to my present five hundred and forty-six pounds. He'd like me to break six hundred, but I think I've reached my limit."

"You're marvelous as-is."

"Why thank you, sugar. So Jimmy and me, we got married pretty damn quick. In fact, we got married over and over, once or twice in every town we stopped in. It seemed to amuse the sucks, Jimmy being such a long and lean type. And things were good for the first six years or so." Bea paused for a moment to recall the way her husband's hands still thrilled her years after the honeymoon, how his tongue melted her into a puddle and his body soaked her up like a sponge.

"Yeah," she said, "things were real good. But after a while the marriage changed to more yelling than kissing, and Jimmy didn't stick to his vows. Not the ones about being faithful, anyway."

Indelible images flashed behind her eyes. The skinny blonde who ran the cotton candy concession, the chubby redhead in the cooch show. Bea had walked in on Jimmy rutting with one and then the other, each time in her own marriage bed. The sight was not a surprise; although Jimmy hadn't made love to Bea for nearly a year, he had emanated the stench of fucking like a musk that only grew thicker as she grew lonelier. It had made the emptiness hurt so much worse to witness what she'd already guessed, yet she stayed with him another twelve months—hoping, yearning, mourning—fueled by a foolishness she pretended not to recognize.

"When I heard about Dugan's Cabinet of Wonders, I figured a Freak-run Freak Show had to be the cream of the crop, and after I found out that the Starlight Carnival Royale was just across town—in Hurford, Alabama of all places—I figured it for a sign. I took off after the last show when Jimmy wasn't looking and didn't slow a lick until I found y'all. I'm shocked as hell that I didn't drop dead."

"You're quite a woman," Saffron said. "And so young! You're, what…" she paused for a second to do the math, "twenty-one?"

Bea nodded. "Being with Jimmy emptied me out, so I came here to fill up again." She sensed that Saffron would understand. It wasn't difficult to see the loneliness in this woman; its hollowing presence, without a hint of color or warmth, was as familiar to Bea as her own body. She asked, "You ever been married, sugar?"

At this question, Saffron's yellow eyes receded, becoming far away, her formerly potent presence thinning, diffusing. After a silent minute passed, she looked at Bea and said, "My husband Benjamin died five years ago. He was an expert aerialist with the MacHenry Circus where we both worked. One night, for no reason anyone saw, he fell from the trapeze, and of course there was no net. He was badly hurt. At the hospital, the nurses kept staring at me. *What do you think it is?* they kept asking each other. *It*, they called me. And I was so frightened that they wouldn't let me see Ben when he got out of surgery that I cried—I actually cried right there in front of them while they hissed to each other that they didn't think it was sanitary to allow something like me inside the hospital."

"Oh lord, sugar. That's awful."

"They finally did let me see him. We had a few nice minutes, then all of a sudden his eyes bulged out and his breathing, it sounded bubbly, like he was underwater. I screamed for help, but no one came. They looked at me and saw a beast, not a wife. He died right there in my arms. Later I was told that his lungs had filled with blood from an internal hemorrhage that the surgeons didn't staunch. He drowned in his own blood."

Bea kept silent out of respect, and after a few minutes Saffron's golden eyes came into focus again. She looked at Bea with her lush eyebrows knit together and said, "I don't usually—I'm not someone who…." She lay back on the hay, half-smiling with chagrin. "I mean to say I surprised myself by telling you all that just now. I suppose it must be your friendly face."

"Must be."

Saffron shifted in the truck bed so that hay dust rose on the wind, tickling Bea's nose into a sneeze. "Sorry," she said. "Bless you."

Bea sniffled, nodded.

Saffron said, "I'd like to tell you another story, if you'd like to hear one."

"I would," Bea promptly replied.

"Have you heard of Julia Pastrana?"

"I think so. Maybe."

"She was very famous sixty or seventy years ago, known as the Ugliest Woman in the World. She was very hairy, like me, and she was from Mexico. I think sometimes that my parents were Mexican, but I was a carnival baby and never knew them."

"You were born in a carnival?"

"No, but I can't remember life outside it. My parents sold me to a show passing through their town when I was an infant. A border town somewhere in South Texas, I think." She cleared her throat and continued. "Julia was four and a half feet tall, with very large ears and a very large nose, and although I can't say for sure if it was true, many people said that she had a double row of teeth in her upper and lower jaws. She was always singing in Spanish and dancing like Lola Montez, and she spoke three languages fluently. She made a lot of money. She ended up marrying this man, Lent, who toured her around the U.S., telling everyone that he loved her for her own sake. Soon she was pregnant and wanted very much to have a normal, healthy child. But her son was born deformed and covered in black hair like her. He died at only thirty-six hours old. Brokenhearted, Julia soon followed. She was twenty-eight, a year younger than me. Right away her husband sent out for a mummification expert, a man called Professor Sokoloff, to preserve their bodies. Then Lent went back on tour, showcasing the mummies of his dead wife and son—Julia under glass in a red silk gown, and their baby, wearing a red velvet suit, mounted beside her. On a bar, like a parrot."

Saffron stopped speaking, and the rumble of the truck, the rush of air as they rattled down the road, and the calls of whippoorwills and tree-frogs skimmed across the wake left by her words.

"That is one terrible story," Bea said.

"Lent eventually married another hairy woman who he tried to pass off as Julia's sister. Not long after, he went insane. Died of a brain disease."

The sound of Saffron's sigh was lost in the louder exhalation of the truck as it sped on towards the next lot. Bea could tell that Saffron had spooked herself by sharing the memory of her husband's death with someone she'd just met, and telling Julia Pastrana's story was a way to share more without having to say anything directly. Bea wasn't exactly sure what that more *was* yet, but she had faith she'd figure it out in time.

Overhead, the Milky Way was a trail of ivory dust, the slender new moon a silver pendant. Bea breathed in the balm of wild roses beside the road, and despite the sad, sick poignancy of the story, she felt peculiarly happy and light, buoyed on a wave of hope; she smiled up at the moon and stars.

"You know something?" Saffron asked. "I've decided to call you Bumble-Bea. Because bumblebees, according to the law of aerodynamics, shouldn't—"

Still smiling, Bea interrupted to ask, "The law of arrow-what?"

"Aerodynamics. It's the law that explains why some things can fly and some things can't. People used the law of aerodynamics to figure out how to build an airplane."

"Have you ever been in an airplane?"

"No. Have you?"

"No. But I saw one once."

"Well," Saffron said, "according to the laws of aerodynamics, bumblebees shouldn't be able to fly. They aren't built right for it."

"That true?"

"Sure. Dugan read it in some science journal. See, scientists just can't understand why bumblebees are able to fly. It should be impossible. But they *can* fly, and they *do*."

Bea had risked everything to find a home with integrity, and in her need, she willfully overlooked the fractures and dents all around her, deciding to believe that integrity was exactly what she had found in Dugan's Cabinet of Wonders. She wanted that security almost as much as Dugan did. Eager to grab hold of everything good that had happened that night, she clenched a fistful of hay in each hand, the hollow stalks crackling then snapping in her ardent grip.

"They fly because they believe they can," she whispered, but Saffron didn't hear her over the onrushing wind.

Chapter three

Blood on his Boots

April 13ᵗʰ, Columbus, Georgia

O n the Wednesday night after Baby Beatrice joined Dugan's Cabinet of Wonders, Shadrach, the tattooed man, turned his last tip of the night (persuaded the final group that watched him pitch the show to buy their tickets) then sat on a folding chair under the painted promises of the banners to put on the boots he kept hidden under the bally platform. He always pitched the ballyhoo to the rubes while barefoot, to complement the loincloth that showed off the majority of his skin without being indecent—after all, saints wore loincloths. But he did love his boots. Two years of scuffs and knocks had lost the footwear their youth, but not their beauty or usefulness, and as he tightened the laces, he admired the sturdiness, the good craftsmanship, the mahogany patina of the aged, polished leather, and attempted to quell the restless energy that twitched in his muscles despite repeated prayers asking God to give him strength and calm.

Finch—photographer, bookkeeper, bouncer and friend—was sitting in a chair beside Shadrach. Pulling a bag of tobacco from his pocket, he pinched a wad of chew between his fingers, and tucked it into his cheek. "Want some?" he asked, proffering the bag.

Shadrach scowled at the way his restlessness turned a desire for chewing tobacco into a physical sensation, a jactitating muscular need that made sitting still almost painful. He forced a smile and replied, "No thank you."

Shadrach had indulged in too many sensual pleasures lately. The cook at the Pie Wagon had recently acquired an oven and was always baking these days. Weakened by wafts of vanilla, lard and sugar, Shadrach found himself requesting slices of pie or cake with both lunch and dinner, and now a modestly round belly cast a shadow over his ubiquitous loincloth. This evidence of gluttony, this visible confirmation of the failure to restrain a sensual nature, shamed the twenty-five-year-old man.

Blaming his agitation on the sparse attendance these past few days, Shadrach reminded himself that it was only Wednesday, and soon word of the carnival would spread. The town was known to be profitable, a real red one, so the rest of the week was sure to be busy. That night, however, because he hadn't enjoyed the catharsis that came from conquering and corralling the anarchic masses, the purple quiet of the midway unsettled him; his restless toes wiggled inside his boots. With so few rubes scuffing through the sawdust-paved midway path, with no one tossing rings or balls in rigged games that would never reward the players with the best of the brightly-colored slum—the huge stuffed bunnies and bears, the occasional gold-plated pocket watch; unwinnable prizes that the concessionaires were now packing up, same tonight as every night—and with so many shows finished or nearly finished—the last pitch over, the last swish of tassel and jiggle of flesh, the last grease-painted pratfall, the last furry hindquarters through the last hoop—the lot was bleeding out, losing the vitality that day to day saved Shadrach from himself.

But poor attendance and the late hour were not the only sources of Shadrach's clenched muscles and jittery skin; he would have been agitated no matter how crowded the grounds were. Next week the Starlight would stop in Augusta, Georgia, a town that sat twenty miles or so outside Clarence, South Carolina, the place where Shadrach had been born and raised—soil he hadn't touched since leaving home at seventeen, no longer able to withstand the painful memories that haunted his father's house.

"I'd like to take a new portrait of you soon, if you don't mind," Finch said.

Shadrach stood, unable to keep still a moment more. "Fine with me," he said, pacing in front of the bally platform. "Just let me know when."

He didn't enjoy posing, but he wanted to be supportive of Finch's photography—a noble and blessed art that honored God by recording and preserving the Wonders of His creation. Of course, Shadrach didn't think of himself as a Wonder. He was a *made* Freak, not a born Freak, remarkable enough to draw a crowd of suckers, but not so remarkable that the tip might satisfy themselves by watching his ballyhoo, and then leave without buying a ticket to see genuine prodigies. The very existence of those authentic others in the Freak Show was sacred, and Finch's photographs would permit future generations to witness the myriad variations of human form that so many doctors now wanted to eradicate from the human race. To Shadrach, the science of eugenics was the worst sort of blasphemy. To institutionalize your fellow man in order to remove him from the general population or to rob him of his ability to procreate with compulsory sterilization was to spit in the face of God.

The righteous anger of this train of thought made Shadrach clench his fists. His restless muscles propelled him up onto the stage with one fluid leap, then right back down again, his boots making satisfyingly definite imprints of sawdust smashed into dirt. Finch, preoccupied with counting up the day's take, scarcely noticed this behavior, and so Shadrach did it twice more, his blood thrumming, a sheen of sweat coating his skin.

When Finch dropped the coins from his hand into the lockbox and snapped the lid shut with an unusually loud clank, Shadrach asked how they'd done that night. Finch didn't answer. Shadrach followed the direction of his friend's gaze and saw a group of young toughs approaching, rolling along with the slouching, asymmetrical saunter typical of their kind; they looked as if they traveled on mismatched wheels instead of feet. Funny how he could spot the type so quickly now. Before his years as a carny, Shadrach would have only seen a gathering of farm boys still wearing their work clothes; he would have seen a certain pathos in the pairing of hair slicked perfectly into place with heavily perfumed pomade and overalls rusted at the knees with red Georgia clay; he would have found the line of demarcation between the boys' clean-scrubbed faces and their still dirty necks sad and endearing. But Shadrach used to be a preacher's son, a position which imparted the privilege of seeing people generously; now he looked at the boys and saw their reckless youth and clumsy anger; now he saw danger.

As Shadrach watched the group of boys step into the light haloing the Freak Show top, he crossed his arms over the Byzantine cross and dove of the Holy Spirit inked onto his chest, while his nerves pulled as taut as the highest strings of a piano.

"Evenin'," he called out, forcing a cordial nod. Usually Shadrach let Finch handle encounters like these, but tonight's tightened nerves and restless muscles demanded that he take some sort of action himself; to simply step back and sit still would have been impossible.

The farm boys' leader was easy to spot, because as he moved forward the others followed behind in V-formation, like a flock of migrating birds. "Evenin'," the boy replied, smirking, donning his mantle of confidence for the carnies who didn't belong in his town, who didn't belong anywhere. His face was a pitiful collection of sallow scar pits and fresh red acne—burgeoning whiteheads rose amid the sparse hair of his eyebrows—and above his craggy pink cheeks, a band of white skin across his brow betrayed the angle at which he wore his hat.

"Is there something we can do for you?" Shadrach asked.

The boys heard the 'we', but didn't even glance at Finch. Segregation had made them complacent, unaware. It had not yet occurred to them that a Negro with the carnival would not care who their daddies were.

"You can tell me a little about that diaper you got on," the leader said. His crew shook with laughter at their captain's wit.

Shadrach smiled. "This is a loincloth like those worn by the great John the Baptist, who heralded Jesus's coming, cleansed the souls of sinners in the river, and sustained himself in the desert by consuming locusts and honey."

The leader blinked. Shadrach uncrossed his arms to allow the boy to examine the illuminated manuscript of skin, and to note the significance of the tattoos for the first time.

"I was gonna tell you that it ain't Sunday," the boy said, "but I guess for you every day is Sunday." As his flock twittered again, the leader shifted his attention to the box in Finch's hands. "How much money you got in there? Enough for me to buy my girl somethin' pretty?"

"You have a girl?" Finch asked, slowly standing, stretching himself up to his full height.

The flock fluttered nervously; they had begun to realize that they might be out of their league. But their leader motioned with his hand and said, "Hey Abel, how about you come up here and tell this nigger about my girl."

Abel, a dirty-blond boy in back, walked forward. Though he stood taller than Finch by an inch or two, Finch must have outweighed him by fifty pounds. Abel seemed all too aware of this discrepancy.

"You know," Shadrach said, "it isn't that smart of you to rob a show on a Wednesday. The week's barely begun—how much money could we really have at this point?"

The leader's head swiveled towards the tattooed man. "Don't call me stupid," he said.

Shadrach furrowed his brow in a show of affable confusion. "Well, now, I didn't call you stupid. I said that you weren't being that smart. But I suppose after you've heard folk call you something enough times—"

"You shut the hell up!" the farm boy shouted. "Abel, you take that box of money and let's git."

Abel's hands inched nervously towards the lockbox, giving Finch plenty of time to toss the money over to Shadrach and land a solid punch on the boy's jaw. Abel lurched backwards, then fell flat on his tail, his eyes looking down at his splayed legs in dumb disbelief. Shadrach caught the metal lockbox with ease, and when the pockmarked leader rushed him, he slammed it flat into the boy's face. With the moist and meaty impact came a sound like cracking ice which sent an electric current through Shadrach's blood—his veins lit up with power, his body engorged with strength—and while this relieved his agitation, it simultaneously introduced a new and violent need. As the blood gushed from the farm boy's nose, crimsoning lips and chin and shirt collar, Shadrach felt himself swell to the size and scope of the universe, and what he wanted more than anything in the world was for this hoodlum to charge him again, to try just one more time. But the boy only huffed, sucking in air and coughing a little on an inward trickle of blood. He staggered sideways a few steps and cast his eyes upon Abel, who still sat, legs splayed, on the ground. The leader's eyes rolled in his head with bovine fright as he turned and fled down the midway, past rows of darkening tents and empty concession stands, the herd galloping close behind him. Abel got to his feet and took up the rear, rubbing his jaw as he loped along.

Tickled by the encounter, Finch laughed and spit an arching brown stream of tobacco juice. "Shadrach, you surprise me. I didn't know you had it in you."

Everything began to fade for Shadrach, first the need and then the strength, his body dwindling until he became a very small, very fragile creature. How blasphemous that feeling of power had been, and how despicable was that hunger for violence! When he looked skyward, the stars rushed backwards, trails of light marking their paths through the universe, a million sparks of starlight swallowed by the vacuum of God's displeasure. Shadrach dropped his eyes, aware on some level that Finch was speaking to him, but he felt as if he'd shrunk down too small and moved too far away to respond.

His sturdy boots, still laced tight to his feet, were splashed over the right toe with blood.

Long ago, back home in Clarence, South Carolina, Shadrach had committed a terrible act of violence. Tonight he had let himself forget that. He could not allow himself to give in to bodily sensation, to earthly rage; he must always watch himself—for was it not true that a man who has killed once can easily kill again?

Quickly, he loosened the laces of his boots and tugged them off his feet.

"I'm going for a walk," he told Finch, unaware that he had interrupted his friend mid-sentence.

"Do you want some company?"

Shadrach shook his head. "I need some time to meditate." He turned and strode barefoot over the dry sawdust, refusing to look down even as the rubbish discarded by the local marks crackled, crunched, or splintered painfully against the tender soles of his feet.

"What about your boots?" Finch called out.

"You take them," Shadrach replied, spitting the words over his shoulder as he continued to walk away. "Take them or give them to someone else, it doesn't matter. I don't want them anymore."

Chapter four

How Do They Fuck?

April 14th, Columbus, Georgia

lex:

Better than anyone else with the Starlight Carnival Royale, I know the reason you pack my indigo tent for the blow-off after every show, each of you slavering for a taste of Alexander/Alexandra. Every time you rubes see a Freak, every time you lay eyes on anyone different from yourselves, there's that question itching too deep in the flesh to scratch: *How do they fuck?* Maybe you won't admit that's why you scramble to buy a ticket to see me perform, but it's true.

What most of you marks can't seem to get is that fucking is really nothing more than a pleasurable *insert Tab A into Slot B*, maybe with some paint and glitter thrown in for decoration.

All right, fine. There's a little more to it than that (whenever I take in the array of faulty fetuses floating blindly in the formalde-hyde-filled jars of the pickled punk tent, then look at my own hands and feel the pulse at my throat, it always strikes me how amazing it is that I exist, or that anyone exists). But when you talk about sex as *fucking*, it's mostly insert Tab A into Slot B. I just have more A's and B's than your average sheik or sheba, which is why I get more offers than I have time to accept. Everybody wants sex; the ones who think they don't just haven't been given the right choice—and with me, there's no end to the choices.

Specifics? I can tell you're like the rest. If you can't see it, touch it, taste it, smell it, at the very least you want an up-close, detailed description.

So here we go. Starting with the overview, I'm tall for a woman, short for a man, and my build isn't a definite this or that; it's neutral, like a young boy or girl in that heartbeat between childhood and adulthood. Small bubs, nice and perky, and people tell me I've got a peach ass. Most seem to find as much femaleness or maleness in my face as they want to see there, and my hair is blonde and cut boy-short, my eyes blue. And between the legs, you ask? You wish you could get down on your hands and knees and look, don't you?

After a lengthy examination by a doctor (not an official examination, just a handsome Midwestern doctor who came up to me after my show and begged to get to know me in my trailer), I was told—and this is damn near a quote, because I have a memory almost as good as Dugan's—that I possess what appears to be either a very large clitoris or a small penis, with the same erectile function of both, and which exhibits an impressive range of size according to my arousal. It's capable of ejaculation as well, but the doctor explained that the juice was most likely infertile. Just below my clitoris/penis is my vagina, which he told me is only a psuedo-vagina, because it doesn't lead to the female reproductive organs but ends abruptly in what he called a *cul-de-sac*. Fascinated by me as a specimen, he proved to be as creative as he was educated, and we spent the next few hours trying out as many variations as were physically possible with our combined Tab A's and Slot B's.

The doctor was fun, and I remember his words exactly, but not much else, not even his name. I only remember that I met him in the Midwest because I can still hear his accent in my head. Most of my lovers blur, then fade from memory in a week or two. Unless they're part of the Starlight, it's doubtful that I'll ever see them again, and that's the way I like it. I don't want all the shit you sucks try and shove off on me. By fucking the Amazing Alexander/Alexandra, you want to get rid of something, to be distracted, to forget, to lose yourselves in my mystery or in your own fear of the unknown. You think that you can make me into what you need. If you're a girl who likes girls, I can give you what you really want while also giving you a cock to help you pretend you want boys. Same thing but opposite if you're a boy who likes boys. And if you're a wife cheating on the hubby, you focus on my female parts to feel you betrayed your man a little less. If you're a man who's fucked too many people in too many ways, I can be the first new experience you've had in years. If you feel guilty for wanting anything whatsoever to do with sex, my male parts and female parts can cancel each other out, letting you fuck me then pretend you've done nothing at all. The variations of your endless needs are matched only by those of my flesh.

Place your fears, your lust, your secrets on me—looking between my legs, you see room for all that and more. I'm brimming with possibilities; I'm more than complete; I'm infinite space. Cram it in and free yourself, and don't look back to see if I'm torn apart.

But that's all right. Every six days brings a Sunday, the day I knit myself back together in preparation for the next week's rip and unravel.

Now, let me tell you about Zimm, and if you're patient, I'll give you more of an answer to your itchy, deep-down question. Zimm is the man who runs the Starlight Carnival Royale's Girl Show—which is a huge moneymaker for the carnival, second only to Dugan's Cabinet of Wonders—and he always tries to pay off the local cops to allow as much cooch in the act as possible. The girls have performed in everything from bathing suits to nothing but skin, and in the strong shows where the bribes go all the way, the handful of girls who do more than pose have a few surprises for the lucky ones able to afford the fun—a private bottle dance is just the beginning. Seeing as Zimm has a thing for me, he always drops in a little extra kale to cover my blow-off, which has its own range of possibilities, but not so broad a range as some of the girls in his show. I'm no Kelsey. Not these days, anyway. I perform for money; I fuck for fun.

To show my gratitude to Zimm, and because I enjoy it, I allow him to worship me in private after-hours sessions. He likes to kneel before my body, taking my erection in his mouth while sliding his fingers inside me at the same time, thinking that by merely putting a part of my body into his body as he puts a part of his into mine, he can know me, posses me, pocket me like a souvenir. His eager fingers tremble, thinking that they're going somewhere, reaching something. But there's no end to me. The road circles to meet itself at my borders, and there's no point when he can say that he's been inside Alex, that he knows my geography. When he can't stand to wait another moment, I let him fuck me, and when he spurts, his seed goes nowhere; it shoots up into my cul-de-sac only to ooze back out onto his own flesh.

I know you. You want to claim me, to cage me, to drain me of all I have to give. And as each week disappears, so does my ability to restore myself. So for now I'm taking away the mystery, the possibilities. Tonight, I'll remain untouchable, and insist that sex with me would be nothing more than the action of interlocking parts—a pleasurable insert Tab A into Slot B.

You want meaning, absolution, a reason to live? Go look somewhere else. I've got a show to do.

Give Daddy Dugan a nickel, and you can watch.

Chapter five

Preferring the Ghost

April 22ⁿᵈ, Augusta, Georgia

When Dugan awoke long before dawn on that Friday in Augusta, it was because of Shadrach's hand beating frantically against the door to his trailer. Shadrach had been overwrought since the fistfight in Columbus the week before last, but he wouldn't talk about it, or about why he had given up shoes. Dugan was quite concerned for the man, and knew immediately who was pounding on his door.

"One moment," he called out, his voice thick with sleep. He rolled out of bed and onto his feet with one quick, unfortunate movement that made him gasp from the pain that seized his spine and left him panting beside his bed, unable to move for several minutes.

Shadrach, impatient, hearing Dugan awake inside, let himself into the trailer and knelt at his employer's bare feet. Dugan dropped back down onto his cot, the pain of movement made worthwhile by the relief of sitting. Rubbing sleep from his eyes with a trembling hand, he said, "Please, Shadrach—get up. I feel like you've come to court to kiss the royal ring. Come on, now. Sit up here."

Shadrach settled on the cot beside Dugan, his eyes glowing far too brightly in the dark room, his sweaty skin stained an agitated ruby at the apples of his cheeks. Dugan considered turning on the light, but decided against it; Shadrach's appearance disturbed him enough when illuminated only by moonlight.

"Tell me what's wrong," Dugan said, a father's love and concern in his voice. "Let me help."

Shadrach opened and closed his mouth once, twice; the third time he leaned in close as if to whisper in Dugan's ear, then pulled back quickly and shook his head. His desperation changed, receded; a veil was drawn across the surface.

"I believe," Shadrach said, "that I must have had a nightmare." He gave Dugan an uncertain smile. "In fact, I don't fully remember coming here. Perhaps I was sleepwalking."

The embers in Shadrach's wild eyes faded to black. Knowing his carnival children as well as he did, Dugan knew that Shadrach had something to confess, an old something buried so long that even a flare of panic as violent as this could end quickly, the secret burrowing back into the loamy earth of the soul. Dugan watched as Shadrach's coloring slowly evened out (a random pecuniary thought suggested that perhaps Shadrach should begin tattooing his face now that his body was nearly covered). His uncertain smile became bashful, like the grin of a grown man who has behaved like a child. Dugan didn't press the issue. He was scared of losing Shadrach, but no matter how paternal he felt, his pain, his insecurity, had made him accept that he was not the tattooed man's father, he was not anyone's father, and he had no right to demand confession the way that a parent would of a child.

And now Shadrach was standing, clasping Dugan's hand in farewell and stepping towards the door. Dugan wanted to call out, to stop him from going, but the memory of the pain it took to stand brought hesitation, giving Shadrach enough time to flash one more bashful smile then slip out the door.

Sighing, telling himself that he had done all that could be done, Dugan lay back down to go to sleep, but the father in him continued to fret. Soon he climbed out of bed, this time slowly, and the pain was not so bad. He put on his robe. Taking an apple for his stale breath and growling stomach in one hand, and a small stepstool in the other, he went outside.

The pre-dawn air was cool. Setting down the stepstool, Dugan clenched the apple between his teeth and used his freed hands to tighten the silk belt of his emerald green robe as he looked around. For security, the Starlight Carnival Royale always arranged the sleeping trailers like a wagon-train coiled snake-like onto itself, an ouroborus of shelter. The living quarters of Dugan's *phenomènes* rested in an arching row near his own. As he finished eating his apple, he regarded the row with pride. To have so many Wonders, and to have been successful enough (in the past, at least) for them to all have private quarters! There were even two spare trailers in case of expansion—he'd given one to Bea, but the other remained empty. Meanwhile, other shows packed in their performers six to a trailer, layered in bunk beds like sardines.

Feeling better, he tossed the core of the apple aside and went from trailer to trailer, a paternal Peeping Tom, using the stepstool to peer into windows, looking for blanketed lumps on cots and listening for steady breathing or snores, satisfying himself that his loved ones slumbered safely and peacefully. This was what he'd been created for, why he'd been born—to father this magnificent family, to guide and protect them. To have so much filled Dugan with a joy that poured from his body like light; he felt himself become an ambulatory, earth-bound moon, a sun—

Until he reached Saffron's trailer, and the light was extinguished.

He checked her quarters last because she had frequent insomnia, and previously, when he'd found her awake at strange hours, the two of them had often sat up together, talking amiably through their insomniac fogs as the dawn slowly bleached night into day. But not tonight. Seeing and hearing nothing through her windows, he opened her front door and discovered the woodsy musk of her skin and the sharp-sweet scent of Florida Water lingering on the air like the residue of a dream; the woman herself was absent.

This upset Dugan, but did not surprise him. Although the two previous stops had been a little slow, this week in Augusta had been quite profitable, and a sudden increase in funds always allowed Saffron to justify her gambling. Blanket games often transpired within the Starlight, but not too many this early in the season; few of the carnies would feel flush enough for regular poker until summer, which meant that she had more than likely gone into town for a game. Anger and worry fought for dominance behind his ribs; she knew better than to go into Augusta alone—for every five successful trips a solitary Freak might make into a town that doesn't know her, there were ten unsuccessful trips wherein she risked her dignity, her skin, her very life. He'd made plans to go out of town this weekend to celebrate his birthday with Mario, his oldest friend, but it pained him to think of leaving Saffron alone when she was behaving so foolishly. Sitting on the front steps of the trailer, he resolved to have a talk with her when she returned—if she returned. Such a terrible thought on such little sleep exhausted him, and he leaned his chin on his hand, closing his eyes to rest them for just a moment.

Dugan woke an hour later to early daylight, his cheek uncomfortably pillowed by a raw-wood step, and Saffron standing above, her head cocked at an inquisitive angle, her lovely shadow falling across him like a blanket cut to match the bewitching taper and curve of her silhouette.

She laughed and said, "That's a pretty goofy smile, Dugan. What were you dreaming?"

He sat up and put a hand to his mouth. In his pleasure at waking so close to his beloved, his lips had been acting of their own accord. "I didn't realize that I was smiling. And I don't believe that I was dreaming."

"Sure you were," she said, sitting beside him on the steps, creating a waft of Florida Water, musk and whiskey. "People always dream when they sleep. A person's brain has to entertain itself somehow, and I imagine that *your* brain in particular likes to stay occupied."

"Alright then," he said. "But if I was dreaming, I don't remember it."

"You were waiting up for me."

"Well, someone woke me early, and since I was already awake—"

"You made your rounds to see if everyone was tucked in all safe and cosy in their beds."

"How well you know me."

"You worry too much, Dugan. I was in town."

"That's where I presumed you were. And that's precisely why I was worried."

Her puzzled expression renewed his anger. She knew full well why he might be—why he *should be* worried. And just look at her. Nearly matted hanks of hair hung clumped around her head like she hadn't combed it in days, her beard and the fur of her forehead and cheeks swirled down flat or stuck up in ragged patches like she'd been rubbing her face in worry or weariness, and delicate red veins threaded the whites of her eyes.

"It simply isn't safe," he said. "It's positively foolish, in fact, for you to go out alone just to gamble. You can't risk yourself like that."

With her voice wrapped up tight the way an angry lover might wrap a robe around her body during a post-coital fight, she said, "I'll risk whatever the hell I choose to." Then she sighed, rolled her stiff neck around in a circle, and waved off his concern as if she were waving off a fly. "It was fine. *I'm* fine. But really, Dugan, you should try to remember that I'm your employee, not your property."

She had tried to make her words sound teasing, but she spoke too forcefully for Dugan to dismiss the comment as a joke. It saddened him that she might believe he saw her as property, and disturbed him, too, because wasn't she the tiniest bit right? He did see her and the other performers in his show as belonging to him. But not like property.

He placed a hand on her shoulder and said, "Please don't think that way. I care about you, Saffron. I worry. If you simply cannot control your compulsion to gamble, then at least ask Finch, or me, or Beatrice to accompany you when you go into town."

She twisted her body so that his hand tumbled off her shoulder. "And why should I?"

"Saffron, you know perfectly well that it isn't—"

"Calm down, calm down. I didn't go alone. I went with Armenante and his son, all right? From the duck shoot concession. We all looked after each other, and we all came out just fine."

The relief that came from discovering that she hadn't been alone was not enough to stop his tongue. "You don't look as if you came out fine. How much did you lose?"

"That's my own business."

"How much?"

She shrugged. "All that I took with me. Why should I care? I have a home, a good job. My job *is* my home. I'm not going to be made destitute by a single night of cards."

"But it never is a single night with you. You always—"

"What about you?" She jabbed his chest with the hard point of her index finger, and he slapped it away without thinking. Her eyes blazed for a moment then banked down to a controlled smolder. "You have no business lecturing me like this when you're planning to take off this weekend to gallivant around Savannah for your birthday. Aren't you afraid that your precious Wonders will perish without your guiding hand?"

The honest answer was, *Yes, a little,* but he said nothing, stood and moved a few steps away; it no longer felt pleasant to sit so near to Saffron. "I told you, I'll be back by the first show on Monday. And I'm not implying that you or anyone else in my show is not capable or self-reliant. I'm simply saying that when you disappear like this, I can't help but be concerned."

She stood also, defying his desire to keep his distance, stepping close and glaring down at him. "You're not my father, Dugan. Or my husband."

Jealous venom saturated his swift reply. "Of course not. I can't possibly be your husband, because I still live and breathe, and you prefer to make love to the ghost of a man five years dead."

The ensuing silence hummed like the metallic soundlessness after a cymbal crash fades. As Saffron's expression evolved from pained surprise to loathing, Dugan stepped further back, his body recoiling from the reckless words he could not retract. The sun had risen higher in the sky, spreading light that almost cut with its brightness; the exposed skin of his face, neck and hands felt dreadfully vulnerable.

He parted his lips to apologize, but Saffron lifted a hand that closed his mouth without contact. Shaking her head, forbidding any attempt at restitution, she turned away. Helplessly watching her climb the short stairway and slam her trailer door, Dugan smelled the fumes of failure all around him like a cloud of truck exhaust.

He choked on his own weakness. Alone again, endlessly alone.

Chapter six

Birthday Whiskey

April 24ᵗʰ, Savannah, Georgia

Neither Dugan nor Mario knew the actual date they had been born, but they still celebrated every year on April 24ᵗʰ because that was the birthday assigned to them by Professor Marshall Clinker, a strict taskmaster who had falsely billed them as fraternal twins in his Freak Show and kept them locked in their trailer between performances. "No showman worth his salt would risk giving a free show," the Professor used to say, tossing his ring of keys, which spun and flashed and jingled through the air, clinking as he caught them behind his back. Mario and Dugan had the Professor to thank for their names as well, since their real names, like their real birthdays, had been lost to an early childhood that Dugan either could not or would not remember.

Dugan and Mario had been eleven years old—or at least that's what they were told—when they met twenty years ago, and became friends from the start, bonded by their common situation and their common enemy, Professor Clinker. Clinker had purchased Dugan and Mario from different sources within the same month (April, of course), and considered them to be his property, same as his banners, his stage, and the garters that held up his socks. Playing Dugan's *dwarf distortion* against Mario's *midget magnetism*, the Professor made quite a profit, packing his sideshow for years, traveling from coast to coast, until he died on one very special Sunday while fishing in Louisiana. Clinker's swamp guide, a bold, old Cajun, liked to ram his walking stick down gator holes, causing the reptiles to rush up out of the ground and whoosh by the legs of shocked fisherman. This thrill had proven too much for the Professor's dickey heart, which stopped on the spot and set Dugan and Mario free to pursue more lucrative, and less confining, employment. That was in 1914, when the friends were eighteen (give or take a year), and though they soon went their separate ways, they never lost touch, and they never missed a single birthday celebration.

On April 24th, 1927, Dugan parked the Cadillac he'd borrowed from his colleague Zimm back in Augusta—the Caddy's sleek lines and shiny chrome had lured more than a few townie beauties to join Zimm's Girl Show—and stepped out into the foul fumes of the paper mills along the Savannah River, feeling nervous about the annual meeting for the first time ever. Last year Dugan's pain had been mild, negligible, something one could chalk up to the cold or to insufficient sleep. Not now. And he didn't know if he should tell, if he'd even be capable of speaking the words, and really, what good would it do? But despite his inner turbulence, as he walked along the sidewalk he found himself chuckling at the sign which designated the dirty, narrow road as *Shady Lane*. No doubt this had originally referred to shade cast by glossy-leafed magnolias, or live oaks dripping with Spanish moss, but now that the trees were gone and the lane ran perpendicular to a juice joint, the name remained appropriate—only with a different connotation.

In honor of the celebration, Dugan wore a smart suit in a

houndstooth check of cream and kelly green, the colors complementing his pecan-brown hair and eyes, and in the lapel he had tucked a yellow rose with orange-tipped petals. Although aware that others seldom noticed the effort, he never failed to pay attention to detail.

As Dugan approached the speakeasy's door, he heard a familiar voice call out, "Snappy suit." It would have seemed like a child's voice if it weren't for the ragged hoarseness that worsened with every passing year.

"Thanks. Yours too," Dugan said, shaking his friend's hand.

Something looked different about Mario this year, but Dugan couldn't place it. Mario's suit was pink seersucker with dapper, tapered lines that made it clear he had employed a costly tailor, but that wasn't out of the ordinary.

After a hacking cough, Mario said, "I cut a fine figure, if I do say so myself."

Dugan gave up trying to determine what was different and focused instead on his friend's tremulous grip. "Your hand is shaking. How long since your last drink?"

"Too long. And wipe that pruney look off your face."

They rapped on the door and the sliding eye-window clacked open to reveal a pair of narrowed gray eyes. "Who is it?"

Dugan and Mario stepped back a few feet; they had been too close to the door to be visible. When the doorman saw who had knocked, he gawked a moment, then laughed and said, "Sorry, this ain't a place for kiddies."

"Stop beating your goddamn gums and open up," Mario said.

Although the doorman continued to chortle, he did open the door. Mario swept past the man without a glance, but Dugan noticed the long jagged scar puckering a path down the man's cheek to where it tugged at the corner of his mouth and twisted his smile. He noticed, too, the doorman's missing right hand, the knotted shirtsleeve hiding the stump.

"If you ever grow weary of this gig, old boy," Dugan told him, "just look me up. Name's Dugan. Any carny'll know me. I could spin a marvelous tale about your little peculiarities, put you up on a stage, and make you a star." He smiled broadly. "Like me."

"Fuck off," the man said.

Still smiling, Dugan walked on.

Dugan and Mario surveyed the room. They chose a corner table, near a hearth that sheltered a whispering, popping fire that overcame the stink of the factories and warmed the cool dankness stemming from the lack of windows and the proximity to the river; the corner also rested far enough from the crowd at the bar to assure the men a little peace while they drank and caught up on the past year's happenings—although Dugan had not yet decided how much of his own happenings he would share. Gleaming from the grease and wear of a generation of use, the table's unfinished wood had a lovely natural patina, but it sat too high, or the chairs too low, for the tabletop hit the men at chest height. Still, they'd often had worse, and rarely had better, so they made do.

When the waitress, carrying a bottle and two tumblers balanced one-handed on a tray, saw Mario, she squeaked in greeting the way a woman might for a baby or a puppy, then reached out and ruffled his hair, causing both men to recall the private parties that Professor Clinker had them play off-season: Mario gritting his teeth as the women cooed and pinched him, passing him from lap to lap, while Dugan argued politics with the men, seething because the more astute his observations were, the more they patted Clinker on the back, congratulating him for having such a well-trained monkey.

"Oh, my goodness!" the waitress gushed. "Aren't you just the cutest, sweetest little thing?"

Mario's eyes turned to flint and struck sparks against the firelight. "You don't know how sweet," he said, grabbing his groin and giving it a squeeze, "but I could give you a taste if you'd like."

The woman quickly stepped away, as shocked as she would've been had the exchange occurred between her and a five-year-old child. Regaining her composure, she looked at Dugan and said, "We got moonshine whiskey. That's it. But it's pretty clean and pretty strong." She set the whiskey and two tumblers on the table. "The level's marked on the bottle. We charge you by the inch." With a sneer directed at Mario, she said, "Guess we won't be charging you much."

As she turned and walked off, Mario studied her closely. "Her ass is alright," he said. "Too bad she's a dumb bitch." He looked at his friend. "That never happens to you, now does it, Dugan. That cutesy wittle woogy-woogy routine. I'm a grown man, for Christ's sake!"

"I'm too grizzled for anyone to want to baby me," Dugan said. "And my figure's not half as cute as yours."

Mario barked in laughter, an almost painful sound.

"You've been drinking too much of the harsh stuff," Dugan said, as he did every year when they met. "I can hear it in your voice."

"The harsh stuff is the best kind," Mario said, as he did every year in return. He uncorked the plain brown bottle and began to pour the bootleg liquor, which was, if nothing else, whiskey-colored.

"Just tell me you don't drink Jake," Dugan said. Jake, the fluid extract of Jamaican ginger, was ninety percent alcohol and the cheapest booze a man could buy.

Insulted, Mario shot back, "I can afford better than Jake!"

"It paralyzes the extremities, you know."

"No one's actually proven that."

"Come on, old boy. I know you've seen it." Dugan pictured the people he'd witnessed walking with that distinctive Jake-baked motion. Unable to properly work the muscles of their fingers and toes, they dangled their feet as they took each step, smacking the pavement toes first, then heel, with a disconcerting tap-click, tap-click. "Not that this panther sweat is much better for the constitution."

"It's fucking wonderful for the constitution. Keeps the blood flowing nice and smooth." Mario raised his glass. "Here's to Birthday Whiskey."

"Here's to the steady attrition of your throat's lining."

Mario grinned and downed the amber liquid in one long gulp. Dugan choked down half, his eyes watering. "It's got quite a kick," he said.

Mario took a huge cigar from an interior coat pocket. "Want one?"

Dugan declined.

Mario clipped and lit the stogie, exhaled a pungent cloud as gray and viscous as wet cement, then clamped the cigar between his teeth and slid a photograph out of his wallet. "Here, take a look at my latest baby vamp."

"She looks like the rest of them. Big and blonde."

"Hollywood keeps itself well-stocked with my kind of tomatoes."

"Big cigars and big blondes," Dugan said. "The two favorite pastimes of all professional midgets. Mario, you're a parody of yourself."

"Nothing wrong with living up to the stereotype if you enjoy it, which I do—immensely." He tucked the photograph back into the wallet, which he returned to his coat. "Don't be bitter 'cause I get all the girls. You could bag quite a few smarties yourself if you were a little more open-minded."

"Why would I care to be open-minded in regards to curiosity seekers?"

"Nubile young things, longing to discover if it's true what they say about dwarfs…why not? Especially since I happen to know that it *is* true in your case. I say hop off your high horse and grab yourself a girl."

"Nubile young things, my ass! I used to partake as much as you, and I know full well that they're nothing but a gaggle of quiffs with a fetish for—hey, hold on. How do you know if it's true or not? I don't recall us ever playing doctor."

"Well, I have been known to have a few *tête-à-tête*s with your ex-lovers. I run into them on my travels and the pattern never changes. It always begins with them asking after your health and ends with them crying drunkenly on my shoulder, pouring their hearts out and wondering what went wrong."

"And who gets them drunk?"

Smiling mischievously, Mario shrugged and poured another few inches into his glass before topping off Dugan's. "Here's to embarking upon our thirty-first year!"

"Or as near as we can guess to it. We could be thirty-two, or only thirty—who knows? We probably aren't even the same age," Dugan said. He took another gulp of the homemade hooch. "This shit is like petrol."

A gust of foul river stench swept in from outside, and the chatter at the bar rose, punctuated by outbursts of nervous laughter. When Dugan and Mario looked to see what was stirring up the drones, the two experienced carnies stared slack-jawed for a moment before recovering their nonchalance. Half a man taller than the tallest person in the room, the man who had just walked in had to stoop to avoid colliding with the ceiling's support beams. Broad through shoulder and chest, he was built proportionately to his height, except for his head, which, no larger than your average man's, appeared tiny atop his towering frame.

"Your friends are already here, Freak," the doorman said, eliciting more uneasy laughter from the barflies.

The giant stared for some time in Dugan and Mario's direction, and Dugan wished he were close enough to read the stranger's face—if only to help clarify what it was that he himself felt at that moment—but he could not discern the man's expression, only the shrug of his great shoulders as he approached their corner table by the fire.

"Do you mind if I sit with you?" the giant asked. "I could really use a drink, and you seem to have the best seat in the house for those with our—"

"Special talents?" suggested Mario.

"Sure. Special talents. I like that." Though the giant's voice was calm, it resonated in his enormous ribcage like thunder through a cave. He pulled a bench over from a neighboring table and sat with his back to the room. When the waitress brought his bottle and glass, her hands trembled.

Once she'd gone, Mario said, "I'll bet she's right to be scared. I'll bet you're no gentle giant—thank the Lord. I can't stand a big man who's chicken."

The giant shook his head. "I'm not chicken, and I'm not exactly gentle, but I'd never hurt a woman."

"Why not?" Mario asked. "What's so special about women?"

"Well, everything. Everything's special about them," the big man said, his eyebrows quirked in bafflement.

"Spoken like a virgin and a mama's boy," Mario said.

"How about we introduce ourselves before we proceed to disparage one another? I'm Dugan. This uncouth midget here is Mario."

Dugan extended his hand in greeting, but suspended the motion in mid-air when confronted by the giant's vast hand, the palm nearly the size of a dinner plate. Without having touched, the dwarf and the giant let their hands drop and swiftly assigned them other duties—Dugan lifting his tumbler for another gulp, the giant uncorking the new bottle to pour a few fingers of whiskey into his glass.

"Call me Sean," the giant said, looking up again, and the three men studied one another and their surroundings, absorbed the extremes of scale, and felt themselves grow and shrink according to which segment of the room they appraised.

"Well," Dugan said, after a long silence. "I can see why people like you and people like us have always had a peculiar relationship."

Sean smiled. "Am I the first giant you've met?"

Dugan answered in the affirmative, but Mario said, "I briefly toured with Ken O'Brien. They paired us together. You know—World's Smallest and Tallest; the usual bit. But he had to give up touring when his legs gave out. Couldn't hold up his weight anymore."

Sean nodded. "Comes with the territory. I've been lucky. My legs and feet are pretty strong. Can't really feel my toes, though. They're a few yards from my brain, so it's hard for me to keep up with what's going on down there."

As they continued to drink, the giant became drunk before Dugan, but not before Mario, who drank twice as much as Dugan in half the time—Mario never allowed socializing to hinder his drinking, and liked to brag that he could make a speech, kiss a woman, and swallow a dram all at the same time.

"I've got no tolerance for alcohol," Sean said. "Always shocks folk to discover that, but it's true. And you there, Dugan... seems you've kept your head entirely together while Mario and I are half seas over."

"I may not be inebriated, but I've got an edge."

"The giant I knew," Mario said, "was a terrible hypochondriac. Every day he thought he had a new fatal illness. A sap through and through."

"Don't be so harsh," Sean replied. "It can be pretty awful knowing you probably won't reach middle age, feeling your bones ache all the time, just waiting for your legs to give out. It's no cakewalk being a giant."

Dugan thought of his own bone and joint pains, and the increasing exertion required for him to merely stand up straight and not give in to the pull of his spine urging him to hunch as he walked. But he said nothing and took another swig of the whiskey, which was probably laced with iodine, or embalming fluid, or who knew what else. Still, it was birthday whiskey, and that made it good.

Sean lit one of Mario's cigars, holding it between his index and middle fingers like a cigarette.

Dugan watched him closely and asked, "So you live the life too, Sean?"

"You mean, am I *with it*?"

Dugan nodded.

"For a long, long while I was the blow-off for this little sideshow where I was the only real Freak. I made sure I got a hefty cut of the take and saved most of what I earned. Now I'm retired. I'm only thirty-four, but I doubt I got too many years left in me."

"What do you do now?" Mario asked.

"I've been traveling. I tried living in a house with this real doll I met in Kentucky, but waking up day after day in the same place really got to me. Too used to carny life, I guess. Had to give her the icy mitt."

"You'll find another," Mario said. "Dames are a dime a dozen. I like to keep a few bushel's worth of 'em spread out across this fine nation of ours."

"I couldn't do that," Sean said. "I'm a one woman man. I just need a gal who'd like life on the road. If I found the right one, I'd marry her."

"Good *God*, are you a sap. No manacle for me."

"A man doesn't know true happiness until he's found his mate."

"Like I said, a sap."

Sean took another nip of whiskey and turned his attention to Dugan. "What about you? What're your thoughts on the fairer sex?"

"On the whole," Dugan said, "I'm not sure of their worth. They're good for the domestic business, but I've got no interest in nesting, so who needs that? But there are a few"—Dugan pictured the Wolf Girl's golden eyes, recalled the silky softness of the russet pelt he'd so rarely been able to touch, and hoped that she wouldn't still be angry with him by the time he caught up with the Starlight on the new lot in Paris, Tennessee— "a few who're worth a little more." Remembering Saffron's expression of pained shock evolving into loathing, Dugan wished that he'd managed to apologize before he left for Savannah. Then he commanded himself to stop wishing and hoping. To stop thinking of Saffron altogether. He refused to get bogged down by sentiment tonight. "Anyway," he said, "a few diamonds in the rough still don't make the coal sparkle."

"You two are quite a pair," Sean said. "You don't know what you're missing. See, the trick about women is, you've got to prove that you're a good man before they'll show you the very best they have to offer. With your attitudes, you'll never know the way a woman can really love you. One woman like that is worth a thousand of Mario's dames."

Dugan smiled and said, "Let me tell you a story."

"Are you changing the subject?"

"No," Dugan said. "Now, listen up. This story is about a man named Matthew Buchinger." He swigged another scorching mouthful of whisky and began. "During the reign of George I, Buchinger was exhibited all across merry olde England, thanks to the little flipper-like hands and feet that sprouted directly from his torso. He had no arms or legs whatsoever. But he was very accomplished with those flippers; he could play instruments, and juggle, and draw very well; he could load and fire a pistol, and was an excellent shot. He also married four times and fathered eleven children. But there was one wife in particular who gave him a great deal of trouble. Licentious, disloyal, and insubordinate, she was also terribly cruel. Some say that she once sat him up on the mantel and forced him to watch her betray him with another man. Soon after this, Buchinger decided he'd had enough, so he leapt into the air, knocked the woman to the ground with his head, and thrashed her viciously with his flippers until she promised to reform and become a dutiful wife."

Sean sat thinking for a moment, looking down at the table. Then he met Dugan's eyes and said, "I've got no clue what you're trying to tell me with that story."

"What he means," Mario said, "is that a gal won't act like the same gal on my arm as she will on yours. That it, Dugan?"

"Close enough."

Sean shrugged and poured Dugan and Mario a couple inches each from his own bottle. "Well, it doesn't matter much what I think of women, because my days of romance are over."

"Why do you say that?" Dugan asked.

"My bones're too weak. Women may be wonderful, but they don't flock to a fragile man."

"Why do you travel then? Why not stay put somewhere and take good care of yourself? The road-fever might pass. You'll settle down, become accustomed to waking up in the same place."

"Maybe. But I can't afford to try. The doctors'll find me."

"What doctors?"

"Any of them, all of them. Gleetin' ghouls. They can't wait to get their goddamn mitts on my corpse. They want to cut me open and see what my insides are like, boil the meat off my bones, study my skeleton, then display it in some museum that's no better than a dime museum, but is supposed to be highbrow because it'll have scientists talking about me instead of showmen. True, I can't exactly hide out anywhere looking the way I do, but if I never stay in one place for more than a week, then the doctors won't have enough time to work out a plan and enlist the locals."

"You think they'd kill you?" Dugan asked, all thoughts for himself eclipsed by the giant's troubles.

"Some would, I think. But mainly they'll just watch and wait like vultures." Sean shuddered, then slugged back another shot of whiskey. His voice began to slur. "My plan is, when I feel myself getting sick, or if anything happens to me, I'll head straight to the nearest body of water. Out of their reach."

"But what if," Mario said, looking sideways at Sean, "what if you collapse, and you aren't able to get to a lake or the ocean or wherever by yourself?"

"Then I'll give whatever's left of my money to whoever'll help me get it done with a promise not to tell a soul. I'll just have to pray they're honorable."

"Well, good luck to you."

The men hoisted their glasses and drank a wordless toast to Sean's future.

"You want to know something else terrible?" Mario asked. Without waiting for a response, he said, "I'm growing."

Silence descended. All three men stared somberly at the half-empty whiskey bottles.

"It's true. I've grown two inches in the last six months, and if it continues, I'll go from a marvelous midget to a run-of-the-mill short man."

"Is that possible?" Sean asked.

Dugan nodded. "Sometimes it happens when a midget hits thirty. They simply begin to grow. Might not be much, but—"

"It's enough to put me out of the Freak business," Mario finished.

"Hell," Sean said, "that's awful."

"It certainly is," Dugan agreed. Until Mario said it aloud, Dugan hadn't allowed himself to realize that this was the specific change he'd noticed earlier. To think of his old friend growing taller was awful;

to realize that all three men were being betrayed by their own bodies was devastating. The air grew heavy, the room dimmed.

After a while Sean shook his head and said, "Aren't we a couple of wet blankets. We sucked all the fun out of this fine birthday celebration."

"Not much to celebrate," Mario said.

"Sure there is. It's Dugan's birthday, too. Your old friend, your pal. Let's toast to the long career and long life he'll enjoy for us both."

The two men, short and tall, got to their feet and held their glasses aloft. "To Dugan," they said.

With awkward resignation, Dugan got to his feet as well, his curving spine and weary legs constricting in pain, demanding that he voice his own troubles. He worried that he was becoming less able to tend to his family and their livelihood. He worried that he would cripple himself trying to keep up his old pace and be forced out of carnival life after the '27 season. He worried that he'd never have the chance to explore the moist, silken mystery between Saffron's thighs. But he could not allow himself to kill the reborn smiles of his oldest friend and his newest friend.

"All right then, gentlemen," Dugan said. "To me."

He swallowed the last gulp of birthday whiskey in his glass and the harsh drink scalded a path over his tongue and down his throat, spreading its fire through his chest, where it warmed his heart with tonic, transient conviction.

"I'll do you proud," he said, and for the few precious hours that followed, in that blurry time between drunkenness and unconsciousness, he actually believed that his body possessed the strength to live a life grand enough to satisfy the ambitions of three men.

Chapter seven

Safe Now, Safe Here

April 24ᵗʰ, Paris, Tennessee

Suddenly awake, panting as one, Molly and Faye sat up in bed with their skin coated in sweat that reeked of yeast and rotten lemons. They kept their eyes closed, afraid to look until the nightmare faded enough for them to regain the awareness of two beating hearts and four hands gripping the dread-dampened sheets. Once they were reconnected, they embraced, opened their eyes, and returned to their trailer on the new lot in Paris, Tennessee. Here, with the Starlight Carnival Royale, they were protected.

"Everything's fine," Molly murmured.

"There's no mother here, and no doctors," Faye responded. "We're safe."

The nightmare had concerned the two things that the girls feared most. As for the first, it wasn't certain if the woman they grew up calling mother was actually their mother, but sometimes she said she was, telling them that giving birth to two babies at the same time was so painful it nearly killed her. Whenever Molly and Faye complained about the dime museum in which she exhibited them, the woman would say, "After what I've been through to give you life, you're mine to do whatever I want with."

Sometimes she told the girls that she wasn't their mother. She'd say that her body—normal and comely with no part out of the ordinary—could never have created monsters like them; that she had bought them from a woman at the side of the road. She'd say, "The woman must've been a monster, too, because she was completely covered up in a cloak, and she only came out at night. I never saw what she looked like, but she must've been hideous."

Faye was positive that the woman they called mother was, in fact, their mother. "Normal people can have Freak babies, just like Freaks can have normal babies," she'd say to Molly. "And sometimes good people like us get born to bad people like her. You can't choose your parents, and they can't choose you."

Molly preferred to believe in the mysterious night woman by the side of the road. She loved to speculate about the woman's identity: a fairy woman, or a beautiful princess forced to hide her illegitimate pregnancy, or a solitary twin who'd lost her sister tragically and could not bear to keep babies that were a living reminder of that grief. Molly would say, "Whoever she was, I know that she was kind and good. My heart tells me so."

And Faye would ask her sister, "What does your heart say about her selling us at the side of the road like a watermelon?"

They weren't certain of their father's identity either; they never knew him. But during the times their mother felt like claiming the twins as her own flesh and blood, she told them that he was a doctor, and if Molly and Faye didn't behave, she'd send him a telegram immediately, and he'd arrive in the middle of the night with a scalpel in hand to cut them apart in their sleep. Even now, years after fleeing their mother and her threats, the twins slept thinly, waking at the slightest noise that might signal the approaching menace of separation.

In tonight's nightmare (the twins did not usually dream the same dreams at the same time, but when it came to nightmares, their fears were synchronized, identical), they'd been drowning in their own blood, choking on a torrent that spilled from the freshly severed joining place at their hips. Mother and doctor were washed away by the crimson deluge, and the twins flailed separate and alone as their throats clotted with the taste of hot copper, each unable to sense the other, unable to discover if her sister were already dead, or still alive, struggling nearby. When Molly and Faye awoke, their tongues tasted acidic, metallic, and they climbed out of bed to gargle away the taste. They knew that sleep would not return soon, so they threw their peacock blue shawl over their shoulders and left the trailer in their nightgowns. Faye suggested that they put on shoes, but Molly objected.

"Let's feel the grass and dew under our bare toes," she said.

"What if I put on shoes and you stay barefoot?"

"No, Faye, please. You know it's not the same if only my toes feel the grass. I want to feel your toes, too."

After the lice problem back in Alabama, Molly and Faye were wary of going to Saffron for comfort, and Dugan was celebrating his birthday in Savannah that night, so they decided that they would have to shake off the nightmare on their own. Outside, the air was so clear that when they tilted back their heads and stared at the bright and numerous stars in a sky as deep as the ocean, Molly and Faye felt themselves falling into the universe, into fathoms of starlight and eternal night. It gave them chills; goose bumps hatched at their joining place and traveled outwards from their hips to their bellies, across adolescent breasts and over soft, unmuscled arms.

"What do you think it'd be like?" Faye asked, as they left the circle of trailers containing crowds of slumbering carnies and followed the path to the creek.

"What would *what* be like?" Molly returned, knowing what Faye was asking but hoping her sister would just say *never mind*, so they could talk about something as far removed from the nightmare as possible.

But Faye didn't say never mind. She asked, "What do you think it'd be like to be cut apart? I bet it'd be horrible. I mean, at first it might be nice to be independent and all, but that wouldn't last long. We'd be miserable. Even if we weren't, I think that pretty soon we'd get pos-i-lute-ly bored. Everything would be half as interesting if we didn't have each other's feelings to feel."

"But we don't have to feel them," Molly said. "Like right now I'm feeling all four of our feet on the grass, but I don't have to. I can block it out and just feel me. All you have to do is to block me out, and you'd know what it'd be like to be separated."

"Nah, it wouldn't be like that. When I'm blocking you out I know that I can start to feel you again whenever I want to. So it isn't like losing something, it's more like not paying attention."

"Why are we talking about this, Faye?"

"I bet if we were cut apart, we'd still think we felt each other sometimes. You know how soldiers who get their leg blown off sometimes think it's still there? They'll get an itch and try to scratch it, but it drives them crazy, because the leg that itches isn't even there anymore? I think that being separated might be like that."

"You're givin' me the screaming meemies."

"I'm givin' *myself* the screaming meemies."

"So why don't we change the subject?"

Faye shrugged and stopped speaking altogether, which was just fine with Molly. In the ensuing quiet, she could concentrate on their senses, inhaling the bouquet of early blooming crapemyrtles and feeling the satin confetti of fallen blossoms under four bare feet. Even now, out in the cool night air, the twins felt hot and sweaty from panic; the sour smell of their fear mingled unpleasantly with the fresh fragrance of the flowers.

"I wish we had some of that scented soap that Dugan gets us sometimes," Molly said.

"He doesn't get it for us," Faye said. "He gets it for Saffron, only he has to give some to us too, so she'll accept the present."

"No, I think he buys it for us more than her. Doesn't matter, though, since we don't have any now."

The small river just a few yards off the lot was called Wild Woman Creek, and Molly and Faye wished they knew someone from the town who could tell them the story behind the name. After carefully folding the blue silk shawl, the twins placed it on a patch of clover beside the broad stream, planning to swathe their naked bodies in the silk when clean. They peeled off their clinging nightgowns, which were custom-made like their dresses, and because they had their hair pinned up in twists to create the pin-curl ringlets which were their current fashion trademark, they had to open the necks of the gowns wide as they lifted them off so as not to catch the hairpins on the lace collars. Then they dropped the sweat-soaked garments to the ground and eased into the cold water.

With the pin-curl twists anchored close to their scalps, Molly and Faye could dip down shoulder deep and splash their faces and necks without wetting their hair. The cold caused the girls' collective goosebumps to multiply and disseminate until bumps occupied nearly every inch of their skin. The stench of fear was gone; they smelled only the flowers, the wet stones at the edge of the creek, and the sweet, astringent tang of pine.

"You're pretty chicken, you know," Faye said.

"So's your old man," Molly said, scowling.

"Naw, it's okay, Moll. Sometimes I'm chicken, too. But mostly I'm braver than you."

"Gee whiz. Thanks."

"Don't get yourself in a lather. I don't mean it in a bad way. I think we were made like this on purpose. I was made braver than you so I can look out for us and make us do the scary stuff we need to do, like getting away from mother. And you're nicer than me, and believe in stuff more than I do, so you can keep us from getting too bitter and cranky on account of the world being so lousy."

Molly's fingers swirled a whirlpool into the cool creek water. She shrugged. "Well, I guess that sounds all right."

"It's the bee's knees," Faye said, nudging her sister with an elbow. "We're a good team."

Molly smiled and nodded.

Before running away from the dime museum and their cruel maybe-mother, Molly and Faye used to daydream about finding a girl's school that would take them in as a charity case. They imagined befriending girls their own age with whom they'd sneak out of school to have adventures and play fun pranks. But it was just a daydream; in truth they knew that the girls would be snobby and mean, staring and pointing without having paid for the privilege. And supposing the place was run by women who felt a great pity for Molly and Faye and decided to try and help them? Then there'd be worse possibilities. Tall grim physicians with ghoul-white skin dressed in funereal black would be summoned to poke at the twins' naked flesh and guess how much of their internal systems were shared, some of the coldhearts wondering aloud if it'd be worth sacrificing one girl to free the other. Molly and Faye had heard stories. They knew what it'd be like. And throughout the callous examination, blades gleaming deep in a black leather bag would wait for a doctor's hand to choose the weapon best suited to slice the sisters apart.

So when Molly and Faye fled the woman they called their mother, they ran not to a silly girls' school, but to the first Freak Show they could find. Far better to be a Freak in the carnival than to be a Medical Conundrum out in the world. From the very first night the twins found him, Dugan promised that he would protect them from doctors and from their mother, that the circle of his protection would let no one and nothing ever come between the sisters. But now, three years further from childhood and closer to adulthood, the twins yearned to be independent, to prove to Dugan and the world that they were nearly grown women. And yet they knew that being Dugan's little girls helped keep them safe from doctors and mothers, helped keep them free to feel their sharing, not only at the joining place, but all the way out to the tips of twenty wiggling fingers and twenty pink toes.

The sisters reached the cold, sternum-deep center of Wild Woman Creek, and decided, wordlessly, that they no longer cared about their hair. Without even meeting eyes, they ducked under the icy stream, their toes wedged between rocks to hold themselves in place as they hurriedly yanked out the hairpins. The pin-curls untwisted in the rush of the current, the pins skittering along the stones and silt of the creek bed, startling the crawfish awake. Molly and Faye held their breath for as long as they were able and endured the cold for as long as they could bear while the water's icy prickle flowed through their hair and over their freed scalps. Usually after sleeping with the mild pain of pins pressing into the roots of their hair, when they uncoiled the twists, they felt light and fuzzy as if they had clouds for heads, but this water was so cold that their unpinned heads felt real and solid, with impenetrable edges, two heads kept safe and kept close thanks to Dugan. Molly and Faye, barely able to see each other through the dark surge of liquid, turned and pressed cold lips together in a grateful kiss. Laughing in an explosion of bubbles, they shot upwards—free, joyful, choate—and broke through the water's surface into night, exhaling breath that felt as warm as morning sunlight against their creek-chilled skin.

Chapter eight

The Decline of the True-Life Pamphlet

May 2ⁿᵈ, Andalusia, South Carolina

For Finch, the marriage of lens, shutter, paper and chemical that comprised photographic portraiture was the truest and best way to capture the real, to make the tyrannical lies that he'd lived with since he entered this world, naked and squalling, wither and fall away. Today he intended to capture the twins; they were being less than cooperative.

"Didn't we just do this a couple of weeks ago?" Faye whined to him.

"I really liked that one," Molly said. "Our hair was curled then, but it isn't today."

"We lost most of our hairpins last week, and Dugan still hasn't taken us to get new ones, and Molly's too shy to let me ask one of the dancers in the Girl Show to lend us some."

Molly and Faye were difficult subjects, prone to twitches, rolled eyes, a refusal to keep silent and a gleefully stubborn stance on anything that struck their fancy in the moment. But Finch, just as stubborn, always stood firm when it came to taking portraits. "It's been over three months since the last time I photographed you," he said, "and yes, the photograph was very good, but that's not the point. It's time for a new one to capture who you are now. Stand up here."

The twins clambered onto a wooden fruit crate that Finch had artfully draped in amethyst-colored velvet, the nap worn flat in patches like the coat of a mangy dog. "But our hair—" Faye began again.

"Your hair is perfect."

The twins' hair swung in braids tied with matching pink ribbons that dangled against the fat pink roses on their long, modest dresses. Dugan had selected the outfits. He supervised the costuming phase of most of Finch's portraits, which Finch accepted because Dugan's vision almost always allied with his own. As for the photographs Finch took of the Girl-Show girls, he allowed Zimm to supervise those, which usually involved more skin than costume.

"We look like little girls," Faye said, "but we're almost sixteen."

"It's wrong," Molly said.

Sensing Finch's desire to define them with his photographs, the twins instinctively rebelled; they had no desire to be *captured*.

"We're old enough to have our hair bobbed and wear dresses with fringe and drink champagne and go out dancing," Faye said.

"If Dugan would let us," Molly added, while Faye smirked, pretending that Dugan's restrictions didn't affect her one way or the other.

Tuning out the twins and their protestations, Finch loaded his film, adjusted the height of his tripod, and scrutinized their image through the lens. Dissatisfied, he left his camera and began arranging the girls, moving elbows to hide glossy brown scabs, tilting chins to help the girls reflect more angel and less anger, positioning and repositioning Molly and Faye until their appearance harmonized with his supposition of who and what they were, form and idea superimposing themselves upon each other until what he believed and what he saw became one image—the synthesis necessary for all good photographs.

With his portraits, Finch sought to capture those that the world categorized and dismissed, using film and chemicals and paper to reveal a deeper truth, a significance beyond the easy assumptions of words like *Freak* or *nigger* or *whore*. Assumptions like those had murdered his mother, the burden of white men's words weighing her down until, at only forty-three, she no longer had the strength to shoulder her heavy load. She had been eight years old when slavery ostensibly came to an end, but was told by her own mother that they could not survive off the plantation; worn down by beatings and condescension and captivity, they chose their master over unknown alternatives.

How differently had Finch's mother stood than the twins were standing now—her back and shoulders stooped, curved into a shelf for her burdens; theirs straight but supple, like young saplings. Her face cast downward, looking away from eyes that glared and mouths that shouted and spat; their faces turned to look up through the trailer ceiling as if boring through it to the blue sky beyond. And yet the twins possessed a certain insularity that had also been present in his mother. Like Molly and Faye, Finch's mother had been her own flesh-contained world, difficult to know and impossible to change.

Finch heard the elephant's trumpet call outside, and the joyful blast soothed his troubled mind. The head animal trainer took the pachyderm out some afternoons, riding on its gray-brown back over long distances with a speed that would have been too frightening for the rubes who paid a nickel for their ride. Finch liked the elephant—so large, solid and powerful. When he was born, his mother had tried to feed him the same lies that her mother had told her, but he was different, solid and powerful—he had fought to trumpet words of his own.

The twins' bored expressions while he picked lint and stray hair from the yellowing lace of their collars reminded him of their

foolish resistance to Dugan's attempts to educate them. On the plantation Finch had grabbed and consumed every bit of education within
reach. Late in the evenings, after the sun had switched places with
the moon, he had attended secret lessons given in the local schoolhouse by a dauntless, freethinking schoolmarm. He liked arithmetic
best, but valued reading more, for a mastery of language helped him
to better communicate to his mother the truths that he'd been born
knowing—the truths that stood in opposition to the legacy of lies
passed down through generations. And yet, no matter how eloquent
his arguments became—debating like a man of twenty while still
only twelve, giving her a thousand reasons to take her freedom and
go with him—his mother would not accept the truth. In her own
way, she was as strong as her son.

As he took his handkerchief and rubbed a gray smudge from
Molly's cheek, Finch heard his mother's voice regurgitating the white
man's fabrications, saying that she was too slow for sharecropping
and too stupid to make it out in the world, that she had been born a
house nigger and would die a house nigger. On and on he had tried
to convince her otherwise, but the ugly lies remained impervious, even
as she clutched the worn sheets that shrouded her deathbed. After seeing his mother safely interred between his father and grandmother in
the rusty earth of the old slave cemetery, Finch had left the plantation
alone, only fifteen years old, the same age that the twins were now.

Years later, when he discovered photography, Finch immediately realized how superior it was to debate; a good, honest portrait
repelled falsehood by presenting a single individual too unique and
alive to allow tired old words touting tradition as truth. Portraits were
images to be used as armor against words used as weapons. Calling
Molly and Faye *Freaks* and then moving on, most people preferred to
see the twins as less than human, as a species distinct from themselves,
an isolated occurrence as removed from their lives as a shooting star.
But Finch knew better, and his photographs would show the world
what he knew. Except for their conjoined bodies, the twins were no
different from any other fifteen-year-old girls, their relationship more

intimate than that of most sisters simply because they had no choice but to spend every waking moment together.

Yet as Finch hurried to toss Faye's braid over her shoulder, his finger caught and yanked the gleaming brown hair, causing Molly to shout, "Ow! Don't pull!"

There it was, the flaw in his theory: he pulls Faye's hair and Molly cries out. A vertiginous sensation unsteadied the floor as Finch's stomach and head swirled, queasy. This was exactly why he never watched the twins do their act. Finch saw his art as a quest for the real, for the truth within each individual, but Molly and Faye defied definition, defied individuality while at the same time embodying it.

Molly giggled, and Faye said, "Come on, Moll. You know it gives Finch the heebie-jeebies when we do that."

"In my entire life, I have never had the goddamn heebie-jeebies," Finch muttered. "Now shut your yaps."

"You're a silly-billy, Finchy," Faye said, fluttering the thick fringes of her eyelashes at the photographer. She and Molly had been practicing in the mirror, just in case they met a boy worth pursuing.

"Just stay still," he said.

Molly laughed and sang out, "Silly-billy, silly-billy."

"Good Lord!" Finch shouted. "What are you, five years old?" Both girls snapped their mouths closed and widened their eyes as they drew themselves up tall, indignation swelling behind their ribs until their growing breasts strained against the cabbage rose print of their old cotton dresses.

He sighed. "I'm sorry. But if you deliberately provoke me while I'm working, I can't help getting angry." In order to avoid the retort knitting itself behind the girls' clenched teeth, Finch quickly continued. "This is important—I need these photos to choose a new souvenir postcard for you two, and it needs to be recent and good. It needs to tell as much in a single image as the True Life Pamphlets used to. Do you know what those were?"

"Of course we do," Faye said with lingering vexation. "Dugan wrote one about us when we first joined on, and you did the picture for it."

"That was hardly anything. Used to be that the great Freaks had booklets that were forty or more pages long."

"Damn," Molly said. "I don't think forty pages worth of stuff has happened to us yet."

"Doesn't matter," Finch said. "Most of it would be made up, anyway. It'd say that your mother saw a double tailed comet on the night you were conceived, or that you were kidnapped by gypsies as babies and they bound you together with magic. You see, centuries ago, when children like you were born, people thought that the gods were sending them messages and all they had to do was interpret them and they'd know about famines or if the king would die. But later, when people stopped believing in signs from the gods, they still didn't know what Freaks were or why they existed."

"We exist because we do," Faye said, her nostrils flared. "Why should people need a friggin' reason?"

"We're special," Molly said. "The world needs special people."

Finch continued as if he hadn't heard either girl. "People wanted the sort of stories that the True-Life pamphlets gave them because those stories made sense of things and made everything seem more definite, more real. But my souvenir postcards are better than forty pages of lies—or forty pages of truth, for that matter—because my photographs of you will be real in a way that words can never be."

"But it won't show who we really are if our hair is in these stupid braids," Molly said.

"Maybe the braids aren't who *I* am," Faye said, lifting one of the plaits and using its tail to tickle her sister's chin, "but I think they suit *you* just fine."

"Stop that."

"Make me."

"If you don't stop it," Molly said, swatting at her sister's hand, "I'll throw you right off this crate!"

After a moment's pause, body-shaking laughter demolished the girls' silence and threatened to ruin Finch's careful arrangement.

"Come on, now," he said. "Stand still."

Surprisingly, Molly and Faye obliged, giving Finch two beatific smiles. He swiftly snapped a picture, saying, "Great," but inside, his sense of vertigo mounted. All he wanted was to puzzle out the twins' pieces, fit them back together, then fix the solution on paper. He knew they weren't the alien creatures that the world perceived, but what exactly were they? Sometimes Molly and Faye appeared to be two separate girls, and sometimes they appeared to be one; moment to moment they transformed. Finch wished they were as easy to capture as Shadrach, who had transcribed his truth onto his skin, taking control of his surface, preempting the world's judgments with tattooed illustrations of faith.

After leaving the plantation and before becoming a carny, Finch had lived as a hobo, the rushing locomotives and unending miles of space a balm to the wounds inflicted by his heritage of captivity. And he had loved the cool green seclusion of the hobo jungle, the impromptu bustle and bargains of hobohemia, riding the rails when the itch to move took over, the drama when some rangy types would try to incite him to bloody his teeth and knuckles, and the camaraderie of traveling with other free men. While he lived as a nomad, the lies and assumptions didn't cease, but at least the faces behind the voices changed, as did the scenery behind those faces.

Then, one day, a handsome photographer with green eyes offered him five dollars for the chance to take his portrait. Finch tried to recall the exact smile on the man's face, but the bright mossy eyes and ivory grin kept dissolving and reconstituting into the identical faces before him now. If jobs hadn't been so scarce at the time Finch wouldn't have accepted the offer, but five dollars was a whole lot of money—a resourceful man could live on as little as sixty cents a day. The photographer explained that he was working on a series portraying the true identity of the hobo—as he saw it, the hobo was the new American frontiersman—and Finch's heart warmed towards this man who could look at his surface and see not just an unemployed Negro or an unshaven nomad, but a brave, self-sufficient adventurer.

With an irresistible desire to know if the photographer had

really captured the truth with his camera, Finch took the man's address and went to his large, sunny studio the following day. Gratified by the freshly developed, true depictions of himself, he begged the handsome photographer to teach him anything and everything about the craft, and to his shock and delight, the man agreed to take Finch on as an apprentice. Eventually they became lovers, and though Finch was pleased with the arrangement, within a year the wanderlust hit and he decided to leave. He was done riding the rails, however. The life of a hobo was not conducive to photography, but carny life was, and as he traveled with various outfits, finally settling on the Starlight Carnival Royale, Finch believed that like his kindred spirits from the past journeying bravely into the American West, he, too, traveled through unknown frontiers, searching, working towards and growing ever nearer to a perfect revelation of human truth.

A lengthy interlude passed during which Molly and Faye said nothing. Finch could tell that they were actively percolating something behind their flushed foreheads, but they were standing so obligingly still that he didn't dare ask them to share their thoughts. He clicked the shutter, changed the film, clicked again.

After a while, as he re-arranged the twins and gave them a white wicker basket filled with dried, dusty sunflowers to hold, Faye asked, "Finch? What's a french kiss like?"

Flinching as if Faye had actually tried to kiss him, Finch loudly replied, "Why ask me something like that? You girls are too young to ask questions like that." Finch was unable to compare himself to teenage girls, unable to remember that by the time he was the twins' age, he knew exactly what a french kiss was like, and then some.

"We're almost sixteen," Faye reminded him.

"There are girls that go naked in the Girl Show that are only sixteen," Molly added.

"Well, there shouldn't be," Finch said.

"But there are. And some girls are already married at sixteen," Molly said.

"So we don't see," Faye said, "why we shouldn't ask about french kissing. If there were any decent boys around we could practice with, then we wouldn't have to ask you about it!"

"Ah hell," Finch said. "Just stay still and let me do my job."

His frustration caused the twins to foam up with laughter that made their cheeks shake and braids jump, and would surely blur any photograph, so because he'd already taken four portraits and film was expensive, he decided that the session was finished. He took away the wicker basket, hurried Molly and Faye off their fruit crate pedestal and ushered them out of his trailer.

As he swung the door closed, Faye said, "Sheesh, you ask a guy a question…."

Gripping the top rung of a ladder-back chair against the vertiginous swirl of the floor and his stomach, Finch focused his eyes on the tightly wound clock ticking beside his cot and told himself that he would feel better as soon as he developed the photographs. With Molly and Faye directly in front of him, chattering so capriciously and refusing to remain still, he couldn't grasp their truth, and how could he liberate them from lies without first seeing their truth? They weren't little girls, but they weren't quite women; they weren't one person united, but they weren't exactly two separate beings; their age and number were mercurial, chimerical. Developing the film remained the only way to secure what was true and what was real. In his photographs, he told himself, Molly and Faye would present themselves concretely. He pinned a heavy black cloth over his window, switched on his red light, got his developing trays and chemicals in order, and began.

Of one thing, he was certain: photography possessed the power to expose the life palpitating behind every surface, to reveal the true selves of the men, women and children who were—like Finch himself—exiled to the curling edges of maps. Image by image, his photographs would erode the authority of that spidery script inked onto parchment borderlands by generations of ignorant cartographers:

Here Be Monsters.

Chapter nine

Evaluations

May 11^{th,} Perseverance, North Carolina

lex:

Although I did acknowledge the truck's importance to the show's well-being, I wasn't terribly fond of it. Still, though, I couldn't help but respect the stubborn fortitude of its crabbiness. Made in 1909, the vehicle had recently celebrated its eighteenth birthday. It had once been baby blue, but the cab boasted more patches of bare steel and flaking orange rust than it did blue paint. When you started up the engine, it hacked and sputtered like an old smoker waking, then took its time transitioning from that deep cough to the thick, hoarse rumble that indicated you should simply go ahead and drive, because that was as good as it would get. The truck accelerated at a brisk crawl, and after five or more solid minutes of driving, could hold its own quite well at twenty-five miles per hour—any faster than that, and the trembling under the hood became a shudder, then a quake, and then a choking that led directly to the engine dying and being unwilling to restart until after it had clicked itself cool for fifteen minutes like a gigantic metronome.

I let Dugan drive, of course. Whenever I drove I liked to *drive*; I didn't want to have to baby the truck, taking everything easy and listening to all its little sounds to interpret its ever-changing needs. He was already sitting in the vibrating beast, shaved and bathed and ready to go, before I had taken my first sip of black coffee.

"I hope you don't mind if I go like this," I said, over the steaming rim of my coffee mug.

From the driver's seat, which he had adjusted so far forward that the steering wheel pressed flush against his chest, Dugan looked from my mussed bed hair to my white cotton shirt and brown drawstring pants—men's clothes that discreetly accented what few curves I had in a manner alluringly, if ambiguously, feminine—and down to my bare feet. "Fine, Alex. But you might want some shoes. What if you need to use the bathroom when we get there? A mechanic's bathroom is almost guaranteed to have a filthy floor."

I shook my head and climbed into the cab. "If I feel the urge, I can piss behind a tree, darling, just like you. Well, maybe not *just* like you, but close enough."

Dugan shrugged, and as soon as I slammed the truck door—which made a horrible grating sound accompanied by a high pitched squeak—we began our palsied journey from our lot in Perseverance, North Carolina to the new truck we planned to buy in Raleigh. In any fully functioning vehicle, the drive would've taken thirty to forty-five minutes, but we expected the trip to take an hour and a half, which is why we were up and on the road at the ungodly, carny-hostile hour of ten A.M.

"So where'd you get the money?" I asked, arranging myself cross-legged on the truck's cracked and torn passenger seat.

"What do you mean? These past few weeks have been extremely profitable."

"Yes, but I know you recently ordered Molly and Faye a new

wardrobe, and since they can't buy ready-made, I'm sure that it didn't come cheap, and on top of that, their birthday is next week, and they'll expect something more than just new dresses—especially considering how demure and boring the dresses you picked out are bound to be. I also know that last week you had to pay to have three of the curtains in the Freak top repaired after mice chewed holes in the fabric."

"The cost of repairing the curtains is negligible."

"The point is, trucks cost more than a bit of money, and I'm guessing that a bit of money is all we've got in the till at the moment."

Dugan drummed his thumbs against the steering wheel, white Bakelite yellowed at nine and twelve o'clock, then exhaled a puff of frustration. "All right, I confess. We didn't have the money for a new truck, but Shadrach donated generously to the cause. He insists that it be considered a donation, but I plan to regard it as a loan."

"Why? What the hell does Shadrach spend money on? I love the man, but come on—his only interests are tattoos and God. He doesn't have much blank skin left, and God is free."

Dugan made an amused but non-committal noise, and I rolled down my window to let some fresh air into the cab, which smelled strongly of Finch's cigarettes and the souring milky residue of a chocolate malt that Faye had spilled on the floor two weeks earlier. The intensity of the sun rising through the morning sky reminded me that it was almost the middle of May, the time of chill spring warming towards summer. My favorite time of year. I drank the gritty, lukewarm dregs of my coffee then opened the glove box, planning to store the mug inside, but a fat leather-bound book already occupied the space. I smiled at the odd, yet commonplace sight, my head swimming with a surge of love for Dugan; he was as unlikely to go somewhere without a book as he was to go without clothes.

"Well then," I said, closing the glove box and resting my mug on the truck's floorboard, "are we going to address the real reason you asked me to come along on this errand?"

"I didn't ask you to come along. You invited yourself."

"Yes, well, I suppose that's true. It's nice to take a little jaunt into the city, maybe lure some lovely sheik or sheba to drive out to Perseverance and take in the carnival before we leave for Virginia, but I know that you were hoping I would ask to come along when you told me about the trip."

"And why, pray tell, would that be?"

"Because, my darling, we haven't had a chance this season to really talk, just you and me. You must be terribly anxious by now. And since we've only got about an hour left on the one-way to Raleigh, we'd better get started. My keen insights are priceless."

Dugan shook his head and laughed, his strong white teeth flashing, his cheeks pushing his shiny, dark eyes into happy, squinting arches. It was lovely to see the solemn cast of his face abandon itself to laughter, even if just for a moment—he had been far too serious lately. For years now, Dugan had been my closest friend, close in a way that my lovers with their vampiric needs could never be. Perhaps I had too many lovers and not enough friends.

"Fine," he said. "Please share with me your priceless insights."

"Hmmm…well, now, who shall we begin with? Who might Dugan be the *most* eager to hear about?"

He shot me a warning look. "Start with whomever you please, Alex. I won't waste your time by designating a set order."

I leaned over the gulf between our seats and ruffled a hand through his thick brown hair. He hadn't combed it back with Silkum pomade that morning, so his curls slipped dry and soft between my fingers. "Saffron is doing just fine," I said, "but she's still too stubborn—or stupid—to realize the caliber of man she's rejecting."

Dugan cleared his throat in protest, his mouth shrinking into a pursed, old biddy frown.

"I think it's a terrible shame," I added. "Not for her, but for you. For all the time you've wasted on her. She's not worth it."

"She's worth a great deal," he said.

I kept quiet.

"Why do you dislike her so much?" he asked.

"I've told you already—some people are simply not meant to like one another."

"That's no answer, Alex."

I shrugged, unwilling to admit my uncharitable reason for disliking the long-suffering Saffron.

"She's really an amazing woman," Dugan said.

"If you say so. But either way, this chaste devotion of yours isn't healthy. I saw that luscious redheaded townie who tried to chat you up in South Carolina last week. She was practically licking you with her eyes and you just shook her hand and sent her on her way like you always do with the local lusties these days. Be in love with Saffron if you have to be—fine—but don't deprive yourself by keeping faithful to a woman you've never even kissed."

"How do you know I've never kissed her? Do I make you the confidante of my love life?"

"Not now. You used to. Anyway, Saffron would tell me. Everyone tells me just about everything."

Dugan frowned because he knew it was true, even with regard to Saffron. I may not have liked her, but for some reason she insisted upon liking me. "Well, I'm not sure that you're the best person to counsel me on chastity," he said. "I doubt that you've ever deprived yourself of a single moment's pleasure."

"Not since I was fourteen and the whole adventure began."

Dugan still radiated displeasure, so I sighed and said, "All right, we'll talk about Saffron and leave you out of it. She actually *is* fine. She and Bumble-Bea are bosom buddies these days, walking around chattering like a couple of sisters."

"Does Beatrice discourage Saffron's gambling?"

"I don't know how much Bea knows about it yet. Anyway, Saffron only gambles because of Benjamin, and maybe Bea's friendship will help her miss him less."

Both Dugan and I scowled at the mention of the dead husband's name, Dugan for obvious reasons, and me because Ben was why I could hardly stand the sound of Saffron's beautiful voice some days. Five years and she still behaved like it happened a month ago, floating around like a sad, furry rain cloud, as if grief gave her nobility. She only acted natural when she gambled like a fool. I saw nothing amazing about her; if you gave her a full body shave, she would be nothing more than a widowed gambler who could carry a tune. But most of all, I hated that she wouldn't even give Dugan a chance when he loved her so much and so well.

I yawned and stretched; my joints were stiff with displeasure. I noticed that Dugan wasn't looking his best that morning, with purplish bags under his eyes and new creases, downturned, at the corners of his mouth.

"Let's talk about someone else," I said, speaking quickly to try and shake my ill temper. "We covered Shadrach—God and tattoos and money for the truck—so what about Finch? Still pining for Shadrach of course, and Shadrach still oblivious. Same old, same old. Except that he seems restless these days—Finch, I mean. Like he's got a yen for something. Now I don't mean sex, Dugan. Not everything I talk about has to do with sex—besides, Finch can and does come to me regularly for that—this is something else."

"Let me know if you figure it out."

"Of course." I took a deep breath and resumed speaking at a more normal pace. "Now, how about Bumble-Bea? I don't know her that well yet, but she seems to be as happy as she can be. Delighted to be apart from her cheating husband and with us instead."

"So you think she'll stay?"

"Oh yes. She's just as much one of us now as Saffron is."

"What about Molly and Faye?" Dugan asked. "They're getting awfully headstrong these days. Much more argumentative than they used to be."

"There's nothing wrong with Molly and Faye that the passing of three more years won't cure."

"Dear Lord."

"They're burgeoning young women—"

"Please don't say *burgeoning*—"

"And they're hungry for new experiences. Don't judge them too harshly for their little rebellions. It's natural for adolescent girls to seek independence from their father."

"Their father?" Dugan's smile returned.

"Of course, their father. Don't act as if you don't know the part you play."

His smile widened. "It's just nice to hear the words."

"Well, don't worry about the twins, Daddy. They're sharp cookies, and they look out for each other."

Dugan reached into a crumpled paper bag on the dashboard that I hadn't noticed before and pulled out some lemon drops. He nodded towards the bag and said, "By all means."

"Don't mind if I do." I took a handful of the sugar-dusted candy, then popped a single drop into my mouth, my cheeks puckering then relaxing as I sucked past the sweet dust down to the sour and then to sweet again. This morning was turning out very differently than I'd hoped. Suddenly I felt like taking the whole bag of lemon drops and tossing them out of the window just so Dugan couldn't have any more.

"It seems that we've covered everyone in record time," he said. "I thought you said this would take a full hour."

"That's because I only gave you the short versions." I gazed out the window at the passing greenery, which didn't seem nearly green enough, and too sparse for late spring. And the air was too hot, too heavy, even at this early hour. I sighed at the stubborn downturn in my mood. I'd woken up cheerful, but now even the pine trees with their bony, spindly branches irritated me.

"It turns out I'm not feeling too chatty today," I said.

Earlier, I had been excited to gossip about everyone with Dugan. He'd been distant, even cold lately, and I'd hoped that with the two of us alone in the truck I could get him to open up his damn mouth and talk to me like he used to. Now I wished that I had stayed on the lot and slept late like everyone else.

But I wasn't quite ready to give up.

"Hold on a minute," I said, "we haven't covered *everyone* yet." I reached out and gave Dugan's earlobe a quick tug—probably a bit harder than I should have—and asked, "What about *you*, darling? Don't you want to know what I have to say about *you*?"

He arched his eyebrows. "Not in the slightest."

"Well then, don't *you* want to tell *me* how you're doing these days?"

I spoke playfully, but he knew that was my way, and he should have answered sincerely—or answered something—but he simply shook his head and repeated, "Not in the slightest."

"Such a spoilsport," I said, struggling to keep my voice light.

"Well, what about you?" he asked. "If you think you should explain me to me in the name of completion, then don't you think you should tell me about yourself as well? In detail, mind you. I'm tired of this newfound inscrutability of yours."

"Oh, really," I said, popping a few more lemon drops in my mouth, wanting to scream like a child that he'd started it.

I wasn't a topic that I was eager to embark upon. Like Finch, I had also felt restless this season—or not restless, exactly. Discontent. The normal patterns of my life had become less and less satisfying to me, and I felt less and less capable of feeding the insatiably hungry men and women in my audience and my bed. I didn't understand what was happening to me, but whatever it was, I had put a great deal of effort into giving it as little thought as possible.

After crunching and swallowing the last shard of candy, I reached out to grab another handful of lemon drops from the bag. "All you need to know about me is that I'm a great old trouper, and while I have come to value inscrutability in myself, I still detest it in others."

"You could say the same of me," Dugan replied. "Which must be the reason that in spite of our deep friendship, we presently find one another so remarkably frustrating."

As I sucked on my mouthful of sour-sweet pebbles, Dugan met my gaze with the sharp, pecan brown eyes of a stranger. Questions filled my mind, my thoughts shouting so loudly I felt that only Dugan's stubbornness would keep him from overhearing. Why couldn't we just be easy together like we used to be? Why had he withdrawn into this cold, hard shell? Something was wrong, something more than his ridiculous infatuation with Saffron. He even spoke and moved differently now. In the past, he had always engaged so completely in every action—even if that action was simply standing still and silent—that his calm, warm presence filled the Starlight's trailers and tops to overflowing. But as we rattled down the road to Raleigh, as long as I kept my face turned toward the window, it felt as if the truck was driving itself and I journeyed alone.

Chapter ten

Drunken Carousel Kisses

Kisses, kisses, kisses! What foolish delirium filled the Girl Show undressing top at just past midnight on May 19th, 1927, with Molly and Faye's hopes flying dangerously close to the sun. Now that they were sixteen at last, now that they had new dresses, which, though ankle-length, were at least drop-waisted and plain blue with no flowers or ruffles or bows anywhere, and now that they had Roxy—barely seventeen, but still a thoroughly modern jazz baby as well as a dancer in Zimm's Girl Show—helping with their hair and makeup, they were ready to have an adventure, ready to be kissed, ready to fall in love with a handsome boy and learn all the secrets of the world of women. Sixteen, the twins felt certain, was the age when life truly began.

"We need to look sophisticated, but Dugan'll cast a kitten if we show up with too much on," Faye said.

"I understand," Roxy replied.

"Just a little lipstick maybe."

"Yeah," Molly said, "and a little powder, and with our hair you could do one of those little knots in the back with the sides looping over our ears so it looks like it's bobbed like yours."

"Yeah, do that first," Faye said. "I want to see how we'd look with short hair."

Molly and Faye were sharing a wide, black-enameled stool in front of the Girl Show undressing top's mirrors, preparing for the carnival-wide party in their honor. The carnies had banished the marks from the midway (after emptying their pockets) and closed the lot to outsiders, but most of the rides and some of the food and game concessions remained open for a carnies-only celebration. In the Starlight Carnival Royale, sixteenth birthdays were benchmark events, surpassed only by matrimony and parturition.

Roxy finished styling the twins' hair just as Bumble-Bea entered with a large birthday cake—yellow with chocolate icing—on a tray. "This cake's just for you two, and Roxy if she wants some," Bea said. "The cook made a big layered one for the rest of those animals out there."

As Molly and Faye eagerly took a slice each of the cake, Roxy's mouth opened and shut like a goggling goldfish before she managed to say, "Animals?—Do you mean the Freak Show people?"

Bea laughed. "Don't be a silly twat! I meant the gazonies and the ride operators. If there weren't any women looking, they'd just stick their faces in the cake like pigs at the trough."

Faye took note of the word twat, which she'd heard before but never from the lips of a woman, and decided that it would be a good addition to her vocabulary.

"Speaking of the ride operators…" Molly said around a mouthful of cake, "what's the name of that new boy running the Ferris Wheel?"

"You mean the one who came on in Andalusia?" Roxy asked. When the twins nodded, Roxy said, "His name's Charlie, and he's about twenty, I guess. He's handsome alright, but he's also an ass. Charming, though. He doesn't have a sweetheart yet, but only because none of the girls've kept him interested. Well, except June. Everybody wants June. That's why she's our star."

"But June is practically married to Jed, right?" Molly asked.

Roxy nodded. "Yep. I never saw anybody move so fast."

"Don't put too much lipstick on those girls," Bea said, watching suspiciously as Roxy dotted a deep raspberry stain onto Faye's lips. "We don't want them looking as trashy as you."

Roxy's mouth compressed and twitched, holding back a sharp response. Molly and Faye had witnessed Roxy mouthing off to Zimm or to other dancers a multitude of times, so they didn't understand why instead of calling Bea a bitch—or a twat—she said, "Nah, just a little touch of red, light and classy," without meeting Bea's eyes.

Bea shrugged and headed out the door, saying, "Well, hurry up. Everybody's waiting to sing Happy Birthday, and there's a nice stack of presents out there, too."

"Go ahead," Roxy said quietly. "I'm finished."

Molly and Faye gave the dancer a ferocious hug and thank you, then ran outside towards the waiting crowd of fellow Freaks, glamorous cooch dancers, boisterous ride operators, showmen, concessionaires, and the gazonies, the men of all work, standing with their rough, laborer's hands clasped behind their backs. The twins hurried the singing and cake cutting, then tore through the packages, most wrapped in newsprint or pages ripped from back issues of *Billboard*, while shouting thank yous left and right. Among their favorite presents were two long strands of blue glass beads from Saffron and Bumble-Bea, and a record of hit songs with a note promising Charleston lessons from Alex. Still, it stung Molly and Faye that everyone who gave a gift either chose doubles of the same object or else a single gift meant for them both—*we aren't interchangeable*, they wanted to say—but they kept smiling politely until they had unwrapped their last present and said their last thank you. As the rest of the carnies scattered over the fairgrounds, Roxy lagged behind with the twins.

"Time for you to open my present," she said, with one hand hidden behind her back.

"Is it what we hope it is?" Faye asked.

"Yep." Roxy swept her arm out, revealing a cork-stoppered glass bottle with cloudy liquid inside. "It's gin. Or close enough, anyway. Enjoy, but take it slow at first. It's strong stuff. And don't let Dugan see it! The last thing I want is him mad at me."

"Don't worry, we'll be very sneaky," Molly said, taking the bottle from Roxy and handing it to Faye to open.

Faye uncorked the gin, brought the bottle close to her mouth, then jerked it away. "Sheeeeesh! That nearly scorched off my nose hair." For her second pass, she held her nose closed, then gulped and swallowed as fast as she could. "Holy hell is that horrible!" An unfamiliar, warm lightness began to seep through her chest. She wondered if perhaps she and Molly weren't ready for this particular new experience, but quickly smothered the thought and said, "Thanks, Roxy."

"Least I could do. Did you see which way Alex went?"

"No," Molly said, "but it was probably to the Carousel."

"It's his favorite," Faye added.

They waited until Roxy was out of earshot to laugh at how obviously goofy the girl was for Alex, crediting their unusual restraint to their growing maturity. Molly took her turn at the gin, pinching her nostrils as her sister had done, and the twins began to feel pleasantly swoony, simultaneously lighter and heavier, courageous and frightened. Time to face the Ferris Wheel, and Charlie, and their grand, romantic future. Although the twins' memories were well-stocked with images of desire's darker side—Zimm spitting blood from a tooth-torn mouth while a dancer's husband dragged his screaming wife offstage by the hair, or Saffron sitting like a statue and staring at her wedding ring while Dugan tried, and failed, to engage her in conversation, or the girl from the hot dog concession lying at the edge of the lot, stripped naked and pinned belly to grass by a sweaty stranger, counting out fresh bills as she lurched in time with his thrusting—they chose instead to believe in the silver-tinged images of desire they'd seen after the lights went down, the curtains parted and the projector began clacking away. The twins had had very few opportunities to go to the movies, but every film they had ever seen was burned onto their consciousness like scar tissue from a branding.

They weren't some cooch dancer; they weren't Saffron or Dugan or the hot dog girl. They were Lillian Gish, Mary Pickford.

Molly and Faye found the Ferris Wheel already revolving, its thick arms and metal support webbing resembling the structure of a bridge coiled end to end to form a circle. Outlining the spokes in the wheel were glowing colored strips of neon, in shades of lime and orange and cranberry. Some of the neon had burned out, and as the wheel continued its revolutions, reflected light slipped up the length of the darkened tubes like sparks or imprisoned fireflies. The music of the Tilt-a-Whirl and Carousel carried through the whooshing Ferris Wheel arms and emerged with melodies wavering like words spoken into a fan. Here was the setting of Act One, Scene One; Molly and Faye walked towards it with self-aware starlet grace, tilting their faces towards the multicolored lights as if preparing for a close-up, their stubborn, romantic illusions softening their expressions like vaseline smeared on a lens.

Only half of the cars were occupied when the birthday girls clattered from the metal steps onto the platform and right up to Charlie, who stopped the ride just for them. Irresistible with his dark, shiny hair a little too long and his cheeks pink from the day's sun, Charlie maneuvered his mouth into a broad, controlled smile. Older, more experienced women would have been wary of that smile, knowing that a man this young, handsome and charming had probably not been given much reason to develop his character. But Molly and Faye, sixteen for less than an hour, had never even held hands with a boy, and they allowed Charlie's smile to infiltrate their eager bodies right down to the bone; there was nothing inside or outside their skin but him.

Faye clutched a pretty lace bag, a present from Dugan that now concealed the illicit bottle of bathtub gin, as she and Molly climbed into the bottom bucket.

"Hey there," Charlie said, as he lowered the safety bar over their laps. His gaze dropped to the twins' inner hips then bounced off, his smile faltering under a wave of confused desire that Molly and Faye could not identify but that Alex would have known at a glance.

"You've never seen us up close before," Molly said. She didn't mind his obvious fascination, or that unidentified something in his eyes, and neither did Faye, who beckoned for him to lean in closer. "If you're real sweet," she whispered, "we might show you where we fit together later." Faye spoke confidently, but inside, she was shaken by her own boldness; she felt a balloon inflate in her stomach, an expanding cavity of air that meant the slightest gust of wind could carry her off into the sky and away from the carnival—away, even, from her sister. Moments from panic, Faye met Molly's eyes, which glistened with nervous tears even as she nodded in approval. They had to make something happen tonight—they were sixteen, after all.

Charlie didn't speak, but only grinned wide and steady, show-ing large, straight teeth slightly yellowed by coffee and cigarettes. His walk back to the controls had a hip-centered swagger, his eyes held the gleam of a man with a new idea. He pressed a button and moved a lever, and the ride resumed its motion with the sound of a dragon grating its teeth. As the twins rose into the air, with neon colors slip-ping over their skin, they slid the lace from the shoulders of their gin bottle and each took another swig.

"Damn," Molly said, feeling her and her sister's limbs grow fluid and fuzzy. "Maybe we should lay off the gin for awhile."

"Chicken?"

"I'm not chicken. Just look out there." Molly pointed to the Carousel, feeling her arm and hand stretch and flow through the cool air of the late spring night like pre-pulled taffy. "Don't you see how all those lights look like a big bright circle with the sides all blurry, and—Oh God, I don't feel so good."

"Stop looking at the friggin' Carousel, Moll, or you'll make us sick."

As their bucket dipped toward the ground, they concealed the bottle once more within the lace bag and looked at Charlie. Still grinning and gleaming, he gave the girls a quick wink. They wanted to wink back, but felt as if they'd lost control of their facial muscles; their entire heads felt numb, and they could only hope that they were smiling as the wheel hefted them skyward again.

"We have to kiss him tonight," Faye hissed, dewing Molly's ear with spit. "This is the perfect day for a first kiss."

Molly wiped her damp ear with her palm and asked, "But how're we going to do it?"

Faye shrugged. "I don't know. But we could just stand around nearby until we get an idea. The ride operators are switching off with some of the other carnies for the party, and he'll have to go on a break eventually."

"And we do look swell tonight."

"Damn straight we do."

When they stepped off the Ferris Wheel a few minutes later, they were pleased to see Charlie arranging for Jed—ring toss concessionaire and fiancée of June, the much-admired star of the Girl Show—to take over the ride operation. As he spoke to the older man, Charlie stretched himself tall, chest out, seeming as young as Molly and Faye in his desire for approval. The twins rolled their eyes. Jed had only been around for a couple of months, and was still considered an outsider, not *with it* at all; the only thing special about him was that he'd managed to woo and win June.

"Sure, I'll take over," Jed said, "but find another guy to relieve me in a half hour or so. I'm supposed to meet my girl at one-thirty."

Charlie nodded, then walked over to Molly and Faye, sauntering in a way that made them conscious of the place where his long thighs met his torso. "Where're you two headed?" he asked.

"Don't know yet," Molly mumbled. When he stood close she could smell his cologne, and under that, a distinctly adult male scent. Becoming aware of him as a man instead of a boy, she felt the same expanding balloon sensation that Faye had felt earlier; it made her want to flee Charlie's presence and run off to somewhere safe, somewhere closer to Dugan.

"I was thinking of going to the Carousel," he said. "Wanna come along?"

Too eager to sense Molly's panic, Faye hurried to answer yes before her courage gave out. They began to walk.

When they reached the Carousel, Charlie suggested that they

ride in the sleigh, and as the trio climbed up onto the wooden slatted floor, inhaling air sugared with caramel apples and brimming with the tinny piping of the calliope, the familiarity of the setting calmed Molly. They sat on the bench inside the sleigh, and Molly was pleased that Charlie wedged himself on the outer side, next to Faye. That was plenty close enough. She felt him place a hand on Faye's knee.

"Hey Charlie," Faye said, slipping the gin bottle out of the bag and waggling it in the air, "we're on a toot. Feel like joining in?"

"Always," he said, taking the bottle and gulping with gusto.

"Take another, and we're even," Molly said, still frightened, but learning how to enjoy the feeling—it was like squinting your eyes at a candle and watching the flame starburst into rays of light. Her fear was a beautiful starburst; she felt tiny stars, clusters of sparks, at the tips of her fingers, on the tip of her nose.

He took two more swigs. "Now I'm ahead. Your turn."

Faye took the bottle, then hesitated, her courage wavering, but Molly smiled and nodded at her sister, making everything all right again. They so very much wanted to stay close to this lovely and terrifying creature, his warm skin redolent of gear grease and Old Spice Cologne. Faye took one more gulp of gin, her and Molly's heads wobbling as she swallowed. Like the fear, the drunkenness had its own beauty—it cast a spell that made the present moment feel like revisiting a vivid memory. There was no such thing as choice; they had lived all this before. And what a lovely memory, too, so graceful and colorful. On the central piston of the ride, mirrors ringed with pink, yellow and blue bulbs flashed in rhythm with the calliope's piping, and on either side of the sleigh, unmanned horses frozen mid-gallop—a palomino pony, a tan cowboy horse and a big, white Arabian—glided up and down on poles, their square, ivory teeth straining at the bit, their raised hooves clad in gold-painted horseshoes. As the cool, green-enameled metal of the sleigh gradually warmed from the trio's body heat, Charlie looked from Faye's eyes to Molly's, back and forth between them, and the twins felt a startling new sensation between their legs—a heated, opening feeling that caused them to long for a kiss, and then for more than a kiss. Exactly what that *more than* might be, they weren't sure, but as their virgin bodies flushed with blood carried by two palpitating hearts, Molly and Faye wanted to find out.

"I never saw anybody like you two before," Charlie whispered.

"You like what you see?" Molly asked, widening Faye's eyes.

He nodded. "You're a couple of real dolls. I mean it."

"You're pretty keen yourself," Faye said, attempting a casual laugh that squeaked itself silent as Charlie used his knuckles to brush a stray curl back from her cheek. The sparks had traveled from Molly's fingertips to Charlie's knuckles to Faye's cheek.

Molly tingled along with her sister, feeling an almost painful expansion of the yearning sensation between their legs, a sensation that complemented the fear, blurring the border between dread and desire. She wouldn't dream of running away now—and besides, hadn't all of this already happened long ago?

Charlie placed his hand on Faye's shoulder and kissed her cheek. Pausing, he waited for her to smile before he leaned over and kissed Molly's cheek. "You two like to neck?" he whispered, his breath warming Faye's ear, and there were the sparks again, buzzing over her tender earlobe.

"We've never done it before," Faye said, realizing how low the three of them had sunk on their seat. Without standing directly beside the sleigh and leaning over to look inside, she knew it would be nearly impossible for anyone to discern what the three of them did as the merry-go-round spun merrily around. They were on their own private island; all of this had already happened.

"You'll like it," he said, then he pressed his lips against Faye's.

Molly started when Charlie's tongue nudged apart Faye's lips—more than sparks now, a sustained electrical charge—but Faye caught on quickly, slipping her own tongue into his mouth. The kiss, tasting of bathtub gin with a hint of yellow cake and chocolate frosting, proved to be more than expected and far from enough, and the twins wished that they could take Charlie back to their private trailer to discover the secret, waiting world of *whatever happens next.*

"What the hell're you doing?"

The sudden loud voice sent Molly and Faye's already racing pulses flying into their throats, their heartbeats like wings buffeting their necks. Charlie pulled away so quickly that he hit his head on the back wall of the sleigh.

"Ow! Nothing," he said, suddenly a boy instead of a man.

Jed leaned over the side of the sleigh with the gorgeous June, who smirked and popped her gum. Jed had never really looked at Molly and Faye before, and the twins felt nauseated by the way he looked at them now.

"I got Stumpy to take over the Ferris Wheel. So…" Jed ran his fingers over his brush-cut hair, "keep doing what you're doing, I guess." Slinging his arm around June's insouciant, slouching shoulders, he said, "Come on, baby. Let's find a more *regular* spot to cuddle in."

With the flames in their bodies doused and the eager unfolding sensation between their legs shut tight, Molly and Faye felt a new sort of fear, that of a cornered animal, and if Jed and June had lingered a moment longer, crowding the sleigh and smirking, the twins might have clawed all four staring eyes out. As the couple turned and left, the fear receded, replaced by a relief so intense it felt almost like joy.

Faye said, "Jed's really not *with it*. He's only been on the Starlight a month or so."

Charlie didn't respond. Even with Jed gone, he remained like a boy, a sad boy, and there should be nothing to fear from one so young and so sad, and yet the twins did feel frightened again, and the fear was not beautiful.

"He doesn't get yet that we're the stars of the carnival," Molly said. "All of us in the Frea—" She stopped, suddenly unable to say the word that she wouldn't have thought twice about saying while she was still only fifteen.

"All of us in Dugan's Cabinet of Wonders," Faye supplied quickly.

Charlie shrugged and said, "I'm not sure that I'm really *with it* either." Looking away, his eyes fixed upon Roxy flirting with Alex over a pink puff of cotton candy. He watched until the Carousel revolved them out of sight.

"Sorry. I should go," he said. "Stumpy's over there and…" A weak smile flickered over his face like a guttering candle. "Anyway, I should go."

He stood and hopped off with the Carousel still moving. Both Molly and Faye noticed that he didn't head toward the Ferris Wheel, but ran in the opposite direction, past the Tilt-a-Whirl with its tubs tossing like small crafts on a stormy sea. By the time the sleigh revolved away from Charlie and back towards the cotton candy booth, Roxy and Alex were gone.

"He'll never talk to us again," Faye said.

"Why do you say that?"

"You know why."

After the passing of a stubborn, painful minute, Molly finally nodded, then lay her head on Faye's shoulder. "I didn't even get my turn."

"It was disgusting anyway. Clumsy and sloppy. Disgusting."

Quietly, Molly said, "No it wasn't, Faye. It was really nice."

Faye sighed and conceded, "Yeah. It was."

The twins sat up and looked at the rest of the carnies on the ride—laughing gazonies passing a flask, the head animal trainer and his wife holding hands in the space between their horses—and spotted Roxy and Alex astride two chocolate brown mares, Roxy's wearing a silver scar where its raised front leg had been amputated then welded back on. Opposite the sleigh on the far side of the Carousel, Jed and June kissed and clung in the Model T.

"Come on, Moll," Faye said, standing up with her sister.

They went to the biggest horse on the ride, an ebony stallion with a streaming black mane and a purple and blue saddle. A favorite among the many visitors to the Starlight Carnival Royale, the stallion's enameled hide was caressed silver in patches, the ridges on the stirrup footplates worn smooth. Faye grabbed the pole, Molly took hold of the tail, and they heaved themselves sidesaddle onto the horse. As their stallion rose and fell, and as the Merry-Go-Round rotated, the calliope began to pipe a medley of popular radio tunes, starting with "Sweet Georgia Brown." The lively chirping scoured their skin like sandpaper while the combined motion of the horse and the ride caused the stationary string of lights encircling the Carousel to draw queasy squiggles on the darkness.

"Your lips are still tingling," Molly said.

"Don't be a twat," Faye snapped, but the word was not as satisfying as she had hoped it would be. She softened her voice to say, "Just forget him and have fun, okay? He's not even good enough for us. He just runs the Ferris Wheel and he's only been a carny for a few weeks."

The tune of the calliope changed to "Yes, We Have No Bananas", and as people began to sing along with the melody, Molly and Faye detested every note. They despised how much feeling Charlie had aroused in them, and that they'd let Jed's reaction disturb them so badly. The twins were the stars here, far above men like that. Unbidden tears began to trickle down their cheeks, which were drained of color; their skin, bled out by hurt and embarrassment, glistened a translucent white marbled with delicate blue veins. At first the tears brought Molly and Faye a rush of panic at the thought of being seen, but soon they began to *hope* to be seen. They would never, *could* never, seek out Dugan to tell him of tonight's events, but if he were to walk by and see them weeping miserably, then surely he would rush to their side with a look of concern and force them to confess everything. He would hug them, say the perfect things—maybe recite a poem, maybe vow revenge against Charlie and Jed, or maybe just whisper that everything would be fine as their tears soaked through his shirt—and for a little while Molly and Faye would feel grateful to be his little girls again. But they couldn't go to him; their legs felt weak and useless.

As more people climbed onto the Carousel to join the sing-along, laughing and yelling in tune—*Yes, we have no bananas! We have no bananas today!*—their feet stirred the sawdust and straw that covered the ground, lending a warm woody aroma to the light sugar scent of cotton candy and the heavier, greasy perfume of frankfurters. Not even the wafts of animal dung on the wind could make the smell less pleasant, and this made Molly and Faye cry harder, as did the rising volume of the chorus; they kept their wet eyes fixed on the surrounding landscape as the Tilt-a-Whirl, the cotton candy booth, and the duck shoot concession passed by once, twice, three times, with no sign of Dugan.

Yes, we have no bananas, the crowd sang, stupidly persisting even as the calliope began to pipe the tune of a different song. *We have no bananas today!*

Faye's lips still tingled, and thanks to two more generous gulps of gin, both girls felt dangerously close to throwing up, but they could not move until someone—it didn't even have to be Dugan anymore, it could be Saffron or Alex or Roxy—noticed their pain and hurried over to clasp their hands and beg to know what was wrong. Molly and Faye needed someone desperately, but they couldn't move, they wouldn't, even if it meant vomiting right there on their favorite black horse and steeping in the mess of their own gorge. On and on everyone sang but no one saw them, as tears dripped from their cheeks and chins onto their pretty blue dresses, as gin and humiliation rose threateningly in their throats, as they waited alone, together, enveloped by a drunken, starlit carnival that bled and blurred in constant flux.

Chapter eleven

Fernglade Methodist Church

1:30 A.M.

Tormented by the twin's never-ending birthday celebration, Shadrach could not abide remaining on carnival grounds.

It wasn't that he disliked Molly and Faye; on the contrary, he liked them very much and considered their conjoined state to be a beautiful way in which God sought to preserve the sisters' chastity as well as their intimacy. The party, however, he wished to avoid. The rollicking shouts and cackles, the eye-stinging fumes of illegal beverages, and the seductive scent of rich, savory sausages and fried pastries with butter cream filling—there were too many temptations to resist, including the powerful temptation to testify as the crowd's flirtation with debauchery would inevitably descend into bacchanalia. In his mind, the celebration resembled a Hieronymus Bosch painting, with twisted acts of violence, greed, gluttony and lust making few distinctions between man, plant and animal. His thoughts often worked this way, going to unrealistic extremes in order to ward off temptation; he was a healthy young man, after all, and extreme measures were often necessary to keep his vigorous spirit restrained.

At first, wandering past the rides encrusted with light bulbs like rainbowed jewels, Shadrach had considered joining the party. Lingering near the Carousel, he observed the stiff mechanical gallop of the horses and the steady glide of the sleigh, the Model T containing two unseemly young people, and the open, unsheltered bench that no one except the very old ever chose to occupy. Molly and Faye rode their favorite black stallion, their faces miserable, their cheeks glistening with tears—but no, not tears, Shadrach decided; it was just an effect of the distance and the twinkling colored lights. What could they possibly have to cry about on their birthday?

As if approaching a dangerous beast, Shadrach had moved toward the ride slowly and carefully, dazed by the heat generated by so much light and so many bodies—strange that in all his years as a carny, he had never ridden a Carousel—and he paused halfway up the steps, arrested by the sight of his own unstable reflection slipping across the enameled hides of the horses. Such passing glimpses obscured his tattoos, and he could only discern the general shape and form of his body, which even in these speeding heat-shimmer reflections remained somehow unmistakable. The piping of the calliope, like a church organ hollowed of its somber center and filled with phosphate, sounded too airy and light to carry the weight of hymns, and wheezed in mockery of worthier music.

It was then that Shadrach knew with certainty that this gathering was no place for a man of God. He turned on his heel while voices sang a popular song he knew from the radio, and used distance to quiet the chorus. Escaping through the field behind the carnival's lot, he ran through the long grasses sprouting between fallen and desiccated stalks of corn and stopped when he reached a darkened grove of pecan trees, a gathering of thick trunks and winding branches far from the heat and noise of the lot. Now that he could breathe again, he sat on a patch of clover to pray for the strength he needed to dispel the Boschian images still winking behind his eyes. The green spring breeze carried the scent of caramelized sugar along with a hint of skunk, and the chirping of night creatures surrounded him, the singing at the Carousel still faintly audible.

He forced his mind away from his environment, turning his thoughts inward to contemplate the self, then outwards, his mind shooting past the pecan grove, past the starry sky, then plunging deep into the wondrous universe, where he searched for the loving presence of God, but found only a disapproving absence. God was still angry at him for hurting that boy in Georgia, for relishing the violence, and for the blasphemous feeling of omnipotence which followed the act; but more than that, God saw down into the center of Shadrach's murdering heart. Overwhelmed by this certainty, Shadrach opened his eyes, got to his feet, and hurried into the field of silvered grass, the night outside the shadowy grove bright by comparison. Through the field and then beyond, his bare feet propelled him onto the dusty gravel road that cut through the center of Galax, Virginia. He had to find guidance, a confessor, a mediator between himself and God, or else freeze to death under God's cold glare.

He found Fernglade Methodist Church a half a mile away, the name hand-painted on a swinging wooden sign. The stained glass angel above the chapel's entrance, illuminated by the flickering candles inside, seemed to flutter her wings. Entering the chapel, he saw a row of tall, white tapers burning on either side of the pulpit down front, and at the sound of the chapel doors closing, a man silhouetted by candlelight called out, "Hello, there."

"Hello," Shadrach called in return, making his way down the aisle slowly, giving the man plenty of time to take in the illustrated expanse of his nearly naked skin. As he approached, the man's face became more distinct, and Shadrach gradually perceived a pair of widening eyes in a ruddy, chubby face. He stopped two feet away and nodded.

"Look at you," the man said. "A cross over your heart, the dove descending at Christ's baptism beside it, the hill in Golgotha on your stomach…" Shadrach obligingly turned around, and the man continued, "…the soldiers of heaven and Jesus preparing to battle the Beast, and on the back of your thigh, there—what's that? Paul on the road to Damascus?"

Shadrach faced the man and nodded. "Yes. My name is Shadrach."

"As in Shadrach, Meshach and Abednego, I presume."

Shadrach pointed to his front, right thigh.

"Ah yes. There they are. You must be from that carnival set up down the road. Well, it's nice to see that the word of God is present even at carnivals—no matter what unusual form it takes." The man grinned. "I'm Reverend Gerald Cartwright." He didn't offer to shake hands. "This is my church."

"Nice to meet you, Reverend Cartwright."

"Call me Gerald. I'm off duty right now."

"If you don't mind my asking, Gerald"—to call a preacher by something so casual was an awkward but pleasant experience for Shadrach—"what are you doing awake at such a late hour?"

"Insomnia. I get it a few times a week, and I always come here to light some candles and think in the quiet. Eventually it wears me out enough that I can go home and fall asleep. I live in the little yellow house next door with my wife Louise."

Soothed by the buttery sputter of candlelight and the Reverend's gentle countenance, Shadrach quickly forced out the words that, once said, would allow him no choice but to go through with his confession. "If you don't mind, I have something I have to say. A story I've kept to myself for too many years."

"I'm a good listener," Cartwright said. "Lots of practice, you know." He motioned toward a front pew.

Sitting on the polished pine bench, feeling God's presence urging him on, Shadrach took a long, full breath, and began. "My father was a preacher at a Baptist church in a small, South Carolina town called Clarence." The story was almost easy to tell, now that he'd begun. "One winter night, while he was away on a hunting trip, my mother and I were spending a quiet evening alone, Mother knitting sweaters for the poor while I read to her from the scriptures—perfect and sweet, like an illustration from a child's picture book. Soon the fire grew low, and seeing that we had scarcely any firewood left, Mother asked me to carry more in from the woodpile. Once outside, rather than immediately obeying, I began to play, kicking my boots through the snow, rearranging the face of the snowman I'd built the day before, and throwing snowballs at the side of the house. Nine years old and carefree, I played until my mittens were soaked through with melted snow, and my fingers grew numb. Only then did I finally gather up an armful of firewood and re-enter the house through the back door.

"I noted how much colder the house had become, and feeling a draft I saw that the front door had been forced open, so I ran to the living room and found my mother pinned against the window seat by a large man with his pants dropped down around his ankles. The man had forced her skirt up and was violently thrusting himself against her. I didn't fully understand what was happening, but I was terrified of the man and horrified by my mother's pained face, so I screamed and dropped my armful of wood.

"The man turned his head, and without stopping his hideous thrusting, pointed a gun at me and said, 'If you want to live, you better keep still and keep quiet.' His eyes were the eyes of a demon.

"Mother nodded, her mouth swollen, her lower lip split open and bleeding. 'Do what he says,' she pleaded, but in a few moments, when I saw the demon close his eyes and begin to groan, I rushed forward and attacked with a large piece of firewood. As I bashed in his skull, the gun went off, firing into the ceiling, leaving a small hole ringed black with gunpowder. Plaster sprinkled our heads like a dusting of flour. The demon cursed from where he fell to the floor, and before he could untangle his feet from his pants, I grabbed a poker from the fireplace and used it to stab the thing through the heart."

Shadrach paused, then began again. "The man was killed, of course. Mother and I took the body to a frozen lake in the woods, dragged it onto the ice, broke through near the lake's center, and with its pockets full of stones, rolled the body into the water, where it sank without a trace. Then I led Mother back to the house and cleaned the blood from her face, anointing her cuts with Mercurochrome. While she was upstairs bathing, I took Father's toolbox, and with great effort, fixed the broken lock on the front door. Then I set to cleaning the clotted blood and gore off the poker and the hearth.

"Mother and I slept in the same room that night, as she shivered uncontrollably. Teeth chattering, she said, 'You must never tell your father about this. God will give us the strength to carry the burden on our own. You killed that man to save us both. There's no sin in self-defense.'

"By the time my father returned home, most of her cuts and bruises had healed, and she'd perfected the art of smiling through pain. Obedient to my mother, I never told, and my father never knew. And he never seemed to notice the plaster patch I'd made for the tiny, scorched bullet hole the demon's gun had made in the living room ceiling. Perhaps I'd done a better job with the concealment than I thought.

"As I grew older, I thought often of the murder, of how difficult it had been to yank the poker out of the man's chest, while the gore that spattered as I worked it free was surprisingly easy to clean off iron and brick. I thought of how my mother had said that what I'd done was not a sin, but I knew that killing in self-defense means the desire to prevent harm without the desire to cause a death, and my motives had not been that pure. I had acted with only one thought in my mind: that any man who would hurt my mother was the same as a demon, and did not deserve to live."

Shadrach fell silent and studied his naked feet, cracked at the heels and throbbing with splinters and cuts, barely visible in the light cast by the altar candles. The pain in his feet pleased him, as did the ringworm he'd developed on his legs—scaly circles encrusting hosts of cherubim and seraphim. He had not worn his boots since the fight in Columbus over a month ago.

"You see, Reverend Cartwright—Gerald—I was forever marked by this experience, and eventually I discovered a way to make the mark visible to the world. I made myself into a spectacle, into something much harder to overlook than clumsy patchwork on a ceiling. This was the path I chose, hoping it would help me atone for my wrongs while making people see the things which must be seen. But I still never knew if my penance was pleasing to God. No voices came from on high or from burning bushes, no angels visited in the guise of lepers. God kept His own counsel."

Cartwright nodded and sighed. He began to reach out a hand to clasp Shadrach's shoulder, but suspended the gesture, stopping to stare at the tattoos as if he'd forgotten that they existed outside the story. Shadrach's skin ached for the affection. His mother had died a few years after helping him sink the corpse of her rapist, and ever since, Shadrach had been starved for her comforting touch, so warm and real; his father never touched him, not even at her funeral.

The Reverend's outstretched hand dropped without making contact. He said, "You're not a murderer, son. I understand why you believe that what you did wasn't exactly self-defense, but I don't think that Jesus, a man who showed such generous compassion to the outcasts of the world, would hold such a thing against a decent Christian like yourself. You were only a boy, and it was a very brave thing to do. You may have saved your and your mother's lives."

Shadrach could not respond. His mind felt empty, scoured clean by the deluge of confession.

Cartwright smiled wryly and said, "I'm not telling you anything you haven't thought of before."

Shadrach nodded. "Thought of, rejected, reconsidered, re-rejected—"

"Come on," Cartwright said. "Let's go make some tea."

The tattooed man followed the Reverend to his little yellow clapboard house, with its green shutters and gray slate roof, and then inside, both men walking quietly on the maple-wood floors so as not to wake the Reverend's wife. In the kitchen, Cartwright motioned for Shadrach to sit, and they didn't speak until the preacher placed two full, steaming mugs of peppermint tea on the table.

"So your father never noticed the patch in the ceiling, and you made yourself into a spectacle. Isn't that how you put it?"

The reductive summary scurried over Shadrach's skin. "Not

quite. I didn't get my first tattoo until my mother died, and that one was of her name, right here." He pointed to the small name inscribed in dark blue ink on his shoulder, barely noticeable next to the large and colorful portrait of the Virgin inked below it. "Then I began to think about the pain of getting tattoos, and the way that they represent a commitment to an idea beyond the power of speech or writing—a tattoo forces you to proclaim that you're committed, physically committed, to a certain image or philosophy, and if later, you decide that you aren't anymore—"

"It's a moot point."

"Precisely. You can say something and not mean it later and it doesn't matter, but a tattoo is a permanent statement. And so I began to get religious tattoos. They were a penance, but also a cel-ebration. They made me feel closer to God. My father wasn't happy about it. He didn't understand when I explained that it was a way I could spread the word of God without speaking. He said I looked like I belonged in a sideshow instead of in his church. I took his words as an indirect message from God, and left home, taking some odd jobs to pay for a few more tattoos before I joined on with my first carnival."

Gerald Cartwright concentrated on drinking his tea while he stared at the charred bricks of the hearth beside the stove. After a while he said, "Those are all admirable reasons for doing what you've done, Shadrach, but I have a question. It's clear that you feel a calling to witness to people about the miracle of Jesus Christ. But do you believe that the life you are presently living fulfills that calling?"

"I used to," Shadrach said.

"What do you believe now?"

Shadrach took his time before answering, the words even more painful in his throat than his confession had been. "I've always wanted my body to be a visible link to the existence of God, but over time I've begun to realize that I can never be more than an imita-tion—not a link, but a link to the link. You see, I'm a spectacle, but I'm not a Wonder. The Freak Show where I work is overflowing with the evidence of God. Every individual on every stage in that top is an original, bearing the mark of the Creator's hand on his flesh. But the marks on my flesh were created by the hands of men."

Shadrach stood and slowly pivoted, revolving to show the Reverend the landscape of his body. For a moment, his hand alighted over his heart, shielding the cross from view. Then, dropping his hands to his side, he said, "Each body in Dugan's show speaks wordlessly with the voice of God. I speak with the gracelessness of human symbols, my voice no different than the voices of a thousand others. So I have to ask you, Gerald, do you think I am heard by my fellow man? Do you think God hears me?"

Cartwright looked solemnly into his mug, saying nothing.

"That's what I think, too," Shadrach said, dropping down onto his chair.

The Reverend held up a hand and said, "Wait a minute. Don't put words in my mouth. I didn't rush to speak because I don't think that anyone can really answer questions like that. Certainly not with a simple yes or no. We might also ask if God hears *me*, or if my congregation hears me. Only God knows for certain. But I keep believing, and I keep preaching, and my heart rests easier to know that I'm doing my best."

The Reverend pushed aside his mug and leaned across the kitchen table. "Have you ever considered leaving the carnival and following in your father's footsteps? Delivering a full sermon to the same congregation every Sunday?"

Shadrach blinked in surprise. "I suppose I have thought of it on occasion, but I never seriously considered it. I've marked myself for the carnival. My path is already chosen."

"Ah piff..." Cartwright swatted the air with his hand. "There's no commandment that says a man has to stick with one profession his entire life. Go ahead and consider it! Maybe you could find a preacher like myself who'd be willing to take you on and teach you the trade. You could cover up your tattoos and let your voice and your actions in the community be heard and felt for their own sake, not for the sake of pictures on your skin."

"You would be willing to take me on as your apprentice?"

The question startled Cartwright, but as he looked into Shadrach's vulnerable eyes, he thought it over and then shrugged. "I might be," he said. "You have the air of a preacher about you, and you speak with authority, and just by looking at you I can tell that you have a thorough knowledge of the Bible. You'd be as good a novice as I could find outside a seminary."

While Shadrach quietly considered whether he would ever, one day, leave the carnival, the Reverend's wife, a lovely plump woman with long black hair, came yawning into the room. As she drew near, Shadrach saw that the iris of one of her eyes was brilliant blue while the other was bottle green, and the quiet wonder contained within this singularity captivated him. He expected her to be alarmed when she saw him, but her sleepy, mismatched eyes registered nothing unusual about his appearance. He wondered if the Reverend had a habit of taking in strange people when he couldn't sleep; maybe the same thing had happened last night, and the night before, and Shadrach ranked as the least bizarre visitor yet.

Cartwright smiled sweetly at his wife and said, "I'm sorry, darling. Did we wake you?"

"Not at all. I woke up on my own and smelled the tea. Decided I'd like a cup." She smiled at Shadrach and held out her hand. "I'm Louise."

"Oh forgive my rudeness, honey—this is Shadrach. He works with that carnival that's in town this week."

"Lovely to meet you," Shadrach said. The warm softness of the woman's grip sent happiness shivering over his skin. He let go of her hand, forcing himself to look away from her entrancing green and blue gaze, studying instead the cozy kitchen, picturing it lit by sunlight. But he could not resist returning to those extraordinary eyes. Azure and emerald, they held a direct, unflinching beauty that made the complicated webbing he'd used to trap his youthful passions seem suddenly ridiculous. Shadrach had spent a lifetime focused on an unending series of *No*s, but here was a loud, defiant *Yes* that shook the walls with the power of all the life that he'd resisted. But as powerful as this *Yes* was, the net he'd woven was not so easily escaped. He wanted everything, but felt unable to allow himself anything. He no longer knew what God wanted from him. Imagining what it must be like to have a church, a congregation, and a marriage to a loving woman like Louise, he envied the Reverend's life with a bitter fervency that released bile onto his tongue, the acid dissolving the calm relief he'd found through confession and the happiness inspired by Louise Cartwright's hand in his. Then Shadrach's mind, fueled by years of thwarted passion and the fear of a life outside the net, spat out a terrible image: he saw himself throwing his mug of tea at the Reverend, then plowing his fist into Louise's lovely, kind, and singular face. Shadrach hungered to destroy what he wanted, what he feared.

Horrified by his wild, violent mind, he leapt to his feet. "I should leave. Let you get back to bed—to sleep."

Either his panic didn't show, or Cartwright didn't notice it, because the Reverend's expression remained unchanged as he nodded and said, "Well, anytime you're in town, come by, and please think about the things I've suggested." With excruciating slowness, Cartwright forced himself to extend his hand the way that his wife had done quite effortlessly a moment before.

Shadrach accepted the uneasy handshake and whispered, "Thank you."

It was difficult, but he managed to leave the house without running, his heart pounding from the enormity of the waiting world, his mind flooding with possibilities. Under the hissing chorus of stars, his fear grew so large it felt fatal. He sensed the swollen immensity of creation, the awesome mystery of the planet and all living things, and sensed, too, the fragile meniscus barely separating each living thing from its death—how easy, how simple it would be to pass through that skin to the other side, where perhaps God waited, or perhaps only oblivion. Shadrach's certainty frayed along with the net that ensnared him, and a great, hungry maw opened in his chest, a powerful emptiness that sent him running over punishing shards of gravel and back to the lot.

He had to hurry and find Finch, who proved the reality of God's universe by capturing it with his photographs. Only Finch could keep Shadrach from feeling frightened or envious or fragile; only the photographer's definite presence could halt the fraying and leave no room for doubt.

Chapter twelve

The Comfort of the Real

3:47 A.M.

A pounding of fist against wood woke Finch from a light sleep and a wonderful dream at the precise moment he was kissing a tall, handsome stranger as black and slender as a licorice whip, a stranger who brought to mind a man he had loved even before he knew about love between men. Disgruntled by the interruption, he yanked the trailer door open, prepared to shout that he wasn't interested in returning to the birthday party, when Shadrach breathed an exhausted word of thanks and fell against him. Finch flooded with worry and arousal in equal measure as he drew the tattooed man inside and closed the door; he knew that Shadrach's touch—always with the quality of a child reaching out to a parent—would never mean what he hoped it would, but as usual, his body responded as if things were otherwise.

"I'm frightened," Shadrach whispered, sitting on Finch's bed. As Finch sat down beside him, the cot creaked under their combined weight. "I feel terribly alone, and when I feel that way I always start to fear that there is no God, and I fear the oblivion that must come after death in a Godless universe, and I fear that my death is at hand."

"Shhh. Quiet. Don't be frightened." Finch pulled the object of his desire against his shoulder, tortured by the expanse of warm, bare skin trembling in his embrace.

Shadrach quickly pulled away and crossed his arms over his chest, panic arresting his face, and for a moment Finch wondered if the man knew more than he pretended to. Then Shadrach said, in an imploring whisper, "Tell me about photography," and Finch sighed; worry overtook his suspicion.

"Photography?" he asked, even though this was an old routine; Shadrach frequently used Finch's talk of photography as an antidote to doubt.

"Yes. Please."

Finch waited, drinking in Shadrach's presence with as much thirst as a man sucking juice from a split desert cactus, and in that moment, as he inhaled the fragrance of Shadrach's illustrated skin—a raw blend of green apple peels and freshly turned earth—he wanted Shadrach almost as much as he wanted to take his photography to those heights that would destroy all lies by capturing the truth that palpitates behind every surface.

"Photography is the art of capturing what is real," Finch began, his voice precarious with longing. "The camera can't lie unless a photographer sets out to deceive. Truth is revealed through the lens, recorded by the film, then preserved on paper for anyone who wants to see and know."

"Truth, yes," Shadrach whispered. "God's truth."

Although Finch didn't believe in God, he nodded and said, "Any person or thing God creates, I can record."

Finch believed in truth, he believed in the real. To him, God was not the puppet-master; he was a false hope, an easy answer. It saddened him that Shadrach only wanted to perceive reality through the mendacious lens of the Lord his God. However, he never tried to disabuse Shadrach of faith; Finch refused to be responsible for the shattering that would accompany his love's acceptance of a godless universe; he would never undermine the power of those tattoos with such a brutal revelation.

"If I can record God's truth," Finch continued, "Then I know that it's truly there. I believe in nothing that can't be shown in this way. Anything I can't photograph can't be real."

"God creates, and you record."

"Yes."

"You take what is real and you preserve it. Your albums are filled with real things. With God's things."

"Yes."

The tattooed man nodded, soothed by the photographer's words and proximity, by the photos framed and hung on the walls and tucked into piles of albums accruing in the corners like layers of sediment. He placed a hand on Finch's shoulder, patted it twice, then crossed his arms protectively over his chest once more.

As he watched the gesture, furious desire clogged Finch's throat like a half-swallowed scream. Did Shadrach know or not know? Finch couldn't ask, of course, but to be entirely ignorant seemed unlikely for a man who'd been *with it* for as many years as Shadrach. Nearly everyone in the sideshow (except perhaps Molly and Faye, who were still children, and Baby Beatrice, who had only recently joined on) was aware of Finch's preference for men, and Alex and Dugan had long ago guessed his feelings for Shadrach. Finch didn't have to declare it verbally; it simply floated in the air around him, a heartsick aura that Shadrach either could not, would not, or pretended not to see. Not knowing was convenient for Shadrach, allowing him to run to Finch as often as to Dugan for comfort. Or perhaps Shadrach sought him out precisely because of how Finch felt. Perhaps ignorance allowed Shadrach to guiltlessly feed on Finch's desire like a parasite.

The speculation was torture. Finch rose to his feet and said, "You have to go." He tugged Shadrach up off the bed and went to open the door. "You're feeling better already. I can tell."

Shadrach. An infuriating paradox of strength and weakness. Finch was sick of feeling the man's warmth and inhaling his scent; the ridiculous futility of desire itself now sickened him. Shadrach's face filled with pained disbelief, his was the face of a man being betrayed, and this turned Finch's sickness into anger. He could not stomach another minute of the tattooed man's presence.

"You'll be fine," he said. "You'll sleep, and it'll be better tomorrow."

Shadrach moved too slowly, so Finch propelled him outside with a firm hand against the back. He whispered, "I'm sorry," but had no way of knowing if he was heard because he shut the door firmly before Shadrach could speak.

Although a swift flare of guilt made him long to, Finch did not look through the window and watch Shadrach walk slowly away, but turned and leaned his back against the trailer door, wondering why he was wasting his love on a man who would never return it. He thought of the slender licorice lover that he'd dreamt of earlier, and though it was true that the man had reminded Finch of someone that he had loved—and had been loved by—long ago, the man in the dream had not been recreated out of the past, but rather, existed as an individual and unique being, the dream a premonition, or a promise. How happy it had made his dreaming self just to be near the tall, tenderly smiling man.

Finch was moved by the way Shadrach's tattoos made faith flesh, bringing Shadrach's inner self to the surface in much the same way that Finch sought to reveal the inner truth of those he photographed. They were both men of passion, dedicated to making the unseen seen. But was that connection where Finch's love began and ended? Or was there something with roots that reached even deeper? Perhaps if Finch abandoned the Starlight and made a new life, his love for Shadrach would fade into a fond, remembered kinship. Twenty-five years had blown past, like leaves on an autumn wind, since Finch had lain a lily on his mother's grave and left the plantation forever. He no longer felt the need to move that had spurred him to ride the rails and then to join the carnival; he'd grown weary of rolling from town to town, his surroundings clicking from old to new like an endless American slideshow. Engendering the inner stillness he needed to create honest, revelatory photography became more difficult with every week, and the idea of a home without wheels sang a siren song promising an ever-expanding space for art.

Perhaps the time had come for a change. For a death and rebirth.

Chapter thirteen

A Visit from Hollywoodland

May 25ᵗʰ, Wayhow, Tennessee

"There you are. Finally," a familiar, whiskey-worn voice rasped at Dugan. "These two didn't have the balls to break into your booze, so they kept us high and dry for nearly an hour."

As he made his way back from a tense meeting presided over by the carnival boss, and attended by the big shots of the carnival, including Zimm, the head animal trainer, and Dugan himself, Dugan was surprised but pleased to encounter Mario sitting beside the ticket booth where Finch and Shadrach had just finished counting up the take from the night before. Even more surprising, Sean the giant sat there, too, beside Finch, who seemed to be fascinated to observe that Sean cast a shadow massive enough to shade him from head to foot.

Dugan called out to Zimm, who had been walking past on

his way back to the Girl Show top, his face still grim with the worry induced by the meeting. "Hey there, Zimm, old man," Dugan shouted. "Come over and meet some friends of mine."

As charming as always, Zimm swiftly traded his scowl for a smile as Dugan introduced him to Mario and Sean. A nondescript white man at first glance —average height, average build, average coloring—when Zimm smiled, he became like no one else. All of his smiles were delightfully wicked. Even his *welcome, nice to meet you* smile gleamed as roguish and conspiratorial as the smile of that one kid in the neighborhood capable of seducing even the best behaved child into any salty scheme, parents and consequences be damned.

Introductions were made with eyes squinting into the glare, handshakes exchanged around fans made from route cards, postcards, and programs—only Finch, sheltered from the sun thanks to Sean, was protected from the unseasonably sweltering May afternoon. The Starlight Carnival Royale was in Wayhow, Tennessee, one hour outside Memphis. Last season, the town had been a red one, highly lucrative, with rubes cycling through the midway in a constant stream, but the cannery in town had shut down nine months ago, and now, the few rubes that did come to the carnival wandered around, sweating in the heat, looking at everything without buying anything. Ulcers were burning in the carnies' guts from swallowing the urge to scream at the dismal penny pinchers. The next stop on the route was Tupelo, Mississippi, followed by Pine Bluff, Arkansas—two excellent stops that should have eased Dugan's mind—but during the past week the Starlight had received word of terrible muddy floods that had stranded at least one major carnival in Arkansas, so there was no way that the route could go as planned. Unfortunately, neither the boss nor the advance man nor anyone else had found an alternate stop within driving distance, and a hole in the route meant money pouring out, not in—a stream of cash flowing into the hands of the proprietor of whatever motel or travel park would lodge the carnival while it waited out the lull. Dugan peered squinny-eyed at the bright sky, the arrival of Mario and Sean feeling like the last thread holding his frayed seams together.

"The sun truly is brutal," he said, forcing a smile that felt nearly natural after a few minutes of holding it. "We'd better get you a dram. I'd hate to see you wither up from thirst."

"God forbid," Sean said. "He hasn't had a drink since his breakfast pint."

"Half-pint, old boy," Mario countered. "I never drink more than a half-pint before noon. Unless I've been up all night, that is."

"A kindred spirit," Zimm proclaimed, winking at Mario.

Dugan led their small assembly to the Freak Show's picnic table beside the Pie Wagon, stopping first to grab a bottle of Canadian whiskey from the supply he had purchased from an entrepreneurial acquaintance in Florida; he thought he spied Alex, a glimmer beyond the sunbursts flaring on the front window of her trailer, but as he motioned for her to join them, the glimmer disappeared behind the glare, and Alex never emerged. They walked on, Dugan noticing that Mario, who had stood an inch shorter than him in the old days, presently sauntered nearly three inches taller. With that breed of obstinate compassion which old friends often wield against one another's miseries, he told himself that while they were in motion it was impossible to know if the growth was truly that dramatic. He put it out of his mind. If he continued to stare, his friend would be able to read his face, and Mario despised pity almost as much as Dugan did.

At the weathered old picnic table, Dugan set up tin cups and a few fingers of whiskey in front of everyone but Shadrach, who disapproved of liquor even more in daylight than he did in darkness. The drinking men lifted their cups in a silent toast, then slugged them back.

While Dugan poured another round, he asked Sean and Mario, "So you two are traveling together these days?"

"After we met back in Savannah," Sean said, "Mario offered me a place to stay if I wanted to try my luck in Hollywood. I took him up on it right away, and spent the last month working on some comedy shorts—you know, the kind that come before the feature. They crank those things out fast, so I kept myself pretty busy."

Mario grinned. "My tall friend was attempting to follow in the impressive footsteps of Mr. Jack Earle."

"Impressive? My thumb leaves more of an impression than that so-called giant's foot," Sean exclaimed, the alcohol seeming to have already gone to his head.

"Sure, sure," Mario said. "The shorts are similar to Earle's is all I'm saying, lots of sight gags and such—"

"Isn't that what all movies are?" Finch asked.

"I'll have you know there are some real artists in Hollywood. As a photographer, you should keep an open mind. This is a new art form. Just ask the French."

"And how much art were you involved in making, Mario?" Zimm asked.

"None at all. I don't go in for that hoity-toity, froggy garbage. I was in it for the vamps and the vino."

The men chuckled as the May sky shone, peppered with sun-drunk starlings that veered and spun through the vitreous blue. Between the sun and the sky and the surprising but welcome company, Dugan began to feel rather good. But still, he doubted this nascent sense of well-being, worrying that it was an illusion, a front-lit scrim strategically placed to distract and conceal, and at any moment, the lighting would change and he'd see through the good feelings to some new, worse trouble lurking behind. Dugan had become too accustomed to pain and fear to trust convivial contentment, no matter how natural it seemed.

Mario took a few cigars from the side pocket of a dingy tow sack on the ground by his feet, and Dugan shook his head. "Fire hazard, old boy. Dry sawdust? Paraffin-coated tents? You know better than that."

"There's a bucket and a pump right there," Mario said. "Fill her up and bring her on over. We'll be as careful as careful can be."

Despite his suspicion of his emotions, Dugan felt too happy to wield an iron fist, and relented. After setting the bucket of water on the picnic table, he accepted a cigar, as did Finch and Zimm; Sean and Shadrach declined.

"All ashes in the water, do you hear me?" Dugan said. "This is a dangerous proposition."

"Yeah, yeah, Pops," Mario said. "We got it."

"So, back to Hollywood," Zimm said. "What did you do there?"

"I appeared in a few pictures for this one producer," Mario said, "and I made a few bucks, then after Sean moved in with me and I got us paired in some shorts, we pooled our funds and bought the little house I'd been renting outright. Sean wasn't sure how long he wanted to stick around, but we knew we'd be able to resell it for a nice price, which we did just a couple of weeks later. Things can move real fast out there, and this house was awful cute, directly under the Hollywoodland sign—"

"The sign is up in the hills," Sean said, "built as an ad for real estate. These huge white letters, over fifty feet high, spelling out Hollywoodland. At night they're lit up with thousands of light bulbs, and there's this one guy whose entire job is just to replace the ones that burn out. He lives in a little cabin behind one of the Ls."

"So if things were so good out west," Dugan said, a dangerous new hope rising in his chest, "why are you here?"

Mario said, "The well ran dry, my friend. At least temporarily. The producer we were working with got goofy over this jazz baby—nothin' but a quiff if you ask me—and he decided to put her in all of his pictures."

"She didn't take to Mario and me. Told him we gave her the screaming meemies," Sean said.

"So out we went."

"We couldn't find much else around town—"

"But we were sick of staying in one place anyway. Weren't we, Sean?"

"That's true."

Dugan smiled to observe the easy intimacy between Sean and Mario. It was good to know that his old friend had someone looking after him—and someone to look after, too, which could be even more therapeutic. Yet beneath Dugan's pleasure coiled a slippery jealousy, not of Mario's affection for the giant, or how quickly the closeness had developed—he could have accepted that sort of jealousy as young green shoots off the trunk of his passionate nature—rather, Dugan felt jealous because no one looked after him in that way. It was his own fault, of course. He had fought hard to conceal his troubles, to ward off nurturing, to make it clear to his family that he alone was the patriarch, protector and caregiver.

"So we set out from Hollywood and came here," Mario concluded, "because we knew that you would never turn us away."

Suddenly Shadrach leaned across the table, his pupils tiny specks centered on two vast expanses of wide and blazing eye. "Any of those producers ever make a religious picture?"

Mario blinked, Sean and Zimm looked down, and Dugan flicked his ashes into the bucket where they hissed against the water, the charcoal flakes dispersing as they sank to the bottom.

"Not that I know of," Mario said. "Religion ain't flashy enough for moving pictures, you know what I mean?"

"Religion has plenty of flash," Shadrach said. "Some of the most thrilling stories ever told can be found in the Good Book." He sprung up from the table, walking swiftly past the Pie Wagon toward the loop of residence trailers on the other side. Lately his moods tossed like tubs on a Tilt-a-Whirl—his thoughts even more so.

"Did I offend him?" Mario asked. He didn't care much if he had.

"You have to understand," Finch said, "Shadrach is a very passionate man."

When Mario began to appraise him with a smile and a knowing look, Finch scowled and added, "He's just a moody bastard, that's all. Don't worry about it."

"I'm not," Mario said, clanking his pinky ring against his empty tin cup. "Shall I pour my own, Dugan, old boy?"

"By all means. I'm not conditioned to keep up with your pace."

Snorting, Mario poured himself a generous serving of whiskey.

"So what do you want with the Starlight, Mario?" Dugan asked, trying to toss a blanket of nonchalance over his shivering hope. "I thought you were too high class to tour with carnivals anymore."

"I never said such a thing... well, maybe I did, but you know I'm a damn boozer—I say all kinds of things all the time, and more than half is horseshit. Anyway, we'd like to join you for a few stops to earn some extra kale before we head down to Florida. I bought some land there."

And though Dugan had tried to prepare himself, the words still struck like a blow to the stomach, knocking him woozy with disappointment.

"Florida? Are you daft?" Zimm asked.

"He bought it years ago," Sean said, "before the big boom and bust. And he went out to inspect it and saw that it's real nice beach-front. He didn't buy any big money swampland."

"I'm no fool," Mario said. A fit of coughing scrunched and contorted his crabapple face, and he dunked his half-smoked cigar in the water bucket. "I've got to quit smoking these things."

Dugan slapped his old friend on the back with more force than was necessary. "While you're at it, quit the bad whiskey. It's worse for you than those damn cigars."

"We don't all have the grade-A prime connections that you do, dollface. Some of us take whatever we can get our hands on."

"So tell me, how will you occupy yourselves in Florida?" Dugan asked. Hope leaked from his chest like air from a pinpricked balloon.

"Well," Sean said, "I had the idea we should build an off-season settlement for people like us, a real nice place for winter quarters—"

"Nicer than that pit y'all stay at in Valdosta," Mario said to Dugan, who shrugged and replied, "Hell, it's only for three months a year."

"Anyway," Sean continued, "we'd make it real swell, and we'd keep it real quiet, so that just those who are *with it* will know, and the doctors will be less likely to find me."

"Are they still after you?" Dugan asked.

In a surge of volume and vehemence, Sean said, "They sure the hell are. You seen my fucking foot yet?"

He hefted up his left leg, and dropped it on the table with a thud that sloshed whisky over the edges of the cups, and dingy water over the edge of the bucket. Pulling his pants leg up and his sock down, he exposed a thick, hairy calf strapped into a wooden prosthetic ankle and foot.

"I lost it a week and a half ago," he said. "Almost two weeks, now. As you might've noticed, I've grown even since that night we met."

Dugan hadn't noticed; he'd been too busy noticing Mario's height.

Sean continued. "I'm so tall now that I've stopped feeling much at all below the knee, nearly nothing in my feet. Didn't even feel it when I stepped on a penny nail. It must've been in my foot for a week, and the wound went septic. I only noticed it was there after Mario commented on how much trouble I was having trying to shove a boot over my swollen foot and told me to take off my sock so he could have a look."

"Nastiest thing I ever saw," Mario said.

"Had no choice then. I had to see a doctor. Funny thing was, Mario goes out to find one, and he's barely half a block away when he runs into this fellow who says he heard that we were looking for medical help."

"I was so worried—and disgusted, I mean, you should've seen that damn foot—it didn't even occur to me to wonder how the hell this guy knew I was looking for a doctor when I'd just set out to find one a minute ago and hadn't told a soul about it yet. Anyhow, the guy says *he's* a doctor, and he shows me his black bag and stethoscope and everything—"

"And Mario brings him back to the house, where the doctor dopes me up with a shot and saws off my whole goddamn foot."

"He told us the infection would spread and likely kill Sean if he didn't amputate. The doc said it was a miracle it didn't get into his blood."

"Of course I barely remember any of it. Mario had to retell me most of it once the shot wore off."

"I thought it was real nice how the doctor didn't charge us anything. He even left a big bottle of pain pills and a stack of fresh bandages and a sheet of instructions for cleaning the wound, but no bill."

"But he took my foot with him when he left," Sean said, his face shadowed by a rage that chilled Dugan under the blazing spring sunshine. The pain in his joints and spine, which usually burned, now ached as if rubbed with snow; Dugan understood how it felt to have one's body betray you, but the consequences for him had never been so extreme.

"And he must've boiled it down and assembled the bones awful goddamn quick," Sean continued, "because less than a week later we heard that our buddy the doctor was delivering a lecture on the skeletal structure of giants, using the display of my fucking foot to draw in the crowds. Charged a quarter a head for admission."

"Probably had no idea that he was running a third rate Single-O that no experienced carny would touch," Mario said. "At least not without claiming it for a Sasquatch foot and fleshing out the tent with a few pickled punks."

Sean lifted his artificial extremity and let it drop back onto the ground. "So yeah. I'd have to say that the doctors are still after me."

He turned his head at the sound of scrabbling and chittering coming from a nearby tree, and took a few long, deep breaths as he watched two squirrels run, spiraling nose to tail up the trunk like stripes on a barber's pole.

Dugan placed a hand over the giant's enormous fingers and said, "My family and I will do our best to look out for you, old boy. I promise that unless you request it, no doctor will come anywhere near you while you travel with the Starlight Carnival Royale."

"I won't request it," Sean said, "but thanks. You're a good man, Dugan, and a good friend."

"Enough with the sweet talk, ladies," Mario said. "Tell me about the Janes here in Wayhow, Tennessee. Any adventurous bits of calico been dropping by yet? It got a little lonely on the road here from Hollywood."

Dugan laughed. "None yet, but I doubt it will take long for you to inveigle a few diverting encounters." He spoke without listening to himself, his mind weaving, darting back and forth like the shuttle of a loom. The pain mounting in his bones kept him from giving as much to his show as he used to, and more new Wonders—fresh blood—could help compensate for that. Sean's lost foot and his fear of doctors were the keys to keeping him; Dugan only needed to think of how to keep Mario. Sean was a first rate curiosity, and even if Mario continued to grow, the fact that he could take over for Dugan as host and announcer if that became necessary made him an invaluable asset; his drunken energy would invigorate the flagging Freak Show like a long-needed transfusion, prolonging its life in these unhealthy times. If Dugan could have, he would've locked both men inside his Cabinet that very afternoon, then dropped the key into the ocean's deep.

Dugan decided, resolute, that nothing he loved, nothing he had created, would end without his permission. His carnival family had been made, not born, and held its present structure through craft, through Dugan's careful fitting of tongue into groove. The family had been built, not born, and therefore was exempt from natural laws such as death. As its creator, Dugan would guard and preserve his family into eternity, watching it grow, thrive, and even change in small ways, but never die. He would never permit it to die.

Chapter fourteen

Moonshine Gamble

May 31ˢᵗ, Tupelo, Mississippi

The scents of home-brewed liquor, mildewed socks, and heavy floral perfume infused the basement of the Tupelo, Mississippi sheriff's office. Saffron downed half a mason jar of moonshine while playing two hands of poker with her new gambling buddies—Deputy Little, a pale, blond man with a belly aping a nine month pregnancy; Kraunk, a swarthy, handsome man who owned a grocery in town; and Harlon, a tall, wiry, rat-faced fellow who rarely broke a smile—before she finally asked about the incongruous scent overlaying the basement's damp rank.

"The wife makes potpourri," Deputy Little explained, patting his belly as if that was where he kept the little woman, "and she sends me off to work with a fresh batch every couple months. Sheriff doesn't like to have the smell upstairs, but he says between the damp and the still, it can't stink any worse down here."

"He knows about the still?" Saffron asked.

Kraunk laughed, exposing his crooked teeth, the only part of him not straight and sharp and handsome. "Do you think that a sheriff don't know what's happening in his own building? He knows, and he drinks. It's like this saying I learned from my poor ol' momma, who left Poland to come to Mississippi and give her children a piece of the American—"

"—I thought you said you were German?" Saffron interrupted.

Kraunk shrugged, then continued, "My poor momma, she always said that anything a lawman likes is no crime for him."

"Yeah. Great saying," Harlon said, stretching his skinny, rubber band limbs. "Don't know why it didn't catch on here. Are you gonna ante up, or keep yapping about your German-Austrian-Polish mother?"

As Kraunk tossed a quarter in the center of the table, Saffron felt an overwhelming urge to laugh, so she took a large swig of the white lightning, which struck fast and razed the impulse. She wasn't usually a silly drunk. In fact, because of how quickly her body processed anything she ingested, she rarely became more than mildly intoxicated. The tipsiness aroused by a few shots of alcohol would fade and be gone in thirty minutes, just like the muscle aches she relieved by taking a few aspirin were sure to return an hour after departure, and the way that after eating, her hunger always revived two hours later, on the dot. But in spite of the unfamiliarity of being so extremely drunk, Saffron was having a fine time. At first she'd been disappointed that Armenante and his son, her favorite gambling companions, had to stay behind to repair the malfunctioning duck shoot, but now she was pleased. It was fun to keep these strange, amusing men to herself, and she preferred to win without having to take money from a fellow carny.

The moonshine made her wobbly on her seat—*no, I'm wobblier than wobbly,* she thought, *I'm jiggly like gelatin*—and the urge to giggle struck her again, but this time she didn't dare drink more moonshine, so her laughter spilled out, splashing the basement with mirth.

"What're you sniggering at, Wolf-Girl?" Harlon asked.

Kraunk said, "She's laughing 'cause the white lightning's gone straight to her head. If she didn't have that beard, we'd see her cheeks all red with liquor."

This made Saffron laugh still more. Deputy Little looked at her and then at the other men with a slow, sly smile which should have made her wary, but she'd already won a great deal of money for her and Bea, for their plans, and in her experience, losers at poker often appear conniving in their determination to turn the game to their favor.

"Well, this certainly is some damn fine corn whiskey," the Deputy said, "even if I do say so myself."

The chipper way that the men nodded at one another and raised their glasses in agreement endeared them to Saffron. All men were really just little boys, and these boys were her new friends. She felt entirely at home; she wanted to tell them everything about her life. She liked the white lightning, but it seemed so awfully potent that she wondered if perhaps her body couldn't process moonshine as swiftly as it processed other varieties of alcohol.

"At the Starlight," she said, "we're lucky when it comes to drinking. We get this really smooth Canadian whiskey because of Dugan. He gets it from this friend of his who has a boat in Florida, and sometimes the guy brings cigars too, which I used to like, but not anymore—I got sick one night from smoking too many too fast. Anyway, Dugan's really good at getting anybody anything that they want, because of all the people he knows, and because he's so smart."

She recognized that she was talking too much, but it felt so good to relax and be free and open, even around rubes, that she couldn't halt the flow of words. "Of course I don't think that Dugan is half as smart as he thinks he is. He's twice as smart as most people, don't get me wrong, but I don't think he's a genius like he claims. If he were a genius he would've helped to find us somewhere better than Dry Fork, Louisiana to replace our Arkansas stop next week."

Picking up her mason jar, then setting it back down without drinking, Saffron jostled her head from side to side and said, "Jesus! What the hell do you put in this moonshine?"

"A little bit of this and a bit little of that," the deputy said.

"Sugar and spice and everything nice," Harlon added. "Just put your feet up and enjoy it."

Saffron laughed, and laughed even more when she looked down and saw the cards in her hand; she had forgotten they were playing poker. She didn't remember whose turn it was or if anyone had taken cards yet, and she would have asked, but the floor seemed to be listing to the left, and she needed to put down her cards and hold out her right arm as a counterbalance.

"The floor in this room is very unusual," she said, her right arm extended.

Kraunk's lips formed a voluptuous smile as he said, "That isn't everything around here that's unusual."

Deputy Little threw his cards on the table and said, "Hell, she's more than unusual, she's a goddamn Freak!"

Saffron frowned and said, "A goddamn Freak who...who..." Speech, which had spewed forth so uncontrollably a minute ago, was now difficult to summon; her tongue had thickened, the muscle weakening as it swelled, turning soft and spongy. "...a Freak who...who is taking all of your money."

Harlon leaned back in his chair, dropped his cards to the floor, and said, "The night's still young, sweetheart. Who can say what'll happen next?"

An icy gust scoured the laughter from Saffron's body. *He dropped his cards to the floor.* She looked at her mason jar. It hadn't occurred to her until that moment that they may have added some sort of opiate to her drink.

She tried to grab her pile of winnings with two torpid hands, but her loose-knuckled fingers didn't want to grip, so she had to slap one hand on top of the pile and slide the money off the edge onto the other. With the bills and some of the coins sandwiched between her palms, she shoved both hands into the right pocket of her Levi's, awkwardly stuffing the money in while a few of the coins pinged to the concrete floor at her feet. When she looked up at the men, they only smiled wider. She knew that she should have run the moment she recognized the danger, but some of her gambling money was actually Bumble-Bea's—money they were saving together, money that Bea didn't know Saffron had taken—so she couldn't leave without it or her winnings. If she returned with more cash than she took, then what she had done was borrow, not steal.

Saffron commanded her body to stand and run for the exit, but when a minute passed and she still hadn't reached the door, she looked down and discovered that she still sat slumped in her chair. Trying again, concentrating on propelling her muscles through space, she raised her rear an inch or two off the chair and slid one foot out as she bent forward to bring herself to stand, but then she slipped sideways and landed on the cold, unyielding concrete, barely feeling the impact. A white mist rolled in from the corners of the basement, a stealthy fog rubbing against her like a cat, then stretching and expanding as it smothered her body in thickening cotton clouds that cloaked her sight and stopped up her ears until everything disappeared into white silence.

When the mists parted, she saw Harlon's skinny face smirking as Kraunk dug her wad of money from her jeans pocket. His rough hands hurt her, but at a remove, as if she were feeling the reverberations of another Saffron's pain. Her awareness guttered and went out.

When the room returned again, she wiggled the fingers of her left hand and checked to see if her wedding band was still there. It was. The thin band wasn't obvious on her hairy third digit, easy to miss. But what about Bumble-Bea, what about her friend's money? A new, distant sensation distracted Saffron then, and her eyes made a small jump to the right, seeking the source. Deputy Little was pulling her pants and underwear down to her ankles.

"I don't know if I'm up for this," Harlon said.

"It'll be a once-in-a-lifetime chance. You'll regret it if you miss out 'cause you're yellow," Kraunk said.

"I'm not yellow, but she's so damn furry—how the hell are we supposed to find her gash?"

"Ain't you ever banged a woman with a hairy hole before? You just shove your way in. She'll help. Deep down they all want it."

The fog began to return, and desperately Saffron flooded her body with energy, willing it to kick her legs and thrash her arms, but her feet only tick-tocked back and forth while her left hand flopped like a landed fish.

She slipped off into nothing again, and when she blinked back into the room, she was lying on her side with her cheek pressed against the concrete. A few inches from her nose, a tooth floated in a pool of blood. Was it *her* tooth? She probed her mouth with her tongue, and only after she had traced the contours of every tooth and found them all still rooted in place did she remember the men. She couldn't see anything, but she heard distant grunts and thumps and meaty thuds, as if she had her ear pressed to a wall, listening to strangers brawling in the next room. Feeling safe with the violence so far removed, she didn't resist when the nothingness returned.

She came to like a flash of light at the sound of a slamming door. No longer on the floor, she was outside now, under the stars. Something hard and lumpy cradled her, carried her: muscular arms with the certainty of stone. Feeling things less distantly now, she tried to kick her right foot and succeeded. Her pants were back on.

"Goddamn crooked town," the man who carried her muttered. "Can't call the law because the cracker lawmen are criminals. Goddamn stealing, raping ofays."

It was Finch. He was taking her away. But how would they escape without a car?

"They picked me up and drove me here," she said sadly, but her voice emerged distorted, her words transformed into, "*Ay-pih-meeuh n dro-meehe.*"

"Shhh. Don't be scared," he said. "We're going home."

Her head flopped to the side, and she saw the new navy blue truck under a streetlamp just a few yards away. Relieved, she drifted off to sleep and dreamed of a sunny, dusty road scored into the side of a green mountain. The air was hot there, and surrounding her were people whose skin gleamed the same brassy, golden-brown as her own did, beneath her fur.

She woke to find Finch helping her out of the truck, and she was happy to feel her feet hit the ground, her hands holding on to him for balance, and even the pain at the tip of her nose beginning to spread. But added sensation meant added awareness of what had happened, that she had allowed herself to become helpless, to need rescuing.

"Do you want me to carry you?" he asked.

"No," Saffron said, ashamed.

As he helped her to limp along, he kept turning his head, his eyes darting to either side. Then he expelled a hard breath and swept her up in his arms. He carried her up some stairs, opened a door and took her inside a dark place; after setting her on the floor, he kicked the door closed behind them.

A bulb hanging from a cord overhead clicked on. Light flooded the room, and Saffron said, "This is not my trailer."

"No," Finch said. "It's not."

"What happened?" a strange man asked. Even though he spoke softly, his voice was as broad and deep as the sea. "Is she hurt?" A large, gentle face with prominent cheekbones bent down into Saffron's range of vision—Sean. She smiled at him. They had just met the week before, but she liked him very much already. She looked around for Dugan's friend, Mario, but he seemed to be out.

"She's been drugged, I think," Finch said. "Her nose is bleeding and a little swollen, but the fur makes it hard to tell where else she might be hurt. Sorry to wake you, but this is the furthest trailer from Dugan's. Plus, I heard you and Mario are well stocked with first-aid supplies."

"You heard right. Why don't you want Dugan to know?"

"He knows some already. He found out where she went from a concessionaire and sent me to go get her, but I'm hoping to get her cleaned up and in her bed before he finds out she's back. He doesn't need to know the rest."

"Thanks," Saffron mumbled. "Dugan can be suchapaininth-eass."

"I'll go fill a pail at the pump," Sean said. "If she was drugged, she probably needs some water. Maybe we can help flush it out of her system."

My system flushes things out just fine, Saffron said, realizing a moment later that she hadn't spoken aloud. Sean thumped out of the trailer using a cane. He only had one foot; she hadn't noticed that before.

As her sense of touch grew stronger, she began to feel an ache through her muscles. Her nose was throbbing and her head pounding; she barely felt drunk or drugged now, just incredibly tired and bleary, as if she had been bedridden with illness for days and at last her fever had broken.

Sean returned with the pail, dropped his cane to the floor and hopped over to Finch, who dipped out a mug of water then pressed the glazed rim to Saffron's lips. "Come on. Drink up."

"What happened to her?" Sean asked, lowering his long, lean body onto the floor.

Saffron took the mug, drank the cold water and watched the men continue to talk about her as if she weren't there. She hoped they wouldn't mind if she went to bed soon.

Finch told Sean that she had gone off alone to play poker with three local men. "And they slipped her a Mickey," Sean guessed.

"They gave her something. I don't know what. Mixed with moonshine, I think. When I got there she was unconscious, and one of the men had her pants down, and—Well, I kicked him across the room before he forced..." The severe lines of Finch's face faltered. His eyes widened. "Wait, but how could I really know if—there were three of them. How the hell can I know what they did before I got there?"

Shaking her head as the empty mug clunked onto the floor, Saffron reached clumsily for Finch, draping her arms over his shoulders and embracing him as firmly as her weakened muscles would allow. "No, stop," she said. "You don't have to know because I know. You got there in time."

"But *how* do you know?" Finch breathed against her shoulder. "You were unconscious."

"I would feel it now, and I don't feel it. Okay?"

She had spoken to comfort him, but when she closed her eyes

and explored her throbbing nerve endings, she knew she'd told the truth. She had not been raped.

"You got there in time," she said. Gratitude and shame welled up in her body, turning to salt water and blurring her vision, but still, no tears spilled onto her auburn furred cheeks. "Oh, God. Thank you, Finch."

Finch pulled back and grabbed her upper arms, shook her. "Why do you do this?" he asked. "Why the *hell* do you do this?"

She stared in surprise until he let her go, crossing the room to sit on Mario's rumpled, empty bed.

"I wanted to win a little extra money," she said. Surprise made her honest, but her answer embarrassed her, so she continued, "I've been saving up. I want to put together my own Freak Show and tour through Mexico." Her thoughts garbled, tangled with images of a hot yellow sun and green mountains. "Here in the U.S.—people, they're more skeptical, and there—people have more faith, and they're more open to wonder."

Sean scooted closer to Saffron and said, "But when you gamble, you're just as likely to lose big as win big."

"I don't know about that. Poker isn't all luck, it's a game of skill. And I'm very skilled." She was tired of sitting up, and she wished they'd stop talking; if she stretched out on the floor, maybe she could go to sleep right there.

"But—" Sean began.

"Oh, hell," Saffron said. A trickle like ice water ran down her back. "They got all of the money."

Finch grunted. "Of course they did. I was lucky to get you out of there without attracting the sheriff and a few more men with guns to the scene. Did you think I'd stop and try and figure out what money was yours? Be thankful you didn't lose anything more important than money."

"But it wasn't just my money. It was Bumble-Bea's, too."

"She loaned you poker money?"

Saffron slowly shook her head.

"You took it?"

"Well, we've been saving it together. Bea's coming with me to Mexico."

"Goddamn it, Saffron!"

Her voice came out very small as she slowly, carefully said, "It wouldn't have been stealing if I'd been able to give back more than I took."

As Finch and Sean stared, she grew sick with doubled shame. Twisting the gold band still on her finger, she said, "I get sad sometimes, you know? Poker makes me feel better."

Finch sat on the floor and took Saffron's face in his hands, studying her eyes as they glistened; then he pulled her against his shoulder, folding her into his arms again.

"If I give you the money to replace what you took," he said, "will you promise not to do anything stupid like that again? No stealing, no going off alone anywhere—in fact, I want you to promise that if you feel like you have to gamble, do it here, with other carnies. I'll give you the money to repay Bea if you promise."

Too tired to do anything but accept, Saffron wrapped her aching, somnolent arms around Finch and replied, "All right. I promise."

Pressing her cheek against his warm, cement-hard shoulder, she sank towards sleep like a pebble through fathoms of dark, welcoming water, while Finch spoke the words that would wheeze incessantly through her dreams that night and for weeks thereafter.

"I know you still love him, Saffron, but he's dead. And you're alive—no matter how much you fight it. Life's no trifle, so stop acting like it is."

Chapter fifteen

A Short Walk from the Girl Show

June 5th, Dry Fork, Louisiana

On the first Sunday in June, over twenty pots and fires turned the sultry Louisiana air into a sauna replete with dirt and horseflies and pollen. Wading slowly into lake water scummed with algae so brightly green it nearly glowed, Roxy, the Girl Show dancer who had bestowed makeup and gin upon the twins for their birthday, squished her bare toes through mud while slimy underwater snake grass slapped her calves. The lake—tepid just above the mud, warm midway, and hot at the water's surface where a stale and sour smell rose—possessed a shoreline aureole of dried black sludge left by higher water.

"Can we even get ourselves clean in a lake like this?" Faye asked.

"It's creepy," Molly said.

"Probably filled with diseases," Sean added.

There was a well on the lot, but the carnies had been warned to pump sparingly, as Dry Fork, true to its name, had been in drought since early spring. The Starlight had avoided floods in Arkansas only to encounter drought in Louisiana; it seemed that their bad luck was growing like kudzu, spreading like a brushfire. After a thorough search, no one had discovered another lake, or a pond, or a creek flowing at more than a trickle, so it was foul water scummed with hot algae or nothing.

Dugan, Zimm and the other carnival bigshots decided that though it would be a tight fit, only half of the pots would be used to boil clothes, and the other half would boil the impurities and bacteria from the stagnant lake water, which could then be used for rinsing.

"A nice splash of hot water for a nice hot day," Zimm muttered to Dugan before wading across the water to a gaggle of naked cooch dancers pouting in the green and brown muck.

In the midst of the discomfort and grumbling (a quiet surface reaction that camouflaged the carnies' growing concern for the unlucky turn the season had taken), Roxy stood out as the only smiling trouper. As she waded deeper into the lake, parting the algae that formed a glistening, pulpy ring around her body, determined to remain with the Freak Show performers rather than join the other Girl Show dancers, she laced her fingers with Alex's under the water and smiled, and smiled, and smiled.

I belong here, she thought. I belong here with you, Alex.

"If staring filled your belly," Bea said, pointing to the clusters of carnies in and around the lake, "then every carny here would be as fat as me."

"Why *are* they staring, anyway?" Sean asked. "Shouldn't they be used to Freaks by now?

"Well," Saffron said, "it's not every day that they get such an up-close look."

Bea shook her head. "Nope. I don't think that's it. I think they're staring because Roxy's here. They're shocked as hell that one of the sweet tomato Girl Show girls is here with us Freaks. Just 'cause our canvas is set up a short walk from theirs don't mean they think it's fine for us to socialize together."

"Whyever not? I don't believe they see themselves as especially different from us," Dugan said. "If you think about it, the Girl Show has a great deal in common with the Freak Show. Many of the same principles that ensure its success ensure ours. And we are the pinnacle of carny success—the top of the heap as far as profitability is concerned. Even in hard times we do fairly well for ourselves."

Roxy said, "Probably only half are shocked, and the rest are jealous." She hadn't felt this little loneliness in four years. She squeezed Alex's hand, hoping that soon, maybe, she wouldn't feel lonely at all anymore.

"I wouldn't be so sure about the jealousy," Mario said. "Sure, they'd like to take in the heavy sugar like we do. Everybody gets jealous when it comes to money. But most aren't eager to buddy up with individuals like ourselves."

"They're carnies. They like being our friends just fine," Saffron said. "They just don't want to *be* us. And *with it* or not, they're still just as fascinated by our bodies as everyone else."

Bea said, "I think Sean's right. They should be used to it by now. No matter what kind of fuckin' wrapper you put it in, a peppermint's still a peppermint. We're no different from any of them."

"Oh, but you are," Roxy said. "You're different, and you're better."

"Better how?" Saffron asked.

Roxy hesitated; she knew that Saffron's late husband had been a normal-bodied aerialist, not a Freak, so she was unlikely to see the world as clearly divided as Roxy did. Still, Roxy's true feelings on the subject, which were all tied up in her feelings for Alex, were too feverish to contain.

"They're all the same," she said. "They're no different than all the rest of the worthless sheep out there in the world."

"They *are* different from the sheep," Finch said. "They're carnies. Carnies are a breed apart."

"Well, okay. They're a little different," Roxy said.

"So we're better just because we're different?" Saffron asked. Still bruised beneath her fur from the trouble in Tupelo, she latched onto the opportunity for angry debate like a leech.

"We aren't different," Bea insisted. "Not inside, anyway."

"But you *are*," Roxy said. "You're special. You don't belong out there in the boring world full of people all trying to live the same life. You belong in your own world, a better world."

Saffron shook her head. "But you see, the boring world out there is scared of us. It doesn't want us. We make our own world because we *have* to. So how does that make us better?"

Saffron's eyes flared so brightly that Roxy realized she must've been angry already, the discussion merely providing her with a way to vent. Roxy wished she had kept her mouth shut and just enjoyed Alex's company in silence.

Shadrach, who had scarcely spoken that day, wading chest deep through the scum before removing his loincloth and handing it to Dugan to be dropped into the pot, suddenly spoke up. "Saffron, your distinction makes you better because it shows that God has marked you. He has made you living proof of his creative power. The difference is a sacred one."

"I asked you a question, Roxy," Saffron said, ignoring the tattooed man. "What exactly is it that makes us better than everyone else?"

"You're better because… you're just…." Roxy's voice trailed away. A headache pricked at her temples. Dropping Alex's hand, she massaged her head with fingers stinking of bog water. All around, carnies worried about lagging profits and unpleasant stops, and whether the health benefits of the lake water outweighed its potential health risks, while Roxy lived in a much smaller world with a much narrower, and entirely personal focus—she was a tiny planet, orbiting Alex's sun. She began to speak, thinking that maybe, if she talked about herself first, she could make Saffron understand.

"I'm weird, okay? I talk to myself without realizing it, and in school my mind used to drift as if I was dreaming and then I'd wake up and be standing at the classroom door with my teacher shouting at me. I couldn't handle school at all, really, so when I was twelve, I left and started cleaning houses with my mother."

Saffron stared at Roxy with her mouth slightly open and the silky brush of her eyebrows arched crookedly; this explosion of overly personal information was not the sort of answer she had expected to get. Every other Freak either stared at Roxy with amusement, or looked deliberately away, embarrassed by her candor. And though Roxy observed these reactions, she still continued to speak, unable to stop herself.

"I've always felt different, all the way deep down in my bones. It wasn't until I saw a photograph—it was a souvenir postcard, I think—of Laloo—do you know him?"

Saffron smirked. "Not personally." At Roxy's exasperated sigh, she said, "Yes, I know who you mean."

Roxy could still picture the sepia-tint photograph of the Indian man with the dead twin buried in his chest like an ostrich with its head in the sand, the twin's tiny lifeless body—wearing a diaper for modesty's sake—dangling near his brother's beating heart.

"Well, I saw myself in that picture. I'm a Freak just like Laloo, only on the inside instead of the outside. That's why when I left home, I ended up with a carnival. So I can be near the Freak Show. Because really, I belong with you."

The anger in Saffron's eyes grew dim with pity, and Roxy suddenly wished she could take it all back. She had volunteered too much of herself, laid her heart right there on the chopping block. Roxy clung to the idea of Freaks as a talisman against pain, and to the Freak Show as if it were a brave new world containing only peace and acceptance. Being *with it* for several years now had not diminished her rube naiveté.

"But you *don't* belong here with us," Saffron said, denying Roxy access to her imagined utopia. "You belong with the Girl Show. Looking different and being different aren't automatically the same thing, Roxy, even if you want them to be. Nothing about people is that simple or obvious."

After giving Roxy a final, dismissive look, Saffron waded to shore, the lakewater coursing down her fur, leaving tracks of shiny green slime along the heavy curve of her breasts, the sinuous line of her furred waist and hips. Roxy closed her eyes, feeling young and foolish, flat-chested and ordinary; she still did not fully understand what had been said to her.

Then she heard Saffron call out casually, cruelly, "That act was a gaff, you know. Laloo's twin was a decapitated doll stuck to his chest with plaster."

Alex slid a hand down Roxy's back and cupped her small, round ass under the water, giving it a squeeze. "She's probably just saying that, Roxy darling. She's been a complete bitch this entire week."

Roxy opened her eyes and whispered in his ear, "Let me come see you tonight. Please. I need you."

After Alex nodded, Roxy pulled away, and with the rest of the Freaks staring after her as if examining a strange, pesky bug, she swam across the fetid lake to Zimm and the other dancers in the Girl Show, resigning herself to the pain of an ordinary existence, already counting the minutes until she and Alex would be together and the labyrinthine possibilities of their lovemaking would once again free her from herself.

Chapter sixteen

A Bag of Bones

June 16th, Marshall, Texas

Bumble-Bea's old friend Mr. White turned up in Texas on June 16th, 1927, the tenth anniversary of the day that Bea's sister Ethel had perished from scarlet fever. Eleven-year-old Bea had cried unceasingly for a week after. Unable to eat, she panicked her parents by losing twenty pounds so quickly that death's bony hand seemed to grip her dwindling (though still substantial) frame, pulling her steadily closer to her lost sister. But the fast didn't continue for long, and soon she had regained all that weight and more.

Losing Ethel had gouged a hole in Bea's spirit, an empty space that begged to be filled by food, by Jimmy sweeping her off her feet, by seven years of carnival performance. Every June 16th over the past ten years, Bea had found it difficult to eat for twenty-four hours, an annual fast that allowed the hole left by Ethel's death to gape unfilled, hungry, howling. This anniversary was no different, and so she performed with twice her usual enthusiasm, regarding the Texan marks with her ornamental smile daubed firmly above her chin, feeling the hollow in her chest begin to fill with their attention. Like a bucket with a hole in it, she remained sated as long as the intoxicating gaze of the masses continued to pour in, and soon felt depleted once the flow had stopped.

"Can you move around?" a girl from the front row asked.

Bea laughed and stood, fluffing the ruffles of her skirt as she twirled.

She hated these frilly dresses with gathers that pinched her fat into corrugated patterns that remained engraved into her flesh for hours after she'd shed the Baby Beatrice costume; she hated simpering and dancing and pretending that her girth made her jolly, wide-eyed and powerless, but seeing an enormous woman costumed as a little girl amplified the dramatic effect, and the conceit was Freak Show tradition, so Bea resigned herself to the daily sting of a hundred fluffs of her ruffles and battings of her eyelashes, flourishes supporting her image as a doll full of giggles, empty of sense, and completely blank, smooth, and sexless between the legs. Still, though, however much she hated it, all those eyes upon her, and all the words, both kind and rude, managed to flow past her humiliation and into her pierced tin bucket of a heart until there was no emptiness left to spawn grief.

Yes, she hated Baby Beatrice, but she loved her more.

"That all you in there?" a man asked.

"Sure is."

"You sure? There isn't any padding filling you out?"

Although Bea refused to show much skin on stage, she had a way of satisfying this sort of rube. Sliding the puffy short sleeve of her dress up to her shoulder, she swatted her left upper arm with her right hand so that the sucks could witness the smack, then swing and shudder, of fat-packed flesh.

Someone shouted, "That's repulsive!"

Bea couldn't tell where the voice came from, but it was when she scanned the crowd for the speaker that she first noticed Mr. White, an emaciated form with skin like a wet sheet clinging to bone, and a head like a living *memento mori*, standing before her and staring. Surprised, she gave him a smile before she could stop herself, then looked away when someone else in the crowd shouted, "It's not repulsive, it's *beautiful*."

The man who spoke was the same man who had asked if she were padded, now looking up at her misty-eyed and star-struck—nice that at least one mark seemed aware that she was a real, grown-up, fully functional woman. Such instant adoration was a regular occurrence; there were a fair number of men in the world who relished not quite wrapping their arms around a jumbo-sized serving of warm woman, but as usual, most of the audience craned their necks to look, their faces revealing incredulity and mild revulsion as their eyes came to rest upon Baby Beatrice's newest, biggest fan, who in turn noticed nothing but her.

Bea winked and said, "Well, well, well. Maybe I'll see *you* later, sugar." She pulled her curtain closed against an uproar of laughter and applause.

The shows after that one proceeded in much the same way for Bea, while the skeletal Mr. White, in a loincloth not unlike Shadrach's, remained standing near her platform like a birch in winter or a half-naked scarecrow. No one seemed able to perceive him and no one interacted with him—not the suckers, not Dugan, not even Finch as he broke up a fight only inches from where Mr. White stood. Returning White's gaze from time to time, Bea had to wonder how the man—his flesh even more extraordinary than her own—could pass unnoticed among people who'd paid good money to see Freaks. If by force of will, or strength of mind, or simply by how little of him there was to see, she couldn't say, but for whatever reason, he was as unseen as she was seen.

The sideshow top filled, emptied, filled again, and as the evening continued, the rubes streaming between the Fat Lady and the Skeleton Man became no more substantial than intermittent fog. After the final show concluded, Mr. White approached, taking Bea's hand and guiding her slowly down the platform stairs.

"It's been too long," he said, his voice like wind rushing through a field of desiccated sugar cane.

Waiting for the crowds to disperse and for the lot to empty

itself of outsiders, Bea and White stood beside the platform, unseen, unspeaking, while Bea tried to not be happy to see him. They held hands as she purposefully thought, *We may've been friends, White, but I never liked you.*

At last, the crowds scattered and melted away. The Fat Lady and the Skeleton Man ducked through an opening in the tent's sidewall and took to the road, walking slowly. Beneath the light of a high moon, their shadows led the way: Bea's rolling like a pile of boulders downhill and White's darting like a minnow, two swift and eager shadows restrained by a dependence upon their fleshy sources. Eventually they came to a crossroads, and after examining every direction, including the road behind them, they decided to sit in a patch of clover that grew undisturbed in the center of the crossing. All around, treefrogs and crickets sang creaky rocking-chair harmonies from the dark interiors of trees and the shadows between blades of grass.

"I went back to Jimmy's show," Mr. White said, "and he told me how you disappeared on him."

Bea only nodded.

"Inevitable," Mr. White added, and Bea nodded again.

"Do you still have the pain?" he asked.

Bea felt her heart catch and falter at the question, although there had been no pain for a year. Towards the end of the time she had worked alongside Mr. White, she had become unable to exert herself beyond her minute per show dances and her walks between trailer and tent without sweating and panting, her heart and lungs in a rictus of pain. At first she had assumed the pain was a warning that fat might kill her as it had many a Fat Man and Woman before her, but that wasn't the case. It was Jimmy. The worse her husband's philandering became, the more physical pain she experienced. The condition only improved when she began to confide in White. She had made a few friends since Ethel, who had been Bea's best friend as well as her sister, but by the time Jimmy's cheating reached its zenith, there were no women around that she could trust. Both her body and her soul needed the relief that came from confiding in

White, the relief that finally convinced her heart to allow her body to move with ease again.

"Not even when I ran from Jimmy's show to Dugan's," Bea told him. "My heart pounded, and my breath came hard, but it didn't hurt, not at all."

"Your place in Dugan's Cabinet of Wonders was meant to be, you know. It's your destiny. I can see it."

Although she'd had the same thought herself, she said, "Don't give me that all-knowing horseshit, White." She let go of the knobs and twigs of his hand and wiped her damp, cushiony palm on her skirt. "You don't know my destiny—if anybody's even got a destiny."

Mr. White didn't argue, but as if to prove his omniscience, he said, "You haven't eaten today. You still miss Ethel terribly, don't you?"

Bea nodded. It was nice, at least, that she didn't need to tell Mr. White those things she hadn't even attempted to explain to Jimmy or Dugan. Still, she wasn't going to praise White for his insight; praise would only puff up his already swollen head, and his pencil neck was barely strong enough to support his thick skull as it was.

"I do miss Ethel," she said, "but not half as bad as I used to. I have a friend here. Her name is Saffron."

"Ah, the Wolf Girl with the lovely voice."

"Yeah, her. We're talking about maybe going out on our own. She's got it in her head that the Freak business in the States is swirling down the shitter, so she wants to go to Mexico. She asked me to go with her and I said, why not? If destiny has fuck-all to do with anything, it's not that I belong in Dugan's show, but that I was meant to come here to meet her."

"You aren't happy here?"

"Oh, I'm happy enough. I just don't think that the show's what it used to be, or what it should be. Saffron says that something's missing lately. And that Dugan is different than before, that he used to be warmer and more energetic, so something's missing in him, too."

"I sensed the same thing, Beatrice."

157

"Oh, shut your pie-hole. You did not. You just don't like me proving that you don't know everything."

Mr. White smiled. "Well, I'm glad to hear you aren't too lonely."

"Not lonely at all, sugar," Bea said, although that wasn't entirely true. Sometimes, in spite of Saffron, in spite of herself, she missed Jimmy; she had an unopened letter from him in her pocket at that very moment, and she planned to read it as soon as she had some time alone.

Continuing to smile, Mr. White said, "We didn't actually have sex that night, you know."

Bea's stomach shifted at his words, bile stinging the back of her throat. She remembered the lust she'd felt for White, fueled equally by her loneliness and her anger at her husband's infidelities, but her desire had faltered as White's bones pressed cruelly into her flesh, as his dry, thin lips kissed her, and as his hard penis attempted to burrow between the twin columns of her thighs. She realized that she was moments away from becoming as despicable as Jimmy, and all at once the horrible pain returned, gripping her chest and stealing her breath.

Mr. White was a stage name, selected because White agreed with those cultures which see white, the color of bone, as the color of death, and death is the language every skeleton speaks. But his real name was Smythe. And Bea knew that even if she could justify cheating on Jimmy because Jimmy had cheated on her, nothing could justify sleeping with her husband's brother.

"If we hadn't stopped, I would've died," she said.

Mr. White shrugged. "Maybe," he said. "But maybe not."

"I didn't think you approved of maybes."

"I don't. Still, everyone has to deal with some, even me. Most people are swarming with maybes, yet fortunately, I have only three or four. My mind is quite an orderly place."

"I don't like you," Bea said. "Never have."

"Yes, you do."

"Just 'cause you're a good listener, and back then I needed someone to listen more than I needed air."

"You see nothing else about me to like?"

Bea smiled. "Maybe one or two things. Doesn't matter. I don't belong with Jimmy anymore, and you do. Blood is blood. Still, I'm grateful for the friendship you gave me. If I hadn't had you to talk to, the pain in my heart would've only gotten worse, and I would've never been able to leave like I did. Though it took me another damn year after you left to do it."

"You're very welcome."

The kiss that followed wasn't at all sudden; it was a gradual inclination of two faces meeting in the space between body and body, tips of tongues touching and hot breath mingling. Flushed from head to toe, Bea felt the dampness of desire in the triangulation of her inner thighs, and then the pain returned, hot iron bars closing in on her heart and lungs. She pulled away, heart strangled, breath stolen.

When he saw that the worst had passed, White said, "You're suffering. I thought for sure that this time we'd be able to follow through, and then everything would be different."

"I guess deep down," she said, catching her breath as the pain abated, "I still believe that sex with you would make me no better than Jimmy."

"You aren't with Jimmy anymore."

"Doesn't matter."

He was quiet for a spell, but finally acceded, "I know," and took her hand.

"You won't believe it," Bea said, "but he's been writing me letters."

White raised his eyebrows, but did not seem surprised.

"After he figured out what show I'd joined on with, he started writing me one or two a week, care of *Billboard*. I'm not about to take him back, but still… the apologies are nice. And I think that it's good for me to be without a romance for a while. As for you, even if you weren't Jimmy's brother, I still don't think you'd ever be good for me. Or vice-versa."

Although Mr. White looked as if he wanted to object, he said nothing; he already knew that Bea didn't change her mind easily.

The Fat Lady and the Skeleton Man left the crossroads, and on the walk back to the lot, their shadows dragged behind—hers a massive wood stove, his an attenuated flag pole—giving the impression that if they weren't tethered to their sources at the ankle, the shadows wouldn't have moved at all.

Saying goodbye beside Bea's trailer, they shook hands while White looked longingly at the door. She followed his gaze and shook her head. "You go on back to Jimmy. It's where you belong, and you know it. Family is family, after all."

He took hold of her dimpled hand, placed a papery kiss on her knuckles. "Maybe," he said.

"There's another one of them maybes! You should be more careful. Before you know it, you'll be swarming with maybes like the rest of us, and then you'll have all these knowing looks stored up that you got no damn use for."

He laughed with a sound like the snap and fall of withered stalks of sugar cane. "Goodbye, my dear."

After Mr. White left, Dugan emerged from the shadows clumped between the trailers. Trying to sound casual, but failing miserably, he asked, "Who's the Skeleton Man?"

Bea's eyes bored into the darkness that no longer revealed nor hid the gaunt form. "My brother-in-law."

Dugan sighed and shook his head. "Ah, I see. Well, I had intended to ask if you thought he might want employment, but I suppose he still works for your husband."

"Off and on."

"In that case, perhaps you could find out if he might be interested? He'd be a marvelous addition to our show."

The White-less darkness possessed a vacant quality like the Ethel-torn corner of Bea's soul, the old wound that she now knew would heal. If she'd had the strength to leave Jimmy, she should have the strength to let go of her sister. Besides, Ethel wouldn't approve of never-ending grief—she had been such a happy, funny girl. Next June 16th, Bea would pick a flower for Ethel, cry a little while, remembering, then continue on with her life.

She uprooted her gaze from the distant dark, turned her eyes upon Dugan, and said, "He'd be a marvelous addition to any show. But he's also a horse's ass."

She paused, then said, "You might like him, though."

Bea winked and left Dugan alone in the moonlight as she went into her trailer. After she undressed and turned off the light—she decided that she didn't care to read Jimmy's letter just yet—she glanced through the window and saw Dugan still standing where she had left him, his neck and back hunched, his shoulders curling as if he were slowly folding in on himself. He looked so different, so strange and constricted and fragile, that she decided to go outside and ask if he was all right.

But when she opened her trailer door, he was already walking away.

Chapter seventeen
Alteration

June 20th, Bell City, Oklahoma

lex:

From first light on that Monday in Bell City, Oklahoma, a dismal, continuous rain fell, like a dingy gray sheet hung from a line hidden by clouds, but by early evening, when I arbitrated a fight between Dugan and Roxy, the sheet and clouds had uncurtained a bright, freshly washed sun. Silver sparks spun off the clean metal rides and water-beaded canvas, while golden light glistened over Molly and Faye's skin as they emerged from the Girl Show undressing top with freshly bobbed hair, wearing skimpy, sleeveless, good-time dresses. Their shorn heads seemed overly large on their slender, exposed necks, and as they began to flee our gaze, *Dugan's* gaze, really—running awkwardly, unaccustomed to so much flesh and bone uncovered and unprotected—the swishing fringe over their torsos and the wind-ruffled fringe of their hair transformed them into fragile baby birds shivering in ungainly flight around the side of the tent and out of sight.

"I don't blame them," Dugan said to Roxy, continuing the argument and still ignoring me, his index finger stabbing in the direction of the twins' disappearance. "They're children. They want modern hair and fashions the same way that they used to want rag dolls and taffy. You're older, Roxy. You should know better."

"She's only seventeen," I interjected, stepping between Dugan and Roxy as a barricade.

Frowning and furrowed, Dugan peered over my shoulder. "I didn't realize that."

"Thanks, Alex," Roxy whispered as she hugged me from behind, pressing her face against my back, a tough young woman transformed into a frightened and miserable child. If Dugan weren't a Freak, she would've already dismissed him with an easy *fuck you*.

"And even if Roxy were thirty-five," I said, "Molly and Faye aren't children. They're old enough to choose how they want to look. It's about time they started showing some flair."

Dugan said, "That isn't just flair. They look like flappers off the cover of *Life* magazine! You had no right to do this, Roxy."

Roxy started to apologize again, so I spoke over her. "Molly and Faye look wonderful. Roxy gives such fantastic haircuts that Zimm has her bob the hair of every girl in his show."

"And do you know why he does that? Long hair is too sweet and respectable—"

"It's old-fashioned—"

"And it reminds men of their mothers and sisters, or their wives and daughters, and Zimm wants his sucks to be titillated without guilt, all the better to empty their pockets. The hair is a visual cue, a signal that these are not women that men need to worry about respecting, that these are women willing to be objects of desire, possibly willing to offer gratification."

I smiled. "So that's what's bothering you." I turned and kissed Roxy's tear-salted lips. "Run along, sweet girl," I said. "You can come by my trailer later."

Roxy scurried off and I returned my attention to Dugan. "You're attracted to them. You look at Molly and Faye and you're suddenly aware of them as sexually appealing young women. That makes you uncomfortable."

Dugan shook his head. "That isn't it at all."

"That *is* it. You're attracted to them, and that confuses you because you're the closest thing to a father that they've got."

"You're wrong, Alex."

The sad calm with which Dugan spoke let me know that he was telling the truth. He wasn't the one who suddenly found the twins attractive; I was. After Roxy worked her magic, when I first saw the twins it was without recognition, drinking them in like I would any pair of sweet young creatures. Realizing that it was Molly and Faye who had stirred my interest discomfited me, almost frightened me. If they had been strangers to me, I would have made a quick and easy conquest of them.

"Fine," I said. "Tell me the real reason you're so upset. You used to be able to roll with the punches, you know. You take everything so damn seriously now." Speaking the words, it occurred to me that this was the first time I had directly confronted Dugan about the change I saw in him, and I wondered why I'd refrained for so long; the lack of his friendship haunted me like a phantom blowing a cold, mournful wind against my neck.

Dugan rubbed his face with his thick, short-fingered hands, and said, "Walk with me to the Freak top. It's almost time."

Although sunset was at least an hour away, the blue midsummer sky was bleeding cerise at the horizon, visible in glimpses between tents and rides and carnies preparing for another night's work. In a few minutes the arch would open and the rubes would start to roll in with bulging pockets begging to be emptied.

As we walked, Dugan said, "To see Molly and Faye bobbed, nearly naked and coated in cosmetics alarmed me. They were in the middle of a metamorphosis from girl to woman, and Roxy helped them to break out of their chrysalis too soon. The men who come to my show will only perceive what is presented to them; fully-formed women, not the half-evolved, tender little girls underneath the lip-stick."

We reached the Annex, where my indigo blow-off top squatted behind the larger tent for Dugan's Cabinet of Wonders.

"Molly and Faye aren't ready for the world of women, Alex. It isn't safe for them to appear otherwise."

I looked down at my sandals peeking out from under the hem of my blue silk performance cape. Dugan was right, up to a point. Despite being born as oddities, which had certainly given Molly and Faye some hard knocks in life, the twins remained very soft, unprepared for the adult world. The year between their age and Roxy's age may as well have been twenty years. Roxy was a passionate girl with a weakness for Freaks, but she was also as tough as boot leather; Molly and Faye were as susceptible as silk.

"Maybe they aren't ready," I said, speaking to myself as much as to Dugan, "but how many girls are really prepared when they're thrust into the world of women? No matter how long you try and keep a girl away from haircuts and modern fashions, it can never change the fact that becoming a woman isn't just about appearance, and it isn't a skill to acquire. It simply happens. A sink or swim proposition."

"So I'm supposed to stand aside and simply watch to see if they drown?"

"Yes. But they won't drown."

Dugan's smile was a hard, thin line. He never used to smile that way; he never used to confront every happening of every day with such a dour refusal to alter his life or his perception. He used to have more faith in Wonders.

"You're different," I said, my voice low, muted. "You aren't the same person you were last season."

"I could say the same of you," he replied.

"We aren't talking about me."

"Of course not. We never are."

We stared at each other in a stubborn caesura—unflinching, inscrutable—until eventually Dugan shook his head. "And we aren't talking about me either," he said. "Go inside your top, Alex. The arch should be open by now."

It was dark in my blow-off tent—very little light could permeate the indigo blue canvas, and the only illumination inside was a spotlight rigged to switch on and off with a foot pedal—but I didn't need to see in order to find my way through the top and onto my stage to wait quietly in the gloom. The way that Dugan had dismissed me stung like lemon on a paper cut, but I promised myself that it wouldn't interfere with my performance. The stage was my birthright; I would make men marvel and yearn with or without Daddy Dugan's support.

As the sucks begin to file in for the blow-off, congregating around the stage then gradually filing into eager rows, I kept to the shadows, unseen and silent. I never spoke when I performed. Speech would break the spell of mystery, and the men never really listened anyway. Dugan leaned in stiffly through the parted sidewall and gave the signal that all the ticket-holders were present and accounted for, then ducked back out, dropping the flap of indigo canvas behind him. As I kicked off my shoes, I slipped a carved jade penis out of a pocket inside my cape and held it tucked in my hand, the shaft hidden behind my wrist. It was time for the show to begin, and I was ready to give one hell of a show—or so I told myself. In truth, my talk with Dugan still troubled me, as did my momentary lust towards Molly and Faye. An unfortunate way to begin a night of performance.

I did my best to clear my mind of all disturbances as I traveled slowly towards center stage with the blue silk of my cape swirling around my legs, and I could almost hear the creak of the rubes' eyes straining to see in the darkness. Then one graceful, bare foot extended like a ray of moonlight from behind a deep blue cloud and fell upon the pedal.

—Click—

Lights up. Alexander-Alexandra, marvelous morphodite, revealed to the awestruck crowd. They grunted, too manly to gasp. I extended the foot further, extended the ankle, calf and knee, the silk spilling aside to expose an alluring inception of thigh. I pulled the leg back; the cape closed. Then I raised a hand to my neck, unfastened the hook and eye closure, and let the blue silk slide off one shoulder, then off the other, and then off my tits. Whistles and hoots whirled through the top, and a few cried out for more, but I covered myself, hiding everything below my clavicle. I turned my back to the crowd and let the cape slide down again, down past my shoulders, past the gentle V of my back and waist and the start of my narrow hips. The cool silk draped over my round ass, exposing the faintest shadow of a cleft as I looked over my shoulder at the crowd that hissed with inward breath, their need to see the rest of me ardent, unrelenting.

For a moment, I hesitated; the eagerness that I used to feel along with the rubes at this point had been waning all season, and tonight I felt none at all. What I wanted most was to hold my cloak tight as a cocoon against my breasts and run for my trailer, but I was a trouper, one of the best, and as the saying goes, the show must go on. I took a deep preparatory breath, and let go; the cape poured into a glistening blue pool at my feet. Then slowly, ever so slowly, I turned to face the sucks. Hushed by fascination, they became as silent as me, these marks with their eyes beady and piercing, or glazed in awe, or even crinkled from contained laughter; these rubes with their mouths tightened by fear or disapproval, or loosened by imbecilic grins, or dry from nervous lust with tongues darting out to wet parched lips. For a little while, I felt like myself again. They belonged to me, I to them. We engaged one another in a distant seduction, my flesh calling to every man, even to those who feared ambiguity, multiplicity: a thousand eyes caressed my body. When the hush gave way to a gentle murmuring, I knew it was time to give them more.

I stepped out of the silk puddle and drifted further downstage, swiveling my wrist and hand to reveal the carved jade penis, which I held aloft by my fingertips so that it shone in the spotlight, the outline of the shaft crisp against the indigo backdrop. Anticipation steamed the air, and my movements became fluid, my body swimming through their expectancy. I slid the cold phallus across my collarbone and between my breasts, my nipples stiffening into painful points, then rolled the jade back and forth across my belly, warming the smooth stone with the heat of my navel. I waited a moment longer, savoring their hunger to discover what I might do, how far I might go.

As I moved my feet into a wider stance, I felt their eyes between my legs like a warm breath, like a pink tongue an inch from my flesh. Becoming still more aroused, I sank into a deep plié and penetrated myself with the jade shaft, my penis erect, engorged. The marks watched the green jade nearly disappear inside of me as my cock extended its reach, nearly as hard as jade now and eager for its own depths to plumb. Unchecked groans of disgust, fear, but most of all longing, came from the most affected marks in the crowd, every gaze locked between my legs, eye-licking me as I dropped my head back in silent ecstasy—this pack of sucks were especially hungry, their need exquisite. What a beautiful communion this was, between a Wonder and a gathering of common men.

I don't recall what exactly it was that broke the spell—it could have been something as insignificant as a cough from the crowd or a hot breeze leaking through a gap in the sidewall—but I suddenly lost the feeling of communion and became terribly aware of the sheer number of men I had engaged. Their throat clearings and murmurings and the shuffling of their heavy, booted feet became the din of an approaching storm. They were too many, too much; they wanted more than I had to give, and rather than leave hungry, they would tear me down to bone and pocket the shreds of my flesh as souvenirs—not the first time the image had crossed my mind, but the first time I had felt it could be literally true. As I backed away from the edge of the stage, I dropped the jade phallus, which clunked to the floor and tripped me, sending me clumsily to my knees. Reaching swiftly, I smacked the light pedal with my palm. Welcome darkness descended as the rubes booed and cheered for more, but I scrambled for my cloak, wrapping it around my body like a blanket. An inexplicable film of disgust spread over me like a membrane sheathing my skin, and I shuddered, dismayed by the inescapable fact of my flesh. If I could have gathered up my spirit and flown from my body like a hawk or a great owl, I would have soared through the darkening sky and left the indigo tent behind forever. I didn't want a different body; I wanted no body.

But now Finch began to usher the present crowd out of the top and the next crowd in. Another blow-off performance was required, and after that would follow another, and then another, because the shows must go on—and on and on and on. Meanwhile, something had gone wrong inside of me, terribly wrong. I still saw the beauty of my act in an abstract sense, and longed to feel physically the way my mind told me I should, but my body rebelled, sickened by what I had once found sublime.

And yet I stood, and adjusted my cape, listening as this new herd of sucks shambled in, their excitement once more rising on the air like steam. Vowing that I would not be ruled by my body's whims, that I would not allow this sudden caprice of skin and blood and bone to change my feelings for the calling I had relished for over half of my life, I retrieved the jade penis from the stage floor and cleaned it with the edge of my robe, stepped up to the foot pedal, and though the feel of it made the sole of my foot crawl with revulsion, pressed down and—

—Click—

Lights up, Alexander-Alexandra revealed.

I forced my body to endure every successive performance, and hours later, after Finch ushered out the final rube from the final blow-off, he targeted me with the beam of his flashlight and said, "Damn, Alex. You look terrible."

"Don't worry about me, darling," I replied. My voice was scratchy, off-pitch. "I can take care of myself."

Before I could muster my signature rakish smile, I collapsed to my knees, gripped the edge of the stage, and splattered the sawdust with a reeking pool of vomit, the fumes bringing tears to my eyes. It felt as if I could never spew forth enough bile to disgorge the filth that had pirated my body. In that moment I knew that I would do anything, change anything, to free myself, and be reborn.

Chapter eighteen

The Morning After

June 21ˢᵗ, Bell City, Oklahoma

A lex, what would you do if you weren't a carny?"

In the hours since witnessing his friend's collapse in the blow-off top, Finch had been cradling Alex's head in his lap as they sat beside the consoling flow of the White Bluff River. Catching the night unaware, the morning sun, with claws of pink and gold, was creeping stealthily up the cobalt sky while Alex considered how to respond to Finch's previously unthinkable but suddenly practical question, and Finch tried not to wonder what it meant that his mind was always thinking of art while he worked the show, and thinking of the show while he created his art. That Tuesday dawn in Oklahoma wasn't nearly as hot as the last week in Texas had been, and Finch tried to enjoy the pleasant morning air, but thoughts of a studio, and peace and stillness in which to work, possessed his mind. He lit a stout, hand-rolled cigarette and passed it to Alex, then lit another for himself, drawing the tobacco fumes deep into his lungs. It was late June, now, with the season half gone. Summer rushing toward Fall, ready or not.

Alex finally answered, saying, "I've been a carny so long, I hardly know what I'd do."

"I know what *I'd* do."

"What's that?"

"Open up a photography studio. A place where any person, no matter their race or social standing, could have a respectable, quality portrait taken. A revealing, *truthful* portrait of who they really are."

Alex sat up and moved closer, kissed Finch's forehead with a sad smile. "My dreams aren't as admirable as yours," he said. "I don't have any dreams, really. I've been a proud carny for years, and a skilled and rapturous lover, if I do say so myself, for even longer than I've been a carny. Until recently, those two things made me happy enough."

"You aren't happy anymore?"

Alex was quiet a moment, watching their exhaled plumes of smoke braid and furl skyward. "Didn't the regurgitation after my last show cue you in?"

Finch sighed. It had been terrible to watch Alex, usually so serenely composed, retching and heaving. "I'm sorry."

Alex shrugged, then shivered, as if physically shaking off Finch's sympathy. "I've been trying not to think about it, but the fact is, I haven't been really, truly content all season."

"Neither have I."

"You should open your photography studio. Maybe you're not meant to be a carny anymore."

Finch nodded. "I've lived most of my life on the road—moving from town to town doing odd jobs, riding the rails, working carnivals—but I don't have the restless need to move that I used to. Now I think I'd actually be happy to live in a home without wheels. Think you'll ever get to that point?"

"Maybe one day," Alex said, though his face betrayed that he might have already reached that point.

"And what would you do?"

Footsteps accompanied by the smell of cigar smoke interrupted the conversation, and Mario appeared. He sat on the riverbank beside Finch and Alex, a cigar in one hand, a nearly empty whiskey bottle in the other, and as he spoke, his voice chafed out from his throat in its usual fashion. "I just got back from visiting the sweetest baby vamp I've tasted in quite awhile. She was somethin' else. What're you two yapping about?"

"I was just asking Alex what he'd do if he wasn't a carny," Finch said.

"And what did you say, Alex?"

"Honestly, I don't have a clue."

"I'll tell you what you should do. I've been waiting for someone to jump out at me as perfect for this, and you just did. You know that property I own in Florida? Sean and I decided to build a little development there, a trailer park on the shore to serve as winter quarters, and a nice retirement place for carnies to live near other carnies—especially Freaks. Finch already knows about it. Anyway, we'd need someone with charm and a knowledge of carnival people to run the place. You'd be perfect."

"Wait a minute," Finch said, "you're speaking as if Alex is planning to leave right away. We're just talking about possibilities, you know. We're still with the Starlight."

"And I'm just tossing my ideas into the basket, is all. Besides, it would take me a few months to be ready to open the park, and I'd need to put an ad in *Billboard* first."

"Sounds like you really plan to do this."

"I do. I don't have much longer as a successful Freak." He scowled at his small hand clamped around the cigar, as if it alone were responsible for his terrible growth; he had gained a treacherous three inches in the last eight months.

Mario took another long swig of whiskey. "I need a new business enterprise, a profitable one. Something that will support me in the style to which I've become accustomed—vamps and vino, you know. Dugan's right. I do wallow in the stereotype, but I have to stay true to my tastes. I might be forced out of the Freak biz, but I refuse to give up everything."

Alex smiled with a faraway look in his eyes. "I've only been to the beach once. There's too much competition there for carnivals, you know? And the lots are too expensive to make much of a profit. But I remember the one time I went swimming in the ocean. I mean, I *really* remember. I can close my eyes and still feel it," he said, closing his eyes. "The waves pounded against me with such power—it reminded me that I don't have to try to be all things to all people. That I can't be, because I'm only one single being, and hardly that, in comparison to the sea. Wondrous I may be, but years after the last carnival breaks up and disperses to the four winds, the ocean will still be exactly the way it was at that moment."

"Very poetic," Mario murmured, confident now that his offer would be accepted.

Alex opened his eyes and asked, "Your property is right on the beach, isn't it, Mario?"

"Of course. And you should see it. White sand, blue-green water, pretty shells, squawky seagulls. Paradise."

Finch bristled that Mario hadn't offered him the job, although if he were honest, the seashore would never be paradise to him. If he were to live in one place, it would be in a city filled with thousands of people waiting to be revealed on film. Still, it would've been nice for Mario to make the offer, so Finch asked, "What about me?"

"What *about* you?"

"Am I not good enough to run your carny neighborhood?"

"Of course you are, but you're overqualified. You're a great photographer and a good accountant, but I can handle the books, and we won't need any portraits taken on the beach. There's got to be a better fit out there for you."

Finch nodded, satisfied with Mario's response. "There is. I've decided to open my own photography studio. Soon, more than likely. It's about time I moved on."

"A Negro photography studio," crowed Mario, "I love it!"

"What's so funny about that?"

"It's not funny, old boy, it's marvelous! That's what's so wonderful about this country. A race that starts its journey in bondage can wind up owning businesses and changing the way people see each other. Finch, men like you will pave the way to equality."

"Where the hell have you been hiding this idealism, Mario? I took you for a dyed-in-the-wool cynic."

"Well, I am cynical about most things. I'm cynical about people in a specific way, because most people are idiots and assholes. But I sincerely believe that the United States of America is a place where great things can happen." Mario shrugged. "I'm not saying Uncle Sam is perfect—far from it—but I give credit where it's due. When I start up my little Floridian community, I plan to sit on the beach every day at sunset, drinking a beer and saluting our nation. Ours is a country that reached great heights in the art of the Freak Show while Europeans were still pushing Single-Os in basements and back-alleys. Never forget that Phineus T. Barnum was an American."

Finch snorted and clapped Mario on the back. "I can't share your patriotism, old boy, but I find this side of you very amusing. If I ever come to visit your little settlement, I'll drink a toast to the beach and the carnies while you salute the rest of the nation."

Finch imagined such a visit, but his mind skipped ahead to afterwards, to leaving Florida and returning to a big, sunny studio in a teeming, sprawling city somewhere. At the thought of abandoning Dugan's Cabinet of Wonders, homesickness dragged across his skin, but more so at the thought of leaving Shadrach. He ground out his cigarette before it burned his fingers, suddenly angry with himself. Was it really Shadrach keeping him from leaving the Starlight Carnival Royale and pursuing a new life? As a made Freak, Shadrach was only an outsider by choice; he was still a white man, and Finch would hate to think that any white man could dictate his actions, even one he loved. His green-eyed photography teacher had been white, and he and Finch had loved each other, but when the wanderlust resurfaced, Finch didn't hesitate to leave—not for a moment. He could not permit his feelings for Shadrach to influence this decision. Out of loyalty, Finch would stay the season, and come fall, he would bid the Starlight farewell and head…to New York City. Yes, that was it. The dream burned brightly in his mind. A studio in New York, that most impressive of cities, a place heaving with masses of humanity begging to be revealed.

But if he and Alex and Mario bid farewell to Dugan at October's end, and if by then Saffron and Bumble-Bea had pulled together enough money to tour their own Freak Show through Mexico, and who knows what changes the twins might go through now that they were all dolled up and interested in men, would there be anything left of Dugan's Cabinet of Wonders to greet the '28 season?

"What about Dugan?" Finch asked. "What will he be doing while we're out in the world taking pictures and housing carnies and making toasts at sunset? We aren't the only ones likely to leave, you know."

Neither Alex nor Mario spoke. The White Bluff River, bubbling swiftly and merrily over smooth stones, shimmering with the fluid reflections of sunlight, sky, and leaves, was the only answering voice. But its answer was wordless, careless, and as impossible to capture as the summer itself, rushing headlong toward the fall.

Chapter nineteen

Golly Wow

June 29th*, Sulphur, Kansas*

Every time it seemed that business was improving for the Starlight Carnival Royale, some new variety of disaster hit, splat, like a pie in the face. Less than halfway through the stop in Sulphur, Kansas, disaster struck; its sticky origins in sex and the local authorities.

Rumor, with its many forked tongues, hissed that the carnival was told to vacate the lot in Sulphur because Alex had cuckolded the sheriff; rumor also murmured that it was because June from Zimm's Girl Show had accepted cash from the sheriff for a certain favor which she then refused to perform; and further still, rumor (helped along by a very small, very bold minority) whispered that Finch had been caught in a lodging house with his pants dropped to his ankles, his eyes rolled back in his head, and the sheriff's winsome son on bended knee between his legs. Rumor is often conceived in truth—how much, in this case, the carnies couldn't say. But no matter the reason, something had angered the sheriff, who ordered the Starlight to pack up and leave town on Wednesday.

Shadrach believed the rumor about June, because he would believe any tale of harlotry and deceit among the dancers in the Girl Show, and although he hated to admit it, he felt certain that the rumor about Alex was true as well. As for the rumor about Finch, Shadrach did not allow himself to believe it for a second. To label Finch a sodomite simply because not one of the multitudes of eager women along the road had ever successfully seduced him revealed how puerile people could be.

On that Wednesday afternoon, under a sun hot enough to bake a pan of cornbread on a slab of granite, Shadrach joined Dugan and everyone but Alex, who was still slumbering, naked in her tangled sheets, to help strip the show. In the relative cool of the tent, as he packed the folded black curtains into steamer trunks, a pattering sound turned his attention to the canvas overhead, where a squall of stones showered the top, casting swift shadows across the carnies' faces.

"Goddamn kids," Dugan muttered, quickly sliding Finch's orderly account books and the lock-box of money into a hidden compartment under one of the platforms. Packs of rowdy children had been roaming the lot all morning, looking for ways to annoy, succeeding when they threw rocks or stole food from the Pie Wagon, failing when they tried to rig up ropes to make the surefooted carnies trip and fall.

"Finch, Shadrach, I'd appreciate it if you would scare off those urchins outside. And Molly and Faye, I think it would be best for you two to wait in your trailer until we're ready to make the jump."

"But why?" Faye whined.

"You know why," Shadrach said. "Dugan doesn't want y'all here if a clem breaks out between us and the townies. It won't be just kids hanging around today, looking for trouble."

Faye turned her back on Shadrach. "But we could hold our own in any clem, I know it! We're strong. We can fight!"

Although less certain of this, Molly nodded her support.

"All arguments are futile," Dugan said. "Bumble-Bea, please go with Molly and Faye to their trailer and keep an eye on them."

Bea frowned, but agreed. "All right tough girls," she said, guiding the twins out of the tent with a resigned hand on each of their backs. "Come on, and don't argue. It tweaks the hell out of my nerves when you whine."

Finch and Shadrach exited the top behind Molly and Faye and Bea, watching the twins flounce past a group of boys who had their fists predictably stuffed with stones and acorns. A little towheaded boy—freckled, barefoot, with skinny shoulder blades draped in a pair of overalls but no shirt—sighed as the girls passed by, "Those Siamese twins sure are pretty."

The ringleader of the group stepped up, with the other boys flanking and following his lead just a few steps behind. He asked the towhead to repeat himself.

"If we wait a minute they might run themselves off," Finch whispered to Shadrach.

Because the freckled towhead had his eyes stuck to the disappearing sway and swish of Molly and Faye, he didn't heed his friend's expression and simply replied, "I said that those Siamese twins sure are pretty."

Shaking his head in disappointment, the ringleader said, "I never took you for a Freak-lover," punctuating the statement with a punishing right hook to the boy's left eye.

Shadrach stepped forward with Finch, and when the ringleader and his gang saw the men, they turned and galloped away, whooping their little boy war cries. Forsaken, his eye swelling shut and his cheeks greased with tears, the towhead stared pitifully at the ground, sniffing and swallowing his slick shame.

Finch smiled and slapped Shadrach on the back. "I'm going back inside to help. I'll leave you to handle this little punk on your own."

The towhead stiffened at Finch's words, but relaxed when Shadrach smiled and said, "You took that punch well."

The boy's tears began to slow. "I did?"

"Sure you did. It looked like a pretty hard knock, but you're still standing."

The boy swiped at his cheeks, wincing a little as his knuckles grazed the puffed red and yellow flesh of his injured eye. "That's right. I am."

"What's your name, kid?"

"Olaf."

"Really? I thought that was a name for fat old men."

"Oh, it is," the boy said. "It's my grandpa's name."

"Do you want me to help you get your face cleaned up?"

The boy hesitated while his eyes raked Shadrach's skin, head to toe. "You must like God a whole lot."

Shadrach nodded and Olaf said, "Okay, then."

The tattooed man led the boy to the spare trailer where Sean and Mario slept, so they could make use of Sean's first aid supplies. Shadrach washed the boy's face with water, then alcohol, then took a cool wet cloth and instructed Olaf to hold it pressed to the rapidly swelling, rapidly purpling flesh squinting up his left eye.

"That's going to develop into a serious shiner," Shadrach told him.

"*Really?*" Olaf asked, smiling again. "Golly-wow, that's swell!"

Shadrach shook his head; the boy sounded like an *aw-shucks* kid from the funny pages. He'd never met a child who actually spoke like that before.

Mario, who had a policy of making himself scarce during times when manual labor was required, and Sean, who wasn't strong enough to work very hard for very long, returned to the trailer, and when Shadrach explained what had happened, Mario winked at Olaf and said, "You've got good taste, kid. The twins are too young for me, but they certainly are a pair of sweet tomatoes."

Sean opened a candy tin on his bedside table and offered the boy a glossy red and white peppermint stick. Olaf accepted and sat on Mario's bed, grinning around the stick of candy and looking back and forth from Sean, who had stretched out as well as he could on his extra long, but still insufficient bed, to Mario, who sat by the window like a costumed, weathered child smoking a cigar.

"Jeepers, you sure got some swell Freaks around. Where're those cute Siamese girls? They were worth getting punched for!"

Sean chuckled and said, "Atta boy, Olaf."

As if responding to a summons, there came a thumping on the door and Molly's voice squealing, "Let us in—Faye's getting blood all over!"

Shadrach opened the door to find Molly and Faye, and Bea. Faye had a hand cupped under her ear to catch a slow drizzle of blood.

"I tried to pierce the damn thing," Bea said. "They wouldn't stop begging, so I agreed, to shut 'em up. But then Faye had to go and move right when she shouldn't, and I hit it all wrong. Can we patch her up here?" She grimaced. "Hell. Dugan's gonna kill me."

Sean heaved his vast frame out of bed and went to examine Faye's ear. "There's really not much blood," he said.

"Don't worry, Bea. We'll tell Dugan that we did it ourselves," Faye said.

"Yeah," said Molly, "we won't even mention you."

"Unless you're mean like yesterday when you made fun of us while we practiced our Charleston," Faye added. "Then we'll say it was all your idea."

"The Charleston is old news, anyway," Bea muttered.

Olaf dropped the cold cloth onto the leg of his overalls as even his swollen eye widened. "Hey," he called to Molly and Faye, "you can come sit by me."

The twins sat beside the towhead, who sighed and said, "Golly-wow, you two are pretty."

The twins giggled.

"And those sure are some pretty blue beads you got on. Bet my mom would love a necklace like that. Golly."

Molly fingered the long strands of birthday beads at her neck while Faye kept her hands cupped over her ear; both girls smiled with pride.

Feeling edgy now that Olaf was taken care of, Shadrach started worrying that there were too many people crowded into the trailer and not enough helping tear down the show. "I think I'll go find Dugan and see what work is left to do," he said.

"Good thing there's troupers like you around to make up for troupers like me," Mario said, leaning out the window, blowing smoke rings like confetti after Shadrach's departure.

With so many of the rides and tents already stripped and loaded, Shadrach could see across the lot unobstructed, and from about a hundred yards away he spotted Dugan and Finch loading the disassembled pieces of the sloughed top onto the back of the show's trailer truck while Saffron stood nearby, with a couple of rubes. Even from that distance, Shadrach detected trouble in the way the men seesawed on their feet and the way that Saffron, standing as rigid and still as a tent stake, had crossed her arms tightly over her chest. He started to run as soon as he saw the baseball bat, but before he could close even half the distance, the rube had cracked it over Saffron's skull. She folded to the ground, clutching her head; Shadrach couldn't see where Finch had gone, but Dugan rushed over, seized the bat and used it to smash the smugness off the rube's face. As the man cradled his gushing nose, Dugan whirled around, prepared to swing at the second rube, but both men turned and fled. Then, after two deep, shuddering breaths, the gallant grace of Dugan's stance contracted, his body shrinking in on itself like the gray accordion carapace of a startled pill bug; he dropped the bat and crumpled to the ground, body bowed, quivering.

Shadrach's feet skidded to a stop.

Finch emerged from the back of the truck, saw Saffron and Dugan on the ground, and hurried over. At Finch's approach, the tremble in Dugan's frame dispersed; he stood slowly and stiffly, reminding Shadrach of an uncle whose bone troubles had forced him to walk stooped over a cane while still in the prime of life—and by the time Finch had Saffron back on her feet, no one but Shadrach could have suspected that Dugan was anything other than the same powerful, capable man that he had been for the past three seasons.

Shadrach saw that Finch was about to hand Saffron off to Dugan, so he hurried over.

"Let me help," he called out. "Dugan has so much to take care of."

Relief ruffled Dugan's grim expression, then was gone.

"I'm pretty sure I can handle the rest," Finch said, but Shadrach was already ducking under Saffron's arm, instructing her to lean her weight on him.

"Dugan," Shadrach said, "why don't you make sure Finch knows everything that needs to be done…"

Finch stared as if Shadrach had lost his mind.

"…and then go get some ice for Saffron's head. I'll take her over to Sean and Mario's trailer and meet you there." He remembered Olaf and added, "Why don't you get some extra. There's a little boy with a shiner over there who could use some ice."

Dugan nodded briskly and said, "Certainly," with reassuring firmness, but now Shadrach understood that the stoniness in Dugan's face and body did not arise from worry or anger or strength, but rather a tremendous effort to dissemble. This pained Shadrach, made him ache. He felt like a child spooning food into the mouth of an ill parent. He turned away and helped Saffron stagger to the circle of residence trailers beyond the midway.

When they arrived, everyone began asking questions at once.

"Some damn townie laid a bat right over my skull," Saffron said to silence them all. "He called me a foul beast and an aberration and then brained me."

Olaf shouted that Saffron was welcome to sit beside him on the cot, but Shadrach ignored the boy and led her to Sean's now empty bed.

"Saffron," Shadrach said, "if we let you stretch out here, do you promise not to fall asleep before we're sure that you don't have a concussion?"

Bea elbowed Shadrach out of the way and said, "*I* promise she won't sleep." She lowered herself to the floor with a groan of effort and said, "I'll sit right here and pinch her whenever she starts to look drowsy. And I can pinch real hard."

Behind Bea's jest was a gentle concern that touched Shadrach, but simultaneously he tasted a familiar bitter envy on his tongue. He had spent so much of his time in solitude, believing that to do so would bring him closer to God's glory, that he had no one who cared for him as tenderly as Bea cared for Saffron.

Dugan appeared with two kerchiefs of ice, walking slowly, deliberately, without a limp or a hunch. "Contrary to the evidence presented by Saffron's head, there isn't much fighting going on," he said. "I had a word with the sheriff just now—he's been out there this entire time, leaning on his car and smiling smugly around a toothpick, and he seemed inordinately pleased by the imbecile with the bat. Zimm is irate, of course. He gave the sheriff a large quantity of money so that the Girl Show could provide a comprehensive performance for the fine citizens of Sulphur, but the sheriff says he's not about to change his mind about ejecting us from the lot, nor will Zimm have his money refunded."

"Rats," the boy said. "So I really won't get to see your show."

"You're very nearly getting to see it here," Saffron mumbled.

"Not at all," Alex said from the doorway. "Performance is what truly makes a Freak. You're seeing Wonders today, little boy, but you haven't seen a Freak Show."

"Where've you been?" Dugan asked.

"Sleeping. I didn't get to bed until dawn, and so I didn't quite feel like packing."

Dugan frowned. "And what care you for the petty trials of men? Or women?"

"Exactly, darling. I'm exempt by virtue of my sexes. Oh, come on now. Wipe that look off your face. No one woke me to tell me what was going on. I only found out for sure we were banished when Finch told me a moment ago. And he said he didn't need any more help."

Shadrach went to stand in the doorway of the overcrowded trailer while Alex went to sit on the cot beside Olaf, who kicked up his feet in delight at the proximity of the marvelous morphodite.

Dugan handed a knotted, ice-filled kerchief to the boy. "Put this on your eye and keep it there."

"Wow, that's some kinda nice watch, mister," Olaf said, tapping Dugan's wrist. "My pop sure would love a swell watch like that."

"Well, maybe one day when you're grown and gainfully employed you can buy him one."

A few minutes later, Finch stuck his head through the door and said, "Everything's loaded up, and the sheriff's issued an order that we clear out within the hour."

There was a lull, punctuated by a few sighs. Then Alex and Finch said in unison, "Sorry."

Shadrach was confused. Of course Alex should apologize, but why Finch? Was there something other than the ridiculous rumor that would motivate him to take responsibility for the sheriff's ire?

"No one blames you two," Dugan said. "It's foolish pride, that's all, the source of most warfare. The sheriff is an orgillous man of little substance." Pushing past Shadrach and Finch, Dugan joined Mario outside and said, "Besides, if I were to place blame, I'd incline toward that quiff June."

"I sure do wish you didn't have to leave," Olaf said. "Golly-wow, I think this would be the best carnival I ever saw!"

"You're probably right, kid," Finch said. "All right, everybody. Let's get the hell out of Sulphur."

While the carnies secured the trailers to the trucks, then lined up the caravan, Olaf lingered, the cotton bundle pressed to his eye dripping in cold rivulets down his cheek.

"Jeepers creepers," he kept saying. "I wish you didn't have to go."

The precious way that Olaf spoke, together with him looking so picturesque, with his white-blond hair, skinny, caramel-speckled shoulders, and dusty overalls, had begun to annoy everyone, even Shadrach. Still, Shadrach felt happy to have met and helped the boy. His open admiration of the Wonders was the same as that of the public that hungered to experience the sacred variations of God's handiwork, and the joy, newness and play of the carnival. Destructive individuals like the sheriff were not among the majority of men, and the carnival should be glad to move on to better climes.

During the past hour the advance man had managed to schedule a half-week's gig in Joplin, Missouri, which would place the Starlight close to Opelika, Illinois, the following stop on the route. Everyone waved goodbye to Olaf, but before they could climb into the trucks to commence the jump, Molly began pleading for them to wait and look around the lot because her string of blue beads was missing. Dugan hurried her and Faye into the cab of the trailer truck Finch was driving, assuring her that the necklace must be coiled safe on the floor beneath someone's cot and promising to buy a replacement if that proved not to be true. Sean and Mario rode in the white pickup with Sean driving, and Shadrach drove the navy pickup with Dugan and Alex beside him on the vinyl bench seat, while Bea and Saffron toasted themselves in the hay-filled truckbed behind. About twenty miles down the road, Saffron knocked on the window of the cab and called out that her deck of cards was missing.

"Does anyone up there have them?" she asked.

"Don't be ridiculous," Alex shouted back. "No one up here took your damn cards. And what do you want them for now, anyway? You can't play poker back there."

"I just like to know that I have them," she said, frowning at Alex before turning away from the window.

Dugan clamped a hand on his left wrist and said, "My watch. I know I was wearing it earlier…and I don't remember taking it off…"

"Oh my," Alex said. "And Molly's beads, too? With this many things gone missing, I say it must be that little pickpocket with the black eye."

Dubious, Dugan shook his head. "That little freckle-faced blondie?"

"I caught him scrabbling on my fingers," Alex said, "trying to swipe my ring. I didn't say anything because I didn't want to embarrass him. And I didn't really think that he'd manage to rip anyone off. We are carnies, after all, and you can't out-grift a grifter."

Taking in Dugan's glower, Alex added, "Well. Most of the time you can't."

Shadrach felt sick. He pictured Olaf walking home grinning, his purpled eye swollen shut, his pockets bulging with presents for his family, his teeth crunching the final delicious inch of peppermint stick into a minty-pink cement which would lodge in his molars, allowing him to suck on candied teeth until dinner. A happy little towheaded thief.

"That is one hell of an act that kid has," Alex said, shaking with laughter. "Golly-wow!"

Dugan scowled fiercely and muttered, "More proof that this season is going to hell in a hand-basket."

"Don't say that," Shadrach said. But it was the saying he objected to, not the sentiment—with which he wholeheartedly agreed.

Chapter twenty

Forget the Rest

July 7-9th, Opelika, Illinois

M ore than a week had passed since the Sulphur sheriff had banished the Starlight, and more than two weeks since Roxy had bobbed the twins' hair, when a handsome young man, his wild curly hair unrestrained in spite of a glossy, unctuous application of Silkum, deftly tossed a note onto Molly and Faye's stage right before Dugan shut the curtain at the end of their act. Dugan didn't notice, and Molly and Faye quickly snatched up the note, unfolding the paper with eager fingers.

Tidy block letters printed in pencil on the back of a torn envelope: *Tonight you two is the best-lookin gals in Illinois. Meet me at westside fence after carnival close. Yor admirer, Lionel.*

The twins read the message, then peeked through the curtains to find Lionel in the crowd. His name suited his unruly yellow mane and the amber-brown eyes that lit up with desire when he saw the twins peeking out at him. Euphoric, exultant, Molly and Faye ducked back behind the black cloth. To stir a man that much simply by being female, simply because your femaleness and your sister's femaleness beckoned to him, without awareness or effort on your part, was more intoxicating than gin. Even if unconscious, it was a kind of power, and the newness of that power was heady.

Not that Lionel had been Molly and Faye's first and only admirer since Roxy transformed them from little girls into young women. They'd witnessed desire in the eyes of scores of men, and some days their skin felt bruised from so many forceful stares. They wished that Charlie hadn't disappeared from the carnival right after their birthday; he'd be sure to regret what he'd done and beg for a second chance (which he wouldn't get) now that the twins had become such sweet, smart, sharp little flappers. And there had been notes other than Lionel's as well, most of them less than romantic, explicitly detailing acts that the girls had never heard of, nor wanted to try. Lionel, young and handsome, with a smile even more thrilling than Charlie's had been, was simply the first admirer they had admired in return. On the night he gave them the note, they rendezvoused at the western border of the lot, leaning over the carnival fence to kiss for hours.

Before he left he asked, "Will you meet me here again tomorrow night?"

Faye looked at Molly and said, "Well, tomorrow is Friday. It'd be our last chance before we tear down and jump Saturday night."

Molly smiled at her sister, the decision made.

The next night, Lionel seemed restless after just a few kisses, his lean and perfectly formed body unable to keep still for a moment, so when he suggested that they take a walk, Molly and Faye agreed immediately, hopping the fence. To the twins' delight, he took Molly's hand and held it, his fingers interlaced with hers as they walked. In a few minutes, he stopped in front of a darkened boarding house. No one seemed to be at home.

"This is where I live," Lionel said. "I rent a room on the first floor. Would you like to come in and talk for a while?"

Despite their inexperience, Molly and Faye well-knew that young men almost never invite young women into their quarters hoping only for conversation, and yet they accepted the invitation. They could still feel his kisses on their lips, and they were eager for more kisses, eager for *more*.

He led them through the front door, pressing his index finger against his full, soft lips and tiptoeing down the hall even though the house was clearly deserted, and took them to an austere, white-walled room containing only a bare desk, a dresser topped with a basin and pitcher, and a bed with white sheets. White curtains billowed on a damp breeze, filtering and distorting the dim moonlight so that the room seemed underwater.

Lionel's hands went immediately to the buttons on Molly and Faye's dresses, and the suddenness of his action, the lack of seduction, vanquished the twins' eagerness; they recoiled, pushing his hands away.

With an embarrassed smile, he knelt at their feet and said, "I'm sorry. I shouldn't rush you like that. But you see, you're all I thought about all week. You're so pretty. I know I'm being too forward, but touching your bare skin would be the most wonderful thing I ever did, I know it. I'll be honest, I've had other women in this room, but I never wanted one as much as I want you two. I never felt like this before. It's like looking at you makes me drunk."

He continued to flatter and cajole until the twins' shyness funneled into their bloodstream, circulating to their blushing cheeks, where it dissipated. They began to fumble with the buttons at the backs of their dresses. They wanted this; they wanted to find out everything.

"Let me help you," Lionel said, then took over the unbuttoning, undoing a few buttons of Molly's, then a few of Faye's, then back to Molly, so that each twin's nakedness kept pace with her sister's, and when he reached the last button at the small of Faye's back, he lifted the contiguous dresses straight over their heads. Standing naked before Lionel, who was still fully clothed, felt exciting, dangerous, delicious, and Molly and Faye kissed him with sixteen years of bottled passion, Molly kissing his lips the way she hadn't gotten to kiss Charlie's, and Faye kissing his neck, the skin there smelling of clean sweat, Silkum and shaving cream. For the first time since their sixteenth birthday the twins felt an eager expectancy tightening their skin, a hot pulse of blood between their legs, and an interior expansion like flowers opening.

Any fear or nervousness melted with Lionel's touch, with his kisses, with his hands cupping Molly's right breast and Faye's left in his hands, the skin of all four breasts shivering on contact, their nipples rising into sharp peaks of pleasure. When his hands slid between their legs, his fingers slipped and slid against a wetness that seeped from their own bodies, and the twins were shocked; they hadn't known to expect this. They knew that some juice or sap came from the man's penis, but they didn't know when, or how much, and they didn't know that women responded to sex with their own succulence. They had noticed dampened underpants on their birthday with Charlie, but mistook it for sweat from their nervousness. They wondered when Lionel's wetness would come, and why feeling their own slippery sap made him moan and hurry to remove his clothes. Once he was naked, Lionel disappointed Molly and Faye by pulling them against his body so quickly that they didn't get a chance to inspect the rigid protrusion now digging into the joining place at their hips. They knew a little about erect penises, knowledge derived from glimpses of the flaccid organs of male carnies during boil-ups combined with indirect information about erections gleaned from dirty jokes and graffiti, but they had never observed one up close.

Urging them onto the bed, Lionel pushed against the twins with his hands, and if it weren't for the allure of desire enflaming his amber eyes and the way that being wanted made the blood beat faster inside them, Molly and Faye would've been angry to be shoved. But they weren't; they were still aroused, and still deadly curious.

"Who wants to be first?" Lionel asked with a sly, almost unappealing chuckle.

"I will," Faye said, and Molly was relieved.

Lionel nodded, spread Faye's thighs with his knees and lowered his weight, crushing the breath from her chest, but before she could complain, he lifted up on his elbows—his left one wedged between the sisters' bodies, above their band of linked flesh—and, with a spike of pain like a driving tent stake, pushed his way inside. As Faye's vision flared red-orange, both girls cried out. But Lionel kissed Faye's cheeks, making shushing noises and moving gently until the red-orange pain softened to a golden ache that seemed always at the verge of evolving into pleasure, but never quite did.

Lionel stopped moving, panting at the crook between Faye's neck and shoulder.

"What's wrong?" Molly whispered.

"Nothing," he said. "I just don't want to finish too fast. You haven't had your turn yet."

After a moment's hesitation, Molly nodded her assent, and Lionel pulled out of Faye's body, slid over onto Molly, then pushed inside her with another red-orange tent stake of pain. Molly stifled a scream, shocked by the intensity, while Faye's initial bewilderment—for her, the pain of the second penetration had been much weaker than the first—gradually evolved into understanding, or perhaps just acceptance. Perhaps she had always known that while each sister felt everything her twin felt, the secondhand feeling wasn't equivalent to direct experience. As the sensation traveled from one body to the other, it became a lessened facsimile of the original. Molly had been prepared for the repetition of an echo, not the direct pain of penetration.

And now Lionel began to pump his hips as if the movement had spasmed beyond his control. With his eyes squeezed shut, his face an ugly, twisted grimace, he battered into Molly, and with one final thrust, released a groan of such anguished intensity that for a moment both girls thought he had hurt himself.

As Lionel's penis throbbed like an artery, pumping something hot into Molly, the final piece of ragged information fit into the puzzle. Faye flooded with guilt. She should've guessed that this was the man's wetness, that this was the baby juice that girls tried not to get inside them by having their boyfriends *pull out*, as they had once overheard June advise another girl to do. Faye had wanted to ease Molly into sex by going first; she had wanted to be the brave, protective sister, but instead, Molly experienced the least gentleness, the most pain, and now this strange and unpleasant oozing heat—a hot sticky glue filling the space where they had felt the sweet expectancy that made them want to do this in the first place.

Lionel rolled over, panting and smiling for a minute, before getting up to cross to the basin on his dresser. He dampened a washcloth with water from the pitcher, wiped himself off, then handed the cloth to Molly. Without looking at Lionel, especially not into his bewitching amber eyes, Faye took the cloth, sat up, and wiped her sister's sore vagina as clean of the clotted paste as she could. Then she tried to hurry them into their clothes, but Molly's fingers were clumsy. She looked over at Lionel, now stretched across his bed with the lopsided *take-a-look-at-them* grin that a thousand other suckers had smiled at her and Molly a thousand times before, and understood that they'd deluded themselves into seeing him as more than just another gawping rube. Humiliation descended; she and Molly had lowered themselves, giving their virginity to a ridiculous nobody. Faye's glare didn't wipe the grin from his face, but he did get on his feet to help her do up their buttons.

When they were fully dressed, Lionel asked, "You all right?" looking uncomfortable suddenly, his supple, leonine body awkward for the first time. Still, even graceless, his perfect and predictable form persisted in its beauty. "I mean, you wanted this, too," he said. "I know you did."

"We did," Faye admitted, but she refused to offer him the forgiving smile she felt him yearning for. "And don't worry," she added, although she didn't actually think he would, "we'll be just fine."

They turned and headed for the door, but Lionel lunged and grabbed Faye's collar, sliding across the hardwood floor and against her back. A few stitches from the shoulder seams popped. The twins looked down; he was wearing socks and nothing else.

"Don't go that way," he said, his eyes widening, appalled that they would even consider such a thing.

Molly recovered her voice and asked, "Why not? It's how we came in."

"Someone might see you now. Didn't you hear that car pull in earlier?" Molly and Faye shook their heads. "And someone turned the hall light on. But since I live on the first floor, you can go through the window real easy. Come on."

He reached beyond them and turned a key in the door lock, removed the key, then shut it inside a desk drawer. At the already open window, he parted the fluttering curtains and gestured towards the frame, his eyes darting nervously between desk and keyhole just in case the twins made a break for the key.

"You said you've had girls here before," Faye said. "Did they all leave through the window?"

"Of course not, but they weren't..." Lionel's voice choked silent.

Just like on their birthday, Molly and Faye felt his shame crowd out desire and make it impossible to speak that word, that prosaic word, inseparable from carny life. But at least it wasn't the twins made mute this time.

"Freaks," Faye finished for him. "They weren't Freaks."

"Please," Lionel said, "just leave through the window."

Molly and Faye complied only because the window appeared to be the fastest means of escape; Molly threw her legs over the sill and sat in the frame, then Faye followed, and they both jumped to the ground.

Seeing no one in the darkened yard of the boarding house, Lionel sighed, smiled, and said, "I had a fantastic time tonight. That was something truly amazing in there. I mean—*amazing.*"

The twins stared at the beautiful young man, too weary to scowl. His shame produced a sour odor like rotting vegetation.

"It really was something else. Thanks," he said, then closed the curtains between them.

The walk back to the lot wasn't far, but seemed long and arduous. Mud from the Illinois rains made Molly's and Faye's feet heavy and slow and the scent of Lionel's seed still clung to their skin, a rank mélange of old custard, gin, and sweat.

Molly knew that she had experienced the worst of the event

while her sister's experience of the final moments, strong as it may have been, remained only an echo, but she did not allow herself to think of it for long—the distinction felt too much like separation. "Most girls only feel it once," she said, "but we had to feel it twice."

More like one and a half times, Faye thought, but aloud she said, "We didn't have to. We could've ignored each other's feelings, turned it off."

"I'd never turn it off and leave you alone for your first time," Molly said. "I'd never do that to you."

Faye's stomach rolled over with guilt. "I'd never do that to you, either. Though it was pretty awful to feel it twice."

"But it got better."

"Yeah, better, but not much better, and then it got worse."

"It'll probably get a lot better later."

"Maybe," Faye said.

A treefrog chorus chirped over the slurp of mud sucking their shoes with every step. After a while, Molly said, "I don't think I like it, Faye."

Faye felt her guilt fill her chest, bloating her heart. "Me, neither. Not yet, anyway. But maybe later."

"Maybe."

The thick, humid heat moistened the residue of semen between Molly's legs and made her inner thighs viscous by the time they reached the carnival's gate, but even with her limbs weighed down with sex, she and Faye climbed over the fence and dropped to the ground with a flawlessly synchronized, resigned grace. Hearing voices in the darkness, they followed the sound to the unlit Carousel where Alex and Roxy sat kissing on the wide bench preferred by the Starlight's few elderly visitors. Flustered, Roxy rearranged her dress, which had been hiked up to her hips, and shifted her legs off of Alex's lap.

"Why, good evening," Alex said, cool and composed. "What've you girls been up to tonight?"

Molly and Faye shrugged and sat on the wooden planks of the ride's floor. "Saw a friend," Molly said. Faye sputtered at the word friend.

"Ah, I see," Alex said. "So now, at last, you are women." The words were spoken with exaggerated formality, intended to be funny. Previously the twins would've giggled, but now they only shrugged a second time.

"Whatever that means," Faye said. As she recalled the feel of Lionel's tongue in her ear, disgust infused her guilt.

In both Molly and Faye's memory, even the nice feelings were corrupted by the grief of losing an innocence that they never really wanted, but which hurt to lose nonetheless. The twins felt too full and too empty at once, their thoughts crowding and crushing in a stampede, their hearts cored like apples.

"You poor babies," Roxy said. "My first time was awful. Just awful. He was old and sweaty, and he didn't ask first. But later, I got to choose who I wanted to do it with, so it got better."

Alex smoothed Roxy's hair back from her forehead with a gentle hand. *He didn't ask first.*

"Was it awful?" Roxy asked.

"Not exactly," Molly said.

"We liked the before part," Faye said. "The kissing and all that."

"But then the—the, you know—that part hurt."

"And we didn't get to enjoy it like he did."

"And then after," Molly said, "we felt weird and bad."

Faye nodded, deciding not to add anything about her regret that Molly went second, or about the washcloth, or about leaving through the window.

Alex and Roxy moved to sit beside the twins on the polished planks of the Carousel.

"It gets better, I promise," Alex said. "And that weird, bad feeling is just an adjustment feeling. It won't last."

Molly and Faye nodded, wanting to believe, eager to wash away the sore, sticky residue that would require more than water and soap to remove.

"The trick," Alex continued, "is to take what you can from sex—which is mainly just a release of tension, some pleasure, and a brief comfort. Then you have to forget the rest, because that stuff always fails. Don't have expectations, because no one ever lives up to them. Enjoy the physical and forget the rest. That's my advice."

Roxy blanched at Alex's words, taking back her hand and scooting away from him.

"Forget the rest," Faye repeated, thinking of the romantic ideas she'd had of Lionel holding them after. Molly had even pictured him on his knees in chivalric worship, begging them not to take the jump to the next lot. But he had only knelt to get them naked, and after he pounded their bodies and squirted into Molly, he had handed them a washcloth, hurried them through a window, and said *Thanks* before closing the curtains.

Molly reached for Faye's hand and they clasped fingers, older now, more experienced; they had learned all about the secret inter-minglings of men and women—at least that was something. And they still had each other. How sad a rough unvirgining must be for solitary girls with no one to truly share the disappointment with; how very sad, how terribly lonely.

Roxy said she was tired, and after kissing Molly and Faye on their cheeks and offering them a shoulder to cry on anytime, she left without looking at Alex, who appeared not to notice.

"How about we sneak over to the Pie Wagon," Alex said, "and I stake you to some late night pancakes?"

Molly and Faye grinned and nodded, but the gestures were hollow; mustering a show of anticipation for the treat was difficult after all that had happened that night—they felt incapable of the eagerness they aped. As they followed Alex through the darkened lot, the twins held hands and thought of the dampened washcloth, of exiting through the window.

Faye whispered to Molly, "If we ever find a man who's not ashamed to be seen with us—who'll love us enough to be proud, even, to be seen with us—then that's who we're meant to be with."

Molly nodded and whispered, "Even if we don't love him."

"Right."

Once this feeling wore off, Molly and Faye didn't ever want

to feel it again. Lionel had infected them with his shame, and now it coursed through their blood, slowing their bodies with sadness, making them uneasy inside their contiguous skin, causing them to sink down to the most ordinary of spaces, where they found themselves wishing, for the first time ever, that they had been born as normal and as beautiful and as cruel as Lionel.

The wish became repugnant after a few moments, but the fact that they had wished such a thing at all made everything in their lives—even their home, the Starlight Carnival Royale—reel and lurch, all of it suddenly strange, suddenly wrong.

Chapter twenty-one

Just Over the Border

*July 10ᵗʰ, between Opelika, Illinois
and Vineherd, Kentucky*

I nching imperceptibly down or up, slowly adjusting the arch or slouch of his spine, Dugan struggled to find a comfortable way to sit in the middle of the navy truck's bench seat. He'd pushed himself too hard during the Opelika tear down, and now he was paying for it; no position felt even remotely comfortable. He wondered, if he were to let his spine relax as he stood, how Quasimodo he would be? A frightening line of thought, but it didn't matter, because he wouldn't find out and neither would anyone else. Even while alone in his bed at night he resisted change: he'd slept poorly for six months before grudgingly exchanging the anguish of sleeping on his back for the relief of sleeping on his side, wound up like a ball of yarn.

He shook the Illinois/Kentucky map spread across his thighs to camouflage a cramp that briefly seized the flesh between his shoulder blades, then realized he needn't have bothered. Finch stared so hard at the road as he drove that it seemed he meant to see right through it, through the dirt and rock and water below, down to the very center of the earth. Meanwhile Shadrach stared out the passenger side window, chin in hand like Rodin's *Thinker*, lost in contemplation of theology, tattoos, or who knew what else. Dugan would have liked to know, but decided not to pry—not yet, anyway. First item on the agenda was finding the rendezvous spot. While the rest of the Wonders were making the jump to Vineherd, Kentucky, Dugan, Finch and Shadrach were taking a side trip to meet up with Lem, Dugan's bootlegger friend.

Finch always came along when Dugan made these exchanges. Shadrach never had before. But earlier that evening, as Dugan was deciding who would ride where for the jump from Illinois to Kentucky, Shadrach had suggested that he join the illicit detour.

Shocked, Dugan had asked, "You do recall that this is a whiskey run, don't you?"

Shadrach had shrugged, looking timorous as he replied, "You're going to do it anyway. I might as well offer my support." Then he climbed into the truck and refused to get out, afraid of being left behind. Dugan had been forced to board the truck from the driver's side.

"Turn left after these railroad tracks," Dugan now said. Not knowing that Shadrach's thoughts concerned a specific decision that had compelled him to join the whiskey run, Dugan wondered if his silence meant that he regretted coming along, but he didn't ask. It was too late to change any plans; they were nearly there. "Egg Farm Road," he called out. "That's it."

"Egg Farm?" Finch asked, taking the turn.

"Lem said the Egg Farm is long gone. Hardly anyone ever uses the road anymore."

"I can tell," Finch said, as the truck began to jounce and clatter down the unpaved, rain-gutted, sparsely graveled road.

A half-mile down, per Dugan's instructions, Finch pulled into the driveway of an abandoned house, disemboweled by fire. Thick brambles and lanky grass fringed a ruined square of foundation, while a brick chimney stretched tall and intact against a cloud-streaked moon. Dugan and Finch were startled when doubled points of light at the summit transformed the chimney into an undersized, landlocked lighthouse, but when Finch switched off the truck's headlamps, they saw that it had only been the reflective eyes of a large bird nesting in the chimney-top. After ruffling then smoothing its feathers, the bird tucked its head beneath a wing and returned to sleep.

The bootlegger Lem arrived soon after, driving a white fish wagon with "Gibson's Fine Seafood" painted in red script on the side. He shook Finch and Shadrach's hands firmly, then yanked Dugan into a manly, back slapping embrace.

"It's been too damn long," he said. "Why don't you ever come visit me in Florida?"

"What else is there to see in Florida besides you?"

Lem chuckled and punched him in the shoulder, and Dugan laughed a little too heartily to mask the shudder that the blow sent down his spine.

"You'll wind up there sooner or later," the bootlegger said. "It's the perfect state for a man to retire in. The warm weather, the curative power of salty air and water, the peace and quiet that comes from a small population, and more than enough nature to go around. An ideal place to grow old."

"That may be," Dugan said, smiling past the confusing amalgamation of sadness, longing and dread brewed by Lem's description, "but I have no intention of ever growing old."

Lem chuckled again, and this time, thankfully, squeezed Dugan's shoulder rather than punching it.

As Dugan counted out bills, Finch and Shadrach loaded two crates of Canadian whiskey onto the bed of the pickup, then secured a sheet of burlap over the boxes using thick jute twine. The ache in Dugan's bones faded some just knowing that he was once more well stocked; although liquor could not give complete relief, it did make his pain easier to bear.

After Lem gave Dugan another firm hug, he climbed into his fish wagon and said, "I hope that you're having as much fun and profit this year as I am, old man."

"Oh, always," Dugan replied. "The twenties are a booming decade. Each year better than the last." A consummate professional, he smiled in a way that appeared completely genuine to Lem; the bootlegger would have been shocked to learn of Dugan's dissimulation.

With a wave from the window of his vehicle, Lem backed out of the driveway and rambled down the bumpy road and out of sight. Resisting the urge to break out a fresh bottle of whiskey from one of the crates, Dugan climbed soberly back into the navy truck, silently cursing his own stubbornness—if he hadn't worked so hard earlier, he wouldn't hurt so badly now. The truck doors slammed, and Finch turned the key in the ignition. Nothing happened. Dugan nodded for him to try again, but again nothing, not even a sputter.

"I thought this was a new truck," Finch said.

"New-used," Dugan said. "But it's a '25 Ford. Built like a tank."

Finch went out with a flashlight and raised the hood. Dugan, impatient with Shadrach, the passenger-side lump, climbed out of the truck through the driver-side door. Dugan preferred to educate himself with books rather than machinery and so knew very little about vehicle repair, and Finch, who spent all of his spare time on photography, knew only marginally more. Shadrach, however...

"Shadrach!" Dugan shouted. "Wake up and get over here!"

The tattooed man had been meditating on the velvety black shadows heaped beneath the thick fence of trees surrounding the yard of the ruined house, and at Dugan's call he slowly, abstractedly, turned his face from the woods and got out of the truck. He placed a hand on the truck's grill, leaning over the engine with the flashlight, his dazed expression clearing. He nodded, then looked up crisply and said, "When you tried to start her up, what sort of sound did the engine make?"

"Weren't you...." Dugan had been about to say *listening*, but clearly Shadrach hadn't been.

"It didn't make any sound at all," Finch said. "Maybe it clicked once, but that's it."

Shadrach nodded. "It's the battery. The truck is fine, Dugan. It's made to last a lifetime. The battery, however, is finished."

"And here we are on a long-neglected road with little to no hope of any passersby, much less a good Samaritan willing to stop and offer assistance," Dugan said, his wry smile somewhere between a smirk and a grimace. If someone, even the local sheriff, should happen by, they would have to repay assistance with whiskey; it was not illegal to drink alcohol, only to sell and transport it, and in Dugan's experience, most lawmen would look the other way for a small-timer willing to share. He retrieved the map from the truck. "Looks like Hiram, Kentucky is the closest town. Right on the other side of the border, about three miles away. Not exactly a pleasure stroll, but possible."

"I'll go," Shadrach said.

"Don't be ridiculous," Finch said. "You aren't wearing shoes."

"I never wear shoes."

"You can't walk three miles barefoot."

"I certainly can."

Shadrach went to the truck and dug out the croker sack in which he carried essentials like his money and his Bible on jumps from one lot to the next. Slinging the bag over his shoulder, he added, "And I aim to, regardless of what you say."

"Fine, fine," Dugan said. "I don't care who goes, as long as someone does."

"You aren't going to let him walk all that way without shoes, are you?" Finch asked.

"It isn't a matter of *letting* him." Dugan lowered himself onto the cornerstone of a ruined garden wall, feeling grateful that Shadrach's insistence had saved him from having to insincerely volunteer to go himself. "Shadrach is a grown man with his own reasons, usually religious, for everything he does. Bare feet included. I agree with Lord Chesterfield on this. 'In matters of religion and matrimony I never give any advice; because I will not have anybody's torments in this world or the next laid to my charge.'"

Dugan smiled. Sitting, even on rough, damp stone, felt

luxurious. How strange it was that a minimum of pain had come to feel like pleasure.

Suddenly Shadrach took his hand, squeezing tightly. "I've been torn lately," he said, his gaze urgent, imploring. "I want to be of help—I care about y'all so much—but I've decided that it might be best if I simply go on my way and allow things to run their course."

Dugan's bafflement held the silvery tinge of rising fear. "What are you saying?" Trying to stand, he grunted, "Come on, help me up." The comfortable seat made him too relaxed, which made him feel vulnerable.

Shadrach hoisted Dugan to his feet, then said, "It's time for me to leave the show."

"You can't possibly mean that," Finch said, stumbling forward as if intoxicated.

"I do. I'll miss you, my friend, and you Dugan, and everyone else, of course, but I have to answer God's call."

"But you can't go," Finch said.

His plaintive tone made Dugan wish for a sidewall to exit through; this was meant to be a private performance.

"Be happy for me," Shadrach said. "I plan to become a true man of God. In the past I've fought against the urge to settle down in one place and preach to my own steady flock, but it's in my blood. And its time for me to think about my future—a family, perhaps."

Finch's voice dropped to a strangled whisper that Dugan had never heard before, and which he felt embarrassed to be hearing now. "But I'm not ready for you to go."

"No. That's not true. You're ready for me to go because *I'm* ready to go, and you're my friend. You want me to be happy, just as I want you to be happy."

Finch frowned for a long while, looking at the ground. Then finally, he looked up and nodded. "You're right. You should go."

Dugan was surprised. If this were his own heartbreaking farewell, he doubted he would part with Saffron so easily.

Then the men hugged, and Shadrach said, "Goodbye."

Goodbye.

The word shocked Dugan. It was standard carny vernacular to bid farewell by saying, "See you down the road." No parting was final in carnival life, the road always led back to old friends and old haunts, and yet Shadrach had told Finch goodbye. This break, this rupture in Dugan's world, was final.

"Goodbye," Finch returned, pounding Shadrach's back before letting go, stepping away from the embrace and turning his face from the other two men.

Shadrach went to Dugan, and said, "I'll miss you."

"And I you," Dugan replied, keeping his voice level, his demeanor stoic. After all, he had been a man of the stage nearly all of his life.

They hugged, and Shadrach whispered in Dugan's ear, "All things end, my friend. Don't try to hang onto the show at your own expense. Stop and take care of yourself."

Dugan's aching spine turned to ice, vertebra by vertebra, as he realized that Shadrach knew of the debilitation he was so desperately trying to hide. But how did he know?

Shadrach stepped back. "Mario can take my place as talker. He'll give an excellent bally."

Dugan nodded. That was true. But Mario would never be able to simultaneously promise sanctification and titillation the way that Shadrach could.

"I'll find help as soon as I reach Hiram," Shadrach said. "I'll take the map with me, so I can show them exactly where you are." He glanced at the truck's flat bed. "I'll be careful who I ask. No lawmen or anything."

Dugan wanted to tell him not to worry about the law, but found himself unable to speak. Then Shadrach turned and left, his body vanishing into the shadows that cloaked the road even before the sound of bare footsteps scuffing over gravel faded into silence.

"You're a stronger man than me," Dugan said to Finch after a while, hoping that he would not have to be more specific.

"Maybe, maybe not," Finch said. "Either way, Shadrach was right. I *am* ready for him to go. I've been doing a lot of thinking lately."

"Would you care to share your thoughts?"

Finch took his tobacco tin out of his pocket, sat on the wall's cornerstone where Dugan had been sitting earlier, and began to roll a cigarette. "No," he said at last.

Dugan sat beside him. Although the jagged rock of that segment of wall did not make as comfortable a seat as the cornerstone, the relief of not needing to support his full weight remained luxurious. "I believe that this might be the best thing for you, Finch."

Finch licked and sealed the tobacco-stuffed tube of paper. "You're probably right about that."

"You know, I often wish that Saffron weren't around, because perhaps then I would be motivated to find someone more suitable to return my affections."

After lighting his cigarette and taking a long pull, Finch exhaled an aromatic cloud and said, "Now that's a lie if I ever heard one."

Dugan didn't respond. Whirred hooting emerged from the green-black woods, followed by a distant train whistle. He caught the scent of honeysuckle on the air, but when he scanned his dim surroundings, he couldn't see any.

With appraising eyes, Finch turned to face Dugan and asked, "So what was that about things ending that Shadrach whispered so loudly to you? What was he trying to say?"

Dugan felt pinned by Finch's gaze, like a shiny black beetle in an entomologist's display case, so he looked away, looked overhead to watch blue cirrus glide over the moon's bone-white face as he replied, "I haven't the slightest idea."

Chapter twenty-two

An All Night Blanket Game

July 13ᵗʰ, Vineherd, Kentucky

My big, beautiful dumpling," Mario said to Bea, "you are far too large to be this drunk on four fingers of whiskey."

"And you, my handsome rum raisin," Bea replied, "are far too old to suck down whiskey like a baby at the teat."

Mario laughed and took another pull from his flask.

It was a few days after the whiskey run, and Mario, Bea, Saffron and Dugan were on the lot in Vineherd, playing poker in the bed of someone's rusty orange pickup. They played until dawn tickled the horizon with rosy fingertips, the supine crescent moon still smiling among freckles of stars. Saffron had lost all of the money she'd brought to the game, but that hadn't been much; since her humiliating night in Tupelo a month and a half ago, gambling wasn't as much fun as it used to be. The quartet were playing poker in a truck bed because the recent rains had left the ground so soggy that card tables and folding chairs sank into the earth, tilting unevenly in the saturated soil, tipping the unwary out of their seats. By midweek the mud had insinuated itself everywhere. Even if the carnies took off their shoes before entering their quarters, layers of dried mud still somehow accumulated, forming trails of dirt along the well-traveled paths between bed and table and door, and however much they washed, it never seemed to be enough to remove the ever-present crust in the nooks between their fingers and toes. In the few days since Shadrach left, morale in the Freak Show had dipped even lower than its previous low, and the weather only worsened the mood.

With the cards now put away, Saffron and Dugan lay on their backs in the flat bed, gazing at the twilit sky while Bea and Mario sat smoking cigars, Bea fitting neatly in the space behind Dugan, Mario in the space behind Saffron.

"They look pretty sweet like that, don't they?" Mario said.

Bea chuckled. "Dugan always looks sweet. He's not a bad lookin' fella."

"Are you expressing an interest?"

"Nah. I'm too much woman for Dugan. I'd snap him like a twig."

"Or maybe he'd snap you. That man's got one great big secret behind his zipper, I'll have you know."

Bea chuckled again and Dugan said sternly, "That's enough about that," but he was pleased when Saffron smiled and raised one questioning tuft of eyebrow at him. He shrugged and smiled mysteriously.

"My Jimmy's jimmy was long and skinny just like him," Bea said, rolling her cigar between her fingers, "but I don't have much to compare it to, since I only saw two others before. One was some rube who flashed me from the crowd, and the other I don't plan to tell you about."

"My dear Beatrice, you are too grand a woman to have had only two lovers."

"Mario, I ain't no piano. If you don't quit calling me grand, I'll have to heave you out of this truck and into the mud."

"Play nice, children," Saffron said, although presently, she had only a passing interest in the activities of the outside world. All day today, which would've been her eighth wedding anniversary, she had been savoring a sweet sadness that made her body feel heavy while the skin at the roots of her pelt tingled. As the whiskey transformed the heavy sensation into a feline languorousness, the tingle made its way between her legs, her memories of her husband becoming her body's demand. She and Benjamin had made love constantly before he died, enthusiastically applying themselves to the work of conception. With Mario's words about Dugan buzzing in the back of her mind, she recalled with fondness that Ben hadn't been too small, nor too large; they had fit together perfectly, their bodies interlocking as if designed as a pair.

"So Dugan," Bea said, "You still sore at Molly and Faye for cutting their hair off?"

Dugan let out a long slow sigh.

"I guess you are."

"Not precisely. I'm simply worried that they're growing up too fast. In many ways the girls have been sheltered. We're their family, and the only other women they know well are Zimm's Girl Show girls, who are hardly paragons of feminine virtue—"

"That's sure as shit the truth," Bea interrupted. Saffron murmured in half-hearted protest and Bea said, "Come on, Saff. You know they're all Kelseys."

"I don't know any such thing," Saffron said, but Dugan spoke over her, saying, "Exactly. Most of them behave exactly like prostitutes, and they don't set a suitable example." Then he looked at Saffron, speaking directly to her, unaware that he had just swept aside her difference of opinion. "You are the only woman that I would have them emulate."

Saffron laughed and said, "What do you know about women? You've never seemed to like them much."

"I like you," Dugan said softly. "More than like, even."

Saffron's laughter died; it was dangerous for Dugan to be so direct, on this day of all days. As the tingling between her legs expanded into a moist heat, she attempted to distract herself by focusing on the drifting wisps of cotton candy clouds, the stars fading out of sight, and the smile of the moon evanescing into the paling sky. A humid breeze carried off the scent of rust and axle grease and replaced it with the smell of wet moss and honeysuckle.

Mario began to snore, and Saffron and Dugan sat up, turning to see Mario and Bea passed out, their slack faces pinked by the sunrise.

"You should drink some water," Dugan told Saffron. "It'll help with the hangover later."

Disconcerted by the way the world continued to rush by even after she'd ceased moving, Saffron sat motionless without answering until the world calmed to the slight sway of a boat drifting on a lake. She had needed to drink an impressive amount of whiskey to become this intoxicated—or at least Mario had been impressed.

"Good idea," she finally managed to say.

That was exactly what she needed. She would get up and go to the water pump, drink water until her teeth hurt from the cold and her belly sloshed full, then lay down in her trailer to sleep, not getting up until fifteen minutes before the Starlight opened its gates for the evening.

Dugan tried to help Saffron off the truck, and when she slipped a little while jumping down, she steadied herself by grabbing onto his head. Embarrassment heated Dugan's face, but he slid a hand around her waist and attempted to salvage his dignity. "You should let me keep you balanced. You've had more to drink than you're accustomed to."

"It'll wear off in twenty minutes."

"Nevertheless, you're still drunk now."

As they slogged through the muddy field where the trucks parked, over to the trailers and the water pump, Saffron wondered why she was putting herself straight on the path to temptation, a path which would only hurt Dugan in the end. She possessed no romantic feelings for him and never would; at times she doubted even her platonic feelings for him, worrying that his every act of kindness concealed an ulterior motive. But as they continued to walk, she became less troubled, reasoning that he was responsible for his own misguided emotions. She had never shared anything truly intimate with him, not even words—no memories of Benjamin, or how she still wanted babies in spite of her determination to never love romantically again, or anything at all about that awful night of moonshine and violence in the basement of the Tupelo, Mississippi sheriff's office. Dugan was a grown man who could look after himself.

After filling a pail with water at the pump, Dugan invited Saffron to his trailer to drink. "Your quarters are over there," he said, "but mine are right here. Why don't you come in?"

There it was then, the moment of choice. To accept an invitation for water that was really an invitation to make love, or to trudge through the mud to her own trailer and drink a toast of cold well water to the crematory urn beside her bed. Five years was a very long time to be faithful to a husband reduced to ash.

Saffron followed Dugan inside.

His trailer was without decoration, but the stacks of books lining the walls made it seem busy and ornate. The drivers used to complain that the extra weight strained the engines of the trucks, but the complaint only inspired Dugan to deliver a lecture on why—as the owner of the biggest moneymaker for the carnival, not to mention as a scholar with a duty to nurture and enrich his great, God-given genius—he could, if he wanted, fill his trailer floor to ceiling and wall to wall with books and sleep on the roof. After a few speeches of this sort, the men stopped complaining–at least within earshot of the magniloquent dwarf.

There was only one chair, and it, too, was piled with books. With the tenderness of a mother for her infant, Dugan lovingly relocated the stack to the floor so that Saffron could sit. He wiped two large pottery mugs with a clean cloth and filled one of them with water; Saffron accepted the mug gratefully, almost draining it, the water going to her head as if she'd had another shot of whiskey. Gripping the arm of the chair, she tried to steady herself while he dipped the second mug into the bucket.

"Fifteen minutes 'till sobriety," he said with a chuckle.

As she drank the rest of the water, its coldness drawing her skin into gooseflesh, she was suddenly reminded of sitting naked in a chair very much like the one she sat in now, with her husband's face between her legs. Stunned by the vivid recollection and already unsteady from the drink, she dropped the mug to the floor—déjà vu layered upon déjà vu.

When Dugan knelt to retrieve the mug, she placed a hand on the side of his neck, feeling the strong sinew stretching down to his shoulder, smelling the unmistakably male musk emanating from his skin. How beautiful Ben's golden curls had been, with his head like that of an angel between her legs, his soft tongue eliciting cries of ecstasy as she sank ever deeper into the mutual worship of body to body. So beautiful she could feel it still.

"Tell me something beautiful," Saffron said.

Already erect from the touch of her hand to his neck, Dugan nodded, and began to recite:

> "Love is a smoke made with the fume of sighs,
> Being purged, a fire sparkling in lovers' eyes,
> Being vexed, a sea nourished with lovers' tears.
> What is it else? A madness most discreet,
> A choking gall and a preserving sweet."

He stopped, breathing heavily.

Saffron nodded and said, "All right, then."

Her body, aroused by memory, opened itself to Dugan, whose touch was more experienced, more assured than Benjamin's had been. Dugan knew well the many techniques of pleasuring a woman with mouth and member, and yet, as his hands slipped over the surface of her body, it was as if he were stroking the fur of a pet dog, discovering the varying textures of her pelt—the silky fur of her back and hips, the bristlier hair of her arms and legs, the fuzzy, barely-there down on her breast and belly—without seeking contact with the skin beneath. When her husband had made love to her, he had never petted her as Dugan did now. Ben's fingers would slip through her fur and down to the roots so that he experienced her in entirety—as Woman and Wonder—and when he slipped between her legs and penetrated her, she would fill up with his energy, with his body, mind and soul, every cell of her body transformed into a vehicle for pleasure, for love.

When Dugan spread her legs and pushed inside, the shock of his size and the startling difference between the feel of him and the feel of her husband split Saffron into two lesser women; she felt like a shadow casting a shadow. One shade responded warmly and naturally to Dugan, to the swell of sensation surging towards climax, while the other lived in memory, attempting to superimpose the love of a dead man over the present love of the warm, palpitating being above and inside her. When she came, her two shadow halves melded into one, but even as she shook and moaned, clutching Dugan's hips between her thighs, she felt like a puzzle piece forced to fit incorrectly. This was not where she belonged.

Whether it satisfied her body or not made no difference. For Saffron, sex with Dugan was little more than a hard baton of flesh thrusting into a hungering, remembering fissure. An act of blunt and desperate nostalgia. She waited for him to drift into sleep, a contented smile curling the corners of his mouth, then swiftly dressed and slipped out of the trailer as quickly and quietly as the shadow of a cloud racing across a setting sun.

Chapter twenty-three

A Tin of Violet Candies

July 21ˢᵗ, Fast River, Ohio

Y ou should corner her," Faye insisted on that Thursday morning in Fast River, Ohio, wondering if she should smack her hand down on Dugan's book so that he would look up from the page and finally see her, and Molly, and the clumps of people sitting at the tables around the Pie Wagon. "You ought to *force* Saffron to talk about it."

"It's been a week and she hasn't said a word to you," Molly added.

"Not for my lack of trying," Dugan murmured, licking his index finger, using it to turn another page of his book.

Molly and Faye sighed. Dugan had been staggering around with a weary scowl ever since he'd made love to Saffron—thanks to the confined and crowded conditions of carny life, everyone had known within an hour of the act's completion—and now he only seemed content and alive when he was reading one of the thick volumes he carted around with him everywhere. Although the twins were glad that something could relieve his sadness, they wished it was something other than his books. Whenever Dugan was reading these days, the surrounding world faded to insignificance, and that was exactly how Molly and Faye felt as they tried to talk to him now—insignificant.

"I don't think you've tried hard enough," Faye said.

Dugan shook his head, still staring down at the page. "This really isn't any of your concern, girls. Not to mention rather out of your area of expertise."

Molly and Faye's throats clogged with emotion, imminent sobs gathering in mass and strength, but before the hurt became visible, Dugan startled away the tears by exclaiming loudly, "Ah, how exquisite! Listen to this."

He tapped his finger against the page and began to read:

> "Fade far away, dissolve, and quite forget
> What thou among the leaves hast never known,
> The weariness, the fever, and the fret...
> Where but to think is to be full of sorrow
> And leaden-eyed despairs,
> Where Beauty cannot keep her lustrous eyes,
> Or new Love pine at them beyond tomorrow."

He sighed, then at last looked up and smiled directly at Molly and Faye. "Keats, *Ode to a Nightingale*. Here—" he pushed the volume of poetry across the table towards the twins, "you two should really read the whole poem. It's absolutely exquisite."

Molly shoved the book roughly back across the table, then she and Faye fled while Dugan, a frown crumpling his forehead, hurriedly inspected the book's leather shell for scratches.

"He's useless. Completely useless!" Molly exclaimed.

Faye nodded, surprised yet comforted by her twin's unusual vehemence. "If he could climb into a book and live there he'd be a happy man."

"Exactly. And Saffron's useless, too. Spending all of her time avoiding Dugan and counting up her and Bea's money."

Faye nodded again.

"Even Alex and Roxy are acting peculiar. We have absolutely no one to talk to!"

They reached the closed arch at the front of the lot, then dropped down upon the grass, sitting cross-legged, not caring about the wet ground or the inevitable stain that would leach into the fabric of their dresses—shapeless, calico sacks that they wore around the lot. They saved their few fashionable dresses for performances and occasions. They hadn't found an occasion since their night with Lionel.

"Well," Faye said, sounding more like Molly than herself, "we still have each other to talk to."

Molly stared hard at her sister, and for a moment Faye expected the worst. Then Molly's eyes softened and she whispered earnestly, "You're right. We have each other, and that's what's most important."

Faye felt tears brim over her lower eyelids and spill down her cheeks. She smiled crookedly and yanked up a handful of dandelions from the damp earth. "Besides, what we have to say is so much more interesting than anything anyone else would come up with."

Molly blinked away her own tears and laughed. "Faye, you're the best all-around person I know. Ab-so-tive-ly, pos-o-lute-ly."

Faye winked and said, "Same but double to you, sweetheart."

The voice that spoke then was sudden, but too mild to be truly startling. "You aren't crying, are you? Oh, I hate to see you cry."

Molly and Faye got to their feet, shoving their knuckles across their cheeks as they studied the man standing on the other side of the fence—tall but too skinny, fancy suit, benign smile.

"We weren't really crying," Faye said. Lying convincingly to rubes was never much of a challenge. "We were laughing. Haven't you laughed so hard that it made you cry before?"

The man looked at them solemnly. "No. But I would sincerely like to attempt it sometime."

In unison, Molly and Faye tilted their heads to the side, and gave the man a closer look. Somewhat handsome, but looking far too serious and as thin as a toothpick doll, he seemed like a man who worried too much and forgot to show up for meals. He also looked rich—creamy linen suit, gold watch-chain winking from his front jacket pocket, blue silk tie, shiny alligator shoes caked with fresh mud.

"Who are you? The arch is closed, you know," Faye said.

"The carnival doesn't open for another few hours," Molly said.

The man nodded. "I know. But I've been here every day this week and I suppose I'm a trifle over-eager. My name is Matthew Harris Henderson. And you're Molly," he said, pointing to the correct sister, "and you're Faye."

The twins were shocked. Only those closest to them were able to remember who was who.

He smiled. "I've seen your show at least ten times so far."

Faye narrowed her eyes. "Why?"

Henderson blinked rapidly in a way that made him seem slightly feminine, but soon he composed himself, and as he lifted his chin to speak again, he became more masculine, but still refined—like an aristocrat in a movie, the twins thought.

He said, "You and your sister are so very beautiful that I could watch your show repeatedly every night of my life. You are the most captivating women that I have ever had the privilege of meeting."

One by one, the key words pealed like bells in the twins' ears—*beautiful, enchanting, privilege*—but the word that rang with the loveliest tone was *women*. *Women*, not *girls*.

"I've been trying to get up the courage to speak to you all week, but until now…." He grinned and shrugged.

His bright, healthy, rich young man's smile made it impossible for Molly and Faye to not smile back, but then they remembered what they were wearing and embarrassment heated their cheeks. An occasion had appeared without warning, and here they were, wearing flowered potato sacks. But then they remembered, too, how attractive Lionel's smile had been, and what had he gotten them other than experience?

"You're not going to get us to go home with you, if that's what you're after," Faye said, crossing her arms over her chest.

Henderson's cheeks slowly stained the color of ripe strawberries. "I would never presume—I mean, to ask ladies such as you to—*Please* don't think me such a cad."

Molly and Faye's smiles returned. They loved the formal way of speaking their new acquaintance had—like Dugan, only more romantic.

"Molly, Faye—may I call you by your first names?"

"Sure," Molly said. "We don't really remember our last name, anyway."

Perplexed, Henderson silently opened and closed his mouth like a trout until Molly said. "Don't worry about it. It's not a sad thing."

Reaching into the right interior pocket of his jacket, he took out a small purple tin. He lifted off the lid and held out the container over the top of the carnival fence. "Would you like a violet candy?"

"Violet?" Molly asked. "Like the flower or the color?"

"Both," Henderson said. "They're my favorite. Try one. They're really quite surprising."

The twins reached out and each carefully selected a violet colored, shaped, and scented candy, then placed them on their tongues. The flavor of the confection slowly bloomed on their taste buds, like plucked flowers, the sweetness as much a scent as it was a taste. It was like eating perfume.

"It's wonderful," Molly said.

"What were you going to tell us before?" Faye asked, eager to hear more complements from the interesting man who had provided such an exotic treat. "You were going to say something else, weren't you? About us?"

Henderson took a breath and began again. "Molly, Faye, you are so amazing, so, so—perfect, that I feel I have to *earn* the right to be close to you. I would never attempt to take advantage of you."

Molly and Faye glanced at one another, then back at Matthew Harris Henderson. "Perfect?" they echoed together.

"I would say you were more than perfect, if such a quality were possible. Oh, how I wish my mother was still alive to meet you. That is, if I'd be lucky enough to have you accept an invitation to my family home."

Molly and Faye's eyes met again, wide and deep, disbelieving. "His family home," Molly whispered. "It's him. We found him."

"Poor Dugan," Faye whispered back, reaching for her sister's hand. "What will he do without us?"

Part Two: The Storm

Felicity, West Virginia

Chapter twenty-four
A Changing Air

I t was the Sunday afternoon after Molly and Faye had met Matthew Harris Henderson, and the Starlight Carnival Royale had reached its new lot. The night before had been a late one, as the jump to Felicity, West Virginia was over two hundred miles, and then set-up had been hindered by a lot so wet that the first layer of sawdust simply churned into the muddy ground and disappeared. The sky was spitting unremittingly from low gray clouds that had arrived before dawn. It was half-past one, and Dugan was breakfasting on an apple as he sat on the bally platform outside the Freak Show top, his head and shoulders growing damp as he assessed the soggy gloom advancing on all sides. It seemed that the dismal weather had hunkered down for an indefinite stay—much like his run of rotten luck.

As Mario approached, rubbing sleepy, bloodshot eyes, Dugan pointed to the sky with his apple core and said, "This exterior matches my interior."

Mario clucked his tongue and said, "Self-pity is not allowed, old boy. But heavy drinking is. I see no reason why we shouldn't break out the whiskey right now, do you?"

Dugan thought for a moment then said, "No, I don't," and jumped off the platform onto a squashy cushion of sawdust and mud. "There's nothing left to do. We are as prepared as we can possibly be for the pitiful crowds tomorrow is sure to bring."

"Don't be so pessimistic. The fine people here in Felicity might come to the carnival in droves to get cheered out of their bad-weather blues."

"Perhaps."

Mario shook his head at his old friend. "Let's call in the troops. You look so pitiful that I don't want to drink with you alone."

Almost two weeks had shuffled past since the morning Saffron had snuck out of Dugan's trailer while he slumbered guilelessly in a post-coital stupor, and in that time, she had managed to avoid him so completely that they'd barely had an opportunity to exchange hellos, let alone confront what had happened between them. That three years of unrequited passion should end in this manner made each day a rank swamp he had to wade through wearing lead shoes—yes, indeed he was pitiful. But alcohol would dispel, or at least blur, his misery, and tomorrow he would restore himself to the strong, family man he used to be—a man who made things happen. As for today, the only thing he planned to make happen was to get himself terribly, irredeemably drunk.

Mario sent out the call, and a modest gathering of men convened beside the Pie Wagon at the Freak Show's customary table, on which Dugan arranged three large amber bottles of Canadian whiskey, a line-up of dimpled and dented tin cups, and a water bucket for cigar ash that seemed unnecessary to everyone but Dugan; deep down, he remained a carnival Daddy even while taking time off. The large umbrella mounted in the center of the table cast the men—Dugan, Mario, Sean, and Finch—into an even deeper gloom. Zimm had indicated to Mario that he would join them after he took a private meeting, which everyone knew meant he was with a girl, or, if he was lucky enough, with Alex.

"Wish I had that kind of meeting on *my* schedule," Mario said.

"Aw, quiet down. You will soon enough," Sean said. "Didn't you tell me you had a choice bit of calico in Florida not far from your land?"

"Sure. I got a girl in most states. West Virginia is one of the exceptions."

"Why?" Dugan asked. "What's wrong with West Virginia girls?"

"High standards," Finch said with a grin.

Mario ignored the jab and said, "The goddamn Alleghenies. I have the worst time with girls in states with lots of mountains. I think they want great big men to go with the great big piles of rocks they grew up on."

"Then how come *I'm* not suddenly a cake-eater around here?" Sean asked. "They don't come much bigger than me."

"It's your approach—you don't have one. Can't be a Valentino if you don't even try. You look at the dolls, but you never try to touch."

"Not *never*."

"Not enough."

"What's enough?"

"*This* is enough," Dugan said. "Let's not talk about women. Why must men always talk about women when they drink?"

"I'd rather be talking *to* women than about them," Sean said. "But I don't see any around at the moment."

Dugan shook his head. "It's better this way."

"You're just sore because of the Wolf Girl," Mario said. "Forget about her. There are other furry fish in the sea. Not many, I'll grant you, but a few."

"I'm thirsty. Somebody start pouring," Finch hurried to say.

Dugan scowled at Finch's deflection of Mario's callousness, but inwardly, the simple but touching act of sympathy pleased him. Nevertheless, he could not leave himself open to more acts of that kind. Even if he had become weak and in need of care, he should not appear so to his family. But as he tried to think of something flippant to say—a clever quotation from Oscar Wilde perhaps, or from Shakespeare: something Falstaff said about drinking, or a piercing line or two lifted from Hamlet and Ophelia's exchanges on love—Dugan found his mind empty. As he visualized his books, the pages flipping in his mind remained blank, the names imprinted on the spines the only identifying marks. Just as lugubrious as the day, and with even less to offer, he downed his first two fingers of whiskey in one gulp.

"You know," Sean said, "Mario pointed out the infamous June to me last week, and I have to say, I really don't think she has it."

"So we're talking about women again," Finch said, chuckling as he reached for one of the cigars that Mario was offering up to the group.

"You're blind," Mario said to Sean. "She has it in spades."

Dugan said, "No, no. Sean is exhibiting admirable taste. June is too obvious, too cheap. She's meat for the common man—for men without ideals."

Mario grinned. "Who needs ideals when you've got a cutie like June for a bed-warmer?"

After struggling unsuccessfully for a full minute to light his cigar, Sean said, "This umbrella's a nice idea, but the rain's so misty it moves from side to side, not just up and down." When he finally managed to light the stogie, the cigar smoke, weighted by the damp air, lingered around his mountainous shoulders like a wreath of clouds.

Dugan scanned the actual mountains in the distance—the rain-fattened smudges above them, the gray-streaked blue overhead—and noticed something changing in the atmosphere, a shift in pressure; again the day mirrored his emotions. He now felt a heavy emptiness constrict within him as if his despair was flexing its muscles, as if his subconscious was preparing to contend with some further, deeper misery. How ridiculous that he should feel this poetically tragic, yet be at a loss to recall a single apt line of poetry. He felt everything, but could anchor nothing, at least not with any words of published literature.

Dugan's eyes continued to drift back to the horizon, where amethyst clouds nestled between the peaks of the mountain range. Finch followed his gaze and asked, "You think those clouds mean a storm's coming?"

"Possibly," Dugan said. "At any rate, we should keep watch."

"Doesn't look like much to me," Mario said. "Remember that storm that hit us back when we traveled with Clinker?"

"I certainly do. That was the most severe blow-down I ever witnessed." To Finch and Sean, Dugan explained, "Professor Clinker was our old boss—I believe I told you about his less than tragic death in an alligator infested swamp?" The others nodded and Dugan continued, "Well, the wind of this particular storm lifted Clinker's top into the sky like a canvas hot air balloon, and it toured the whole town before finally crashing about three miles away from our lot. By the time we found it, the tent was torn and shredded beyond repair."

Mario continued the story. "Clinker takes one look at that ruined top and informs Dugan and myself that he plans to garnish our wages for a few months to pay for a replacement—not that there was much to garnish. But it wasn't long before the bastard took that blessed Louisiana fishing trip—and *that* was the heart-stopping end of Clinker."

Sean said, "I saw this one storm a couple of years ago that wasn't too bad by itself, but the heavy rain stirred up the ground, and since the juice-men hadn't buried the cut-in line deep enough, the electricity shot right through the mud and up into two gazonies trying to put up the big top. One fellow came out fine except he couldn't see too well after that, but the other died. Anybody here thought to double-check our juice-men's work?"

"Don't worry," Dugan said. "The Starlight has its act together. No one will get electrocuted today, or any other day."

Sean shrugged, eyeing the ground with suspicion.

"You know what I'd like to do?" Finch asked, his gaze remote as he answered his own question. "I'd like to start taking some family portraits."

Pleased, Dugan said, "We could gather up our show and dry everyone off for a sitting today, if you'd like."

Finch frowned. "No, I mean portraits of *real* families."

The words ice-picked through the center of Dugan's beating heart.

Mario gave his old friend a solemn wink, then filled both of their cups to the brim. "Good medicine," he murmured under his breath.

Finch continued to stare off into nothing as he said, "I'd like to take my time and arrange everyone in a way that really shows off the family resemblance. You know, one generation leading to the next generation—which might display the same features but in different combinations, or those same features changed by a marriage and the influx of new blood. And you know how there's often someone in a family who doesn't seem to take after anyone? Maybe I'd place that child right in the center, like a single red rose in a bunch of daisies. Could be an interesting effect."

Dugan did not like this at all. He was pleased to see how well Finch had coped with Shadrach's departure, but this sudden happiness, this tipsy artistic enthusiasm for family portraiture, felt as ominous as the purpled charcoal clouds collecting at the horizon.

No. *More* ominous. The clouds might portend nothing more than a continuation of the same, dreary drizzle, but Finch obviously had not been referring to carnival photography. Maybe in the circus one might find a large, extended, *real* family to photograph, but not in the tiny, rag-tag, incessantly shifting world of the Starlight Carnival Royale. The heavy emptiness in Dugan raised its hackles, becoming as sharp and prickly as a porcupine: his old familiar fear had risen up from his sadness like quills quivering with anticipation, and he knew that the final blow would drive the spines backwards through his skin, impaling him in a hundred places.

Despite his instincts, Dugan still refused to acknowledge the danger crouching within the clouds at the horizon; he did not want to be a responsible father, gathering his family (his *real* family, no matter what Finch might argue) to strip and roll his banners and tear down his tops; he wanted to drink, scoff and laugh with his friends, and slowly forget that he'd ever let a woman sink her claws into his heart. From infancy, his mother's example had taught him that women weren't the loving, gentle creatures that the world made them out to be, but he had nonetheless allowed himself to think that he could be happy with Saffron. The very same minute he felt his desire expand into love, he should have forced himself to remember his mother and her cold, cruel heart.

Like Saffron, Dugan had become a carny after being purchased by a showman for a Freak Show, but while Saffron's parents had sold her as an infant, Dugan's mother had waited until he was old enough that even now he could vividly recall the pragmatic expression on her face as she tucked Professor Clinker's money into the front pocket of her apron and then disappeared into a cloud of dust stirred by wagon wheels and galloping hooves.

Wait, no. *No.*

Dugan refused the memory. He did *not* remember his mother. He did not remember his childhood at all. In fact, he had never had a childhood; his life began with the carnival, Professor Clinker, and Mario, his designated twin who shared his assigned birthday. Furthermore, Dugan had never even had a mother. He'd been hatched full-grown from an egg, or fashioned out of ashes like a phoenix, or spawned by the mingling of god's blood and sea foam. No mother and no storm; the bruise-hued rain smearing the edges of the silent mountains did not warrant his concern. Not even as the thunderclouds thickened, darkening and slithering stealthily closer.

Chapter twenty-five

Not a Freak

Vibrations both familiar and strange caused the rain around Alex's trailer to incandesce in spite of the gloom, tickling Roxy's skin with light and movement. Everything had begun to look strange, feel strange, after she dropped by Alex's that afternoon. She couldn't help being drawn there—she was always drawn there—nor could she help backing away without knocking when she heard Zimm's voice through the door, then peering through the trailer's side window, becoming mesmerized as her dress grew heavy from the rain, her hair clinging to her head like a limp and drippy cloche.

As Bea, Saffron, Molly and Faye walked from Bea's trailer to the Pie Wagon, sections of the local paper held umbrella-like over their heads, they found Roxy outside of that carelessly uncurtained window, and the chatter falling from their lips ceased abruptly; all four women instantly knew what sight within the trailer had the dancer hypnotized.

"Oh, no, sugar—don't watch," Bea exclaimed, keeping her voice low to avoid attracting attention from inside the trailer. "It hurts a hell of a lot worse when you've got pictures in your head to go with it."

Roxy made no sign that she'd heard, and when Bea took hold of her arm and pulled, the girl's feet felt stuck in cement.

"Bumble-Bea, you take the twins and go on ahead," Saffron said.

Bea read her friend's eyes, then nodded, took Faye's hand and headed off to the Pie Wagon, the twins looking back over their shoulders, too preoccupied with Roxy to object to being led away like children.

Tossing her newspaper umbrella aside, Saffron permitted the rain to fall directly onto her pelt. Water beaded, skated off. She placed a hand on Roxy's unresponsive shoulder.

"You're only making it worse. Come away from the window. I know you share with a bunch of other girls, but I have a private trailer, and I can take you there and leave you alone if you want to cry, or I can stay and talk to you if that's what you want, but first you have to come away from the window."

Roxy's voice was quiet, but firm. "No."

Saffron felt drops of water wheedle through the glossy barrier of her fur to land coldly and startlingly against her skin. Still, the air was warm and the sensation pleasant. "Come away from there. You've seen too much already."

Roxy shook her head.

Most of the performers in Dugan's show—including Saffron herself—had a mule streak about a mile wide, and she could tell that Roxy would stand beside the trailer for hours, allowing the images she saw to cut so deeply into her mind that even if the wounds did heal, they would form thick scar tissue in reaction to the pain she felt now; at only seventeen years old, Roxy would stop risking her heart, pulling back from romantic love just as Saffron had done after Benjamin died. Saffron sighed heavily, then lifted Roxy, slung her over a shoulder like a sack of grain and carried her away. Once they were a good distance from Alex's trailer, she dumped the girl onto the wet grass, then sat down, her arms, back and legs aching from the strain, her heart drum-rolling. Still, it was nice to carry someone else rather than be carried. Although she remained grateful to Finch for rescuing her back in Tupelo, her pride was still smarting to have needed it. Then there'd been the rube with the bat in Sulphur…except for meeting Bea, it had been a dreadful season for Saffron.

"You're strong," Roxy said with a dull voice.

Saffron nodded, catching her breath.

"Why did you do that?"

"I don't approve of romantic self-torture. Especially not over someone like Alex."

Coming out of her daze a little more, Roxy said defensively, "Alex is perfect."

Saffron shook her head. "No, he's not. She's unique and smart, and full of life, and everyone who knows him comes to love him in one way or another, but she's not perfect. She takes on a lot of people's burdens and gives a lot to people. And that's nice in some ways, but it also means that there will never be one Alex that can be devoted to just one person. It isn't healthy to get attached to someone like that."

With the rain falling harder now, streaming in silvered rivulets down both of their faces, Saffron couldn't tell if Roxy was crying as she stared off in the direction of Alex's trailer. Saffron hadn't altered her opinion of tears, but she thought they might be the best thing in this particular case. To cry over something that's unfair, cruel and commonplace, to cry because you should've known better, to cry to get a foolish pain out of your system, these might be good reasons to cry—good enough for a cooch dancer like Roxy, anyway.

"Let's go," Saffron said. "Get you away from here."

"No," Roxy said.

"At least come with me to the Pie Wagon."

"No."

Saffron sighed. "You really are stubborn."

Roxy shrugged, nodded, then grimaced slightly as she attempted a wry smile. Saffron took this widening range of expression as a sign of improvement.

"It's strange," Roxy said after a while. "Zimm isn't a Freak, either."

Saffron heard, but didn't understand. She asked Roxy to repeat herself.

"I said Zimm isn't a Freak, either. I thought that if something got in the way of Alex and I being together and happy it'd probably be that I'm not really a Freak. I'm not really one of you. I thought that would be the thing to get in the way of him loving me."

"Roxy, Zimm didn't get in the way—Alex doesn't love Zimm."

"*Either*, you mean. Alex doesn't love Zimm, either. I know that. Just like I knew already that I wasn't the only person that Alex made love to—I'm not stupid, not completely stupid, anyway—but I tried not to think about it."

"I'm sure that Alex *does* love you. Actually, she loves Zimm, too, but not in the way you love her. Alex loves everyone in his own way."

"Loving everyone is a lot like loving no one," Roxy said.

Saffron had no response. Her shirt and pants, soaked through, weighed heavily against her body, flattening her fur. In spite of the coldness of the rainwater, the wet clothing and squashed fur functioned as insulation, holding in her body heat. Sweating now, she began to add her own moisture to the terrible, waterlogged day. Water everywhere—inside and out, inescapable.

"I'm sorry," Saffron said.

"Don't be. You didn't do anything wrong." Suddenly Roxy turned and stared hard into Saffron's eyes. "Do you remember that time when you were trying to get me to explain why I thought Freaks are better than other people? We were having a boil up at that awful lake in Dry Fork—"

"I remember."

"Well, I told you then how I felt different all my life, because I'm a little dizzy and I talk to myself—but not just that, I talk to flowers and chairs sometimes, and I start singing while other people are trying to talk to me. I really can't help it, my mind just drifts off, and I do things without deciding to do them. So anyway, when

I was thirteen, because my mother's lover was sick of how weird I was, my mother gave me twenty dollars and her favorite dress if I'd promise to leave and not come back. So then I was different and alone. But when I joined the carnival—because of Laloo, like I said before—and I met my first Freak and saw my first Freak Show, I knew I was where I belonged. Freaks were as alone and unhappy in the world as I was, but inside the carnival they had their own world where they could be together and happy, and I wanted to be a part of that. I'm not trying to say that I'm the same as you, I'm just trying to explain. I really do love Alex, but I think that part of why I do is that by being with him I thought I'd get to be a part of something big and important and special. Magical, you know? I wanted to be magical, Saffron, not just alone and different."

Saffron opened her mouth to speak, but Roxy interrupted, saying, "Don't try and make me feel better. I won't feel better for a really long time. I know that I wasn't born special, that I'm just weird and dizzy, and my mother didn't love me enough to risk losing her man to keep me. There's no fucking magic in that."

Taking hold of her fur at the roots and tugging it hard as she spoke, Saffron's voice rose. "And you think there's magic in this? This—this is some accident, some one-in-a-million combination of egg and sperm. That's all. Don't feel sorry for yourself because you're different inside and beautiful outside, Roxy. Fact is, that's one of the easiest ways to be in this world. Other than getting stuck with a weak and selfish mother, you're pretty goddamn lucky."

At the word *beautiful*, then the words *easiest* and *lucky*, Roxy flinched as if Saffron had slapped her.

"It's true," Saffron continued, "whether you want to hear it or not. And I love Alex, too. Not in the same way that you do, but I understand how easy it is to love her. But he's not faithful, and he could never belong to anyone. She belongs to herself and always will. That's it. You're a carny, Roxy. You have to toughen up and learn to read people better."

Roxy frowned, watching water pool in the crease of a fat blade of grass, then spill off. "I am tough around some people," she said.

Saffron sighed. "But you understand what I'm telling you?"

Roxy nodded, then shook her head. Plucking the blade of grass and shredding it with her fingernails, she said, "I think maybe I do, but you said so much—I can't keep it all in my head. And I love Alex so awful."

She looked up from her grass-stained hands with such a pitiful expression that Saffron's anger deflated and fell away, the emotion becoming as soggy and pointless as the sawdust embedded in the mud of the lot.

Converging clouds darkened the landscape and a shattering boom of thunder shook the ground as the shower became a torrent. Although part of Saffron feared for the carnival and the damage that such a sudden storm might do, she focused her attention on Roxy, pulling the sad girl to her chest and saying, "I'll tell you again when we're both calmer."

Although she was initially rigid in Saffron's arms, it only took a moment for Roxy to soften, relaxing into the embrace, and only a moment more for her to wrap her arms around Saffron and hug back, both women drenched by the almost painful force of the rain. Squeezing tightly, Roxy said, "You know, you'd make a real good mother."

Saffron froze, her pulse tripling in her throat, her veins pulsing in time with the heartbeat of a quietly tenacious dream that still lived after five long years. She felt the world swell and yawn: a huge gaping space with Benjamin nowhere in it, but she remained there, remained alive, and life, more patient and enduring than any grief, still waited for her to re-open herself to the world.

Her eyes filled; tears mingled with the rainwater on her cheeks. "Ah, hell," she said.

Chapter twenty-six

Tearing Down

4:15 P.M.

Looking back, Finch should have realized that he was drunk when his reaction to the first booming clap of thunder was a vague annoyance at having his discussion with Dugan on the social responsibility of art interrupted. And Dugan was just as intoxicated; initially he too felt merely irritated by the din. But then the sky opened up and released a cold flood of rain and an abrupt gust of wind pushed the cigars down the length of the table and onto the muddy ground before the men could catch them. Finch peered through the onslaught of rain into a sky swarming with swiftly moving black billows sewn with lightning like silver thread.

His eyes met Dugan's. Their expressions of sobering alarm were almost identical. "What a pair of idiots we are," Finch said.

Dugan nodded his agreement, and with his wet curls whirlpooling in the rising wind, shouted for Bea to take the twins to their trailer and keep them there.

Finch started running for the Freak Show top, and each step

sank his feet into mud that sucked at his shoes as if attempting to pull him under. Keeping his eyes on the ground, he began to aim his steps at the rocks and sticks and bits of refuse now spread across the lot by rapidly proliferating tributaries of flash flooding; he made stepping-stones of clumps of leaves and pine needles, of chip packets, popcorn boxes, and one of the many spangled fortune-teller costumes belonging to the woman who worked the mitt camp. He began to make better time, passing the Ferris Wheel, where three men were lashing the towering hub in place with extra cables, and the menagerie, where animal trainers pressed against cages tried to calm the braying, squealing, trumpeting, hooting and growling creatures within.

"Tear down for a blow!"

The repeated shout punctuated Finch's frantic journey again and again, taunting him with the knowledge that he and Dugan should have begun sloughing the show and packing it up hours ago. The storm had hit suddenly, true, and most of the carnies had missed the warning signs because many had still been sleeping after the all-night set-up, but he and Dugan had no such excuse.

The first thing Finch did after reaching the Freak Show top was tip the ticket booth onto its side to make it less likely to catch the escalating wind. As he was untying the bannerline, the wind threatened to rip it from his hands, but Alex showed up and caught the other side, and together they rolled the wet, paraffin-coated banners into a man-sized, sloppy, lumpy tube that they tucked inside the ticket booth.

Dugan and Saffron and Sean showed up next, followed by Mario, and everyone went into the top to drag the props off the platforms and shove them underneath, while the rain battered the surrounding canvas like an army of incessant drums. While Dugan, Mario and Alex unstrung the curtains, Finch, Sean and Saffron stood on ladders that were sinking lopsidedly into the soft ground, dismantling the strings of lights hung overhead. Once they were down, they wound the wires and bulbs into coiled masses small enough to fit beneath the stages with the curtains and the props. This was not the ideal way to keep the show's equipment safe from the rising wind and water, but there wasn't enough time to run for the trucks and drive them over and load them up; everything would have to remain where it was.

"Now we drop the canvas," Dugan shouted above the grumble of rain and wind and thunder. "Everyone outside."

"I should take care of my own top," Alex said.

Dugan nodded. "Of course, but we can't spare many hands to help you."

"I know. I understand," Alex said, then laughed and added, "Hell, you bought it with your dime, anyway."

The sound of Alex's laughter soothed Finch. They all needed to laugh a little, to not take the storm so seriously. He took a deep, fortifying breath and told himself that they would get everything done that needed to get done, that he and Dugan and everyone else would withstand the tempest just fine.

Dugan told Alex to take Sean along. Sean nodded and said, "I'm not quite strong enough to help out with the bigger top, but I can certainly help you out with yours."

Finch felt, as always, a grave admiration for Sean's easy admission of weakness. He did not believe that he would be able to face his own debilitation so frankly—but then, his body had never yet failed to perform whatever task he required of it.

Sean and Alex went around the back side of the tent towards the Annex, while Finch and everyone else fanned out around the Freak Show top; it was sixty by twenty, not a huge tent, but not so small as the blow-off tent, which could be dropped by only two people. As the storm whirled, the carnies worked with speed as their primary concern. Any damage they did while tearing down the top would be far less than a storm could do; it would take only a few hundred dollars to repair any holes or ripped seams, but over two thousand dollars to replace the entire top—a hell of a lot of nickels and dimes. They tossed weighted blow lines over the dropped canvas and shortened and staked the ropes, anchoring the tent as securely as possible to the soft ground. The water that was coursing down from the foothills of the Alleghenies expanded the slender rivulets into swollen creeks that made the carnies slip and fall. Despite Finch's days riding the rails, which had honed his balance and control, the water knocked him to the ground more than once; his knees, wrists, and hips ached from the repeated abuse.

Suddenly the few electric lights mounted on poles across the midway flickered and went out; Finch heard someone shout that they'd cut the electric because a man had been shocked by a shallow cut-in line.

"I'll be god-damned," Mario shouted. "Sean was right to be worried about that!"

One of the Girl Show dancers, maybe June (it was June, but Finch wasn't sure because he never could tell one half-naked white girl from another), ran up and said something to Saffron, who nodded, continuing to drive in a stake as she yelled, "It's Zimm. Zimm's the one who got shocked, and his girls are starting to panic without him telling them what to do. They don't ever drop the tent themselves, but there aren't enough gazonies to go around in this mess. There's no one to help them."

"He alright?" Finch asked.

"She said he's conscious, but he's not talking. He's just sitting stunned on the ground."

"Goddamn it to hell," Dugan shouted. "The line could've zapped a useless cooch dancer, but instead it prostrates one of the Starlight's best. Fine! Let's hurry and finish this so we can go offer our assistance."

Thunder growled through Finch's rib cage, but he continued to work in silence while the reverberations cycled through his ribs then shot out through his shoulders and hips and down to his fingertips and toes, his entire body thrumming with the power of the storm. The pummeling rain was cold but the air was warm as the wind whipped his body, gaining substance and shoving vigorously, trying to force him to his knees, but he planted his feet deep into the mud and refused to budge as he double-staked the ropes. With the sky crowded by thunderheads and the electricity cut, the lot was as dark as night. All around, the flood creeks engorged into rivers strong enough to carry larger objects like logs and folding chairs on their bloated current. His thoughts iced over with shock as a heavy steamer trunk washed up and beached itself on the dropped canvas like a great, wooden whale.

Finch could see that he'd been right. Everyone with Dugan's show would get done what they needed to get done, but that was still no guarantee that they and theirs would be safe from the storm, which continued to bluster and scream, pounding its fists against the mountains and disgorging floodwater over the land. In the sky above, Finch saw no sign of retreat, no emergence of light, and not a single spot of blue.

Chapter twenty-seven

Can Trailers Fly?

Ordered by Dugan to hide from the storm that now quaked the trailer walls around them, Bea and the twins rattled along with the collection of kitten figurines that Molly and Faye kept arranged on a shelf. As thunder rumbled through the three womens' bodies, the edges of their skin felt fizzy; flares of lightning seared their eyes, dulling, by contrast, the illumination from the single naked light bulb convulsing on a cord overhead.

"He knows we're not babies anymore," Faye said, "so why does he do this to us?"

Bea snorted, "What? Send you off while everybody else has to do hard labor in the middle of this nasty old thunderstorm? He did it to me, too, and I don't mind."

"But Dugan made you do it because he wants us to have a chaperone," Molly said.

Bea shrugged. "Maybe a little, but I reckon it's mainly 'cause he knows I'm too damn fat to work that hard. Besides, the only one

245

who has a right to be upset in here is me. I'm the one stuck baby-sitting two little girls who like nothing better than to whine and complain."

"We're not little girls," Molly said at the same time Faye said, "See! You do think that he treats us like babies."

Bea sighed. "Just relax, sugars. You're safe in here, and that's what's important. And isn't it better to be in here than out there?"

Before Molly or Faye could respond, the trailer shook from an explosion of thunder just as a white flash of lightning seemed to strike the roof above their heads. When Bea looked out the window at the rain-mottled, blackberry dark, fear twitched beneath her calm façade; she worried about Saffron, who she hadn't seen since they had found Roxy staring so mournfully outside Alex's window.

Faye asked, "Bumble-Bea, do you think that this trailer could get blown over? Or picked up by the wind and carried off to crash into something somewhere?"

Although Faye's question bolstered Bea's fright with an extra jolt of adrenaline, she affected indifference, lowering herself to the trailer's floor with a grunt and saying, "This friggin' trailer ain't going nowhere, you dope. Not with me weighing it down." Any comfort that the words may have given were undercut by the tremors of the flimsy box containing them and the continuous violence of the weather.

Molly and Faye sat on the floor beside Bea, all three smiling thinly and sitting quietly, trying to conceal their fear. After a few strained minutes, they heard a pounding at the door, barely perceptible over the gusts and growls of the storm: the twins went to answer it.

As the door swung open, Faye said, "Holy hell, he actually came," while Molly shouted, "I'm so happy it's you!"

A rain-drenched, bedraggled but snappily dressed man entered the trailer, and the twins shut the door behind him.

"Are you alright?" he asked, placing his left hand on Molly's cheek and his right hand on Faye's.

"I can't believe you followed us here!" Molly said.

"I said I would, didn't I? I know you didn't want me to come by so early, but I got so frightened about what might happen to you two during a storm like this that I had to come and see if you were safe."

When Bea stood up and cleared her throat, the man whirled around, his hand flying to his chest in a graceful, fluid show of shock. "Oh," he said. "I didn't realize that my girls had company."

"*Your* girls?" Bea asked, deciding that the man was older than she had first guessed. He had a boy's narrow-hipped build, but now that they were face to face, she could see shallow lines striping his forehead and spidery creases fanning the sides of his eyes. "How old are you?" she demanded.

"Don't be rude, Bumble-Bea," Molly said.

Faye looked from her sister's admonishing frown to Bea's angry surprise, then threw her head back and laughed.

"This is not funny, and I'm not being rude," Bea said. "Who is this man and why the hell is he calling you his girls? I've never seen him before."

Molly said, "We just met him last week."

The man took Molly's hand and smiled. "But it felt like we'd known each other forever. That's how it is with soulmates."

Faye rolled her eyes, but her cheeks flushed and her mouth inched into a small smile. The fearful tightness that had inhibited the twins' expressions had evaporated; the storm still raged outside, but Molly and Faye seemed to no longer hear it, to no longer feel it.

"Tell me your name," Bea commanded, wishing for a shotgun or a baseball bat. Her own fear of the storm distilled into a bitter mistrust of the rain-soaked stranger.

Smiling, he stepped forward and held out his hand. With the worry lines smoothed from his face, he seemed a bit younger. "Matthew Harris Henderson, at your service."

Bea did not accept the handshake. "At my service," she said. "More like at *their* service. Or your own service. What do you want with Molly and Faye?"

"I love them."

Bea snorted. "Not after one week's acquaintance."

"Oh, yes," he said. "Sometimes it only takes a moment to know. I fell for Molly and Faye on sight."

Bea narrowed her eyes. This was the same kind of prattle that Jimmy had cooked up when his show rolled through her hometown all those years ago, and of course she'd gobbled it down just like Molly did now. She could see that Faye was more skeptical, but her blush and smile revealed that even though she knew it was prattle, she still lapped it up like cream.

"And you plan to start following them from town to town?" Bea asked. "Make yourself the Starlight's caboose?"

"I hope to convince Molly and Faye to leave the Starlight, actually, and to marry me. I proposed the first night we met."

"You did what?" Bea's heart lurched in her chest. She looked at the twins. "What did y'all tell him?"

"We said we'd think about giving him an answer if he followed us to the next lot," Faye coolly replied, but as an especially brutal clap of thunder shook the trailer she yelped and grabbed her sister's hand.

"And he did follow us," Molly said, moving with Faye to sit on the double bed they shared, "which I think means so much." She patted the cot, indicating to their new beau to come join them.

"Stay right where you are, Mr. Matthew Harris Henderson," Bea said, still wishing for that shotgun. "What do you really want with these girls? You a showman? You wanna frame an act and get rich?"

"Frame what? Listen, Miss—"

"*Mrs.*," Bea said. "Mrs. Smythe."

"Mrs. Smythe, I'm a wealthy man. My family owns several textile-manufacturing plants,"—he switched to a confident, proprietor's tone of voice—"we primarily produce heavy weaves used to upholster furniture"—then switched back upon observing Bea's immobility of expression. "We do very well for ourselves. I don't need Molly and Faye to make me money; I want to spend my money on them."

"Do you realize, Mr. Henderson, that these girls are only sixteen?"

"You think we're too young!" Molly cried, a flash of lightning momentarily washing out her pink face in a glare of white.

"Everybody thinks we're too young for everything," Faye said.

"You forget," Bea said, "that I met and married Jimmy when I was only fourteen. Not that I would recommend that to anybody. But hell, girls—this Joe ain't no spring chicken."

She turned to Henderson and asked, "How old are you, anyway?"

"Twenty-five."

"Hmph. You look a lot older."

Far from offended, Henderson smiled and said, "My mother used to tell me that I'd worry myself to death. It's in my nature. But these two—I think that they could cure my worries forever if they'd only answer yes."

"What a load of bullshit," Bea said, but she was studying the man's warm cow eyes as he spoke, seeing the way that he gestured to the girls with one yearning hand, paying no attention to the storm vibrating through the floor and walls, or to the water that still dripped from his fingers, from his nose and ears, down his neck and body, then puddled around his sodden, mud-streaked wingtips. A ridiculous pose of enraptured adoration.

"By the twenty-four swinging balls of the apostles," Bea murmured. "I think he's actually sincere."

Molly and Faye burst into giggles while Henderson looked steadily at Bea and said, "I am sincere. I mean every word I say. I've remained a bachelor so far because no woman has ever managed to truly touch me. But these lovely angels struck straight for my heart the very first second I laid eyes on them."

"Jesus, man. You could sell bushels of that tripe come Valentine's Day."

Molly wore a look of dreamy vagueness, but Faye cackled.

Bea sighed and lowered her voice, speaking with just enough volume to be heard over the storm. "But don't y'all each want your own husband? I know you share most things, but a man? A marriage? Y'all want to share that, too?"

Faye looked at Bea as if she were slow in the head. "We'd have to share anyway, Bumble-Bea. Even with two husbands, there can't be one that's just Molly's or just mine. We'd never be alone with them."

Startled by the simple revelation, Bea glanced down at the twins' hips. How easy it was to become accustomed to someone different from you—so easy that you sometimes forgot that they were different at all; or, if you were also considered different by the world, it was easy to start believing that your difference and theirs were the same. You could easily forget that while their life was something you could imagine through empathy, it would never be something you truly knew.

Bea sighed again. Then, as if Henderson weren't still standing right in front of her, she asked, "But are you sure he's a nice man?"

"He's wonderful," Molly said.

"He's okay so far," Faye said. "He'll be decent to us, at least. And he likes us exactly how we are."

"I *love* you exactly how you are," Henderson said, kneeling at their feet and sandwiching their hands between two soft, wet, pink paws that had clearly never done a day's work.

When Faye giggled and dropped her eyes demurely, Bea knew that it was far too late. Besides, this was Molly and Faye's life to live. So they might get married too young. Had Jimmy been that terrible? Sure, he followed through on infidelities that Bea hadn't, but she'd come close, and with his own brother, no less—thank the sweet Lord, Jimmy never found that out. And she had been happy with him once. Very happy.

She wondered how Jimmy was doing, what he was doing right then. Every week for about two months now, he had written Bea a letter—some weeks two or three—in shaky and splotched ink, the penmanship of passion, apologizing repeatedly for his wrongdoing, promising that he would never again be unfaithful, and describing at length how terribly he missed his wonderful, beautiful wife. Bea hadn't been suckered in yet, but she hadn't entirely ruled out going back to him; she was a practical woman and knew that Jimmy would give her a hefty percentage of the take—Saffron, too, if she asked for her—and when combined with her newfound strength and independence, a lot of money very fast could open up the world to her in ways that she could hardly imagine.

When another flash of lightning dazzled at the same moment the thunder boomed, Molly and Faye flung themselves at Matthew Harris Henderson, who happily cinched their trembling bodies in his long, skinny arms. The wind rose, moaning, snatching at the floor and walls while the rain pounded against the roof as if the trailer had been relocated beneath a waterfall, that merciless downward force the only thing keeping Bea from becoming convinced that the wind actually *could* scoop up the trailer, lift it high into the air like a boxy bird in flight, then carelessly fling it against the jagged, unforgiving rocks of the Allegheny Mountains.

Oh, sweet Jesus. All at once Bea wanted Jimmy right there beside her. He hadn't been faithful, but in uncertain times, he had always made her feel safe. As the trailer's naked ceiling bulb swung and shivered on its string, then guttered and went dark, she flooded with the desperate, futile longing to rush out into the fray and run without pause until she found her husband, his arms open, eager to recapture her.

Chapter twenty-eight
Indigo Bird

lex:

After Dugan dismissed us from the group dropping the Freak Show top, Sean and I pushed through the downpour against a wind that felt almost as solid as a wall, fighting our way over to the Annex to tear down my little blow-off top. I ducked inside the flapping canvas and dismantled the single spotlight, squirreled it under the platform, then ran back outside just as the electricity cut out across the lot.

"What the hell was that?" I asked.

"I'm not sure," Sean said. "I heard some shouting."

Common sense prevailed over curiosity, and I said, "Well whatever it is, I'm sure we can't fix it, and we'd better get started on my top. It shouldn't take long, but we'll have to be careful not to let the wind snatch the thing up before we get it all the way dropped."

"Alex?" a plaintive voice called out, hardly audible over the rain and wind and thunder.

I turned and peered through the slick, membranous dark and spotted Roxy, but before I could ask what she wanted, Sean turned as well, and slipped on the shifting earth, hitting the ground with a slick splatter of mud and floodwater.

I rushed to his side. "Are you alright?"

He nodded, but his grimace told me otherwise.

"Listen," I said, "Roxy can help me tear down."

Roxy appeared a little frightened by this claim, but she nodded anyway.

"And I think you should go back to your trailer. If you break a bone I won't be strong enough to carry you to safety."

"I need to do my part," Sean said as he struggled to his feet.

"You will. Go check on Bea and the twins. No one has gone to see how they are since the storm started."

Sean kept silent a moment. Then he said, "Fine. I'd only distract you with worry if I stayed."

Although I felt the sting he felt along with him, there was nothing I could do to change what was. "Be careful," I called out as he walked away. Without turning, he waved to show that he'd heard.

Roxy stepped forward and said, "We need to talk, Alex."

"That may be, but I need to get this canvas dropped as of an hour ago, and you're the only person available to help."

"This is more important," Roxy said, attempting to sound stern, but seeming more like a pouting child.

Frustrated, I spat stormwater from my mouth and said, "Do you know how much this top cost, Roxy? A thousand plus. More than you make in a year."

"I don't care how much it cost, Alex. This is more important."

I ran my hands over the rain coursing through my drenched thatch of hair, and glared. "All right, you win. Say what you've got to say, only say it fast, and help me get this thing down."

As Roxy lifted her chin, I couldn't help noticing that even with her hair plastered flat against her skull and melted mascara ringing her eyes like double shiners, she was terribly pretty.

"I need to tell you that I made a decision," she said.

"Yes?"

"I've decided to give you up."

"Give me up?"

"Yes."

"*You've* decided to give *me* up?"

"I just can't be with you anymore, Alex. Don't make this any harder than it already is."

"Dear Lord," I muttered, trying not to laugh at the girl outright. Standing in the middle of the worst, most thunderous and dangerous blow-down the Starlight has ever encountered, Miss Roxy interrupts the scramble and panic to announce that our affair is over. How completely ludicrous. Fluttering and twitching, my indigo blow-off top seemed overcome with silent laughter.

"You're no good for me," Roxy continued. "I saw you with Zimm today, and—well, deep down I already knew about him, and the others, too, but it took until today for me to decide that it hurts too much for me to love you as much as I do when I know that you'll never really be mine."

Such a look of tragedy.

On the one hand, it was funny, but on the other—I felt a creeping guilt. She was so young, and I would turn thirty-two on my next birthday. Forget her life experience; what the hell was I thinking making love to a seventeen-year-old child?

I needed to resolve this fast and get back to work. I allowed myself a moment's thought, choosing my words carefully.

"Please don't be upset, Roxy," I said. "I'll never really belong to anyone. I only belong to me."

"That's exactly what Saffron told me."

That she had discussed this with Saffron, of all people, and that Saffron might choose the same words that I would, burrowed like red-bugs under my skin, an all-over itch I had to fight not to scratch.

Roxy continued, saying, "And I need a man who will be mine just like I'll be his."

"Ah," I said, the itch fading as I finally allowed myself to laugh, "you need a *man*! I've been wrong from the start, then."

Her face stared at me gravely through the pouring rain, then broke. Sobs palsied her shoulders, and my mounting guilt was trounced by anger. I didn't have this time to waste. No lovers under twenty-one from here on out. No—no lovers under twenty-*five*.

I sighed and said, "I'm sorry if I hurt you, darling, but I really need your help right now. We can talk more after the storm clears."

She buried her face in her hands, continuing to sob, of no use now to me or my blow-off top. Why did all her boot-leather toughness have to dissolve around Freaks? If she would just find herself a nice average boy, she could mold him like clay—he wouldn't dare *piss* without her permission. But no, she had to go and fall for someone like me.

Out of the corner of my eye I saw one of the tent stakes pull itself out of the yielding earth, and then that corner of canvas began to tug and dance, as if trying to exhume the rest of the stakes. If I didn't do something soon, I would lose the top.

But then, how bad would that really be? Over the past few weeks, ever since Mario offered me the Florida job, my imagination had been filled with speculations as vivid as a perfectly recalled memory: emerging from the ocean after an evening swim to join my friends as they sat in chairs half sunk into the sand, I could smell the brine in my hair and feel the tightening of my skin as the water evaporated in synch with the sunlight; I could see the booming sea spread out before me—implacable, eternal—and taste the fizzy, yeasty tang of cold beer filling my mouth and easing down my throat. How lovely that new dream had become in such a short time, how filled with the promise of relief. In Florida, blissfully empty of gaping faces and greedy eyes, I could learn to live in a house without wheels, discover where keeping still might take me.

Roxy had stopped crying and now watched me as if she knew I had already drifted far away from the carnival to a place she'd never reach; then the brutal wind unsteadied her feet and she stumbled sideways a few steps, but didn't fall. I shook my head sadly at the girl, then turned and labored through walloping gusts toward my top, but before I could reach it, the indigo canvas shimmied and shuddered, and the entire structure came unmoored, heaving itself into the sky, wavering and altering with liquid grace as it flew off into the storm.

"Son of a bitch!" Roxy shouted as the top ascended through the sky.

My eyes attempted to track its fledgling flight, but the rain distorted my sight and the deep, mysterious blue of the canvas disappeared against the heavy black storm clouds.

I had only one regret—for Dugan.

A chorus of shouts pulled my attention from my indigo gosling and Roxy and I followed the sound of the commotion down the midway to the Girl Show top, where Dugan and Finch and Saffron were helping some of the cooch dancers with the half-down, half-up canvas. Zimm kept trying to help and Dugan kept pushing him away, ordering him to sit and rest.

"Oh yeah, I forgot to tell you," Roxy said. "Zimm got shocked by a cut-in line. That's why they turned off the electricity."

I looked into her impassive eyes. Ah, yes. There was that boot-leather toughness. Right there.

I hurried to ask Dugan what I could do to help.

"Take over for one of those useless quiffs," he told me. "They've been no help at all."

I took one of the blow-down lines out of a frantic Girl Show dancer's hand just as the other side of Zimm's top started to fall, but the wind caught the canvas before it touched down, causing it to buck into a sail that began to drag us through the mud. I looked down and realized that I was ankle-deep in cold, muddy rainwater, while Finch, just ahead of me, was up to his knees. Hearing shouts behind me, I looked over my shoulder and saw Zimm sitting in water rising up to his chest as he shouted curses at the horizontally parachuting canvas I could barely hold onto.

"Goddamn piece of shit fucking storm cost me thirty-five

hundred and no goddamn insurance," he screamed, his face as scrunched, mottled, and red as a rotten tomato, and for a moment I panicked, remembering that Dugan didn't have insurance either, then another jerk of the tent combined with the wind and the rushing water underfoot to knock me facedown. Bitter mud oozed between my lips. I sat up, hurriedly swiping at my eyes and mouth with my face tipped back so the rain could rinse away the slime. When my eyes cleared I saw Finch and Dugan attempting to tackle the slowly skating top. It seemed fruitless—the tent was far too large, the ground far too slippery, and their weight not enough ballast to counter the phenomenally powerful exhalations of the storm—but then a couple of dancers from the Girl Show began to dive on, flinging their slender bodies onto the canvas, attempting to anchor Zimm's top to the earth.

"Worth a try," I muttered, then ran to join the fight, leaping onto the top just as a swift brown tide, surging as if from a broken dam, lifted the tent and sent it speeding through the remains of the Starlight Carnival Royale on a cataclysm of foamy floodwater. I closed my eyes and clung to the canvas as we sailed into the deafening, banshee dark.

Chapter twenty-nine

Wreckage

July 25th, just past sunrise

On that cool morning after the storm, as Dugan quietly left Molly and Faye's trailer where he, the twins, Bea, Saffron, Finch, Alex, Mario and Sean had all slept tangled together like a litter of kittens, he wished he had a jacket or coat, or at least clothes that weren't clammy and damp like the ones from yesterday that he still wore. Last night, Molly and Faye had come up with the admirable idea of hitching their trailer to one of the trucks and dragging it to higher ground, but by the time Dugan tried to do the same for himself and his other Wonders, the ground was far too soft for the trucks' tires to gain traction, and they had to make do with wedging rocks and boards under the wheels of the remaining trailers to prevent them from sinking axle-deep by sunrise.

Finch exited Molly and Faye's trailer just behind Dugan, also moving quietly to allow the others a few more hours of sleep. After a whispered exchange with Dugan, he went to join the men who were fanning out to search beyond the borders of the lot in hopes of recovering objects carried off on the flood before townie scavengers could swipe them. Dugan longed to go down into the valley on the other side of the hill and assess the damage to his own trailer, and in particular, to his books, but he felt that doing so first would be terribly selfish, so he kept that part of the valley out of sight and climbed down the opposite side of the hill, heading for the lot alongside a host of other long-faced early risers.

The dawn shone gold and tangerine, crisply outlining the ragged ruin of the carnival and painfully pricking Dugan's squinting, bloodshot eyes. Every step he took hurt. During the storm, his bones had flowed with lava and ice, but he had pushed past the pain and continued to work. This morning his aching joints felt ossified, his arms and legs moving straight and stiff like a robot, while his spine seemed fused into a single long tusk of pain; again he pushed past it and kept on.

The Ferris Wheel had been tipped off its base. As he passed by, twenty-odd men were struggling to hoist it back upright. He stepped carefully around the refuse and relics scattered over the mud—torn canvas and ruined props, candy boxes piled with acorns and leaves, logs, sticks, stray ropes and shoes, soda bottles, a smashed concession stand, ring-toss rings, stuffed animals, light bulbs, and even a pair of dentures, which he pocketed for safekeeping.

He found the Freak top where they'd staked it down the night before, now half-buried in silt and sludge and bright green leaves that had been torn from the treetops. Still, he preferred buried to the alternatives. The battered canvas would need cleaning and a fresh coat of paraffin, as well as new ropes and replacement stakes, but none of that was unmanageable. No sign of Alex's blow-off top, however, or the ticket booth in which Finch had stashed the banners that had cost over three hundred dollars to have made. With how poorly the Starlight had been doing lately, it would take a couple of months to earn three hundred—unless he stopped giving his family their cut. Last season, he would've been certain that if his savings weren't enough to cover the cost of replacement banners and a new ticket booth, his Wonders would give up their pay to cover the rest, unanimously willing to invest in a show that they loved and that was sure to repay the investment. Now he had his doubts. Shadrach was already gone, Finch seemed poised to leave, Mario and Sean had never quite settled in, and last night, as Dugan drifted into sleep, he had heard Saffron and Bea whispering something about touring in Mexico. Later he dreamed that he was weeping on his knees in Saffron's bare and empty trailer, and when he awoke, he found his face crusted with dry trails of salt. Even without damage from the storm, his family life was inconstant at best.

A shout of laughter drew his attention to a man—Armenante, Saffron's old gambling buddy—and his son, smiling and joking as they gathered armfuls of scattered wooden ducks and piled them with frail air rifles in front of the listing ruin of the duck shoot concession.

"What a grand mess this is," Armenante called out cheerily to Dugan. "How do things look for you?"

Dugan could not allow himself to appear less positive than this hardworking, optimistic man, so he replied, "Fairly bad, but I'm already concocting my comeback plan."

"That's the spirit!" Grinning, Armenante returned to work.

Perhaps there really was a great comeback in his future. Dugan willed himself to feel optimism, his heart forcing hope through his veins as he began to construct around himself a castle bricked with illusions and lies. So, a few of his *phenomènes* might desert him in his time of need—he could comfort himself with the knowledge that Alex and the twins would stay by his side, and those three possessed enough wonder to drive a sideshow by themselves. And although losing the object of his desire would hurt, it would do no lasting damage. Saffron demonstrated many admirable qualities, but she only appeared to be his ideal woman because of her exceptionally prodigious pelt; underneath all that fur, she was just another dame.

But he knew that was the biggest lie of all. Loving Saffron had made Dugan hunger to experience more than the carnal pleasures of his past affairs; for her sake, he would be willing to exchange dominance for symbiosis. Two weeks ago, as he had drifted off to sleep, naked and dewy by her side, he had been prepared to offer her everything he had to give. But she would never accept, would never know the offer's significance, and so he lied to himself now, insisting that she was nothing much to lose, reminding himself that he knew how to work a show, telling himself that he could enlist new Wonders equally as stunning and that his heartbreak would heal just in time for the next dame to twitch her hips in his direction. No matter how tragic things seemed, he remained a survivor down to the marrow; even if his body grew weaker, there were ways to continue onward. Professor Clinker had been an exceptionally lazy man, expert at delegating work to others. Dugan's pain seemed manageable when he rested his body, so if he could get past his pride and remove himself from physical labor, he might be able to continue on indefinitely as the scholar and mastermind behind the show. There was no such thing as an unsolvable problem for a man of true passion and genius—this had to be the truth, had to be. The alternative was unthinkable.

Resigning himself to the idea that he was not going to find the ticket booth or Alex's top, Dugan wound around the side of the midway, making his way towards the living quarters at the rear of the lot, bracing himself for what he might see. The boards and rocks had been a nice idea, but he expected that many trailers would nevertheless need to be disinterred with shovels, and it was also likely that a few roofs may have sprung a leak, so that many possessions would need to be hung out on a line or spread out on a tarp to dry in the late summer sunshine. Fortunately the sky above sparkled a sunny, crystalline blue without a single cloud, and that reassuring sight made Dugan smile.

Until he saw what was left.

At first, he did not trust his eyes. The ouroborus of sleeping trailers was no longer a recognizable ring. Of the trailers that had not been moved to higher ground, only a handful remained standing—three stacked side by side and braced by an ancient oak tree and two more nearby, cocked at crooked angles, buried two feet deep in sludge. Four or five others lay sprawled on their sides, banked by forest debris and carnival refuse, one inexplicably split down the middle, spangled and sequined dresses spilling out from the fissure like glittering entrails. Dugan's heart fluttered in his throat, a frantic hummingbird. None of these trailers was his.

Dugan slogged through the mud towards the low side of the field, which sloped into a ravine through which a river rushed from a distant mountaintop source. As his feet slipped down the slope, he did nothing to catch himself, but simply stared with dread as he slid. Wheeled wooden boxes were strewn everywhere, littering the ravine, and damming the flow of water so that the river became a muddy pool. His own trailer, painted a sunny yellow with white trim, lay resting on its side with its wheels kissing the wheels of one trailer and its roof halting the downhill slide of another.

Though his first impulse was to run, Dugan approached without hurrying. It was broad daylight and other carnies were around, laughing in disbelief, cursing, crying; there would be witnesses to his panic. Using the sticks and logs and leaves clumped at the sides as a stairway, he climbed on top of the first trailer, then walked across it to get to his own, which lay door side down.

"Lucky for me the window's broken," he muttered, lips twisted into a bitter smile. He dropped through the window, landing on something soft—his bed, he thought at first, but then he realized that his hand had sunk into the slimy softness of sodden, muddy paper. He was crouching atop a huge pile of books, an island of sorts, surrounded by murky, swampy water. Strident sunlight fell in oblong rays through the overhead window, illuminating the wreckage. When he tried to use his hands to help him get to his feet, his fingers dug grooves through layers of pages as soft as clay. Slipping on paper pulp, bloated cardboard, saturated cloth and slick leather, he fell to his knees as his optimism tumbled off the island of ruined books and drifted away on the tide. Weighted by a heavy heart immune to illusion and lies, he sank like a stone into grief. It had taken him a lifetime to amass this collection. These books were his escape, his balm, his salvation, and now, they were destroyed.

"Dugan? You in there?"

It was Finch's voice. Submerged in a sea of ruined literature, Dugan felt that if he opened his mouth to reply, he would drown.

As Finch peered through the window, the sharp-edged sunlight split into smaller rays in the shape of the man's head.

"There you are," he said. Then he whistled. "Holy Jesus, will you look at this! My own quarters will take a few hours to dig up, but since the trailer stayed upright, very little water got in and none of my equipment was damaged. But this is just terrible. I'm so sorry, Dugan. You must feel awful."

Dugan said nothing. Nothing remained. He kept his mouth closed, losing oxygen at the bottom of the sea.

"I've got some good news for you, though. I found the ticket booth about a quarter mile away, and though it's not really salvageable, somehow the banners made it through intact."

The sunlight at the edges of Dugan's vision began to dim.

"Dugan? Are you alright?"

The dimness spread, an expanding halo of inky surrender swallowing the sunlight while Dugan's mind crawled away from the watery devastation, deep down inside the self, where it was blessedly dark and quiet and dry.

Finch's panicked shouts for help echoed faintly like a voice from another world. Hidden deep within the catacombs of himself, Dugan could not be touched by anyone's worry or fear.

Not even his own. Not anymore.

Chapter thirty

Nursing

Like a miniature alpine village, the tiny honeymoon bunga-
lows of Felicity Falls Campgrounds resembled Swiss chalets grafted
onto the foothills of the West Virginia mountains. Thanks to the
messy divorce between the owners, Mel and Hilda Wiener, every
chalet sat vacant, and thanks to Zimm's charming persuasion and the
carnival boss's offer to pay double the asking price, Mel and Hilda
agreed to put aside their differences and open the campgrounds to
the lingering refugees from the Starlight Carnival Royale. The carnies
needed a place to stay while they repaired what they could and called
in orders for what they couldn't. Many had already left for new acts
with new carnivals, but those who remained—including Dugan's
Cabinet of Wonders—had filled the village to full occupancy for the
past three days and two nights.

Molly and Faye thought the mock-alpine cottages were darling, and if the situation had been different, they would have been
delighted to take a break from a regular week of shows to stay there.

Even the bathrooms, which were separate from the cabins, had steeply sloping roofs and walls with stenciled scrolls of leaves and flowers and colorful shutters flanking fake windows. There was one set of showers and toilets for men and another for women but the carnies simply attended to their bathroom necessities in whichever donniker was closest to their own cottage.

As Molly and Faye guided Dugan back from the showers—the women's was closest—they scowled to see Bea and Saffron swiftly shut their door when they spotted them shambling down the path with the slouching, wet-haired, bathrobed Dugan. Then Finch walked by with a towel slung over his shoulder, giving them a nervous wave and stepping off the path to allow them an inordinate amount of room to pass by. Everyone was behaving as if Dugan's sudden, strange speechlessness was a contagious disease, so Molly and Faye nursed him alone. They had relied upon him for years, and now they attempted to repay his kindness.

"Alright, Dugan," Molly said, "step up now. We're back at our chalet." She had heard Zimm call his bungalow a chalet and had been using the word ever since.

Dugan, remaining just as silent as he'd been for the past three days, climbed the stairs with Molly and Faye's guiding hands pressed to his hunched back. He was able to bathe himself and use the toilet by himself, and feed and dress himself, but he had to be guided from place to place and told what to do. "I'll bet you're ready for the bathroom after such a nice, long sleep," Faye would call out cheerily. Or, "Now it's time for mashed potatoes and gravy," Molly would say. And Dugan would dutifully close himself up in the stall to take care of business or lift and swallow spoonful after spoonful of potatoes, always with his eyes glazed and distant, never making a sound.

Inside their chalet, Molly and Faye handed Dugan his pajamas, told him to get dressed, then looked away from his nakedness, taking their time hanging up his bathrobe. When they turned around again, he was wearing his pajamas. The twins pulled back the covers, telling him it was time for bed, and he obediently climbed in, his head sinking into the plush pillow as they pulled the sheets up to his chin.

"Comfy?" Molly asked.

She thought that maybe there was a slight smile in response, an almost imperceptible nod of the head, or at least a glimmer of acknowledgement that faintly altered his expression, but she couldn't be sure. A hundred times a day for the past three days she and Faye had looked into Dugan's eyes and thought they saw a change; their heartbeats would accelerate and they'd clasp hands, certain that in a moment he would shake off the spell, return to his old self, and be their father once more. A hundred times a day they were wrong.

Then a quiet knock at the door made them jump. They couldn't think who it could be; the other carnies avoided the place as if it were under quarantine.

Molly and Faye went to answer and found Matthew Harris Henderson waiting on the doorstep, sporting a dapper gray suit and fedora, holding a bouquet of flowers in one hand and a ribbon-wrapped box in the other.

"We told you not to come around anymore," Faye said.

"Dugan isn't well," Molly said.

"I tried to stay away," he replied, "but I was in agony without you."

"You're talking too damn loud," Faye hissed. "Dugan's trying to sleep."

He spoke in a whisper. "I brought presents. Not just for you. For Dugan, too."

Faye frowned and took the box, slid the pink silk ribbon off, carelessly letting it drift to the floor, knocked off the lid, and peered inside. A box of chocolates, a yellow candle, and a small vial of liquid.

"The chocolates are all caramel—your favorites—and the candle is lemon verbena. A very sharp, astringent smell. I thought it might be invigorating for Dugan. I also brought him smelling salts."

"That's what's in this little bottle?" Faye asked.

Henderson nodded.

Molly reached into the box. "So we just unscrew this top and then hold the bottle under his nose?"

He nodded again.

Eager smiles bloomed on the twins' faces. They tossed the box onto their bed—the candle rolling off the mattress to the floor, the chocolates spilling across the green blanket like acorns—and hurried to their patient's bedside to hold the smelling salts under his nose. Dugan's eyes flew open and bulged wide, and he quivered from head to toe, but then he turned over, closed his eyes again.

No longer smiling, Faye wrenched the cap back on the vial then clacked it firmly down onto Dugan's bedside table.

"I suppose we should try again later," Molly said.

Matthew Harris Henderson, still clutching the bouquet, furrowed his brow and said, "I'm so sorry, my doves. I really hoped that would work."

"Come on. Outside," Molly said, taking the flowers from his hand and flinging them onto the bed atop the chocolates.

They stood outside in the peach flush of evening, leaving the door cracked open because maybe, just maybe, Dugan would call for them.

"You look like angels," Henderson said. "And don't think by my coming here that I don't respect what you're doing for Dugan. I admire you for it. I do. But I love you, and it pained me to know that you were here having such a sad, hard time while I was back at the inn, unable to help."

Molly and Faye's anger disappeared as the delicacy of the man's kindness and the consoling power of his protectiveness filled them like a light illuminating their darkest, saddest, most hopeless corners. As a cool breeze slipped over their skin and goose bumps rose on their arms and legs, the twins looked into each other's eyes, and started to sob. They embraced as tightly as they could, but because the narrow band of flesh at their hips had limited flexibility, they were not able to hold each other in a close, face to face hug. They could only take turns resting their heads on one another's shoulder as they wept—a small, insufficient comfort, when what they truly wanted was Dugan's embrace, and they had no way of knowing if they would have that ever again. Without having to speak a word, they turned and launched themselves at Henderson's chest. He wrapped his long arms around the weeping girls and held them tight, soothing their fears with sweet words.

"I wish I could spare you your pain," he said. "I wish that you would let me take care of you. I would, you know. If you agreed to marry me, I promise that I would do everything I could to keep you safe and happy. You shine as lovely as the stars in the sky. You're my angels, my dream, my—"

"We don't care about that sappy shit," Faye interrupted, her voice muffled against the lapel of his suit. "What we really need to know is if you'll promise to keep us safe from doctors. If you'll promise that you'll never ever allow anyone to cut me and Molly apart."

"Of course I promise," he said. "I thought that went without saying. I love you the way you are right now, and I want to help you be happy. I'll do whatever it takes."

Molly and Faye took deep, shuddering, synchronized breaths and stepped back, digging their hands into their pockets, then swabbing their cheeks with two identical handkerchiefs, each with a cursive *D* embroidered at the corner in emerald green floss.

"Okay," Molly said.

"Okay you'll marry me?"

Faye nodded. "Yes. We will."

Henderson swept the twins into his arms and twirled them around, whooping for joy, before he returned them to their feet and bent over with his hands on his knees, panting from the exertion.

"Congratulations."

With their hearts stuttering, Molly and Faye turned to see Dugan leaning in the doorway.

"I've wallowed in bed long enough," he said, his voice weak, cracked, hoarse from neglect. "I want you to gather everyone with the Freak Show and tell them that Dugan is calling a meeting. Is there a place for a fire somewhere around here?"

Molly and Faye nodded, too stunned to feel anything, much less the joy that they had expected to feel if—when—this happened.

"There's a fire pit that way," Faye whispered, pointing. "On the far side of the campgrounds."

"Good. We'll hold the meeting there." Dugan placed a hand against his throat—it hurt to speak—then nodded to Matthew Harris Henderson, the twins' new fiancé, and croaked, "You may as well come too."

Chapter thirty-one

Fireside Meeting

The blazing of the fire pit drowned everyone in a wavering orange light that made the gathering seem slightly unreal to Dugan, so recently returned from three days spent burrowed in the center of himself. During that time of silence, as he had walked from place to place, following Molly and Faye's instructions, the outside world had remained a show performed on the other side of a door that he chose not to open. He had surprised himself by feeling no shame or anger at being nursed by the twins, only a vague gratitude for being watched over while he rebuilt his strength from the inside. After the jolt of the smelling salts, and hearing Henderson's proposal and Molly and Faye's acceptance, he knew that it was time to unbolt the door and rejoin the show—past time, perhaps.

Dugan regarded the nervous faces encircling the fire and said, "We need to discuss our future."

Although his Wonders had appeared overjoyed by his revival, they still kept their distance, unwilling to touch him or to even stand close—except for the twins. Once they recovered from the shock, they had hugged him for nearly ten minutes before leaving him to go and gather the others for the meeting.

He continued. "The storm was devastating. Obviously it had a profound effect on me. But it doesn't have to mean the end of Dugan's Cabinet of Wonders. We can rebuild and start making a great profit again soon, if we're willing to make a few sacrifices and be patient. First we need to invest in the show, repairing what we can..."

At this, many of the nervous faces creased with guilt. No one had bothered to try and repair anything yet; Dugan didn't know what they'd been doing all this time, but he could see that they hadn't been working.

"...and purchasing whatever replacement items we may need. Now, I realize that I've left you alone for a few days, but I've returned with renewed vigor, and I feel ready to start fresh. Who's with me?"

Dugan had been trying for a Shakespearean Henry v vitality—a morale bolstering speech, an inspiring example of strength and determination. He did feel badly about his days of silent retreat, but had no regrets; without it he would not have had the spirit or the physical strength to try and rally his troops—after the long rest, the pain and stiffness in his bones had considerably improved.

Mario sat at his right hand and Sean at his left, but he could see that they were not prepared to respond. In fact, as he scanned the golden, flickering faces staring fixedly into the fire, it seemed they had all lost the power of speech.

"The quest looks uncertain for our poor hero," Dugan said dryly. A few titters of laughter were the response.

"Listen," Finch said, standing, his white shirt tinted a fiery orange, his face illumined ominously from beneath.

Here is the first Judas, Dugan thought.

"I can't pretend anymore that I want to be here. I'd like to help you, Dugan—you've been a good boss and a good friend—but for the sake of my sanity, and the sake of my art, I need to leave the Starlight."

"How soon will you go?" Dugan asked, transmuting his heart into cold, impervious iron. This would not be his only disappointment tonight.

Finch sat down, his face front-lit again, no longer ominous, only handsome and sad. "Zimm's hanging it up, too," he said. "Plans to take a few of his girls and get into the burlesque scene. He's going to give me a lift to New York this weekend."

"Who else is planning to go?" Dugan asked.

The fire popped and rose higher.

"Molly, Faye? What plans do you two have with your gentlemen friend there? Will you be August brides, or will you wait out the many months until next June?"

Molly, holding Henderson's hand, hid her face against his shoulder as Faye rushed to say, "We only said yes because we were so sad that you—" She cut herself off. "I mean, just because we said we'd marry him doesn't mean that…." Her voice dwindled. She seemed confused, and turned to Molly for help.

"It *does* mean," Molly said firmly. "We agreed to marry him, and we aren't going to take it back. We don't *want* to take it back."

After a while Faye shook her head. "No," she agreed. "We don't."

Dugan's iron heart grew colder. He inched his log seat closer to the fire and said, "Saffron, Bea? What about you two?"

The women met each other's eyes, communicating a nonverbal message of resolve, then Bea spoke. "I'm going back to Jimmy," she said. "Well, not back to *him*, but back to his show. He's been writing to me, and well, Saff and I have these plans, and they'll take some real money to get rolling, and the son of a bitch wants me back so bad…. Anyway, he telegrammed me a few days ago and promised me a huge pile of mazuma if I rejoin his show, and while the money would be fantastic, to be honest, what I like most is how pitiful he sounds. To watch him grovel for a while would do my heart a hell of a lot of good." She laughed softly and stared into the blue-orange roots of the fire. When she looked up again, her eyes, locked onto Dugan's, shimmered in the firelight. "I'll always be grateful to you, Dugan, for taking me in like you did."

"And you, Saffron? You're going with her?"

He had hoped to read sadness and shame on her face, but she simply flashed a pragmatic smile set off-kilter by sympathy and said, "I am."

She gave no further explanation, saying nothing of Mexico, and smiling with a lopsided pity that arced past Dugan's iron heart and landed heavily in his gut. He could see that Saffron knew she had hurt him. She didn't seem to mind much.

He looked across the fire to Alexander-Alexandra, his marvelous morphodite, and asked, "What about you?"

Before Alex responded, Bea and Saffron got up to leave the circle, and Dugan noticed at the same time that Finch, along with Molly and Faye and their fiancé, had already departed.

Alex moved to sit close beside Dugan on his narrow log bench. "I'm sorry, darling. But it's time for me to move along as well. I'm taking a big leap and getting off the road. I have a new job."

Shocked, Dugan demanded, "What on God's green earth is that?" He had thought Alex a carny to the grave.

"I'm off to Florida. To manage Mario's little settlement."

Mario patted Dugan on the back and said, "I'm only giving the lady—the gentleman—what she wants."

"Please don't think badly of him," Alex said. "I've been out of sorts for a long time. I happened to hear Mario's suggestion first, but I probably would've taken any non-carnival offer that crossed my path."

Dugan shook his head. He had seen the flare of excitement in Alex's eyes when she said Florida. "It isn't necessary to lie."

"I'm not. I just—well, I don't know what I would've done if Mario hadn't offered me this job, but I do know that I've been unhappy. And I'll do whatever I need to do to feel good again."

"So this is what's been behind that inscrutable surface of yours all this time. A secret plan."

"I've only had the plan for a few weeks. The discontent, how-ever, feels ancient. I tried to keep it secret from myself, even, but big emotions can't be contained forever."

"Speak for yourself."

Alex slung an arm around Dugan's shoulders, saying nothing, so Dugan said, "I suppose you're going to get up and leave the fire now too."

She cupped his cheek, gave his forehead a soft kiss, then stood and said, "Don't be so hard on us. We all love you very much, and we feel completely awful about this."

"Nevertheless, you're all going."

"Yes, we are," Alex said, holding her empty hands out, open and apologetic, then dropping them to her side. "But you know, you're not that different from us. We're leaving now, but you—you left before the season began. I'm not angry; I know you must have good reasons for it, just like you have for everything you do. Still, though. I've missed you."

Dugan's iron heart creaked, but before he could reply, Alex turned and disappeared into the darkness beyond the fire.

Mario clapped his hands together and said, "I think it's time to start drinking, don't you?" He produced three battered tin cups, which he set out on the rocky earth by Dugan's feet and filled with Canadian whiskey. Nodding to the bottle, he said, "I just helped myself while you were...*indisposed*. Figured you wouldn't mind."

Reaching over Dugan with one impossibly long arm, Sean took one of the cups and said, "I think that this is just what we need right now."

"Come on. You too," Mario said to Dugan.

"I've done far too much drinking lately."

"Too much is a subjective concept."

"You've been hanging around this bookworm for too long," Sean said. "I don't get that high-falutin' talk." When he chuckled and clapped Dugan on the back, Dugan could feel the guilt radiating off the man like waves of heat. Sean was abandoning him, too, as was Mario. No announcements were needed; it was no surprise.

Mario said, "I just meant to remind Dugan that he's been given a hell of a lot of reasons to drink lately, and therefore *too much* does not apply."

Dugan nodded. "You have an excellent point, sir." He took the proffered whiskey, downed half the cup in one gulp, then exhaled a scorching breath. "Powerful stuff."

"Wonderful stuff."

Dugan felt himself thaw, his iron heart returning to flesh while he drank, flanked by Sean and Mario, conversing about inconsequential things, and used a hickory stick to prod crackling sparks from the fire—tiny, flame-bright cinders swirling up in tandem toward the constellations clustered across the cobalt sky. When an owl hooted someone's name from a branch directly overhead, their laughter faded. They stared into the fire.

"So, tell us," Sean said. "How are you with all of this? Honestly."

Dugan shrugged. "Surprisingly fine considering that my entire way of life has been annihilated. I suppose the grief and desperation will arrive tomorrow in the company of a vicious hangover."

"Dugan—" Mario began.

"No, no. Don't. You are the last person I'd expect to go soft on me. You made it clear that your time in my Cabinet was temporary."

Mario nodded. "But our friendship," he said with a wink, "that's forever."

"Whether we like it or not," Dugan replied, slugging down another mouthful of booze.

"You could start up a new show," Sean said.

"I don't think so. That's a young man's game."

"Come off it. You're barely over thirty. You're young."

"Not in my bones, I'm not."

Although Sean was uncertain what Dugan meant by this, he didn't press. Mario, however, stared at Dugan for a long while, then nodded, his face slack and sagging, the seams weakened by unhappy knowledge. Then he looked down and topped off everyone's whiskey, his face shadowed, untouched by the firelight. "I think it's time for a toast," he said. When he looked up, he wore a dashing smile.

Just then, Dugan felt a tingling between his shoulder blades. He turned and saw Saffron watching from the edge of the fire's orange nimbus.

"Just give me a moment, gentlemen," Dugan said.

He joined her, taking his tin cup with him.

"I couldn't sleep," she said.

"Need a nightcap?" He hoisted his whiskey.

She shook her head. "I couldn't sleep because I've been think-ing that maybe Bea and I gave you the wrong idea about things." She spoke quickly, twisting her hands. "I don't want you to think that I'm leaving your Freak Show for Jimmy's Freak Show. I mean, I am, but that's not what's really happening. Bea's a great friend, and I want her to do what she needs to, and in the end doing this will help us with our dream. Well, my dream, really. I want to go to Mexico with my own show, and Bea and me, we're almost like family. I don't want to leave the country without her. And I'm sorry, but you know as well as I do that it would take a lot longer to save up the money if we stayed here with you."

Dugan nodded, wishing that Saffron's eyes weren't pools of golden honey warmed by a compassion and a strength that he loved even as she abandoned him. There was nothing he could say. He had shed his iron armor for the giddy vagueness of liquor, and now heart-break hovered in his peripheral vision, waiting for the right moment to dive, talons extended toward his defenseless, drunken head. He tried to tell himself that she was just another dame, but this time the lie didn't stick: she was marvelous, incredible, and she would have been a Wonder even without her fur.

Then Saffron said, "I think a kiss is called for," and despite the fact that she had announced her intentions, Dugan was still shocked when her lips met his and her tongue slipped soft and silky against his own. The fur above her lips and on her chin rasped against his bristly three-day stubble, but the contact still felt as soft as velvet. Then it was over—far too soon—and his heart wasn't even there anymore; it was clutched in the center of Saffron's strong fist.

When she left, she left kindly, without saying goodbye.

Returning to the fire and his valiant drinking buddies, Dugan took a hearty breath, shoved his pain aside yet again and said, "So where were we, gentlemen. A toast?"

Mario stood up, as did Sean.

"A toast to the unknowable future," Dugan said. "May it be brimming with Wonders."

"And broads," Mario said.

"With wondrous broads," Sean said, chuckling.

As they raised their cups in toast, a log collapsed in the settling fire, sending a whirlwind of sparks to spiral over their heads and blink out one by one against the infinite, sidereal sky—the universe wide open, waiting for the men to grasp new threads, to weave their lives anew.

Part Three:
Down the Road

Chapter thirty-two

And Baby Makes Three

September 23rd, 1928,
New York, New York

On a beautiful Sunday afternoon in September 1928, over a year after the storm and the dissolution of Dugan's Cabinet of Wonders, Saffron and Bumble-Bea took a small jump (driving a shiny new Ford that Jimmy had bought Bea a few months earlier) from New Brunswick, New Jersey to Harlem—that fervent young city within a city—where they hoped to surprise an old friend. They parked right in front of the brown brick building, and Saffron hurried across the sidewalk with her forehead down and a shawl over her head; she had made the mistake of walking uncovered down city streets before, and now traveled more cautiously.

The door to the brownstone was set with a windowpane that had the name of the establishment and the hours of operation painted on the glass in gold, and a nubbly, white linen blind pulled down on the opposite side. The studio was closed on Sundays, but Saffron

281

and Bea had a feeling that the proprietor would make an exception in their case. They rang the bell and stood back.

"Well, then. Edward Finch Photography," Bea murmured. "Doesn't that sound fine."

"Hmmm. Edward," Saffron said. "It's ridiculous, I know, but I didn't realize he even *had* a first name."

"It's not that ridiculous," Bea said, "after all, you don't have a *last* name. And Dugan—is that a last or a first name?"

Saffron shrugged. She had no idea.

They waited for some time before a corner of the blind lifted and an unfamiliar face peered through the gold-lettered glass. Then the blind dropped again, the locks slid and clanked undone, and a handsome young man, very tall and slender, with olive-black skin and auburn eyes fringed by thick, curly lashes, opened the door.

The man grinned and said, "I'm Nathan. And I know who you are. Welcome."

He led them up a narrow flight of stairs that smelled of sandalwood and floor wax, the staircase lined on both sides with examples of Finch's work: portraits of glamorous people, both Negro and White, and Saffron even spotted a Chinese family, the women in gowns and furs, the men in suits and wingtips, their children topped with stiff bows or hats and bundled into puffy velvet coats.

Bea whispered, "This is one hell of a ritzy joint, Saff. We ain't fancy enough to get our portrait done here."

Saffron patted Bea's broad, soft back and whispered, "We're quality carny people. And so is Finch, no matter what he's doing now. What does fancy matter to us?"

They entered a bright, clean room with soaring ceilings and streaky buttery sunlight that plummeted from a high-up row of rectangular windows onto caramel hardwood floors. Still more framed photographs lined the walls.

"Eddie's in the darkroom," Nathan said. "I don't like to interrupt him while he's developing, but he should be out in a minute. In the meantime—here, look over here. This is how I recognized you."

Mounted along a back wall in the corner was a selection of the original photographs used to make the souvenir postcards for Dugan's Cabinet of Wonders. Every act was represented. There was even an early self-portrait of Finch as the Wild Man of Fiji, a role that had lasted no more than a month because Dugan decided that wild man gaffs lacked class, and felt that Finch's energies would be better spent as a bookkeeper/ bouncer/ photographer. Finch had selected one representative portrait of each performer, except for Shadrach, who was present in three. Two of the portraits were in the same style—the tattooed man stood lock-jointed, straight-angled and stern, hands riveted onto hips in front of a plain backdrop in Finch's trailer—one with his face to the camera and one with his back to it. But the third, blown-up double the size of the others, was of Shadrach out by the Pie Wagon, happy and loose-shouldered, with his head tilted to the side as he lifted a heaping forkful of chocolate cake towards a laughing mouth. Saffron knew that leaving Dugan's show had been the right thing to do, but still, to see the photographs was to be inundated with homesickness.

"I met Eddie six months ago," Nathan said, "and then I began working with him here."

He tapped the frame of the largest picture of Shadrach, his eyes sad as he said, "Eddie hasn't heard a word from him."

"Neither have we," Saffron said.

"But I'm so glad that you two came to visit. He might not say it, but it'll mean the sun and moon to him."

"You love him very much, don't you," Bea said.

Nathan blinked nervously and clasped his hands together. When Saffron met his eyes and smiled, he rubbed the back of his neck, smiled back, and said, "Yes, I do. Enormously."

A door opened and slammed shut, and a booming voice echoed through the studio, accompanied by Finch's heavy tread. "I heard voices, Nate. Tell them to go away. We're closed."

"Not to us, you ain't," Bea shouted.

Finch stopped abruptly when he saw Bea and Saffron. Then, with a delighted laugh, he ran and tugged them into a three-person embrace. "Of course not! I'd never be closed to you two. How'd you find me?"

"You're famous," Saffron said.

Finch snorted. "Well, I'm fashionable. God, can you imagine? Me, fashionable?"

"We don't need to imagine," Bea said. "We can look around and see for ourselves."

"Actually," Saffron said, "Alex told us where to find you. I hear that you two have become serious letter writers now that you both have permanent addresses."

Finch nodded. "It's been nice. Alex can write a really fantastic letter. Now, anyway. They were a little rough at first, but he's developed a real way with words."

The old troupers stood around smiling as they caught up, Finch talking obliquely about the apartment on the third floor that he shared with Nathan, then telling them directly about the terrible photographer he worked for until finding an investor to help him open his own studio seven months ago. Finch's business had grown so rapidly that he now made appointments at least a month in advance and had to turn people away almost daily.

"I keep raising my prices," Finch said, "and at this point, I'm ludicrously expensive, but people only seem to love it more. As I overheard one of my wealthiest clients say to her husband, the twenties have been so kind to the rich that they've gotten bored, and they like to keep life exciting by going to shady clubs to hear *le jazz hot*, or by getting their picture taken by overpriced nigger photographers in Harlem."

"She sounds like a real doll," Bea said.

"Half my clients are dreadful people, but thankfully, not all of them. And one day a month I do free portraits on a first come first serve basis, and then there's the portraits I do in my spare time, just for the art of it, so I do get to photograph more regular folk. Meanwhile, I'm saving every cent I can. Who knows how much longer it'll be fashionable to go to Edward Finch Photography? I'm not banking on it lasting."

"Cynical," Saffron said.

"Realistic," Finch corrected. "So, are you two here for a portrait? I'll take it free of charge as long as I can display it on my wall. You sure have changed, Bumble-Bea. You're skinny!"

Bea laughed, now with only two chins to wobble instead of four. "I'm still fat, and you know it. But Jimmy keeps callin' me a scarecrow."

"So you're back with the hubby?"

"Not *with* him, exactly." She shook her head. "It's complicated."

"Are you on some sort of reduction plan?"

"Hell, no. Not on purpose anyway. See, pretty soon after Saff and I joined up with Jimmy's show, Jimmy put a bun in my oven. A moment of weakness that was not repeated, I might add." Bea smiled, and proudly patted her belly. "I'm almost eight months along. Straight off I had God-awful morning sickness, and I lost some weight from that, but even after it went away, I didn't have much appetite. Not like before. I eat plenty to keep up me and the baby, but I guess it's not enough to keep up Baby Beatrice—I'm just not as interested in food as I used to be. I don't mind losing the weight, though. After the baby's born, Saff and I and a couple of our Freak buddies from Jimmy's show plan to take off for Mexico, and Saff says I don't need to work anymore if I don't feel like it. At least not as a carny." Bea patted her belly again. "I'm sure this little critter will keep me busy."

"Mexico, huh?" Finch shook his head, and turning to Saffron (he knew the source of the dream) said, "Life is rougher there than here, you know."

She nodded. "I know. That doesn't matter to me. A Freak can have more of an impact there."

"You think so?"

"Oh, yes. Also, Mexican doctors aren't as keen on sterilization and institutionalization as ours are. That nonsense is going to kill the Freak Show business in this country. It won't be long before everyone looks exactly the same up here."

Finch laughed as he lifted his chocolate brown hands with

their peaches and cream palms and held them up beside Bea's rose petal cheeks.

"All right," Saffron said, "not exactly the same. But you know what I'm trying to say."

"Sure, sure," Finch said, smiling. "Come on. Let's make a portrait."

Arranging their clothes and hair and posing them in front of a tropical backdrop, in honor of Mexico, Finch took his time as always, stepping back and squinting, striding up to make the tiniest change, then stepping back to squint again—as Nathan bustled around him, setting up a tripod and camera, loading film and adjusting lights according to the photographer's instructions, issued through nods and grunts and hand gestures. The two men kept in perfect synchrony, Finch able to stay deep inside the portrait in his mind because he didn't have to stray from his vision and use language to receive what he needed from Nathan. And whenever Finch touched him—a hand on the shoulder, a graze of hip against hip as he walked by—Nathan smiled sweetly, lowering his long eyelashes with unfeigned coyness.

Watching them move in smooth, choreographed patterns about the studio, Saffron shocked herself by thinking: *They have a good marriage.* It had never occurred to her before that two men could have a marriage, but here it was right in front of her, looking almost as lovely as her memories of her marriage to Benjamin. Then she looked at Bumble-Bea, flushed and smiling with her laced fingers perched on the crest of her belly. Bea had already said that in her mind Saffron was the child's second parent, not Jimmy, who had been too concerned with his wife losing size to be happy when the doctor said that the weight loss would insure a healthier baby and an easier birth. And so Saffron was almost a mother, and she now wore her wedding ring on a chain around her neck instead of on her hand. Maybe one day soon she might take her husband's urn, place it in the bottom of her trunk, and blanket it in layers of clothing, making space enough in her life and in her bed for someone else, a man who wouldn't be her husband's equal, but who could, unlike Ben, love her alive and in the flesh, exhaling warm breath as he lay sleeping beside her. But for now, she was content with her friend, and the baby, and Mexico—at long last, a family act.

"Holy shit," Bea laughed, fingers splayed on her belly, "this kid's got Rockette legs, for sure. Feel this kick!"

Finch and Nathan and Saffron gathered close, the photographer voicing no protest as his carefully constructed pose was dismantled in an instant. Bea placed their hands against her stomach.

"It's over here," she said. "Press down. Can you feel it?"

They all closed their eyes as if in prayer, hoping to feel those Rockette kicks, but were unable to detect anything more than the warm give of Bea's soft flesh. They looked at one another and shrugged, but Bea kept her eyes closed, her gaze turned inward as the foot kicked again, kicked from *inside* her stomach—how amazing it was, a life inside a life! There in the floating dark, the tiny creature sensed his mother's attention, as he tried out new movements with his feet, then his hands, each movement so absorbing as he rotated slowly through the amniotic fluid, like making a fist—so fascinating to tuck and clench his fingers, to make his hand closer, smaller—and punching out against the walls of his mother-home. So entertaining it was, practicing each of these movements, that he did it for nearly five minutes; shift and kick, shift and punch, floating, flipping, this way then that through the liquid dark, communicating to his mother that he was alive, that he was strong and getting stronger, almost strong enough to join her—not yet, but soon—until eventually his movements slowed, and he curled his tiny body into a nautilus and fell into healthy, contented sleep, his dreams embellished by the wonderful sensations that flooded his mother's body whenever someone said the word *baby*, or the word *Mexico*.

Chapter thirty-three

Seaside Requiem

September 25th, Nashville, Tennessee—
September 30th, Tampa, Florida

The phone call found Dugan in Nashville, at the Sweetheart of the South Theater, where Zimm's Girl Show Revue had a three-week engagement. For the past eight months, Dugan had been working for Zimm, whose break from the Starlight Carnival Royale to get into the burlesque scene had proved to be very profitable. As it turned out, June was blessed with perfect comic timing, and she and Zimm put together a great magic show/ comedy/ strip act. Roxy, in addition to her dancing (which wasn't bad, although she did fall down often enough that when she stripped she never removed the thigh-high stockings that concealed her bruised knees), had a pleasant singing voice. A few of the other girls from Zimm's old Girl Show fleshed out the chorus, and in Ohio, Zimm picked up a blonde with killer legs who could flirt with a French accent and do the can-can, and now his show got regular bookings on the circuit. Because Zimm performed in the show in addition to directing, things flowed more smoothly with Dugan managing the business side of things. The job was simple and took little time, so Dugan could concentrate on his research for the book he planned to write about the history of exhibiting little people. The work kept him from brooding. He was slowly but steadily rebuilding his collection of books.

He had heard from some of his Wonders, receiving a letter from Beatrice announcing her pregnancy, in which was also scrawled a painfully brief note from Saffron, and a few letters from Finch and Alex, who each claimed to be very happy in their new, stationary professions. Mario didn't write from Hollywood, where he did a little acting but primarily worked as a talent scout for B-movies. However, he did visit when work was slow, always sitting in the front row of the theater with a flask, always managing to talk one of the burlesque girls into coming up to his hotel room for a nightcap after the show. Dugan heard about Molly and Faye and their beloved Matthew Harris Henderson, but only in bits and pieces through Bea and Mario. The twins themselves did not write. This hurt, and Dugan tried to keep from thinking of them too often. Shadrach sent one postcard, just to say he was doing well, but he didn't say what he was doing. The postmark was from Galax, Virginia.

He had heard nothing about or from Sean—not until September 25th, 1928, when the owner of the Sweetheart of the South Theater interrupted Dugan's critique of Zimm's new act to say that Dugan had a phone call from Florida. As soon as Dugan hung up the phone, he returned to the stage to tell Zimm that he had to leave that night, then packed a tattered leather suitcase and called a yellow cab to take him to the bus station.

Sean met Dugan at the Tampa station the next day, and the two men caused quite a commotion as they walked down the street and boarded a local bus to travel a little further down the coast, but they paid no more mind to the stares and murmurs and gasps than they did to the rumble and flash of passing automobiles or the squawks of citified seagulls overhead. Sean—thin and pale, with eyes sunk into olive-tinged hollows—did not look good.

"Mario sent a telegram saying that he'd meet us at the motel," he said.

Dugan nodded, wishing that he'd done the same; Sean didn't look healthy enough to travel around town like this. He asked, "So how are things, old boy?"

Sean shrugged and said, "I can hardly feel anything below my thighs now, so I stumble and fall nearly every time I try to walk, and my hands get so numb that I can barely hold a pencil. Also, I had to leave my girl Jessie who I love more than anyone I ever knew, just because I couldn't stand for her to watch me die. That about sums it up. How're you?"

Dugan took a deep breath, then replied, "My joints and bones hurt like hell, and if I weren't so damn proud I'd be walking with a cane. I got one of the girls in Zimm's burlesque show in the family way, and although she's simply desperate to have children as soon as possible, she preferred to become intimate with a coat hanger in a dark alley rather than risk birthing a Freak baby she could never love. That's about it on my end."

The two friends were sad for one another, but not surprised—they'd been around too long for surprise—so they exchanged saturnine smiles, then looked out the bus windows, watching the palm-treed landscape hum past under an over-bright turquoise sky until they reached the stop for the Flamingo Motel.

The motel wasn't the nicest establishment, but Dugan didn't mind; he wasn't looking for a luxury vacation, or any sort of vacation for that matter. He was there to help Sean—and Mario, too.

When Dugan and Sean stepped into the hotel's lobby, the first words out of Mario's mouth were, "Hell, you two look like you could use a pint of whiskey each."

They exchanged handshakes and smiles, pleased to be reunited, even under such unhappy circumstances. As they approached the front desk, the man standing behind the counter goggled at the trio, tall, small and small, as they requested adjoining rooms, and before handing over the keys he cocked his head back, narrowed his eyes, and said, "Now, this is a proper establishment for nice, normal people, so I don't want any sorta funny business, you get me?"

Reaching out and snatching the keys from the man's hand, Mario asked, "And what *sorta* funny business do you mean?"

"*Any* sort," the man hissed. "Now, we've got donuts and coffee out here in the mornings, but if you like I can get Patrice to bring you yours straight to your room."

"That won't be necessary," Dugan said.

"You sure? I don't know how comfortable you'd be out here with the other guests—"

Dugan turned on his heel and walked out of the lobby.

"Forget him," Sean said, shuffling behind with Mario. "There's a market down the road, and I brought an ice chest and a hot plate."

Predictably, the rooms had gritty carpet filled with sand, a sour seawatery aroma, and no radios; but surprisingly, they also had clean bathrooms and clean bedclothes over the saggy, lumpy mattresses. Dugan took a long shower while Sean rested and Mario went to the store, coming back with tomatoes, eggs, cheese, mushrooms and potatoes, as well as a few lukewarm bottles of Coca-Cola. They cooked omelets, then ate and talked, elbows propped on the rickety card table in Sean's room, Mario adding whiskey to everyone's coke.

"Her name is Jessica Bell," Sean said, "And we've been together and in love for about four months now. With her, I didn't get restless, not even once. But there's a few doctors in Tampa who look at me funny, and when I found out I was sick, I just knew I couldn't make Jessie handle it all—looking after me while I die, and after, too. When I tried to think of someone I could trust who'd be willing to help me, I thought of you two straight away. At first I was just going to call Mario," he said to Dugan, "but then I worried that this might be a two man job, so I called you, too."

"It's no trouble, Sean."

Earnest and dignified in spite of a tomatoey splotch of egg on his chin, Sean said, "I appreciate that, Dugan. You're a good man."

Sean never explained what was wrong with him, and neither Dugan nor Mario asked him to, but the decline was swift. After a few days, the long, large bones of that skeleton for which doctors had always hungered became visible below a layer of wasted flesh. And then on Sunday, at 2:30 A.M., Sean woke Dugan and Mario and told them it was time.

Dugan didn't ask the question in his mind, but it must have shown on his face, because Sean said, "I just know. Got it? I can barely feel my legs or my hands, but I can feel my organs clanking inside. They're about to break down. They're stalling out."

Under a tarp between the dunes in front of the motel was a boat with their supplies stashed within, all of which were undisturbed, of course: the Flamingo Motel during late September was not the most bustling of tourist spots. Just to hassle the man at the desk, Sean and Dugan and Mario had gone to the lobby for coffee and donuts one morning, and the only other guests had been a withered old couple wearing matching white shirts and safari-explorer shorts. The man, drifting past with coffee and crullers in hand, nodded at their group and murmured, "Very impressive. Very impressive indeed."

Sean wasn't much help pushing the boat, but even with the supplies weighing it down, the craft glided easily across the sand. Pushing off with Sean seated inside proved to be more of a struggle, but they were on the bay side, so the water didn't resist after Dugan and Mario finally got the craft's stem afloat. They climbed in—the boat had two bench seats, so Sean sat on one and Dugan and Mario shared the other—then pushed off with their paddles. The light from a full ivory moon and stars like glitter against blackcurrant jelly gilded the bay's placid waves and silhouetted a solitary fish as it jumped out of the water, flipped in the air, then pierced the sea with a splash of fin and seafoam and moonlight. As Dugan and Mario continued paddling, shadowy coral reefs slipped under the keel of the boat like cloud formations, while the occasional clear, sandy patches without coral or seaweed revealed that the water was growing deeper.

When the bay became too deep to determine if they drifted above coral or sand, Mario set down his paddle and announced, his eyes locked onto Sean's, "All right. This should do it."

Dugan set down his paddle as well, and looked over his

shoulder to where the neon flamingo of the Flamingo Motel sign winked like a hot pink constellation. He turned back to Sean as Mario reached for the rope. After Dugan and Mario each tied an oar to the other's wrist with a length of rope long enough to allow freedom of movement, they cut another few lengths of rope with the knife, hefted the first concrete block onto Sean's lap, and tied the giant's hands to the block. Then they tied a block to Sean's right foot. When they reached for the left, Sean stopped them.

"Take it off, please," he said.

"What?"

"The fake foot strapped onto my leg. I don't want it on me when I go down."

Mario swallowed and looked up at the sky in silence while Dugan nodded, shoving Sean's pajama leg up high enough so that he could see by the dim moonlight how the prosthesis was attached. He unhooked and unstrapped the wooden ankle and foot, and lifted Sean's pale calf—a lumpy-ended stump, shiny with scar tissue—from the hollow. Before he could place the prosthesis behind his own seat in the boat, Mario grabbed it, clutching it to his chest like an infant. As Mario cradled Sean's wooden foot, Dugan rested the last block of concrete on Sean's thigh, tying it close and tight to the flesh like the others to give the man a more stable center of gravity and greater ease of movement. Not that any movement would be easy. Until now, Dugan and Mario had done all the paddling, lifting and tying because Sean needed to save his limited strength for his final jump.

"It's time," Sean said.

"And you're—"

"Don't ask me again if I'm sure, Dugan. You know damn well that I am." Sean rose slowly, straining one-legged against the weight of the blocks, against the mysterious illness that had ravaged his flesh—or perhaps there was no illness, just an overgrown body, too massive to maintain—and the boat wobbled. "I'll try my best not to tip you over," he said.

Mario forced a smile and said, "Don't worry about it. The paddles are tied to us, so we won't lose them, and we can swim fine.

Get in the water however you can. I'd lift you and throw you overboard if you were a little more delicate, but...." His voice trailed off at the sight of Sean's wide, moonlit smile.

The giant hadn't done much smiling recently, and the sight wrenched Dugan's heart and stole the words he'd been about to speak. He had been prepared to say something warm and hopeful; he couldn't recall what.

"You've got the letter for Jessie," Sean said, "and the money I want to give her, and you know where she lives and where she works, and you're going to take everything and put it right in her hands, okay? Her brother's a lowlife bastard, so don't let him—"

"We know, Sean," Mario said. "Don't worry. I remember every bit of your instructions, and Dugan even took notes. We'll take care of everything."

"I left some cash in there for you."

"We don't want your—"

"Just take it, all right? Your just reward and all that."

Dugan and Mario nodded, but as their eyes met, they silently agreed to add the extra money to Miss Bell's envelope. A mellow wash of moon and starlight smoothed the harsh lines of Sean's sunken cheeks and frosted his sickly complexion. Stretching so high above them—a pedestal, a monolith—the man looked almost as grand but twice as sorrowful as he had on the day they first met him in the Savannah juice joint.

"Thanks, Mario. Thanks, Dugan. For everything."

Sean leaned his long body out over the water, still balanced on his one good leg, while the boat canted perilously to the side. "Hold on tight," he said, and in one great burst of strength, he half-dove half-jumped over the edge, barely clearing the side of the boat to land cleanly in the ocean.

He created a mighty splash as he hit the water, and the bay swallowed him quickly, leaving behind a circle of bubbles and expanding ripples that pushed the boat away from the point of submersion, still afloat, but yawing violently close to tipping over. Dugan watched until the ripples smoothed and the bubbles dissipated. Only when he was certain that Sean had sunk to the bottom did he look at Mario, who was watching the sky with one hand covering his mouth and the other still clutching Sean's wooden foot. Dugan moved across to the empty seat, took the oar tied to his wrist and begin to paddle, all at once noticing the pain in his bones that he hadn't allowed himself to feel since he'd arrived in Tampa. Still, he rowed onward, guided by the pink neon of the Flamingo Motel, a tawdry, artificial north star leading him back to shore.

Glancing over at the prosthesis in Mario's lap, he coughed and cleared his throat. His eyes did not well with tears, but his body clogged with heavy sadness.

Mario looked back gravely and said, "You know, as I walked through town on the way to the Flamingo, I passed an antiques shop and thought of you. In the window there's a lovely oak partners desk, and beside it is a large umbrella stand filled with a wonderful variety of walking sticks..." His voice snagged on the words and fell silent. When Mario spoke again, it was very quietly. "Truly lovely craftsmanship," he said. "They don't make things like that anymore."

Dugan nodded, and said, "Perhaps I'll have a look," but in his mind, there was no perhaps. He thought of the Emerson quote he had often recited for the rubes. "And supply to us new powers out of the recesses of the spirit," he now said aloud, "and urge us to new and unattempted performances."

After sunrise, in honor of the vast, unfailing courage with which Sean had accepted challenges both out in the world and within his own body, Dugan would go into town, find the antiques shop, and make a long overdue purchase.

Chapter thirty-four

California Honeymoon

October 2ⁿᵈ, Hollywood, California

Step-step, step-step, in synchronized rhythm.

Mathew Harris Henderson remained impressed at how easily his twin fiancées moved together, and although it wasn't something Molly and Faye had pondered before, they often found themselves thinking it over now. They had always moved this way, but through their fiancé's eyes, they had become fascinated by their old, familiar instincts. Step-step-*stop*—even when one of them decided, wordlessly, to stop walking, the other stopped as well, as if she'd made the same decision at the very same instant. Clumsiness only surfaced when Mario poured them too much wine, or when Faye read a fan magazine as they walked, too preoccupied to heed whatever interior signal forecasted her twin's movements. Molly would halt suddenly on such occasions, causing them to stumble and fall onto the thick white carpet covering the first floor of Mario's house. Falling on the luxuriant carpet never hurt, and as long as the photo of whatever screen star she was in love with that month didn't get wrinkled, Faye didn't stay mad for long.

On that night in early October, Molly and Faye walked to the pool, *step-step, step-step*, the hard gritty concrete pebbling the soft soles of their feet (Matthew paid for bi-weekly pedicures to keep their once hard and calloused feet soft, polished and delicate). The wavering blue light from the pool was the only illumination other than interior light falling from one or two windows of the house; even the moon was blocked by the orange and grapefruit trees, by the bougainvillea encrusted fence enclosing the back yard. The wavering blue tinted the twins with frost and made the edges of their bodies appear to undulate. Tossing their huge, white towels onto a teak lounge chair, they ran to the other end of the pool to jump in so that the splash wouldn't get the towels wet. As they jumped, their squeals filled the air until they hit the water and submersion muffled the sound, making the squeals louder inside their heads than outside their ears.

They loved their bathing suits. On the first day after Molly and Faye had settled in as guests in Mario's Hollywood villa—Mario liked to call it a villa—while Matthew went out to hunt for houses (he was still just a fiancé, because he refused to have a marriage license printed with only one of the girls' names, even though he had been told by six state governments so far that the alternative would constitute bigamy), Mario called one of the costume designers from the studio to come measure the twins and create a wardrobe suitable for up and coming Hollywood starlets; this included, of course, swimsuits.

At first the costume designer had been scared to touch the twins, her bulging eyes staring so unblinkingly that Molly and Faye had thought she might cry, but after the first few minutes of the twins chattering and trying not to laugh, the woman began measuring, her hands slowly becoming steady, until, by the end of the hour, she was telling them dirty jokes and wicked stories about Mario. When she offered them slim French cigarettes rolled in peacock blue paper and flavored with orange oil, Molly and Faye accepted, enchanted. If they had known such cigarettes existed, Faye said, they would've taken up smoking years ago.

The costume lady worked quickly—Matthew was paying her well—and returned with the swimsuits and a pair of pink sundresses a few days later (she also slipped two packages of the elegant French cigarettes into the pockets of the dresses as a secret surprise). Although the bathing suits weren't what Matthew had had in mind—three pieces total: a blue skirt concealing the joining place at the hip, high enough at the waist to conceal the twins' belly buttons, but short enough at the hem to show off their long, slim thighs; and halter-style tops that exposed a line of flesh around their middles and a modest swell of cleavage assisted by padded cups sewn in—he tolerated the suits because they at least reassured him that the twins weren't swimming naked. This was a great concern of his, for he constantly worried that other men coveted his beautiful pair of fiancées.

Every night, before they bathed and got ready for bed, Molly and Faye swam alone in Mario's pool. Fall in California had proven to be warm during the day but cool at night, and once the girls were in the water, they didn't get out until nearly bedtime, when they would blot themselves frantically with the towels, swathe themselves roman-style in terrycloth and, slippery with poolwater and bumpy from cold, sprint inside the house, running for their big, glamorous bathroom complete with an enormous marble bathtub and a gold-plated faucet that never ran out of hot water.

By now Molly and Faye had been in Hollywood for a month; they had had no auditions yet, but Mario had made a lot of calls on their behalf before he left for Florida (he had told them it was a business trip to check on his property). Their swimming habits allowed them to enjoy the early October air while the chlorinated water retained the warmth of a full day's sun, and the contrasting temperatures tightened their skin and flushed their cheeks. Sometimes they swam laps, but usually they just drifted, lazily frog kicking from one end of the pool to the other, either face down to observe the rippling pattern of tiles at the pool's bottom (a pink clam shell ringed in blue tile and surrounded by geometric patterns in blues and greens and pinks) or face up to take in the multitude of crisp, white stars scattered across the cloudless sky.

They had only been swimming for a few minutes that night when Matthew began calling them. Being off house-hunting all day, he missed his fiancées; he wanted attention. Each time he called, leaning out the window of the guest bedroom, Molly and Faye ducked their heads under at the initial *Fffa*, or *Mmmo*, so they could pretend that they hadn't heard him.

"He's as bad as Dugan," Molly whispered when they surfaced.

"He's not so bad," Faye said. "Dugan either. They're both protective is all."

"Yeah, but we don't need a father. Especially not if he's also our husband."

"Of course we don't, but Matthew needs to act that way, and besides, we can do what we want when he's not around, and he keeps us safe and together, and he really, truly loves us. It all balances out in the end."

The twins heard their fiancé close the window. He'd given up for now: Molly and Faye were finally alone. They sighed luxuriously, flapping their arms slowly through the water like gliding birds, swishing their legs like mermaid tails and drinking in the sweet, dry air of another night in Hollywood.

"I mean, you're right, Moll," Faye said, "we did trade Dugan for Matthew, and we're not totally free to do what we want. I agree with that, but the thing is—I don't know if anyone ever is. Free, I mean. Especially not women, and especially not people who're different from whoever's in charge. But what's most important is that we're safe. We're together and safe, and we love each other."

"And Matthew *is* sweet. Rich, too."

"And he's proud to be seen with us."

"And he's very good for some things," Faye said, thinking of their nights together, of Matthew's gentle tongue and hands, of his passion and kind regard, and she thought, too, of the reassuring resonance of his voice when he comforted her and Molly after a nightmare—they didn't even have nightmares very often anymore, thanks to him.

"Yeah. He's good for a lot of things," Faye said, "and we're good for the rest of it."

"What do you mean?" Molly knew what her sister meant, but she wanted Faye to explain aloud. Sometimes it was nice to hear the words.

"We're together," Faye said, "and safe, and we love each other, and we know how to have a hell of a lot of fun. All people really have is themselves, but we're lucky, cause there's two of us. And we're happy, now, aren't we Moll? We're happy exactly the way we are?"

Molly gave this question more thought than Faye expected her to, weighing on one side the various unwelcome reactions from strangers when she and Faye went out in public—those days were bad, sometimes worse than the worst days with the Freak Show could be—and on the other side, all the fun that she and Faye had without even leaving the house. And then Molly weighed the delicious sensation of warm water and cool air, of twenty toes slipping across the tile floor of the pool, and the sharp smell of chlorine that filled her and Faye's bodies and made them feel as peaceful as they did after sessions of laughing until they cried. Most of all, Molly considered the fact that they would never, ever, have to be alone.

She nodded. "I think we are pretty happy, Faye. I think we're good at it."

Without words, Molly and Faye ducked underwater and dove down to the deepest part of the pool, placing their palms flat against the pink mosaic clam shell, kicking their legs to keep from floating back up to the surface. The sisters bobbed as they tried to swim in place, their hair rippling up and down and back with their kicks, and they smiled, their eyes reddening from the chemicals (Matthew wouldn't like that, but they wouldn't have to hear about it until much later), then they kicked forward, dipping their heads down and kissing the pink tiles, the painted ceramic slick against their lips. Looking at one another, the twins laughed, and irregular shimmying bubbles exploded from their mouths, each one bearing a part of their mirth to the surface. Then they turned, pushing off the tile with their

pedicured feet, and shot up to the surface, their strong, young bodies—safe, joyful, choate—thrilled by the shock of breaking through
the warm water into a mild autumn night, exhaling breath that felt
like icy winter against their wet skin.

Chapter thirty-five

Rooted House with Ocean View

October 3ʳᵈ, Mario's Floridian carny camp

A

lex:

Bleached by salt water and sunshine, the near-translucent hair on my tanned arms glistened with sun and sweat as I planted the slender, sway-backed young palm tree, the angular, red-tipped birds of paradise, and the squat lime tree that the woman at the nursery had promised was already capable of bearing fruit. I didn't know if it was the right season to plant, or if I had dug the holes correctly, or placed the plants in locations with the proper amounts of light and shade—et cetera and so on—but I didn't care. I'd always been much better at learning by doing than by written instruction. Mario had bought me books on gardening, but the only book on my beside table, indigo ribbon marking my place, was *The Great Gatsby*. It was published a while ago, and Dugan kept saying I should read it, but I didn't get past the first few pages until after I moved to Florida. While on the road with the Starlight Carnival Royale, I didn't have the patience for the book (back then the narrator seemed like a prig and a bore to me), but since I'd started reading it this time, I saw things differently. It's a glamorous novel, they say, and I suppose that's true, but it's a sad book more than anything else—the story of a performer getting suckered by his own act and by the act of the woman he loves. Half-way through, I could already tell that it wouldn't end happily. Gatsby and Daisy and Nick were clearly their own marks.

So no gardening books, but darling F. Scott made me decide to start reading more novels—even before I'd finished *Gatsby*. The pace of life by the sea was slower, and stillness seemed to inspire activi-ties such as reading, and writing, too—letters for now, but I figured I'd try my hand at something more before long: I had a feeling that at least one book waited inside my head. The trailers were nearly all sold or booked for rental already, but the season wasn't quite over, so the carnies hadn't arrived yet. My little bungalow—the only per-manent structure, a real little house with a yard and window boxes and a cement foundation rooting it to the earth—was the only home presently occupied. The difficult adjustment period I had expected to suffer as I learned how to live in a house passed in a matter of days. I had no restless need to move; I simply swam towards the sunrise every morning and the sunset every night, feeling the immense eter-nal shifting of the ocean, which stretches across more of our earth than the land does, containing countless discovered and undiscovered varieties of life, and carrying, like a substance in the blood, the quali-ties of the countless shores it has met. To swim in the sea is to pull your body through the liquid of all life, of all places, of everywhere and everyone at once.

I finished patting the sandy soil around my lime tree and kissed its glossy leaves, willing it to grow in spite of such an ignorant and clumsy gardener as myself. Standing, I brushed the dirt off my knees and noticed the horizon seeping glimmers of tangerine and cherry, heralds of the approaching sunset. As a concession to the skittish deputy sheriff who periodically stopped by to ask how things were coming along, I went inside to put on a bathing suit for my swim—the sort of old fashioned one-piece worn by grandmothers and grandfathers throughout Florida—and returned outside with a pitcher of sweet iced tea and two glasses. It was strange that I fetched two glasses. As if I already knew.

On the beach, I set the refreshments on the card table I kept beside two similarly half-buried reclining beach chairs. If the wind ever seemed to be picking up, or if storm clouds threatened (I could encounter neither without seeing my indigo blow-off top flapping away into the sky and feeling a nostalgic pang) I took the table and chairs back inside to keep them from blowing away, but they primarily lived on the shore.

At the edge of the sea, I absorbed the simmering pink and orange light and the slowly sinking white-hot ember at the horizon, then ran and dove into the cold waves. The ocean welcomed me as it welcomes all creatures, with an impassive nurturing, for the sea gives when you follow the dictates of its nature, but takes anything and everything when you don't. They say that the sea is cruel, but it is no more cruel than kind. The sea is itself, completely so, and profoundly unalterable.

The ocean filled me up with its power, and emptied me too, scraping away the residue of seventeen years of trying to be everything my lovers wanted, years that had clung to my spirit like barnacles to be scraped off a boat, allowing me to float in its silky, salty arms and feel as free as I had ever made my lovers feel. The ocean became to me what I had been to them, except that the ocean was never too full, never overwhelmed; the ocean didn't have to *do*, it gave and took simply by *being*. It scarcely noticed me as I fed upon its constancy, finding a peace I had never before known.

Trailing my fingers over the sandy ocean floor, my fingertips skipped over the crumbly domes of sand flea houses, the swift spiny back of a hermit crab dragging its new conch home, and a multitude of shell fragments the size and thinness of confetti, but hard and smooth, growing ever smaller as the sea reduced them to sand. They rustled as I stirred them and as the sea shifted and folded their layers, making a *ssshhhhhh* sound: a strange auditory-tactile blending of the rush of blood as the heart pumps, the echo of a cave, and the clack of beads on a string. *Sssssshhhhhhhhh.* I held my breath for as long as possible, then kicked to the surface and blinked away the water that distorted the sunset, trapping its colors in droplets clustered on my eyelashes.

When I finished swimming it was almost dark, and I didn't see the figure reclining in the beach chair until I'd trailed a shivering path of brine halfway up the shore. His voice was as warm and liquid as the last glimmer of sunset, which bled from sky to water, erasing the hard horizontal between.

"Sea nymph or landlord? The villagers wondered, but with no one to tell them the answer, they decided that the creature was both, and they drank in her beauty and her shining at every opportunity, and they were never, *ever*, late with the rent."

"What took you so long, Dugan?"

Although he'd always been suspicious of the southern tradition of cold and sugary tea, refusing to drink it even in Georgia in August, Dugan drank sweet iced tea on that October day at my insistence, begrudgingly admitting that he found it good. Like someone claiming land by planting a flag, he had plunged a polished hickory stick into the sand beside his chair, but still he fidgeted with the silver knob at the top, as if reconsidering. I was surprised by the cane, and yet I recalled that in those first few days after the storm, Dugan's walk had taken on the stiff, hesitant, shuffling quality of the very old. At the time I had thought it was simply another aspect of his strange, silent, inward seclusion.

I didn't want to rush his confidence, but I felt we had reached an important crossroads that I needed to acknowledge, so I tightened the belt of my robe and gave the cane a pointed look and a nod. Dugan nodded back, a signal that we each knew what we knew; confessions were unnecessary.

"I got a letter from Molly and Faye this week," I told him.

"You did? I haven't heard a word."

"I think they're afraid that you'd disapprove of their new life. They haven't been able to legally marry Matthew Harris Henderson— they always write out his full name, I think they find it impressive—at any rate, they can't legally marry him because, well, it's bigamy, so they've decided that they're probably going to simply declare themselves married. They're trying their luck in Hollywood, and Mario's putting them up until they find their own place, which should be soon. I think that Matthew Harris Henderson is a very rich man."

"Well, I suppose I do disapprove. I disapproved of every birthday they had after they first came to me at twelve years old, so of course it's difficult for me to accept them as married women, whether they are officially married or not."

I laughed and said, "Poor Daddy Dugan, his babies are all grown up."

Dugan started. "What was that you called me?"

"Daddy Dugan. I used to call you that sometimes. Remember?"

"I don't recall that."

"Well, maybe I didn't say it to your face."

Relaxing his rigid shoulders, he reached out and twisted his cane clockwise then counterclockwise in the sand. "Daddy Dugan," he said quietly. "I like it." After a long period of silence, he said, "I tried to do my best for all of you, but it wasn't nearly good enough. For some time, I saw it as my fault that the family fell apart. Because I have so much pride and because I wanted to control everything without assistance, I felt compelled to conceal my every vulnerability, and in many ways, that was self-destructive. But now I've learned to admit that even geniuses are fallible. And I've developed a new theory. I think that we were collectively distracted by too many unfulfilled longings—my own included, I confess—a disarray of emotions working at cross-purposes. We were *all* self-destructive. If I'd only noticed sooner, then possibly I would've stopped wasting my energy on trying to hide things, and instead found a way to preserve us unchanging and content, even while we moved from town to town. If I could've done that, then we might still be a happy family of nomads, storm or no storm."

"Listen to yourself," I said. "If you were able to do that, you'd be the first human to know how to stop life with something other than death. Nothing is still, Daddy Dugan. Life is always in motion, always changing, and in any group of people, it's just about impossible to keep everyone content at the same time."

He looked reluctant to accept what I was saying, so I continued. "It's something Finch explained to me in his letters. See, he used to be obsessed with what he called *the real*; by what he thought was real, by what he thought he could prove was real with his photography, creating images that he would use to fight the good fight. You know—using photography to battle against bourgeois oppression."

Dugan raised his eyebrows.

"Don't look so surprised. Finch and I read, too."

"Glad to hear it."

"Well anyway, Finch explained that what he's come to understand is that life—what's real—can't truly be captured in a photograph because *nothing is ever still*. Therefore, a photograph is always a lie. He can try to affect change in the world by preserving a single, true *moment* on film, but he can never really capture life."

I refilled Dugan's glass of tea, and tried to fall quiet, giving him time to digest what I was saying, but I couldn't resist adding, "It sounds like you had a photograph in your mind of a family all safe and warm and permanent. But a moment is just a moment. Things either change and adapt, or they die. Dugan's Cabinet of Wonders died. But each little part of it, all of us, we're still alive, and most of us seem to be fairly pleased with our lives, which is pretty remarkable considering the world around us."

Dugan sighed, and I couldn't tell if it was the sigh of a genius dismissing the ramblings of an ordinary mind, if he was simply releasing air pressure as he adjusted to a new way of thinking, or if there was something else troubling him. I didn't know, nor did I find out—not that night, anyway—because when he spoke, he changed the subject.

"It's quiet here. Not many people. Don't you miss...do you ever...?"

"Are you trying to ask me about sex, Dad?"

He nodded. "In part."

"I haven't had sex in a very long time," I said. "But to tell you the truth, I don't exactly miss it. Not much, at least, and not often. See, I've thought a lot about this—I think an awful lot here—and I've realized that sex has never exactly been something I *wanted*, because really, it's something I *am*. And with a lover or without, I'm still that, I'm still me, but without having to work so hard at it. And here beside the ocean I feel good. Maybe one day...." I smiled. "Sex will always be there if I decide I want it, but for now I like to stretch diagonally across my bed and sleep alone."

Dugan nodded, then finished his second glass of iced tea. I reached for the pitcher, and he waved me off.

"No more. Or I won't sleep tonight." He pointed to the darkened horizon. "That was quite a sunset."

"They're always wonderful here. Beautiful and temporary, but guaranteed to repeat once a day. That's what's great about sunsets. And you get a certain, specific amount of them, but you don't know how many, so they never lose their mystery." I shrugged. "Anyway, it's a great show that doesn't cost a cent. I never miss it."

After draining the last few inches of sweet iced tea, I set down my glass and said, "You know, Dugan, there's this one trailer, right by the path to the beach, that hasn't been bought yet. I was keeping it free for Mario or Sean, but Sean's disappeared, and I doubt that Mario will ever want to leave Los Angeles—he was supposed to come visit this week, but he called and cancelled. So if you wanted a place to live, to try out life in Florida, I could give you a great deal."

He stood, gripping his cane, using it to hoist himself up. The stoop of his back was so pronounced that I had to struggle to hide my shock.

"An interesting offer. Let me sleep there tonight, and then, over breakfast, I need to tell you a story about Sean." He placed a hand on the suitcase beside him on the sand, stroking its handle like one might stroke a baby's head. "Then I want you to take me swimming—I hear that swimming is quite beneficial for individuals with bone troubles—and tomorrow evening, after we watch the sunset, you can begin to tell me what life here is like."

"And then you'll send for the rest of your things and move in?"

"Let's just wait and see what happens."

The beach had grown quite dark by then, our smiles imperceptible to the eye, but palpable nevertheless—a tender affinity wafting on the salty breeze.

"All right," I said. "We'll wait and see what happens."

Afterword

For this novel, I did a great deal of research on carnivals and sideshows, as well as the U.S. during Prohibition, using what I found to try and capture this particular time and place. In order to avoid anachronistic or implausible language, I had to employ terms for my characters and their world that I would never use outside a novel—for example, the use of *Siamese Twins* rather than *conjoined twins*, and the frequent use of the word *Freak*. I had to silence the voice in my head that objected to these words, and find the courage to bring my characters to life with the honesty and respect I believe they deserve.

I would also like to say that in the process of all this research—which I began in hopes of attaining historical accuracy—I encountered wonderful critical works such as *Freakery: Cultural Spectacles of the Extraordinary Body*, edited by Rosemary Thomason, and Rachel Adams's *Sideshow U.S.A.: Freaks and the American Cultural Imagination*, which set my mind on fire with ideas and made me realize that my goals as a novelist and the goals of historians such as James Taylor, the remarkable force behind *Shocked and Amazed!*, are not exactly the same. I decided to create a novel more concerned with emotional authenticity than unmitigated historical realism. I doggedly continued with my research, however, because I respect (and enjoy) the history, and I wanted the world of Dugan's Cabinet of Wonders to *feel* realistic, even to experts who might balk at the central inaccuracy—the fact that Dugan's sideshow has too many human oddities and not enough working acts.

Ultimately, what I hoped for more than anything was to write a good novel, and the stuff of fiction is too big and sweeping to confine in a Cabinet of anyone's making.

Acknowledgments

Thank you:

To all of my writing teachers at the University of Houston, especially Kathy, my undergraduate thesis advisor, and Toni, my master's thesis advisor, and to my unofficial teacher and official husband, Allen Gee, who dutifully read and critiqued this book more times that I care to admit.

To my sister Alice, for being my first reader and for always understanding the worlds I create, no matter how obscured they might be in the early drafts.

To my agent Bill Contardi, my publisher Matthew Miller, and my editor Deborah Meghnagi, for the hard work and enthusiasm that got this novel into print.

But most of all, to my parents Bobby and Margie, for giving me such amazing, unfailing support, and for never once telling me that it couldn't be done.